SMOKE AND SCAR

A SHATTERED CROWN NOVEL

SMOKE AND SCAR

GRETCHEN POWELL FOX

SCARLETT
PRESS

SIMON & SCHUSTER

London New York Amsterdam/Antwerp Sydney/Melbourne Toronto New Delhi

Previously published in 2025 by Hopewell Media
First published in Great Britain in 2026 by Scarlett Press,
an imprint of Simon & Schuster UK Ltd

Text copyright © 2025 Gretchen Powell Fox
Cover illustration © 2025 Kim Cavrak, Spirit of Ebullience
Interior illustration (p. 451) © 2025 Rózsa Vivien / @celestarly
Map and chapter opener illustrations © 2025 Charis Loke

This book is copyright under the Berne Convention.
No reproduction without permission.
All rights reserved.

The right of Gretchen Powell Fox, Kim Cavrak, Rózsa Vivien and Charis Loke to be identified
as the author and illustrators of this work has been asserted by them in accordance
with sections 77 and 78 of the Copyright, Designs and Patents Act, 1988.

1 3 5 7 9 10 8 6 4 2

Simon & Schuster UK Ltd
1st Floor, 222 Gray's Inn Road
London WC1X 8HB

For more than 100 years, Simon & Schuster has championed authors and the stories they create.
By respecting the copyright of an author's intellectual property, you enable Simon & Schuster and the
author to continue publishing exceptional books for years to come. We thank you for supporting the
author's copyright by purchasing an authorized edition of this book. No amount of this book may be
reproduced or stored in any format, nor may it be uploaded to any website, database, language-learning
model, or other repository, retrieval, or artificial intelligence system without express permission.
All rights reserved. Inquiries may be directed to Simon & Schuster, 222 Gray's Inn Road,
London WC1X 8HB or RightsMailbox@simonandschuster.co.uk

www.simonandschuster.co.uk
www.simonandschuster.com.au
www.simonandschuster.co.in

Simon & Schuster Australia, Sydney
Simon & Schuster India, New Delhi

The authorised representative in the EEA is Simon & Schuster Netherlands BV,
Herculesplein 96, 3584 AA Utrecht, Netherlands.
info@simonandschuster.nl

A CIP catalogue record for this book is available from the British Library.

PB ISBN 978-1-3985-6069-7

This book is a work of fiction. Names, characters, places and incidents are either
the product of the author's imagination or are used fictitiously. Any resemblance to
actual people living or dead, events or locales is entirely coincidental.

Printed and Bound in the UK using 100% Renewable Electricity
at CPI Group (UK) Ltd

*To my darling girl and boy:
you are my greatest work
(but this book is a close second).*

*And to every soul wading through the dark:
may you uncover your light.*

AUTHOR'S NOTE

Smoke and Scar is an adult epic romantic fantasy that contains language, violence, and themes that may not be appropriate for all readers.

Content warnings: strong language, graphic violence, blood, gore, murder, torture, grief, self-sacrifice, parental death depicted in a flashback, and prejudice/slurs against fictional races.

While these subjects are important to the story and character journeys, if at any point you find the material distressing or triggering, you are encouraged to stop reading and return only if you feel ready. Your well-being and mental health matters.

PRONUNCIATION GUIDE

Aerithia *(Air-ih-THEE-uh)*
Alouette *(Al-oo-ETT)*
Arcanis *(Ar-CAN-is)*
Artemicion *(Art-ih-MEESH-un)*
Aurelia *(Oh-RELL-ee-uh)*
Belien *(BELL-ee-en)*
Belis *(BAY-lis)*
Cedric *(SED-rick)*
Coralith *(KORE-uh-lith)*
Corlyn *(KORE-lin)*
Cyren *(SAI-ren)*
Daephinia *(Day-FIN-ee-uh)*
DissiduaPyr *(Diss-IH-dew-uh Peer)*
Elyria *(Ell-EE-ree-uh)*
Evander *(Eh-VAN-der)*
Gael *(Gayle)*
Gaia *(GUY-uh)*
Lachlandris *(Lock-LAN-driss)*
Laeliana *(Lay-lee-AH-nah)*
Leviathan *(Lev-EYE-a-thin)*
Luminaria *(Loo-min-AH-ree-uh)*

Lunara *(Loo-NAH-ruh)*
Malakar *(MAL-uh-kar)*
Nocterrum *(Nock-TERR-uhm)*
Noctis *(NOCK-teese)*
Nyrundelle *(NEER-uhn-dell)*
Olyndor *(OH-lin-dor)*
Paelin *(PAY-lin)*
Paideus *(Pie-DAY-us)*
Raefe *(Rayph)*
Selenae *(Sell-in-NAY)*
Solaris *(So-LAH-riss)*
Tartanis *(Tar-TAN-iss)*
Taryn *(TAIR-inn)*
Tenebris Nox *(TEN-ih-bris Nocks)*
Thibault *(TEE-bo)*
Thraigg *(Thrayg)*
Varyth Malchior *(VAIR-ith MAL-kee-or)*
Verdentia *(Ver-DEN-shuh)*
Zaric *(ZAIR-ick)*
Zephyr *(ZEFF-ur)*

Full glossary and character guide can be found in the back of the book.

World of Arcanis

SEA OF SORROWS

DEEPDELVE

IRONPEAK MOUNTAINS

STONEHOLD

HAMMERFELL

Silverbrook

IRONRIDGE

PAIDEUS

THE MIDLANDS

Goldenvale

Briarwood

FOREST OF VALANDOR

Brighthold

Dawnspire

KINGSHELM

LUMINARIA

SEASTONE

Elderglade

HAVENSREACH

PROLOGUE

The end of queen Daephinia Nero's life tasted bright.

It did not look it.

It was chaos and confusion and clashing steel and roaring spells.

It was darkness.

Her eyes blazed, determination and fury warring in them as she stared down the dark sorcerer standing on the other side of the tower rooftop. Rain pummeled them both, plastering Daephinia's golden hair to her forehead. The faint sound of ringing hit her ears as droplets pelted her crown like a warning bell.

"You have brought the realm to ruin, Malakar," Daephinia said between heavy breaths. Her chest heaved; her muscles trembled. This fight had gone on too long. "But your horrific reign ends now. Ends here."

Malakar tilted his head, his shadowy cloak rippling like soft waves on a dark ocean. His eyes darted to the golden crown atop Daephinia's head. "Such conviction, *Your Majesty*," he mocked. "But where was that honorable resolve when you were the one sundering the continent?"

His words were a sharp dagger in her. Guilt bled her insides. "I . . . There is much I regret about my actions."

Malakar paused, assessing the queen with a cold arch of his brow. "Regret, Daephinia? Really? Such a *human* emotion." He let the word hang between them. "I confess, I am surprised."

"I do not pretend that I have not faltered," she said, steeling herself. "But neither should you pretend that the Chasms were anything other than the result of the pain *you* caused."

"Perhaps, Daephinia. Perhaps. But just look at what your *grief* has led to. See how your sorrow has nurtured this chaos." He waved his hand dismissively—almost lazily—at the battle raging outside the castle walls. To the legions of his cultists and the misguided humans fighting against Daephinia's floundering Arcanian forces. She bit back a grimace as she caught sight of a contingent of Malakar's soldiers encroaching upon one of her garrisons.

They were losing.

A slow grin spread across the sorcerer's face. Malakar sensed the queen's faltering will. "Your husband begged me at the end, you know," he said, his voice slithering over Daephinia's skin like a snake. "On his hands and knees, tears streaming down his wrinkled face. Begged me to spare you. Spare your daughter. Even as he cursed my name for my betrayal, still he *begged*. Juno truly was a weak, pathetic human."

Hearing her husband's name pierced Daephinia's heart. Hearing it from Malakar's mouth set her blood on fire. "*You* are human!"

"I think we both know I am something much greater than that now."

Her hands tightened into fists, light flickering weakly at her fingertips. "And just look at what your ambitions have wrought. It is *enough*, Malakar. It ends here and now. I will end your evil and restore the peace I helped shatter." Her anger was a living thing inside her. It begged her to lash out, to use her magic to ruin this evil man. But there was so little of it left. Her palms warmed, and then her power sputtered out.

"Peace?" Malakar's low laugh was a death knell. "Our peoples were *never* at peace—and they never will be, so long as your kind continue to hoard your magic, flaunting your abilities while my people claw their way to whatever pitiful mana stores they can reach."

"That's not—"

"My people fight not for conquest but for the power they rightly deserve. That which they are *owed*. Peace is an illusion. The world was born in chaos, and in chaos it shall end."

Dark magic burst from his chest, and Daephinia raised her hands to defend herself too late. It slammed into her, sending her crashing into the parapet, the back of her head hitting the hard stone. Stars appeared behind her eyelids. Her chin lolled, and she released a strangled cry as the golden crown tumbled from her head—rolling to a stop at the sorcerer's feet.

"The Crown of Concord." Malakar's voice was reverent as he bent to pick it up, his eyes gleaming. Triumphant. "So much power contained in such a little thing."

"Don't you touch it!" Daephinia shrieked, struggling to her feet. "It was meant to be *hers*!"

Malakar rolled his eyes. "What use would a half-breed baby have had for the most powerful object in creation? It is better that her miserable existence was put to a swift end. Truly, you should thank me."

Red flooded her vision. "I will flay the skin from your body for what you have taken from me."

Malakar chuckled darkly. "I think not." He raised the crown, a vicious glint in his eye. "There will be no stopping me now."

It was as if time suddenly slowed. Daephinia closed her eyes, burrowing down deep inside herself, digging out the final scraps of her magic. With the last vestiges of her strength, she called forth a golden light. It enveloped her hands, her arms, her being. The stuttering rhythm of her heartbeat grew more erratic. She did not care. Her light was within her and without her as she forged it, molded it, gave it shape.

The crescent curve of a bow, the luminous thread of its string.

The sharp, focused point of a golden arrow.

With a prayer to Solaris on her lips, she drew the bowstring back, releasing it with a cry of defiance just as Malakar set the crown upon his brow. The luminescent arrow hit its mark, striking the gilded crown right in its center.

"No!" The sorcerer's roar was swallowed by a burst of white as the Crown of Concord shattered. A brilliant flash radiated out in a wide arc—a tidal wave of light that engulfed him, her, the battlefield, the very city around them.

Malakar was nothing more than a wisp of splintered shadow as the crown, cleaved in two, clattered on the stone.

For a moment, there was nothing but pure, incandescent, dazzling light.

And then that light was sucked back into Daephinia, a blinding assault of power that ripped her open.

The end of her life tasted bright.

PART I
FIGHT

CHAPTER 1
THE REVENANT

Elyria

Glass shattered on the wall behind Elyria's head, sticky amber liquid spraying across her neck.

"Not the cider, you fools." She pulled her feet from the stool they'd been resting on as she took a long swig from her tankard. Swaying, she dipped her head to appraise the pieces of the broken bottle that had landed on the bar top beside her.

Waste not, she thought, picking up what remained of the bottom half of the bottle and gingerly tipping it over her mouth. A few drops of cider, sweet and tangy, dribbled onto her tongue.

The tavern was a cacophony of shouts and clashing bodies, though that was nothing new at the Sweltering Pig. Falling mugs clinked and crashed, ale splashing across the floor and nearby tables. Elyria ducked, narrowly avoiding a silver flagon whizzing past her ear. It hit the dark wood of the tavern wall with a clang, more cider spilling out in a wave across the cobblestone floor.

She shook her head—*such* a waste—and caught sight of Artie. The dwarven tavern master shouted unintelligibly as he attempted to break up a pair of wrestling patrons. Broom in hand, Artemicion Bonejaw was every bit the crotchety, if diminutive, proprietor. And he was glaring at Elyria like this was all her fault.

Her skin prickled as she glared back. Sure, energies had run a bit high during the final few songs of her nightly performance. But it wasn't as if she'd been chanting war anthems. If anything, this was Artie's own fault. Surely the crowd would be far less likely to drink themselves into a frenzy if this tavern didn't serve the best cider and third-best ale in Coralith.

And *Elyria* certainly wasn't to blame for the group of six brutes who had barged into the Sweltering Pig during her encore, practically trampling half the patrons on their way in.

So, no, she didn't think it fair for Artie to act like it was *her* fault fists had started flying. This time, at least.

The sound of more glass shattering rang in Elyria's ears, setting her nerves on edge. She'd pay for this in the morning, no doubt. Elbow on the counter, she braced her head in her palm as someone hurled a stool at the bar and it exploded in a shower of splinters. Her eyes darted back to Artie, whose jaw hung open underneath his woven beard, his brow creased with outrage. He'd whittled that barstool himself.

Elyria grimaced. Yes, she would be paying in more ways than one.

"Come on then, Revenant," a man's deep, resonant voice drawled over the chaos. "We've gone through a lot of trouble trying to track you down."

Elyria drew her heavy-lidded eyes—not without effort—toward the man. A strong jaw with a cleft in his chin. Gray eyes. Blond hair that fell to his shoulders. Elyria supposed he was handsome enough, though the garish golden hoop dangling from each of his pointed ears immediately soured her interest. A single ruby-red bead hung from each earring—one of Tartanis's men.

"All this for me?" Elyria taunted, placing her hand over her heart. "I'm flattered, truly."

The man rolled his eyes. "Not our fault you got the crowd all riled up during your little performance." He waved a hand toward his lackeys standing at his back—three men, two women—then to the stage in the corner. "And now you're coming with us."

"Am I?" Elyria sighed, setting her tankard on the bar top with a *thunk*. "And here I thought I'd have a quiet evening."

He had the gall to smirk. "Well, I leave it up to you to determine if that will remain the case."

"How do you figure?"

His eyes narrowed. "You can come quietly, or we can take you . . . *not* quietly."

One of the man's greasy henchmen chortled. "You tell her, Raefe."

"Raefe, is it?" Elyria wobbled as she rose from her seat. She was not precisely the pinnacle of sobriety herself at present, she would admit. Not that it mattered.

Raefe's brow arched. "It is, *Revenant*."

Elyria rolled her emerald-green eyes. Half the people who used her moniker to address her hurled it like an insult. The other half said it like a prayer. She didn't care for either.

"Well, Raefe, your nose is bleeding," she said matter-of-factly.

Raefe's eyes widened. He dabbed at his nose with the back of his hand, then peered down, his brow creased. "No, it isn't."

She cracked her knuckles, giving him a pointed look. "It will."

Raefe scoffed and signaled his men forward. "Have it your way, then."

A duo of brawling patrons tumbled close. Elyria stepped away from the bar, and Raefe sprang into action. He levied a wild swing at her head, another at her gut.

She spun, dodging both blows and managing to stay upright with a wobbly sort of grace. A proud laugh escaped her lips. Even with more than her fair share of cider in her system, Elyria was still a formidable fighter. Anyone else would likely have been flat on their ass by now.

Still, the liquid courage was of no help when it came to the second opponent waiting to her right.

The woman's viridescent hair was pulled up in a tight series of braids, her leathers cut to showcase her shimmering wings and the swaths of pearly skin on her shoulders and arms. She flexed her hand, and a focused gust of air swept Elyria off her feet.

A stormbender. Wonderful.

Elyria flailed toward the ground. As she fell, she couldn't help but take in the woman's sharp features: her pointed jaw, the regal slant of her nose, the jut of the bones in her cheeks. A classic fae beauty, so unlike Elyria.

Were it not for the pointed ears and periwinkle hair that greeted her each day in the mirror, Elyria might wonder if she was fae at all. She couldn't help but compare her own face, with its soft cheekbones and button nose, to the woman's harsh beauty.

Made all the harsher from the sneer on the woman's lips as Elyria's back met the floor. Not for the first time, Elyria was glad she kept her own wings cloaked, that the magic that kept them from view also protected them. She knew all too well the pain that came with unceremoniously crushing a fae's wings.

Elyria was back on her feet in an instant, steady enough despite the way the room seemed to sway around her.

She slammed her arm into the woman's chest—perhaps harder than she'd intended. With a sputtering cough, the woman was on the ground, wheezing as if all the air had been knocked from her lungs. Elyria supposed it could have been.

Poetic, she thought, *for a stormbender to lose their breath.*

Elyria Lightbreaker was not known as "the Revenant" for nothing, after all. She had earned her wartime moniker, hadn't she? Whether she liked it or not. And it was good she was drunk, all things considered. This was the most fun she'd had in ages. Were she sober, she knew it would be coming to an end all too soon.

Raefe lunged at her once more. Her fist connected with his nose, eliciting a satisfying crunch. He stumbled back, colliding with a group of thrashing men, who bowled over as if they were ninepins.

Sadly, there was no time to savor the sight.

A young nocterrian surged forward, their hands outstretched as if meaning to grab her. She darted out of the way, her brow furrowed. The nocterrian wasn't even part of Raefe's gang. They were merely getting caught up in the brawl.

Elyria grabbed one of the thick horns on their head, swinging them around as they screamed in outrage. Her boot swiftly connected with their ass as she sent them careening toward the tavern door. When they finally regained their footing, they were staring at Elyria with wide eyes.

"Boo," she said, and the nocterrian fled into the night.

A cold sting scraped down the back of Elyria's neck. She whirled. Another one of Raefe's people—the *other* fae woman—stood in the middle of the tavern, eyes narrowed.

"Did you just—was that a snowball?" Elyria pawed at the back of her head. Sure enough, her hand closed around remnants of snow. She squirmed as slush slipped down the back of her vest, dancing over her spine. The icy bite sharpened her senses.

"Points for creativity, tideweaver." She hooked her boot through the rung of a nearby barstool. "A snowball in high summer. Can't say I expected that." She kicked her foot up, launching the stool into the woman's face. The collision of wood and bone sounded eerily similar to ice cracking.

"Put that one on my tab, Artie," Elyria said.

A disgruntled grumble came from near the bar in response.

With a crash, a table was overturned to her right. She leapt up, landing on the thin rim with a dancer's grace. "Come on, then." Her voice was bright as she teetered back and forth along the table's edge on the tips of her toes. "Who's next?"

Another tankard soared through the air, aimed at Elyria's skull. She caught it midair with a laugh, took a hearty swig, and tossed it aside. It was cold but stale—she grimaced as she felt it slide into her belly.

Her next laugh died in her throat as her vision went suddenly blurry. For a moment, she saw luminous golden eyes, a curl of dark hair across a strong brow, wings of deepest black and glittering gold.

She grasped at the image as if she could cement it in her mind. As if it weren't a picture of a ghost. A pang of longing stabbed her chest, sharp and painful. She could almost feel Evander's breath, warm on her skin. Could almost hear the whisper of his voice in her ear. It cut through the drink-induced haze in her mind.

The sound of the tavern door slamming snagged her attention, and

Elyria cursed. In the few seconds she'd lost herself to whatever vision had overtaken her, most of the tavern's patrons had fled.

Most, but not all.

Raefe and three of his thugs remained—the men. Something uncomfortable pricked at the back of Elyria's mind. She wondered where the women had gone. Standing watch outside, she supposed. Or maybe Elyria had wounded them badly enough that they had simply fled. As she observed the four men, huddled by the door, leering at Elyria, she regretted that.

The gold links in their tapered ears gleamed in the firelight as they traded tense whispers. Elyria frowned. The men were clearly strategizing about the best way to bring her down. Ten minutes prior, she would have welcomed the challenge. She had wanted to draw this out, give them a good show, have a little fun.

But that vision was . . . unexpected.

And Elyria didn't feel like fighting anymore.

Her eyes found Artie's, and she made a show of looking deliberately at the tavern's back door. As irritated as his constant scoldings might make her, she was fond of the old dwarf. He needed to clear out—she didn't want him getting hurt when she did what she had to do.

Artie rolled his eyes but took cover behind the bar.

Good enough.

Power hummed in her ears as Elyria raised a hand, calling upon her wild magic to bring this to a quick end.

The ground shook. Wood groaned. Dust drifted from the rafters.

And that was it.

Elyria looked at her hand and sighed. Perhaps she'd had one too many after all. The earth below the tavern floor was refusing to answer her call.

A taunt cut through the din. "This is the might of the Revenant?" jeered Raefe. "We're truly to believe this waste of wings took down three dozen cultists during the Battle of Luminaria?"

"Guess the tart's become sloppy over the decades," said one of the men, cracking his knuckles as he leered at Elyria.

She bit the inside of her lip to keep herself from snorting. He wasn't nearly as intimidating as she knew he was trying to be.

Raefe, on the other hand, was a walking column of menace. He huffed a laugh, teeth bared in a bloodstained grin as he stalked toward Elyria. Blood dripped from his nose—the effect of her previous punch.

At least she'd made good on that promise.

He didn't seem to care. "When word reached Master Tartanis that the mighty Revenant had been spotted back in Coralith, he couldn't believe his good luck. Neither could I believe mine, when he sent me to track you down. Imagine my disappointment to instead find a waif spinning musical yarns onstage before getting pissed in this hellscape of a tavern."

Elyria tamped down the growing discomfort in her gut and forced a grin. "You should be thanking the stars the cider tonight was so sweet, or this would have been over before it began."

She hopped off the table and planted her feet on the ground, bracing for the rush of bodies that were surely about to come her way.

They didn't.

Instead, Elyria felt the air around her grow thin. She suddenly couldn't take in breath fast enough. Her vision started to go black at the edges. She reached out to grab hold of something, to steady herself, and recoiled when her fingers found nothing but the sweaty arm of one of her attackers.

Through her bleary vision, she saw two of the men with their hands outstretched—Raefe had brought a near army of stars-damned stormbenders with him tonight.

"Ch-cheater," she stammered as the tavern spun around her. Then, without warning, air whooshed back into her lungs as the men let their magic die down. Elyria gulped down a greedy breath, unable to do anything more before the man nearest to her took hold of her wrists. She yelped as another wrapped his meaty hands around her ankles. The third righted the upended table, and Elyria was slammed upon it, the wood groaning under her back.

"Such a disappointment," Raefe said again, towering over Elyria as he stood next to the table. "Not only have you dashed our dreams of witnessing the legendary Revenant in all her supposed glory, but the fight barely even lasted long enough to count as entertainment." He dabbed at his nose again, his expression darkening. "Sing for us again, then. Your power may have underwhelmed, but I concede I rather enjoyed your performance earlier. You do have a *lovely* voice."

Something about the way he said that made Elyria never want to sing another note again.

"Maybe another time," she managed to grit out. "I think I've had just about enough for tonight." Her glare roved over the faces of the men pinning her down, committing each of them to memory. "And I don't think your boss will be too happy with you roughing up his prize," she added.

The way Raefe's lip curled up at the mention of Tartanis only confirmed as much.

"Get her to show us her wings, Raefe," rasped the man pinning Elyria's wrists. She suppressed a shudder, jerking against his hold. The grip on her limbs only tightened.

Raefe traced a finger around her ankle in slow, deliberate circles. "Ah, yes. Won't you bring your wings out to play? Perhaps if you put on a good show, we'll let you go."

Even if his lecherous gaze hadn't been raking over her body as he said the words, there wasn't a chance in the four hells Elyria believed him. He'd already told her they'd come here for her. They weren't leaving without her. But even if he was telling the truth, there was still no stars-damned way she was unveiling her wings. Not a fucking chance she would reveal the most vulnerable part of herself to these scoundrels.

"Show me yours, and I'll show you mine," she spat.

"That can be arranged," Raefe said, and Elyria had to swallow to keep the evening's libations from making a violent return up her throat.

Her pulse quickened, that feeling of discomfort—of *warning*—stirring in her gut once more.

"Fine," she said quickly. "I'll sing for you—and I'll do it happily, too." Raefe arched his brow. She smiled sweetly. "When your body is cold in the ground, and I'm dancing atop your grave. In fact, I'll put on a whole celestial-blessed concert, motherfucker."

Raefe made a tutting sound before widening his grin. The blood froze in Elyria's veins. "Oh, I think we'll be making sweet music together long before then."

CHAPTER 2
BRUTES, BEASTS, AND VERMIN

Elyria

Raefe dragged the finger that had been circling Elyria's ankle up the outside of her leg, following the seam of her pants. She drew a sharp breath when he reached her thigh, her heart pounding in her chest. His hand snaked slowly over her leather breeches in a checkerboard pattern—back and forth, up and down—like he was trying to memorize the shape of her.

Revulsion coursed through her veins, hot and fierce. She refused to let it show on her face, though she couldn't help writhing as he neared her inner thigh. She was bracing herself for his touch to go further—to go too far—when he stopped. With a wicked grin, he moved to the other side of the table and repeated the same thing on her other leg.

It took a moment for Elyria to calm her thundering heart enough to realize that something wasn't right. To realize that the path Raefe traced up her body prickled—that it *burned*. Her skin was on fire, the leather of her breeches scorching.

Her first thought was that his touch was just *that* repulsive, but it soon became all too clear that the sensation was not in her head.

Her skin *was* burning.

Raefe was a flamecaller, and he was branding her through her clothing.

The guffaws of the men pinning her down were a horrific chorus in Elyria's ears as pain finally dawned on her face. Sweat beaded on her brow, and she thought she might crack a tooth from how tightly she clenched her jaw. But she would not scream, even as she thrashed against the table.

The slightest breeze wafted over her legs as she did, a cruel respite for her scalded flesh that didn't last nearly long enough. It was quickly overshadowed by a dark understanding of exactly what Raefe was doing as his white-hot touch seared through her breeches, leaving them in tatters.

He was stripping her bare, inch by excruciating inch.

If nearly suffocating before hadn't sobered her up, the scorched path Raefe was carving into her skin certainly did the trick.

The stench of charred leather and burnt flesh wafted into her nose. Elyria nearly vomited. She cursed her traitorous body when tears slipped from her eyes, dripping into her ears. Still Elyria refused to give Raefe or his lackeys the satisfaction of hearing a single whimper.

She could take it.

She'd survived worse.

But it hurt. The pain was overwhelming. And while Elyria had no doubt she could survive the torment, she could also feel . . . *it*. Stirring, awakening, deep inside her. That inner darkness that she spent so much of her energy, so much effort to keep contained.

Admittedly, at this moment Elyria didn't mind the thought of Raefe getting a taste of that darkness. He had, after all, sought her out for it. *"This is the might of the Revenant?"* he'd complained. If he only knew what he was asking for.

What Elyria knew was that however satisfying it might feel to let the darkness out to take care of Raefe and his men . . . it would still not be worth the cost.

This needed to stop. Now.

Elyria wrenched her neck, looking around her in a desperate bid to see if there was anyone—anything—left in the tavern that might help her. Any potential ally. Any possible distraction.

The tavern was empty.

Empty, save for . . .

From the corner of her eye, Elyria saw Artie rise from behind the counter. She shook her head, just a degree in each direction. A tiny warning.

The tavern master gave Elyria a purposeful look, placed a small plant on the bar—no bigger than the palm of his hand—and ducked back down behind the counter before any of the men noticed.

A sense of calm washed over Elyria. Her consciousness reached toward the plantling, feeling for its energy, the magic thrumming in its cells. Full of potential, full of possibility.

Full of *growth*.

She did her best to still her body, to cease her writhing, despite the blisters she could feel forming on her legs.

Raefe's finger stilled. He met her eye, his expression shifting. Puzzlement. Wariness.

"What's this, then?" he said, whispering as if speaking only to himself.

Elyria closed her eyes. She exhaled. "It's just that I truly do hate that I've disappointed you. Allow me to rectify that."

Her eyes snapped open. They burned silver with cold fury. Power thrummed along her skin, wisps of energy seeping off her like smoke. The men holding her wrists and ankles inhaled sharply, and their grasp loosened by a fraction.

Raefe's head whipped from side to side as he tried to make sense of the shift in the air, as he searched for the cause of this sudden change in Elyria's countenance. Shadows blurred the edges of her vision as he locked eyes with her once more.

And then she saw it.

Fear.

Elyria smiled.

She flexed her hands, splaying her palms even as her wrists were still pinned by Raefe's increasingly confused henchman. Vines sprouted from the planter on the counter, shattering the tiny terra-cotta pot as they erupted. They split, lengthened, multiplied, and in an instant, all four men were suspended by their feet, wrapped from neck to ankle in thick vines.

"She's a wildshaper!" cried one of the men.

"You bit—" yelled another, but a vine snaked around his mouth, cutting him off before he could get the word out.

Elyria bit back a laugh. That was putting it mildly.

Raefe's gray eyes were wide as the vines curled up the length of his body, but he said nothing. He made no sound at all, save for the labored inhale and exhale of breath as Elyria's vines tightened around his chest. Then a sort of choking, gagging sound as one crawled into his mouth. Elyria shook with the effort it took to be just as slow and deliberate with Raefe as he had been with her.

Elyria sat up with a groan. Ignoring the muffled screams coming from around her, she peeled back the scraps of leather that had once been her pants. She frowned, wincing as she prodded one particularly heinous section of her right thigh.

Artie poked his head up from behind the bar and assessed the scene—a half-dozen men hanging upside down, engulfed in vines—with stony disinterest. "All right then, lass?" he asked Elyria, and maybe she just imagined it, but she thought she saw relief flicker over his face. Thought his voice sounded thicker than usual.

"I'll live," she grunted, pain overtaking her senses as she shifted one of her legs. Her magic was nearly spent keeping her attackers bound, but Elyria called forth what little remaining energy she had. She wrapped her blistered, burning legs in tendrils of healing magic. The relief was immediate. Her thighs still stung, throbbing as if each leg had its own heartbeat, but it was manageable. And it would do until she got to a healer.

"Ye're sure—"

The door burst open. A gaggle of city guards poured into the tavern, interrupting whatever Artie planned to say. They hauled the two female members of Raefe's merry gang in with them, their wrists bound and gags over their mouths.

"Ah, Officers, excellent timing, as always," Elyria said drily. The muffled screams of agreement coming from both the shackled women and Elyria's own vine-bound attackers indicated they either did not understand or did not agree with her sarcastic words.

"What now, Lightbreaker?" said the guard at the front of the pack, sounding tired. He wore a captain's emblem over his left breast. She thought his name might be Zaric, though admittedly, she had not been in a particularly reliable state of sobriety during their past encounters.

Elyria got to her feet, her hands raised in mock surrender. "Wasn't me this time, sir. I swear it."

Zaric snorted. "Regardless, I must insist you release those men."

"They are hardly men, Captain. Cowards? Yes. Brutes? Absolutely. Beasts? Without a doubt. Vermin? In—"

"I do believe we understand your meaning," Zaric interrupted.

"Regardless," Elyria said pointedly, "I am of the opinion that they require a bit more time to consider the consequences of their actions. They attacked me, unprovoked. Destroyed the tavern. Ruined my favorite pair of breeches." She motioned to her barely covered legs, and several of the guards' eyes shot to the ceiling, their faces red. One of the female guards standing next to the captain looked personally offended. "I remain unconvinced they've learned their lesson."

Artie huffed in agreement.

"A likely story." The female guard stepped forward, blowing a lock of short copper hair out of her eyes with a huff. Elyria wondered if she knew her. "Just how much have you had to drink tonight?"

"Taryn," Captain Zaric cautioned.

"For this would hardly be the first time we were called to break up a tavern brawl—called to this very tavern—only to find you attempting to hide all manner of sins," Taryn sneered, undeterred by the captain's warning.

Elyria's gaze turned cold as she assessed the guard. "Do I know you?"

Taryn's jaw flexed, but she barreled on, ignoring the question. "And even were you being truthful, preposterous as the concept may be, the punishment of these men is not up to you. It is to be decided upon by Lord Corlyn."

"Enough, Taryn." Zaric shot her a silencing glare, and she stepped back into line with her fellow guards.

"The girl speaks the truth," Artie offered. Elyria's eyebrows shot up at his unexpected assistance. It seemed to shock the dwarf as well, as he was quick to add, "For once."

Zaric sighed. "Release them, Lightbreaker. I won't ask again."

Elyria glowered at the captain as she curled her fingers in, drawing her hands into fists. The vines retracted, and all four men dropped to the ground with a satisfying *thud*.

"Get them on their feet. We'll haul the lot of them to the jail, question them there," Zaric commanded his guards.

Raefe's voice filled the air, hoarse and labored. Elyria kept her fists clenched tightly at her sides for fear she'd claw his lips clean off. "C-Captain, I th-thank you f-for interce-ce-ceding," he started, though those were the only words he could get out before dissolving into a coughing fit. Doubled over, his hands on his knees, Raefe hacked and retched so animatedly that even his own flunkeys stepped away.

"The others aren't acting like that. What's wrong with him?" asked Taryn, her gaze pinned on Elyria.

"No idea," Elyria said with a shrug, though she grinned inwardly. "Are we done here? I have quite some sewing to do."

"Sorry, Lightbreaker," said Zaric. "You'll need to come with us as well."

"Surely that's not ne—" Artie began to object, but Elyria held up a silencing hand.

"It's fine. No need to shove it down my throat," she said, throwing a wink in Raefe's direction. He paled several shades and began retching anew. "I'll go, assuming you have some spare breeches for me at the jailhouse."

"I imagine we will be able to find you something," said Zaric as Taryn muttered something under her breath.

Elyria whipped around to face the guard. "What was that?"

"Taryn." Zaric's voice was deep with reprimand.

"No. If she has something to say, I want to hear it." Elyria drew up to her full height as she turned to face Taryn. The two were evenly matched in terms of stature, though Elyria was not nearly as muscled. Still, she was the Revenant. Furthermore, she'd done nothing that she knew of to warrant Taryn's ire. If nothing else, surely her reputation warranted a modicum of respect from the guard.

Taryn did not agree.

"I said," she spat, her grass-green eyes shooting daggers into Elyria's emerald ones, "perhaps if you spent more time singing your ditties and less time spreading your legs for every man, woman, and nocterrian in Coralith, you'd have enough gold to buy your own stars-damned breeches."

The air in the tavern was suddenly impossibly thick.

"Well, shit," muttered Artie, shuffling surreptitiously until he was safely behind the bar again.

"Four hells, Taryn, this is not behavior befitting of the city guard," Zaric reprimanded.

Elyria barely heard him. Her heartbeat pounded in her ears. "Is that what this is about?" Her eyes narrowed on the smug expression on Taryn's face. "Did I snub your advances? No . . . something tells me I'm not quite your flavor. Perhaps I stole a prospect from you? Spent my evening with someone who had been of particular interest?"

Taryn's pompous grin melted into an ugly sneer. It bolstered Elyria, who could feel that inner darkness stirring in her chest once more.

"Or perhaps it was someone already close to you?"

Taryn flinched.

Elyria pounced. "Was it someone who made you promises? Who told you they belonged to you and you alone?" she continued. "If so, you can hardly hold me responsible for their actions. Though whatever would possess them to step out on you, I couldn't possibly imagine." Elyria's smile was feline, lethal. "You're such a treat."

"You don't even remember." Taryn's voice was quieter now.

"I've walked this land for two hundred and sixty-one summers. My list of satisfied lovers is longer than the Chasm is deep. You cannot possibly expect me to remember the name, face, and"—she flicked her gaze from Taryn's hair to her toes and back again—"associates of each one."

Elyria found the guard's answering snarl deeply satisfying.

"That's enough," muttered Zaric, though he took no additional pains to intervene. For a moment, however, it appeared as though that was enough. Taryn broke her stare, shooting her eyes to the floor, and Elyria turned toward the tavern doors once more.

"Whore."

A greater woman might have taken the insult in stride, but Elyria was tired. She had just endured the feeling of her own skin melting under Raefe's torturous touch. Her magic was spent. Her patience nonexistent.

Still, Elyria tried. And when the slur was repeated, when the word cut across her ears, sharp as a knife, she took a deep, steadying breath.

Then another.

It was to no avail.

Because there *it* was.

The darkness. The shadow inside her.

Alive.

Raefe's torture had awoken it, and now it searched. It yearned. It begged to be unleashed.

And Elyria didn't know how to stop it.

So, she did what any sensible person would do.

She reared back and punched Taryn, a sworn member of the city guard, square in the face.

The rest of Captain Zaric's squad swarmed—as she knew they would. They descended upon her, pushed her to the ground—as she knew they would.

And when one of them smacked the back of her head with their baton—not once, not twice, but three times before consciousness began to leave her—Elyria smiled.

CHAPTER 3
A BAD HABIT

Elyria

Golden eyes hovered on the fringe of Elyria's awareness, glimmering like stars through a fog. They beckoned her—familiar, distant. A dream she struggled to cling to, to hold, only for it to slip through her fingers like water.

Evander.

Elyria's eyes flew open.

Her head pounded, a steady, walloping beat that echoed throughout her body, reverberating off her bones. Whether it was due to her fresh head injury, having overspent her magic, or the sheer amount of cider she consumed before the brawl broke out, she couldn't say.

Most likely, it was a combination of all three.

The pounding grew louder, each drumbeat wiping the lingering images from her mind as her skull throbbed in rhythm with a nearby clanging. Someone was banging on the bars of their cell.

Someone who clearly yearned for a swift death.

Elyria groaned as she rolled onto her back, her body aching from the unforgiving stone floor beneath her. This was not her first time in a cell. Hells, it was likely not her first time in *this* cell. Which was how she knew not to think about whatever might be coating the stone, about who might have been in here last and what they did while they were. She knew not to think about how long her face had been pressed to the somehow simultaneously sticky *and* slimy surface.

She knew not to think about whatever *that smell was*.

She closed her eyes again. She wanted to go back inside her head, to the visions of Evander that had now come upon her twice. She wanted to gaze unendingly into those luminous eyes, to feel his bronze skin under her fingers, to see his black-and-gold wings shimmer as she lay on her back, his strong body moving over her.

How many nights had she sought solace at the bottom of a bottle, hoping for exactly that? Drunkenly prayed to see him again, even if only as a ghost?

Why was she finally being blessed with it now?

As if in answer, Elyria's mind was awash with images again, only the warm memories of the past were nowhere to be found this time. Instead, she saw only agony. Evander writhing in pain, dark veins creeping from his golden eyes. His beautiful wings, shredded, black blood pooling on the ground.

Elyria's eyes shot open, blinking rapidly to stop the wetness that had begun to gather.

What the quartered hell was that?

"Oi! Lightbreaker's awake!" a rough voice from a neighboring cell whisper-shouted. "How's the head, Rev?"

The words bounced around noisily in Elyria's skull; she winced but didn't answer.

"What's the matter with her?" another voice asked. Smaller, lighter. Curious.

"Dunno. She weren't in such good shape when they brought her in."

Elyria focused on the ceiling directly above her, keeping her gaze locked on a crack in the stone until her eyes began to burn and she was forced to close them again. Blessedly, she was met with the black of the back of her eyelids and not another nightmarish depiction of her former love. She kept her eyes shut and tried to block out the world.

"Perhaps she is ill," the small voice said.

"Couldn't be too ill, not with the fight she gave 'em," said someone new, a third speaker. "Did you get a look at that one guard? Nose bleeding like a faucet, shiner blooming 'round one of her eyes."

Pride unfurled in Elyria's chest at the description of what her singular punch had done to Taryn's face.

"Should we be talking about this?" The small voice was barely more than a whisper. "About her, right in front of her?"

"She's asleep again, innit?" the first person said. "Not too impressive, if you ask me."

"Noctis damn you, watch your tongue, man! You're talking about the warrior who took down two dozen men at the Battle of Luminaria on her own."

"It was three dozen, at least." The small voice again. "And they weren't just men. They were cultists. Malakar's own."

Someone sucked in a sharp breath. "Humans are bad enough on their own, but cultists? They're a special breed of dark."

"Sanguinagi." The word came from a new voice, which could only belong to a nocterrian—somehow simultaneously soft and hard, masculine and feminine. "Blood mages."

"Still a stars-damned bloody nuisance, even today, thanks to Varyth fuckin' Malchior at the helm."

"Heard some members of the Cult of Malakar got picked off outside Crystalfell just the other week."

"They made it that far into Nyrundelle? Four hells."

A few moments passed in tense silence. Elyria's skin prickled under what she felt suddenly sure were multiple gazes focused on her.

"My uncle was on the battlefield on the day of the Shattering." One of the previous voices resumed speaking. "Said it was near a lost cause—Malakar had already taken the castle. His cultists overwhelmed them. Queen Daephinia's forces had all but given up. Until her. He didn't see her on the field, but he saw what she left in her wake . . ."

Elyria stopped trying to keep track of who was speaking. It hardly mattered. She wished they would all cease entirely. She just wanted *quiet*.

I could make them be quiet, she thought idly. Confident that the baffling, unsettling visions had passed, she reopened her eyes and let them drift across the grime-covered stone ceiling, then down the bars of her cell.

A small sylvan girl in ragged clothing that revealed patches of green skin along her arms and legs stared wide-eyed from the cell to Elyria's left. Two fae men shared a large cell next to her. The three of them were locked in their continued discussion of the Revenant's ancient exploits.

Opposite them, a nocterrian with skin the color of the midnight sky sat alone, legs crossed. Their eyes were on Elyria, but they had a vacant look to them, lost in thought as they absently stroked one of the majestic curved horns protruding from beneath their pitch-black hair. The darkness inside her stirred slightly. She shoved it back down.

A sign hung on the wall next to the nocterrian's cell, directly across from Elyria. NO MAGIC it said in large, red letters. Below the words was a crude drawing of a stick figure being struck by lightning.

Alas, Elyria didn't think that being zapped with a counterspell would do much to improve the state of her pounding head. With a sigh, she sat up, delighting in the terrified squeals of her gossiping neighbors as they realized she was awake. Perhaps there was *some* benefit to the persistent myth of the Revenant.

Sadly, it wasn't enough to keep her fellow detainees from starting up their conversation again after a few minutes—in harsh whispers this time, though Elyria stopped listening anyway. She had more pressing concerns.

Where were Raefe and his men? Had they already been questioned? Released? Though the thought made smoke erupt from her ears, it would hardly surprise her. Tartanis had a lot of influence in Coralith. Beyond it, too. A well-placed bribe—or a better-placed threat—and his men would be back on the streets to terrorize at their leisure once more.

Elyria rubbed her temples, assessing herself. She noted with frustration that she still wore her shredded leathers. Which was to say, she wore barely anything at all.

No wonder everyone was staring.

Peeling back a few scraps of scorched leather, Elyria took stock of the mess that was her legs. The long, puckered lines that ran up the side of each limb were already well on their way to healing. In time, she thought that they might fade to near nothing. But it was the map of scars emblazoned upon her thighs that had her sucking in air through her teeth.

The bubbling blisters that had crisscrossed her skin had hidden the majority of the damage when she checked herself in the tavern, so she hadn't noticed then. But Raefe had burned her deep. And when Elyria had thrown that weak bit of healing magic over her legs to take the edge off the pain, she hadn't realized she was setting the marks in place.

Now, with the blisters gone and the burns partially healed, these scars were part of her. Getting rid of them would entail flaying the very flesh from her legs and having a healer regrow it from scratch.

Elyria found herself wishing she had done a lot more to Raefe than shove a few vines down his gullet.

Slowly, the voices around her rose in volume, though her fellow detainees had wisely stopped discussing her so openly now that she was upright. Elyria began to pace. She wondered how long she would be down here this time. She felt it unusual that no one had come to speak to or check on her yet.

On the one hand, she had attacked a member of the city guard.

On the other, the guard in question was *Taryn*.

The woman was horrid. Elyria hadn't missed the glances exchanged between the rest of the guards as Taryn railed at her. Disapproval. Judgment. Irritation. She wasn't sure if it was aimed at herself or at Taryn, who, by their captain's own admission, was hardly behaving as an honorable member of the city guard should.

A wave of pity washed over Elyria as she spared a thought for the rest of the guard, putting up with Taryn and her sanctimonious bullshit day in, day out. Then she wondered how they would feel if they knew what Elyria had been saving them all from by taking Taryn's bait.

Humming quietly, she paced the length of her cell, making a song out of counting each pass she made. Finally—just as her count reached one hundred and seventy-three—a guard approached.

"About damn time," Elyria said with a singsongy flourish, her mental tune spilling out.

The guard chuckled as he unlocked her cell. "I think it's time to find a new hobby, Elle. This is becoming a bad habit."

CHAPTER 4
NO ONE'S MESSENGER

Elyria

Elyria grinned at Olyndor Oleander as the guard held out a mug of water and a corner of bread. She snatched the items from his hands, her thirst and hunger hitting her in a sudden wave. She hadn't given either much thought until this moment, but she was ravenous.

A choked sound rumbled from the cell next to her. She glanced at the sylvan girl sitting against the wall, whose green-skinned knees were gathered to her chest. She was viscerally focused on the bread in Elyria's hands.

With a sigh, Elyria tossed the loaf through the bars. The girl squeaked in surprise as it landed in her hands.

"It's good to see you too, Ollie," Elyria said. It was true. She might've been under lock and key, but it didn't mean she wasn't pleased to have the opportunity to catch up with the guard. They'd befriended each other during one of her early visits to the jailhouse, after Elyria had made the move to Coralith. She was uncharacteristically fond of him, in no small part due to his name, which she found endlessly amusing for what she felt were obvious reasons.

"I was going to bring food for the others after, you know," he said defensively, eyeing the sylvan girl as she scarfed down the piece of bread.

Taking a hefty swig from the mug, Elyria let her gaze roam over Olyndor's turquoise hair, warm brown eyes, and the tanned skin covering thick muscles beneath his uniform. He arched a brow at her leering. She grinned. She was well aware of his preference for the company of men, but that didn't mean she couldn't enjoy the way his presence improved the atmosphere significantly. And she appreciated the physical reminder that there were still handsome men out there who were also *good*—unlike Raefe.

"After what?" she asked.

To her surprise, Olyndor stepped aside, holding the cell door open and gesturing for her to walk through it.

"What's going on?" Elyria asked, truly puzzled. Despite the affection she held for the guard, she'd gone through this process enough times to know better than to think she'd be getting out of here so soon. Zaric hadn't even returned to question her yet.

Ollie shrugged. "You're free to go. Unless you'd rather stay here, of course. I enjoy your company well enough, but I think we both know you've better places to be."

Elyria frowned. "Why would you do this?"

He chuckled. "As much as I would like to take credit, it's not an act of kindness. Your release has been requested."

"By whom?"

He shrugged. "Word's out that the Gate will open soon. Perhaps someone hopes to persuade you to take on the Crucible."

She snorted. "A fool's hope." Elyria stretched her arms as she strode through the open door.

With a shake of his head, Ollie led her out of the cellblock and up a winding stairway. Elyria didn't miss the way her name shot out of the other prisoners' mouths as soon as she was out of sight.

They exited the stairway and made it halfway down the jailhouse's long vestibule before Ollie resumed speaking.

"It wouldn't be the worst thing in the world, you know. If you entered. For you to become a champion of Nyrundelle."

"There are plenty of Arcanians clamoring to enter the Sanctum on the kingdom's behalf."

"None like you."

Elyria shifted, discomfort rolling through her gut. She did not like the fact that they were talking about this. "Are you that eager to be rid of me?" she teased, trying to get their friendly banter back on track.

He didn't take the bait. "If anyone could get through the trials, it's you, Elle. Folk are on edge. They want the Chasm filled. Battles over territory in the Midlands have only gotten worse—the humans continue to fight dirtier and dirtier. Securing the crown for King Lachlandris could finally put an end to it all." His tawny eyes locked on hers. "You'd be giving hope to so many."

"Enough, Ollie."

"The morning star's already been spotted. It was burning so bright, the poor farmer who saw it thought a second sun had appeared. It's never been like that before," he continued, failing to notice the way Elyria's shoulders began to sag. Or perhaps he did notice, and he just didn't care. "The Crucible's magic will take effect soon. All fighting in the Midlands will be forced to cease, and dozens will make the trek to the Lost City."

"Olyndor."

He ignored her, rambling now. Like so many others, he was clearly caught up in the hysteria and glamour of the Crucible. As if it were anything more than a guaranteed means to a violent end for all who attempted it.

"And rumors say the aurora's expected to bloom brighter than ever before too. Some say it's a sign from Lunara, that it means it's time. You know the prophecy, don't you?"

Elyria clenched her fists, her head starting to throb again.

"From shadow and fire, champions rise, forged in the Crucible of fate." Ollie clamped his hand over his heart as he recited the ancient words. *"Strength, spirit, magic, and concord test the trials beyond the Gate. From bitterest rivals—"*

"I said, that's *enough*." Rage sparked in Elyria's veins, compelling her body into movement. Before she realized what she was doing, she had the guard pinned against the wall, her forearm on his throat.

Elyria gasped, pulling back almost as quickly as she had struck. "I'm sorry, Ollie. I didn't—"

"Tsk, tsk." A familiar, disappointed clucking came from behind Elyria. "Still so quick to violence. I see some things truly never change."

And Elyria spun around to find herself face to face with Duchess Laeliana Ravenswing.

She looked just as Elyria remembered. Statuesque. Grace taken fae form. Long white hair that flowed over mahogany skin. Deep-set golden eyes—her son's eyes.

Elyria could barely stand to look at them.

"What are you doing here?" she blurted.

"I think the better question, darling, is what in Lunara's name are *you* doing here? Honestly, Elle, I fear this is becoming a pattern."

Ollie let out a nervous chuckle. "That's precisely what I said, Your Grace."

Laeliana blinked at him as if she'd forgotten he was there.

"That is—er, I mean to say—"

"You are dismissed," said Laeliana.

"O-of course. Good day, ma'am," he stammered before making a hasty retreat, leaving Elyria alone with the duchess.

"What purpose was there in scaring him off? He's my friend," Elyria said petulantly.

Laeliana arched a brow. "*He's* your friend? He's your jailer."

"Close enough," Elyria said, her tone flippant even as a pang ran through her heart. She was momentarily overcome, as though she could feel the warmth of the summer sun and smell the roses in the gardens at the Ravenswing estate. She could hear Kit's laughter ringing as she chased Evander around the fountains, could hear his indignant shout when his sister dove *into* the fountain to get to him. Could still see Laeliana watching over the inseparable trio from the balcony, a cup of tea in her hand.

Elyria blanched. Eager to rid her mind of the unbidden images, she went on to say, "I suppose I have you to thank for my expedient dismissal?"

Laeliana nodded, watching Elyria's face closely.

"You have my thanks. But I confess, I find myself at an utter loss as to what you're doing here. You're a long way from Aerithia, Your Grace."

The duchess tilted her head. "Walk with me."

"Oh. Er . . . I'm not . . . properly . . ." Elyria waved a lame hand at the state of her clothing. Laeliana looked her over with an amused expression. "Didn't know I would be in the company of nobility today," Elyria said.

"I know better than to think you'd go out of your way even if you *had* known, my dear." The duchess snapped her fingers, and a long purple cloak, the color of orchids, soared over on a controlled gust. It landed upon Elyria's shoulders, draping over her legs and hiding the worst of her outfit's offenses.

"Convenient," Elyria murmured, unable to mask the admiration in her tone at the duchess's graceful wielding of her storm magic.

They exited the jailhouse and walked in silence toward the city proper. Day was just breaking, the clouds a kaleidoscope of soft grays, pinks, and blues. Birds sang in the mistwood trees. Elyria relished the moment of peace . . . but that was all it was. A moment. Because as she scanned the sky, she saw the morning star. It was exactly as Ollie described—bright and angry. The Gate would open soon.

It wasn't until they crossed into the gardens beyond the city square that Laeliana resumed speaking. "I won't ask how you ended up here . . . again."

Elyria's cheeks heated.

"But I will say that I was glad when word of your most recent escapades reached my ears. I flew here as quickly as my wings would allow."

"Dare I ask why?"

Laeliana drew a deep breath. "The Arcane Crucible is upon us once again. I think you know this—I saw you watching the morning star. And King Lachlandris's personal oracle and best diviners all agree the aurora will bloom any day."

Elyria swallowed the knot that was forming in her throat. "I mean no offense, Your Grace, but what does that have to do with me? You know better than anyone my feelings about the Crucible. Let the aurora bloom, let the Gate open. I do not care."

Laeliana's expression tightened, her reaction making Elyria feel as though she'd struck her.

"I'm sorry, I didn't—"

"Katerina—Kit. She has decided to enter the Crucible."

The words of apology Elyria had been about to speak died on her tongue. "No. What are you—no. Impossible." Laeliana said nothing as Elyria's words spewed forth in a furious tangle. "She wouldn't. No. Not after—she can't. You cannot allow this. You must *stop her*." Shadows flickered at the edge of Elyria's vision. Her control was slipping.

A memory swept in—fierce, fast. She saw the pride on Evander's face, colors dancing over his skin as the sunlight filtered in through broken stained glass. He grinned as he strode toward the Gate, stopping just before he reached it.

She remembered watching him turn, searching for her as she stood at the front of the crowd of onlookers. She was huddled next to his sister, Kit's hand firmly squeezed in her own. Elyria remembered the way she'd nodded, encouraged him. She had truly believed he would be the one, that he could win.

Evander winked at her, his golden eyes burning with resolve. And then he stepped through the Gate.

She never saw him again.

The vision that had overtaken her in the jail cell prickled in her mind—hideous black veins vining through his beautiful face, the suffering in his voice as he cried out. Was that how he died? A painful, horrendous, lonely death?

"You know my daughter." Laeliana's voice brought Elyria slamming back to the present, eyes burning. "You know if I had any choice in the matter, I would stop this. You know I have *tried*."

"Try harder. Lock her up if you have to. Chain her to her bed. You must not allow her to enter the Sanctum." Even as the words tumbled from Elyria's mouth, she knew they were empty. Kit had always been mercurial. A free spirit—freer even than Elyria. Beholden only to the whims of her heart, she would go where she wanted to go, would do what she wanted to do. To prevent her from doing so would be to snuff out her very light.

Even still, to attempt to follow in her brother's footsteps, to go through the Gate . . . Elyria thought this foolish even for her capricious erstwhile friend.

"I came to ask you—to *beg* you—to talk to her. Please, get her to change her mind. I have done all I can, said all I can. I know the two of you have history to work through. I wish I did not have to ask. But as I said, the aurora is due. I am out of time." The duchess took a breath, as if she expected the next words to hurt. "I cannot lose another child beyond the Gate."

Elyria exhaled through gritted teeth. "You can't ask this of me. Kit and I haven't even set eyes on each other since Ev-Evander"—she choked on his name—"failed to come back. We haven't spoken since . . ." Guilt nipped at the back of her neck. Since she had stopped replying to Kit's letters. Since she had refused Kit's final attempt to visit, so determined was she to lose herself nightly in the fog of drink and distraction. "I can't."

Laeliana's face fell. "I know what it is I ask of you, child. The wounds I am asking you to reopen. I do not pretend it is fair, and I do not take it lightly. But you are my last hope, Elle," pleaded the duchess.

"If Kit wants to throw her life away like her brother, so be it. That is her choice. I am not your messenger." Elyria stalked away, her hands busy with the clasp of the cloak as she shrugged it from her shoulders. "I am no one's."

With a shiver, she released the magic veiling her wings. They burst from her back in a shower of brilliant iridescent purple and green.

Elyria pumped her wings—once, twice. Relished the feel of them, free and open and wild. They shimmered in the light of the dawning sun, a cascade of colors dancing like a miniature aurora on her back. Her feet lifted from the grass.

"Elyria! Elle, please. Please!" Laeliana called after her, but Elyria was already in the air.

She did not look back.

CHAPTER 5
THE KNIGHT

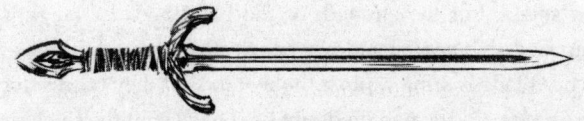

Cedric

Sweat dripped from Cedric Thorne's brow as he moved through the training yard. Tristan's sword whistled through the air, passing a finger's width from Cedric's chest. His mettle was certainly being put to the test today. He supposed he should have known better than to expect anything less when he made a sparring partner of Tristan Hale.

The clangor of sword against shield filled the yard, the knights dancing around each other. Tristan lunged. Cedric spun. Then he struck.

"You're slow today, Ric," Tristan teased, deftly angling his blade to repel Cedric's thrust with a resounding clash of steel. "All that brooding you've been doing must be taxing indeed."

"Hardly," Cedric snorted, deflecting Tristan's next strike. "And what you call 'brooding,' I call staying focused. Not all of us are blessed with the capacity to fight with such happy humor."

"That I cannot deny. Indeed, I am blessed." Tristan laughed, the scarred line on his left cheek curving with his smile, before he feinted to the side. "*Enormously* blessed, so my lovers tell me."

Cedric pushed a lock of damp chestnut hair from his forehead with the back of his hand, a smirk playing on his lips. "What lovers? Pray, tell me his or her name so that I may recommend them to a healer. Clearly, they are in need of aid if they suffer such delusions."

Tristan gasped in mock offense, swinging his sword in a wide arc. Cedric dodged it easily. "Whatever would Lord Church say, should he hear your egregious lies?"

"Alas, how I wish I was lying. But you forget how many times I've had the misfortune of seeing you naked, sir."

Tristan sniffed. "Prick my skin and bleed my body, but never shall you wound my pride."

"As you wish." A laugh burst from Cedric as he threw his weight into his next strike, driving forward with crushing force. Tristan blocked with his shield, but the strength of the blow had the knight's knee buckling. Cedric hammered down blow after blow, the dull edge of his practice blade roaring against the wood. Had they been using their actual weapons, Cedric had no doubt he'd have split the shield in two.

"Aurelia damn you!" Tristan's knee hit the dirt, strands of blond hair falling into his eyes. "I yield."

Cedric grinned as he tossed his weapon aside and removed his gauntlets. He extended a hand to his friend. "Perhaps you might try a bit more brooding. I am, after all, not the one on the ground."

Tristan huffed as Cedric hauled him up, but he was smiling by the time he got to his feet. "And I'm glad for it. Anything that shows me you won't be doing the same when fending off a fae blade."

"It is not their blades he needs to worry about." A booming baritone echoed over the yard. Cedric tensed, turning to meet the keen, assessing eye of Lord Leviathan Church. The nobleman stood next to the weapons rack, robes billowing in the breeze, his dark brown hair, peppered with gray, slicked back from his face.

"No, my lord." Cedric bent at the waist in a respectful bow.

"What *is* the greatest threat posed by the fae?" The lord's cane left pockmarks in the dirt as he limped toward the duo.

"Their magic," answered Cedric.

"And why is that?"

Tristan arched an eyebrow. "Is that a serious question, your lordship?"

Lord Church leveled him with a cool stare. "Fae—all Arcanians, in fact—wield magic as easily as the breath in their lungs. It lives in their veins. They do not require *assistance* the same way we do."

He drew his mana token from beneath his robes, the circular amulet hanging from a chain around his neck, the size of a large coin. The dark—almost black—metal seemed to suck in the light from around it, even as the single crimson gem set in its center glowed bright and lucent. It brimmed with mana.

He must have recently charged it, Cedric thought.

"I would like Sir Thorne's reassurance that he has a thorough understanding of exactly what he'll be facing in the Crucible," Lord Church continued.

Tristan cleared his throat. "Yes, my lord. I only mean to say, even the smallest of children know the dangers of the fae. Of all the races of Old Arcanis. Cedric does not—"

"You may take your leave, Sir Hale," Lord Church commanded, interrupting him.

Tristan's blue eyes widened infinitesimally, but he dipped his head. "Be sure to find me before you leave, Ric," he said, then strode away.

Cedric straightened, pushing aside the uncomfortable feeling their exchange stirred in his gut. "What news, my lord?"

"The aurora blooms. It is time."

Cedric's eyes shot to the sky. The sun burned brightly, but as he squinted, he could see the rainbow of colors shimmering behind the clouds. They would only grow more vivid as night approached.

His heartbeat quickened. "I am ready."

A smile played on Lord Church's lips. "I know you are. This is what you trained for." Then his expression grew stern, his amber eyes darkening. "But remember, the Arcane Crucible is more than a challenge of physical prowess. It is a test of mind and spirit—of your determination.

And the Arcanians you shall meet in the Sanctum will be nothing if not determined. They want the crown."

Heat flared in Cedric's chest at the thought.

"And should they be allowed to claim it . . ." Lord Church trailed off, a faraway look in his eyes. "Space is already scarce here in Havensreach, our mana limited. With the power of the crown, Nyrundelle could finally reclaim the Midlands in full." He frowned. "Worse, should they desire, they could widen the Chasm until Havensreach falls into the sea."

Cedric pressed his lips in a tight line. The races of Old Arcanis—sylvan, dwarf, nocterrian, and fae alike—still harbored deep enmity for humans. The fae, according to Lord Church, most of all. Nearly two centuries had passed since the Great Betrayal, but their desire for retribution remained strong, since they decided all humans deserved to pay for the actions of one evil man.

It was nothing compared to Cedric's own thirst for vengeance.

He brought a finger to his mouth almost absentmindedly. To the scar that cut through his upper lip. "The crown shall *never* fall into Arcanian hands. I swear it."

"Then show me how you intend to win."

Cedric drew his own token from beneath his cuirass, a sense of calm settling over him as he wrapped his fingers around it. He opened his palm to reveal the midnight-blue stone, veined with streaks of gleaming silver—frozen lightning. The emerald set in its center flickered. He would need to recharge it before they departed.

"Show me," Lord Church beckoned again, a challenge in his voice.

Cedric felt the familiar hum of energy course through his veins as he drew the mana from his token. In his head, he recited the ancient words that would allow him to wield its power. Gripping the token in one hand, Cedric threw the other out to the side before pulling it close to his chest. His practice sword soared from the spot where he had discarded it; the next moment, its edge was pressed to Lord Leviathan Church's neck.

"Good." Lord Church nodded in approval. He wedged his cane between the blade and his skin. Were it Cedric's regular weapon, it would have left a bloody slice behind.

Cedric loosened his mental grasp of the weapon. The sword fell away.

A heartbeat later, he was on his back.

"Did I yield?" Lord Church clutched his token in one hand. The other was still wrapped around the handle of his cane, a single finger outstretched. The man had barely moved. But the ache in Cedric's chest was proof of the magical strike Lord Church made against him.

"No, my lord," Cedric wheezed.

"Never drop your guard. Never relent."

Cedric scrambled to his feet. "Yes, my lord."

"Show me your control."

With a clench of his fist, Cedric's sword was in the air again. This time, it was joined by a dozen other blades that had been hanging on the weapons rack moments before. Cedric grunted with effort as the weapons fanned out around the lord, each one pointed at a different vulnerable spot—an artery, a tendon. They were not all practice swords, either.

Lord Church flinched as the sharp tip of a stiletto dagger touched the fleshy divot at the base of his throat. "I yield."

Cedric returned the weapons to their original positions with a satisfied grin.

"Impressive." Lord Church's tone remained measured. "Though I'm afraid these small magics will not be enough if you intend to best your fellow champions."

"Small magics?" Cedric scoffed. A searing bolt of defensiveness flared through him. He bit down on his tongue to prevent himself from saying something he would regret. He knew the lord did not mean to insult him.

"I say this not to belittle your abilities," Lord Church said, as if he could read Cedric's thoughts, "but more than a dozen other champions will be working against you in the Crucible, the least of whom will be spellweavers as capable as yourself."

Cedric leaned against a nearby training post, his face neutral even as he scowled internally. Spellweaver. To equate what he could do with those who used their tokens to light candles and purify well water made his palms heat with irritation. He may not yet have earned an official designation as a sorcerer, nor would his paltry mastery of curative magic name him a saint. Still, Cedric knew his power went beyond that of a spellweaver, even if he wasn't quite sure why he felt so strongly about it.

He said none of this, and if Lord Church sensed Cedric's displeasure, he did not let it show. "Let us put aside the elemental magic of the Arcanians who shall be competing against you. My sources tell me that Cormac and Blackwood will be among those championing our kingdom beyond the Gate."

Cedric pursed his lips. Leona Blackwood was a powerful sorcerer, her magical abilities said to rival even those of King Callum. And Cedric would be a fool to overlook Brandon Cormac. As a sage, he could easily learn of the plans and movements of the other champions. Whether he used his telepathic skills for active sabotage or simply to stay three steps ahead, Cedric would need to remain vigilant and keep his mental walls strong.

"Are there any others I should be aware of?"

Lord Church cocked his head. "Alden Ashford may be worth considering for an alliance. His healing prowess could most definitely be of use."

Cedric made a mental note to keep an eye out for the saint.

"If there are any other humans of note set on entering the fray, though, I have not heard. And as for those from the other side of the Chasm"—Lord Church's lip curled—"I do not have much information. Although . . ." Something that looked almost like chagrin flashed across his face.

Cedric's eyebrows jumped up his forehead. He wasn't sure he'd ever seen that particular emotion from the nobleman in their many years together. He braced a hand on the training post and leaned closer. "Although what?"

Lord Church sighed. "Word has traveled across both Chasms of a great Arcanian warrior—a *fae* warrior—planning to take on the Crucible. There are even whispers of some movement stirring, rallying. The calls have grown louder for the Arcanians to make their move on the Midlands, with or without the crown."

Red flared across Cedric's vision. His hands felt hot. An array of violent images overtook his mind. Blazing fire. A maniacal laugh. The razor-sharp edge of a blade against his mouth. And blood. Everywhere, blood.

He blinked it all away. "You speak of the Revenant."

If that fae demon was entering the Celestial Sanctum, Cedric would have to be on his guard indeed. At the same time, something sparked in his chest at the thought of facing the Revenant. An ember of yearning—a deep *need* to be the one to cut the monster down.

"Only Aurelia knows whether it is all hearsay or not," Lord Church said, pulling Cedric's attention back. "And I see your emotions roiling under the surface. Do not let them control you. There will be no room for distractions in the Sanctum."

Cedric bit back the retort on his tongue. "Yes, my lord."

"Our party departs for the Lost City in the morning. Be ready."

His expression hard, Cedric nodded. "I shall."

With an assessing look that made Cedric feel as if he'd been stripped of his armor, Lord Church exited the training yard.

Cedric sucked in a deep breath, thoughts spinning. He had to finish packing his belongings before they set off on their pilgrimage to Luminaria. He needed to visit the mana forge so the magicsmith could recharge his token before tomorrow. He wanted to find Tristan so he could say farewell. Should there be time, he'd like to visit the local tavern to find some lady with whom to spend his final hours too. He'd heard that the aurora put them in quite the mood.

He peeled his hand from the training post, only for his swirling thoughts to narrow into one of confused curiosity. The wood was charred where his fingers had been resting. He'd never noticed that before.

Something poked at him, lingering on the edge of his thoughts. He frowned, then dismissed the notion. He had much to do and little time in which to do it. So Cedric turned and walked away, the scent of singed wood lingering in the air.

CHAPTER 6
GHOSTS

Elyria

"Stars damn you, Elyria lightbreaker," the tavern master roared. "Ye are a curse on my tavern."

"Artemicion, please save your shouting." Elyria placed her hand at her temple. "At least until the pandemonium in my head has subsided to a dull rattle, hmm?"

"Ye'll never play here again, mark my words," Artie continued at full volume with absolutely no concern for the state of Elyria's head. Rude.

"As I recall, that's not the first time you've said as much," Elyria said with a smirk, even as the movement caused her head to throb. She'd returned to her room at the Sweltering Pig after leaving the duchess—flying straight in through the window—and been holed up ever since. Sleep had eluded her, but she had no particular desire to face the surly dwarf. Sadly, her desire for food inevitably overtook her desire not to get yelled at, and so, here she was.

She winced as one of the tavern maids wrenched a set of shutters open. The midday sun poured into the space, and Elyria's eyes flared as she took in the carnage.

The Sweltering Pig was a mess. Shattered glass had been swept into haphazard piles. Sylvan maids mopped away at the sticky pools of ale and blood covering the floor. A stocky fae man was gathering the splintered legs of stools and tables that had not survived the brawl. Elyria didn't recognize any of them—had Artie called in additional cleaning staff?

She sucked in a guilty breath. "But those men would not have been in here in the first place, drinking your ale and filling your pockets, had I not been performing."

"And right back out of my pockets goes their gold, to make up for this mess," Artie grumbled, though Elyria could tell his temper was fading. "I've a mind to kick ye out of yer room and be done with ye entirely."

"Aren't you even the slightest bit relieved to see me alive and well after all that hubbub?"

"If there's one thing I can count on in this bleeding world, it's that ye'll make it out of a silly little scrape like that." He gave an indifferent wave of his hand, like it was nothing, but Elyria felt emotion behind his words. It sparked something warm in her chest.

A member of the tavern staff dropped something in front of her with a grunt. A steaming bowl of pottage with three strips of salted fish. She hadn't even seen Artie put in the order. She gulped down a spoonful of the stew, cursing as it burned her tongue. Artie barked a laugh, and she grinned behind her spoon.

"So, will you tell me what Tartanis wants with ye?" asked the dwarf.

Elyria hesitated, then shrugged. "What they all want. It's not really me they're after. It's *the Revenant*."

"Why?"

She made a noncommittal noise. "Why do men do anything? Because they have something to prove. Because they have someone to prove it to. Because they want to. Because they can.

"Men more powerful than Master Tartanis have sought me for some manner or another—whether for my name or my power, I do not know." She traced an idle figure eight in the bowl with her spoon. "But every Arcanian babe born since the war has grown up on tales of the Revenant. It was only a matter of time before it followed me to Coralith."

"Quartered hell, Elle." Artie seemed unsure of what to say after that.

Elyria took another scalding sip of stew, wishing it would wash away the memory of a different sort of burn. A heady mix of rage and shame climbed up her spine as she thought about last night. She wasn't sure how long it would take for her to forget the feel of Raefe's flame-touch, but she suspected it would be a while. The physical marks she now bore would not be her only scars from their encounter.

She wished she had killed him.

Her inner shadow stirred as if in agreement.

Perhaps Artie sensed the shift in her thoughts, the sudden darkening of her mood, because it was with forced nonchalance that he suddenly said, "So, what do ye think about the rumors?"

"What rumors?" Her words were garbled, her mouth full.

"About the Crucible. How the aurora's brighter than ever. Poke yer head outside—the sun's brighter than dragonfyre, but ye can still see it. Folks are saying it's a sign from Solaris or some other kind of celestial-blessed shit."

Her hand paused in midair, her spoon hovering just above the bowl. Artie didn't know about her conversation with the duchess, she reminded herself. He didn't know about Evander—no more than the average person, at least. He was merely making conversation.

"I believe I might've heard something about that" was all Elyria could say. Ollie had called it a sign from Lunara, the Time Keeper, not the Light Goddess, Solaris, but it was all the same bullshit.

"Before yer little showdown last night, it was all folks could talk about," Artie continued, oblivious. "Speculating over who might enter this year, trading bets. Odds are looking pretty good for this one champion—some noblewoman's daughter from Aerithia. Fancy name. What was it . . . ?" He drummed his thick fingers on the countertop. "Eaglefeather? Something like that."

Elyria's fist tightened around her spoon. Had she been paying attention to the banter in the bar last night instead of trying to drown herself at the bottom of her tankard, perhaps she would have heard this too. Perhaps Laeliana showing up wouldn't have been such a shock.

Kit.

Just thinking her name sent a shiver of remorse down Elyria's spine. Artie was still talking. The tavern bustled with activity as the staff continued cleaning up. It all faded as Elyria was pulled back to a time when her life was filled with laughter instead of regret.

Golden sunlight bounced off Kit's moonlight-colored hair as Elyria watched her. Her hands were clasped together, brow furrowed in concentration.

"Come on, Kitty Kat. You've got to focus," Evander said. He held out his hand, a swirling orb of water dancing over his palm.

"I am focusing. It's harder than it looks, you know." Kit drew her hands apart, and a ball of water materialized between her palms . . . then dribbled through her fingers a moment later. She groaned in frustration, her mismatched eyes—one blue, one green—swimming with misery when she met Elyria's gaze. "Four hells, I'm never going to master this."

"Chin up, darling." Elyria reached over and gently adjusted Kit's hands. "It takes practice, and your brother has a century on you. Remember what he told you before—you have to feel *the magic. Feel the moisture in the air, the water in your blood." She pointed across the grassy meadow to the small brook babbling quietly nearby. "Feel it there. Then grasp it, embrace it. Let it course through you. But don't fight it. Don't try to trap it."*

Evander chuckled, his deep voice a comforting rumble. He draped his arm over Elyria's shoulders and pressed a kiss to the side of her head.

Kit sighed but cracked her neck and folded one hand over the other once more.

"Your magic is a river. You have to let it flow," reminded Elyria.

Kit loosed a slow breath through her mouth, then parted her palms. A sphere of water formed between them, swirling and eddying just like Evander's— a miniature ocean in her hands.

Her mismatched eyes lit up, her blue iris rippling as if it were made of water too. "I'm doing it!" she exclaimed.

"You're doing it," murmured Elyria, pride flaring in her chest.

"One day, I'm going to be as strong as you, Ellie."

Elyria's lips parted in surprise. Pressure gathered in her chest. She looked at Evander. Caught the sad, knowing look in his eyes.

He cleared his throat. "Not bad, Kitty Kat. Now, just do that a few hundred times more. Easy."

Elyria ducked as the sphere suddenly zoomed toward Evander. The cool water splashed her as it exploded on his face.

"Katerina," he scolded, sputtering as he pawed at the black hair that was now plastered to his forehead. Kit stuck out her tongue at him, and the pressure in Elyria's chest deflated as she doubled over with laughter.

With a jolt, Elyria slammed back to the present. "Damn it," she muttered, her hand shaking as she reached for the mug of water that had been placed in front of her.

"All right there, Elle?" Artie's voice was laced with concern.

"Fine, fine," she lied, "just memories." She closed her eyes, unsure if she wanted to shake the images from her mind or keep them there forever. "Memories . . . and ghosts."

He didn't press further, but she could see the question in his eyes. She pushed her bowl aside and stood, glad she'd shoveled down what she had, when she had. She suspected her appetite would not return for some time, given what she now had to do.

"Taking off, then?"

"There's something I need to take care of." She hesitated before adding, "Not sure when I'll be back."

The tavern master nodded, his expression difficult to read. Elyria wanted to tell him how much she appreciated his hospitality, how much it meant that he'd put up with her these past months. But given the mix of emotion churning in her, she didn't know how to do so without making a blubbery scene. And she knew *that* would have the poor dwarf running to the first quarter of hell in embarrassment. So she simply said, "Until next time, old man."

Elyria took a deep breath as she stepped onto the bustling streets of

Coralith. With her belly full and her thirst slaked, her head was vastly improved, and she threw a quick prayer of thanks up to Solaris, or Lunara, or Earth Mother Gaia—whichever celestial would claim credit for the small mercy. Hells, she would even have been willing to lay her gratitude at the feet of Noctis, Warden of Shadows, for how much better she felt. Any of them would do, she supposed, aside from the banished star god, Aurelia. Even Elyria knew better than to invoke that cursed name.

She squinted at the sky, and true enough, the clouds were alight with faint beams of purple and green. She still had time.

She needed to find Kit. Had to talk to her. Had to try.

She owed her that much.

She owed her much, much more.

CHAPTER 7
IF AT FIRST YOU DON'T SUCCEED

Elyria

Elyria's wings ached as she soared over the chasm, the cold air biting at the exposed skin on her face and arms. She should have hired a gryphon in the capital once she learned that Kit had already left for the Lost City. The flight from Coralith to Aerithia had already taken a lot out of her—she wasn't used to flying long distances anymore. The hours in the sky had sapped her strength. Her wings felt leaden. But Elyria hadn't been willing to wait. Whether flying on her own or as part of a caravan, Kit would be traveling quickly. Elyria didn't know how much time she had until the aurora disappeared, signaling the Crucible's start. She only knew she had to find Kit before she reached Luminaria.

And so, Elyria flew. Her wings beat. Her back twinged. She drew a breath, wound a finger through the air, and wrapped a tendril of magic around her shoulders—a brace. It would do for now.

Her stomach lurched as she glanced down into the seemingly bottomless abyss of the Chasm. The jagged scar separating Nyrundelle from the Midlands was narrower than the one that ran through the human side of the continent, but it still made for quite the sight. Mist billowed along the cliffs, pouring into the gorge like a smoky waterfall. The clouds hung still, as if even they dared not cross the mighty canyon. Above Elyria, the vibrant colors of the aurora mixed and swirled in the sky. Below her, fathomless darkness.

Elyria barely remembered what life had been like before the Shattering. Before the twin Chasms ripped through the continent, from the Sea of Serenity to the Ironpeak Mountains. Before the realm was cleaved in three. To the west lay Nyrundelle—home. To the east, the human kingdom of Havensreach. And the wild, untethered Midlands in between.

Located just south of the Forest of Valandor, the Lost City of Luminaria was the only real landmark of note left in the Midlands. There were, of course, the small bouts of territory marked by encampments and the evidence of battles gone wrong. While the Chasm kept the vast majority of humans tightly locked in their third of Arcanis, groups were constantly infiltrating the Midlands, their sights trained on areas where mana springs had formed.

Elyria thought of what Ollie had said—how the battles over those bits of land were getting worse, how humans were starting to fight dirty. She'd thought by now King Lachlandris would have perfected the art of pushing back the magic-hungry mortals whenever they got too ambitious. But perhaps their desperation had finally reached the point where they felt they no longer had anything to lose.

She recalled the time a dwarven trader, a frequent patron of the Sweltering Pig, had spent an entire evening regaling Elyria with tales of what Havensreach was like. He'd tried to paint the overcrowded streets in the capital city of Kingshelm as exciting, if somewhat pitiable. But one description of navigating through throngs of clamoring, hungry children and all he'd done was leave her with a sour taste on her tongue.

That part was unfortunate, Elyria would admit. Children of any kind—even human ones—were precious. They deserved full bellies and soft places to lay their heads at night. Still, that was hardly a good enough reason to encroach upon what was Arcanian territory by right. Humans could reproduce so easily, so quickly. So unlike the fae. Perhaps if they took that blessing seriously, they might have carved a different future for their progeny.

That thought left an even worse taste in her mouth.

The tips of what remained of the crumbling Castle Lumin appeared in the distance, and whatever feelings she might have had regarding the human situation in Havensreach were erased. Elyria's heart lurched. The last time she'd flown this route, Evander soared beside her. His golden eyes had been full of resolve. Now, the loss of him echoed through her with each beat of her wings.

Her back twinged again. The burden of keeping Kit from following him weighed Elyria down. She couldn't let her repeat his mistake.

She spotted the first wisps of campfire smoke making their way up to the sky—a traveler camp that had been set up on the outskirts of the city. The smell of woodsmoke and roasting meat wafted up to greet her as she approached.

She noted the clear delineation between the Arcanian and human camps with amusement. Not only were they separated in distance, the human camp set up on the far side of the city gates, but the camps could not have looked more different. Where the human tents were plain and practical, set up in orderly lines, the Arcanian tents were a patchwork of vibrant colors, scattered haphazardly.

Typical, she thought. Leave it to humans to suck all the color out of the occasion.

Despite the ancient magic that prevented violence within the Midlands as long as the aurora bloomed, it was clear neither side felt the need to get too friendly. She didn't blame them. They were after the same thing, not on the same team. Each side sought to win the crown. Wanted to wield its power for their own reasons.

Elyria wanted to scream at them all just how stupid that desire was. Neither side would win it. After a hundred years and countless champions lost to the Sanctum, it was clear nobody ever would.

Heart pounding in her chest, Elyria descended into the Arcanian camp. An uneasy silence hung in the air, punctuated by the occasional crackle of fire and murmur of hushed conversation as she hovered. Her eyes darted over clusters of travelers, searching for any sign of—

There. Cropped moonlight hair. Gold-and-silver wings that glinted in the firelight. Water deftly weaving through the air as if at the behest of a conductor's baton. And radiating from her very being, a vivacity that could only belong to . . .

"Kit." Elyria landed with a soft *thud*, folding her wings neatly behind her as she approached with hesitant steps.

Kit stiffened. The water magic she'd been playing with dissipated into mist as she turned with agonizing slowness. Fierce eyes—one blue, one green—met Elyria's. "What are you doing here?" Her voice was detached, disinterested. As if Elyria were a stranger.

Shame crept from Elyria's gut. "I—"

She had rehearsed her speech over and over while in the air. She'd known exactly what she would say to get Kit to see reason. She would appeal to the love and loyalty Kit had for her mother. For the duchy she was one day destined to lead. And if that didn't work, Elyria would say whatever she needed to convince Kit to give this up, to turn back. She would make her understand how foolish this was, that she was throwing her life away. Would remind her that three times, the Crucible had been met. Three times, the strongest in the realm entered the Celestial Sanctum. And three times, they failed. It had swallowed up Evander and it hadn't even bothered to spit his body back out so they could give him a proper Sending.

Now that she was here, Elyria couldn't remember a single word. And so, what came out of her mouth was "You cut your hair."

Kit raked an appraising look over Elyria. She took in the wrinkled blouse tucked under beat-up leathers. The smears of sweat-streaked dirt running down each arm. Her sharp eyes narrowed when she reached Elyria's face—lips chapped, cheeks chafed from the wind. "You look like you crawled out of the first quarter of hell."

Elyria attempted a grin. "Not much time for primping and preening when I'm chasing your ass across the continent."

"And why would you do that?" Kit asked icily.

Elyria wished she had a drink in hand. "I think you know the answer to that."

"My mother has become desperate if she felt the need to seek you out. Truly, I didn't think she would ever stoop that low."

Elyria deserved that, but the words cut, nonetheless.

"All right, give me your best shot, *Revenant*." Kit wielded the moniker like a weapon, hand braced on her hip. "Say what you've come to say, and then go back to wherever it is you've been hiding. You won't change my mind."

Elyria took a steadying breath. "Why are you doing this?"

"Why do you ask stupid questions?"

Elyria's jaw ticked. She had forgotten how quickly Kit could get under her skin. "The Arcane Crucible is an unwinnable challenge. You'll be throwing your life away, and for what? I beg you, don't do this." She hesitated, searching Kit's face for any sign of softening. If anything, her expression only grew harder.

A different tactic, then. "Think of your mother, of *your people*. You can't just run into—"

"Yes, well, you know a lot about running, don't you?" Kit interrupted.

Elyria swallowed the ball of shame that attempted to lodge itself in her throat. Now was not the time to react defensively. She fisted her hands at her sides, digging her fingernails into the flesh of her palm to keep from lashing out. "Yes, I do. I ran. Ran from my pain. Ran from my grief. And I won't lie to you—I would still be running, if I could. But I'm here because—"

"You think I didn't feel pain? That I didn't grieve? He was my *brother*. My best friend in this world." Mismatched eyes met Elyria's for the briefest moment before Kit ripped them away.

Elyria heard the words left unspoken. *My best friend in this world . . . aside from you.* Her heart cracked. All that time spent mentally rehearsing, imagining this conversation from every angle, and she was utterly unequipped. She wasn't sure anything could have prepared her for how this would go. For how this would *feel*.

So Elyria said nothing.

Her silence only fueled Kit's rage-filled words. "And I am here *because* of my people. With your talent for shutting yourself away, perhaps you haven't noticed, but I have. I see the way my people struggle with the Chasm. The cost of maintaining the bridges. The burden of crossing, even for those with the ability to make the journey on their own." She gestured to her wings, then to Elyria's, still folded on her back. "Without the Midlands, we are half a realm. My brother believed in the power of the crown, in the magic it holds to heal this land. And if the humans steal it first . . ." Her expression turned grim. "I cannot allow it. And neither will I toss away my only chance to save him by—"

An immense sadness pressed on Elyria's chest. *Save him?* "Kit." Her voice was soft. "He is long since lost."

Kit's eyes became unfocused. "I see him, you know. In my dreams—my nightmares. He calls out for me. For our mother. For you. For anyone to help him. I see him with black eyes, bleeding. His wings a shredded mess."

Elyria's heart stuttered. "You—you've seen visions of him like this?"

Kit's expression softened as her gaze refocused on Elyria, just for a moment. Then it hardened again. She turned away. "I'm not crazy."

"I never said you were."

"And I am not a fool."

"Kit, I—"

"I know he no longer lives, Ellie." Some of the tension in Elyria's chest eased at hearing Kit call her that—the nickname only she ever used. "But neither is he at peace. It's like his spirit is . . . trapped. He is being tormented in the Hereafter. Unable to move on because his work is not finished. And it will remain so until the Crucible is complete, the crown won. Maybe then, the ancient magic will deign to return his body to us, and he can finally rest."

"Kit . . ."

"How can you ask me to ignore this chance to bring my brother peace?"

"At the cost of your own life? That is not what Evander would want."

Kit whirled, her eyes blazing with anger. "Who are you to say what he would want? You don't get to say that. You don't get to say his name."

The words were a hot poker scraping through Elyria's insides. Her eyes burned, but she continued. "He wouldn't want you risking yourself. If he were still here—"

"Well, he's *not* here." Kit was shaking now. "And you haven't been either. The minute he was gone, so were you."

"Please." The inner corners of Elyria's eyes pricked. "Don't let his memory drive you to your death."

"You know *nothing* about what drives me!" As if acting on reflex, Kit raised her hand, and a burst of water slammed into Elyria.

Twenty-five years of pent-up anger and resentment poured from Kit's hands. The attack was unexpected; it stunned Elyria, knocking her off-balance. She hit the grass, ass-first, with an undignified *thump*. Yelps sounded as nearby travelers scattered.

Elyria grappled with what to do. She'd expected Kit would be angry—livid, irate even. She hadn't expected her to lash out physically. And even if she had, shouldn't the Crucible's magic be stopping this? Wasn't the whole point to prevent fights from breaking out before champions entered the Sanctum?

Another spray of water smacked Elyria in the face. She sputtered, flipping her now-soaked periwinkle braid to her back. Perhaps the magical contract only applied to brawls between humans and Arcanians. Perhaps the celestials found infighting amusing.

Perhaps they just liked torturing Elyria.

She scrambled back to her feet, wet wings flaring out for balance. "You need to stop right this instant, Katerina."

Kit laughed—a hollow, empty sound. "Did you truly track me down after decades of silence only to scold me like a child?"

"When you stop behaving like a child, I shall stop treating you like one."

Scoffing, Kit advanced toward Elyria, each step a threat. Her hands wove intricate patterns in the air as she called upon more magic. Elyria narrowly avoided a waterspout that burst from the ground with such force it would have launched her into the sky had it hit her.

"I don't want to fight you," Elyria said, even as she felt her wild magic gathering in her hands. There was so much nature here. The grass below her feet, the trees surrounding the camp. Elyria could feel it all.

"You want me to turn back because you agree with my mother that I am not strong enough to best the Crucible," Kit said. "Let me show you how wrong you are."

She didn't give Elyria the chance to deny the claim. Kit thrust her hands forward, a torrent of water surging toward Elyria, who raised her arms in defense. Roots erupted from the ground, quickly weaving together into a shield that absorbed the majority of the water's impact.

Kit let out a frustrated screech as a vine snaked up her left leg, wrapping around her wrist and pinning her in place. But it was clear Kit had been training for the Crucible. Training hard. One by one, she curled the fingers of her free hand in toward her palm until they formed a fist. A massive sphere of water appeared, the surface roiling as it advanced on Elyria. She knew that Kit didn't truly want to hurt her. She also knew if she let herself get trapped inside that bloated bubble, there was a very high possibility it would drown her.

Darkness stirred from somewhere deep in Elyria's core, displeased at the thought. She pushed it back down.

"Kit, please," Elyria shouted over the tidal roar. The ground started to rumble, her magic reacting reflexively to the threat. "I loved him too."

"I loved *you*!" Kit cried, her voice breaking. "I needed you. And you weren't there!"

Just like that, the fight in Elyria died. She dropped her arms. The vines caging Kit slithered away. The earth stilled. The sphere burst, water spreading over the grass, a tiny tide that lapped at Elyria's boots.

Kit and Elyria stared at each other, their eyes ablaze with anger and pain, fury and guilt. Elyria's heightened hearing picked up the whispers of onlookers, hoofbeats plodding along the road, excited shouts echoing from the human camp. She blocked it all out as she opened her mouth to speak—then closed it. What could she say? Twenty-five years ago, she had left the grieving sister of the man she loved—*her* sister—to mourn alone. To pick up the pieces of her shattered life, alone, while Elyria sought solace at the bottom of a bottle and in the bed of some meaningless distraction or another, night after night.

No, Kit was not a fool. Laeliana was, for asking Elyria to do this.

Elyria was, for actually thinking she could.

Her mouth opened again. "I'm sorry."

"Don't pretend you care," Kit spat. Then, without so much as another glance, she stalked away.

Elyria felt heavy as she watched her go. She was soaked and exhausted, her back still aching from the flight and the added strain of the unexpected fight. And then there was the matter of the weight on her heart.

She had come all this way. She had failed.

She could not fail.

Evander would never forgive her if she let his sister walk through the Gate, knowing what was sure to happen.

Elyria approached a burgeoning campfire, ignoring the wary stares of the travelers around her. Using a flicker of magic to dry her wings before cloaking them from view, she squatted next to the fire. The woman beside her stiffened, a bottle dangling precariously from her hands as she deliberately avoided making eye contact.

"Are you going to finish that?" Elyria asked.

The woman met Elyria's eye for a single heartbeat before thrusting the bottle into her hands and scurrying off, dragging along a young boy who had been gaping at Elyria.

Dubious, Elyria eyed the contents of the bottle, then shrugged and took a swig. It burned as it went down. Though she shuddered at the bitter taste, it did more to chase away the chill that had settled in her bones than the fire did. She sighed, looking to the sky, where the vivid colors of the aurora blended with the orange hues of sunset. She was running out of time. Soon, the aurora would vanish in a burst of brilliant light, and the Gate to the Celestial Sanctum would open.

Slowly, conversations resumed between the travelers surrounding Elyria. Friends, family, and supporters of the champions who would be attempting the Crucible. Others who made the trek to the Lost City in order to say they bore witness to the occasion—should this attempt finally be the one to become historic. Elyria wondered who among them were here in support of Kit—or if any of them were at all. The duchess wouldn't be coming. Wouldn't be able to face the sight of her daughter walking through the Gate, never to be seen again.

Elyria didn't know if she could face it, either.

But until that moment came, she would try. She would give Kit time to calm down, give her room to breathe after this ambush.

And she would try again.

CHAPTER 8
BOORISH BEHAVIOR

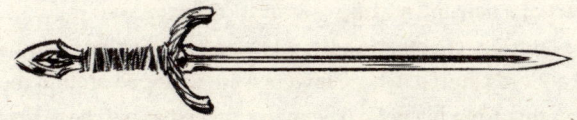

Cedric

Cedric's sword cut through the air with a sharp whistle before it connected with the bandit's crude blade. The thief crumpled, wrapping his hands protectively around his head. "I'm sorry! Please don't kill me. We only—"

"You only what?" sneered Lord Church as he came out from behind the horse-drawn wagon. "Thought you'd find easy prey on the road to Luminaria?"

Hargrave and Thibault, the other guards in their traveling party, towered over three more of the bandits that had attacked their caravan, holding them at swordpoint. The fourth lay bloody on the ground next to the wagon, his eyes open and unseeing.

"On your knees, cur," said Cedric, his sword still trained on the first man.

Lord Church paced closer. "You intended to rob those journeying to witness the start of the Crucible. Foolish though it was, you attacked *us*. Your life should be forfeit."

The man whimpered, his eyes darting to his fallen comrade. "I'm sorry, my lord." His shoulders were slumped, his voice resigned. He knew the fate that awaited him.

But Lord Leviathan Church was nothing if not a man who kept others guessing. A look of surprise flitted across Cedric's face as Lord Church said, "I will, however, allow you to keep your life." The bandit's expression was just as bemused. "Provided you use it to pass along a message. You will warn off any *associates*"—Lord Church's nose wrinkled—"who might be considering similar foolish plans. I will *not* have the road to Luminaria thus polluted."

The man scrambled to his feet, words tumbling from his mouth. "Yes, my lord. Of course. You are so generous—too generous. I will see it done. No others will dare attack travelers on this road, not after I speak to them. And don't think I take your generosity for granted. This is the start of a new life for me, I swear it. You won't—"

His platitudes cut off abruptly, replaced by a choking sound. Cedric glanced at Lord Church, whose fingers were wrapped around the mana token hanging from his neck. The man clutched at his chest, his throat, his fingers clawing at some invisible force. He fell to the ground, his body thrashing. His face turned red. Then purple.

"My lord . . . ?" Cedric asked, his voice low.

Lord Church released his token. The man stilled, then sucked in a life-giving breath.

"Go," Lord Church boomed.

The man ran.

"My lord?" asked Thibault, brushing a piece of ash-blond hair from his forehead. "What of the others?"

Hargrave nodded in agreement with Thibault's question, his left hand bracing his side as he kept his sword aloft. It was pointed at the other three bandits, who wore matching expressions of wary shock. It likely wasn't every day they saw someone wield magic with the ease and strength of Lord Church.

Cedric frowned at the pained expression on Hargrave's

scruff-shadowed face. One of the bastards had gotten a hit in.

"How many men does it take to pass on a message?" Lord Church said, disinterested.

Thibault grinned. "Just one, my lord."

"Just so."

The bandits seemed to come to an understanding of what Lord Church meant at the same time, because all three of them leapt at once. Hargrave's sword met one before he even made it to his feet. Another made it a few steps before Thibault's blade ran him through. The third, however . . .

Cedric had been on the other side of the wagon when he realized the bandits were making a run for it. He hurtled toward the third bandit, but the man was fast. By the time Cedric rounded the wagon, the bandit had nearly made it to the trees.

Cedric cursed, readying himself for the chase.

A sickening crack rang out. The man collapsed midstep, neck broken.

"You default to your physical skills, rely too heavily on your sword," came Lord Church's voice. He released his grip on his token once more. "You forget there is power at your fingertips to be used as well, when blade and bow alone are not enough. Take this as a lesson, Sir Thorne."

The flush of chagrin crept onto Cedric's face. He wanted to protest, to defend himself. He had to endeavor to conserve his mana for the Crucible, he wanted to say. But he didn't. He just nodded.

If he was being honest, Cedric had not even considered using his magic to stop the bandit. Even if he had, he wasn't sure he was capable of snapping a man's neck with a thought. Such magic required immense control. It would significantly deplete his token.

Not that the finite power of his token was the only reason Cedric felt himself incapable of doing such a thing.

"You appear displeased, Sir Thorne," Lord Church said, some emotion Cedric couldn't quite read lacing his words.

"No, my lord," Cedric said quickly, cursing internally for wearing his emotions so plainly on his face.

"You would have acted differently." It wasn't a question.

"I—" Cedric wasn't sure how to respond.

Lord Church pursed his lips. "These men would have slaughtered us all to take what few possessions we travel with. Think of those they may already have done so to, those not as fortunate to have such esteemed fighters in their party. What would you have me do?"

"Yes, my lord, I just thought that perhaps a show of mercy might—"

"Mercy is a luxury of the weak," Lord Church said, his tone even. Like it was just a simple fact of the world. "Power is in hard decisions made, the respect gained from acting with purpose, from being willing to mete out swift justice. You would do well to remember this for the trials ahead."

"Yes, my lord." Face red, Cedric sheathed his sword and turned to Hargrave, who wiped his blade on the shirt of the now very-dead bandit. "How bad is your injury?"

"I've had worse." Hargrave attempted a grin, though it came out as more of a grimace.

Cedric's brow furrowed. "Let me see." He gently moved Hargrave's hand aside to reveal a deep gash that had been cut through the guard's doublet. Blood seeped from the wound. Cedric looked at Hargrave in disbelief. "This needs to be treated."

"Bah, merely a scratch. I shall be fine, Sir Thorne."

"Yes, yes, you are very strong and brave," Cedric said with a roll of his eyes. "Thibault, fetch the healer's kit from the wagon."

With a chuckle, Thibault sprinted off.

"Let us keep moving," said the lord. "We have delayed too long."

Cedric nodded. "Yes, my lord."

Once Hargrave was patched up and the bandits' bodies had been hauled to the side of the road, the men set off once more. Lord Church, Cedric, and Hargrave sat in the back of the wagon, while Thibault held the reins at the front.

Though Cedric kept a watchful eye on their surroundings, noting every rustle of leaves and distant birdcall, the ride was blessedly quiet as they wound through forest and field until they reached the Chasm.

It was then that Cedric's heart began thumping in his chest. He swallowed, staring at the flat expanse of stone—perhaps the length of four men laying head to toe. The bridge that would carry them across the colossal abyss.

Thibault said something—a joke, perhaps, judging by Hargrave's answering guffaw—but Cedric didn't hear it. His gaze was stuck on the cliff ahead, the sun casting long shadows across the rocky expanse. The wind whispered a haunting melody that seemed to beckon from the great canyon's depths. Cedric's cuirass suddenly felt too tight. Suffocating.

"First time making the crossing?" Hargrave asked, humor evident in his voice as he scratched at the dark stubble lining his jaw.

Cedric's eyes dropped to his boots. "That obvious, is it?"

Thibault snickered. "Don't worry your pretty little head, Sir Champion." Cedric sent him a cutting look, but Thibault's eyes were on the road ahead. "This bridge is sturdier than it looks."

Lord Leviathan Church nodded in agreement—a reassurance. But Cedric got the distinct feeling there was amusement there as well. He didn't understand why. Surely anyone who took one look at the cracked stone and the infinite drop below would feel the same way he did . . . wouldn't they?

He swallowed hard as the wagon creaked across the ancient bridge. The Chasm yawned below them, its depths hidden in shadow. Despite the confidence of the rest of his party, Cedric couldn't shake the feeling that came with the knowledge that one misstep could send them plummeting into the abyss.

He rubbed his sweat-slicked palms together and tried his best to distract himself. He fixed his eyes on the thinning tree line, the mixing colors of the aurora in the sky. He tried to drag himself back to the happy memories of his final night in Kingshelm, sated with drink, buried between warm thighs. Tried to focus on anything other than the creak of the wagon's wheels as they dragged over the bridge, the echo of the horse's hooves clopping on the stone.

"Tell me, Cedric"—Lord Church's voice broke the silence—"now that you're finally experiencing it in person for the first time, what do you think of the Chasm?"

So much for that plan.

"Is it all you thought it would be?" Lord Church pressed.

Cedric's gaze flicked to the edge of the bridge, where the stone seemed to crumble away into nothingness. "It is certainly . . . impressive," he managed to say, voice tight. "Descriptions and maps do its vastness no justice. I have never seen anything like it."

He left out the part where he would have been perfectly content never to have seen it at all. He could hear Tristan's mirthful voice in his head.

"Tits up, Ric. You're a champion of the realm. Don't be such a pussy."

Cedric scowled internally. Some champion he was. Havensreach's finest, afraid of heights.

"It is indeed impressive," Lord Church said, a note of awe in his tone, calling Cedric's attention back. "As is this very bridge. A truly spectacular feat of magic. The number of sorcerers and spellweavers required to construct it is a testament to the fortitude of our ancestors. And while the Arcanians might boast that they can accomplish the same thing with a handful of wildshapers"—his nose wrinkled, as if he suddenly smelled something unpleasant—"the comparison is moot. Not as their sad bridges crumble and collapse, while this one has held firm for centuries."

"A lifeline to the rest of the continent," Hargrave said.

"A *mana*line," Thibault corrected.

"Mana *is* life." Lord Church touched his hand to his token. "Which is why, despite how difficult it is to maintain a presence, how *difficult* the Arcanians make it for us, we need the Midlands. Without it, much of the kingdom would be without magic entirely. The singular mana spring near Kingshelm is not nearly enough to support all of Havensreach."

"If only the stars-damned pixies would leave us alone," said Thibault.

The back of Cedric's neck prickled uncomfortably at his use of the degrading epithet. Cedric of all people held no love for the fae, but he didn't think it was very becoming of Thibault to wield the slur so casually.

"As if getting our people across the Chasm isn't difficult enough," Thibault continued, his voice low.

"Why do they even need bridges anyway?" grumbled Hargrave. "When the stars-damned Arcanians can just soar across their wisp of a Chasm whenever they want? Though I suppose not *all* the freaks can fly."

Just the worst ones, thought Cedric. He realized the implication of Hargrave's statement a moment later. "You've seen the Arcanian Chasm?" he asked, his interest piqued.

"Aye," Thibault replied. "It's about a third as wide—"

"—and less than half as deep as this one," Hargrave finished.

These men were well traveled, Cedric realized with a pang of envy.

"And the real rub," Hargrave continued, "is that they don't even *need* the damn Midlands. Their magic doesn't rely on mana. They just *have* it."

"Exactly why we need to get our champion here to Luminaria," Thibault said. "Once Sir Thorne bests the Crucible, we won't have to worry about any of this ever again."

"Hear, hear!" said Hargrave, thumping Cedric's back.

Cedric nodded absently.

"We return to solid ground," Lord Church said, too low for the others to hear. "Be at ease." He patted the back of Cedric's hand, and Cedric looked down at it, white-knuckled on the wooden bench. He hadn't realized how tightly he'd been gripping it.

Relief washed over him as the truth of Lord Church's words set in. The crunch of stone beneath them had been replaced with the dirt road once more. They'd cleared the bridge. "Thank you, my lord."

"When I was your age," Lord Church said, "I, too, feared this crossing."

Cedric had forgotten that the lord had traveled to Luminaria at least once before, to bear witness to the last Crucible. He'd never been able to work up the nerve to ask Lord Church why he made the journey—if he had been close with one of the previous champions.

Was it painful, Cedric wondered, making the trek again now? Knowing that nobody came back through the Gate last time? Knowing nobody ever has?

A pall loomed threateningly over Cedric at the thought. He shook his head. There was no use thinking that way. He made a concerted effort to focus back on Lord Church, who was still speaking. It sounded like he was a far more seasoned traveler than Cedric had realized.

"Growing up, my father would tell me tales of monsters that lived at the bottom of the Chasm—specters that whispered to those who were afraid, attempting to lure them into the abyss. He saved the worst stories of the worst monsters for right before bed, as if he sought to script my nightmares."

"Your father sounds like a right bastard," Cedric muttered, before remembering who he was speaking to. "I mean, that is—I'm sorry, I—"

Lord Church chuckled. "Come now, my boy. After all these years together, I like to think I've earned the privilege of your honest reaction."

Cedric felt his cheeks warm. It had been many years since Lord Church had referred to him so familially. "Thank you, my lord. So . . . did those stories make the crossing easier or more difficult for you?"

"I admit I do not know. I think it made the journey more interesting. I would try to hold my breath from the moment we stepped onto the bridge until we reached the other side."

Cedric's eyes widened. "That seems . . ."

"Impossible? Yes, it is." Lord Church laughed. "But it made for a decent distraction. You might remember it for your return trip."

Cedric smiled, but it didn't reach his eyes.

"There *will* be a return trip for you," Lord Church assured him. "You've trained hard. Learned well. I have no doubt you'll run circles around any foolish Arcanian who dares to try you."

Cedric felt a weight lift from his shoulders. The nobleman's confidence was bolstering. "Thank you, my lord," he said quietly.

Lord Church's expression softened further. "You have a strong heart, Cedric. Stronger than you realize. You can do this. I believe with every fiber of my being that you are the only one who can."

The wagon creaked and swayed as they continued along the winding road toward the Lost City. The landscape began to change, trees thinning to reveal rolling hills and the deserted remains of towns that had been decimated when the Chasms tore through the land. The aurora overhead grew bright as the sun slipped lower in the sky.

"There," called Thibault, pointing ahead.

Cedric's gaze followed a path of flickering campfires to Luminaria's ivy-covered city walls. The broken spires of Castle Lumin poked through the mist, towering over them.

Lord Church took a tremulous breath.

Two separate camps were set up on the outskirts of the city, and Thibault turned the wagon toward the one on the right. But something else caught Cedric's attention, tugged his focus in the opposite direction. A shiver ran down his spine—magic.

Voices that should not have been audible at this distance rode on a phantom wind from the camp at the left—the Arcanian camp, Cedric realized. He couldn't make out the words being exchanged, but the sentiment was clear enough. Anger, rage, hurt. Cedric squinted, recognizing the pointed ears and luminous wings of two fae women. One of them summoned a burst of water that sent her opponent stumbling.

Cedric smirked as she fell to the ground.

"Can they not keep their magic to themselves for even a single night?" Thibault griped.

"Truly boorish behavior," Cedric agreed, even as he found himself wondering what the reason for the scuffle was. Then another thought occurred. "How are they fighting each other?" he asked.

"Far be it from me to understand the intricacies of the Crucible's magic," Lord Church replied, sounding bored. "But I would surmise it is because their intentions are not malicious. Violence may be forbidden during this time, but perhaps we are simply witnessing some sort of . . . family spat."

Hargrave let out a grunt. "They flaunt their magic to intimidate us, knowing Cedric and the other human champions must conserve their mana for the trials."

"Would that we could just go over there and slaughter them all," Thibault said, lip curling as his eyes darted to the sky. "This magical truce forced upon us by the aurora is utter bullshit."

"I do believe that kind of thinking is the precise reason said magical truce exists," Cedric offered. "I imagine the celestials prefer we champions at least make it into the Sanctum before we start killing each other."

"Pay the brutes no mind," Lord Church said, waving his cane dismissively. "Cedric will have the opportunity to deal with them in the Sanctum soon enough."

Thibault nodded as he slowed the horse, pulling off to the side of the road. He kept one eye on the scuffle, looking slightly nauseous, even as he helped unpack supplies from the back of the wagon.

Cedric found it difficult to look away too. His vision narrowed on the second woman—the one who had been knocked down. He couldn't see much—a flash of purple hair, the shimmer of sparkling wings that were a near-perfect match in color to the aurora blooming overhead.

Then he didn't need to look, because he *felt*. Felt a rush of power as the ground rumbled below him. Lord Church grabbed on to the side of the wagon for balance, and Cedric ran to assist him, finally ripping his gaze from the fight.

"What was that?" Hargrave muttered as he helped Lord Church right himself from the other side.

A chill slithered through Cedric. He suspected he would very soon find out.

CHAPTER 9
TYPICAL FAE

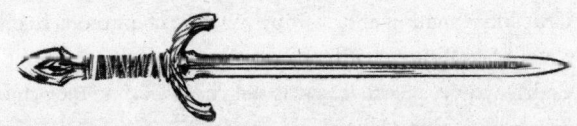

Cedric

Two days later, the aurora vanished.

For one glorious moment, the sky looked like it was on fire. The brilliant, eddying colors of the aurora burned brighter and brighter until they finally coalesced into ribbons of pure white light.

Then they were gone.

And the gates to the Lost City opened.

The tension was palpable as people disassembled tents and packed wagons, readying themselves to make their way to Castle Lumin. Travelers from the two camps converged on the road into the city, humans and Arcanians each keeping a wide berth from the other.

With so many people all heading in the same direction, the crowd moved slowly. Voices engaged in conversation—enthused and apprehensive both—drifted in and out of Cedric's ears as he fell into step beside Hargrave. There was excitement in the air, but trepidation, too. Fear. The combination made Cedric's skin feel itchy, like the very sky was holding its breath to see what would happen. Like he was waiting for magic to strike.

It was the humans who seemed the most eager. It might have seemed ironic, Cedric thought, given their frail bodies and mana-dependent magic—not to mention their supremely mortal lifespans. Stars knew Cedric himself grappled daily with the knowledge of the disadvantages he and the rest of the human champions held when it came to the trials ahead.

But perhaps it was these very limits that also allowed humanity to revel in the excitement and glory of the Crucible. That drove them forward with greater purpose. This was their chance to keep the crown out of Arcanian hands, to wrest power from them—power they did not deserve.

Cedric's jaw tightened. *This time will be different*, he told himself. Maybe not for the scores of Arcanian spectators who would spend yet another Crucible watching and waiting for their champions to emerge.

They would continue waiting.

But Cedric would ensure this was the very last time they did.

Because he was going to *win*.

He'd only had the chance to meet a few of his fellow champions thus far. Lord Church had gone to lengths in advance to ensure Cedric's prowess and abilities were well known among the spectators in attendance. As a result, he'd been rather popular during their time in the camp. The attention had made him supremely uncomfortable—something that came with the title of champion but for which he never felt adequately prepared.

So instead of establishing himself to his rivals and reaching out to potential allies, Cedric had chatted with spectators, graciously accepted favors, and listened politely to unsolicited advice. Advice that, regardless of how well intentioned and well reasoned it might have been, was ultimately useless. Nobody could truly advise on what to expect inside the Crucible. Because nobody had ever made it out alive.

Cedric kept his chin down and shoulders back as he walked toward the castle, offering dutiful nods to the occasional passersby. Even those who only pointed and whispered at him. Though he did think it rude, and by the fifth or sixth time it happened, he'd had enough.

Cedric was about to say something to a pair of wide-eyed gossiping young women when a sudden blur of motion caught his attention. He barely had time to react before nearly colliding with something—no, with someone. He staggered back, his hand reflexively moving to his weapon.

A streak of purple blinked past him. She was moving so fast, he might have missed her entirely if she hadn't stopped. But she did, coming to a halt just a few footspans ahead of him. Periwinkle hair cascaded down her back, elaborately interwoven. An uneasy expression settled on Cedric's face as he followed the flow of her braids to the pointed tips of her ears.

She searched the crowd of spectators before them, stretching onto the tips of her toes to get a better look. No wings, Cedric realized as he looked over her back. Two thin slits ran down the back of a leather bodice, which clung to her lithe frame, a gauzy cream blouse peeking out from underneath that left the pale, peachy skin of her shoulders on display. His eyes darted back to her ears. Fae, without a doubt. So where were her . . . ? Was she *hiding* her wings? Cloaking them with magic?

He hadn't realized that was something they could do.

Cedric found himself wondering whether some of the travelers surrounding him could be fae as well. He'd dismissed them all as fellow humans. But with hair and ears covered easily by hats and cloaks, and now knowing they could simply banish their wings from sight, there was no way of knowing. Not without forcing them to lower their hoods or getting up close and entirely too personal with one.

And what if cloaking their wings was not the only thing they could change about themselves? Cedric had long heard tales of shapeshifters from Old Arcanis—creatures that could transform into beasts great and small. Were they and the fae the same? Or was that something else?

There was much even the most accomplished sages and sorcerers still did not know about Arcanian magic. Despite the long hours spent studying with Lord Church and the best magical tutors from the

Academy in Paideus, Cedric's magical education suddenly felt woefully inadequate.

He suppressed a shudder. He'd already gotten complacent, started to let his guard down. And the Crucible hadn't even begun. He wished he had time to discuss this with Lord Church, to figure out what it might mean for his strategy during the trials. He would have to be extra vigilant. Who knew what a sneaky, motivated fae might be capable of beyond the Gate?

Cedric hated that his experience with Arcanians was so limited, his knowledge primarily formed from study and Lord Church's tutelage. His personal encounters had been limited to meeting the occasional dwarven trader from the Midlands and the even more occasional occurrence of stumbling across one in the course of duty.

That's how he saw firsthand what happened when Arcanians strayed too far from Nyrundelle, saw what happened to the poor humans they bewitched. Turned into Arcanian sympathizers—traitors against their own people. Convinced humans were hurting the planet by channeling mana with their tokens, by trying to claim just a smidgen of the power and magic that every Arcanian was born with.

Idealistic idiots.

As if Varyth Malchior and the Cult of Malakar weren't already enough to deal with.

Cedric had dragged more than one poor sod to the gallows for consorting with the enemy. Once, he even caught a fae in the midst of sowing the seeds of dissent . . . quite literally. The bastard had impregnated a human woman, had defiled her with a mixedborn child. Or perhaps she had done that to herself, being so willing to lie with the enemy. He swallowed hard, remembering how she'd cried, how she'd *screamed*, when Cedric's fellow knights dragged the fae away.

It brought Cedric no joy to think of what happened to the babe—what happened to all mixedborn children when they were discovered. But as for the father . . . seeing him carted off to the castle, his magic bound, his wings clipped . . . Well, that was rather satisfying. Served the fae bastard right for trying to infiltrate Havensreach.

Granted, *this* particular fae did not seem especially interested in subterfuge. The fae woman in front of Cedric loosed a frustrated sound—somewhere between a growl and a whine—that had his attention snapping back to her.

"Fuck," she muttered, the coarse word coming out in a melodic voice that immediately burrowed beneath Cedric's skin.

Why was she here? Was she a champion? With a dagger strapped to each of her thighs and a long, carved staff strapped to her back, she looked like she knew her way around a sparring ring, at the very least.

She was on the taller side of average—didn't have much muscle on her and Cedric still towered over her in height—but he knew better than to judge a fae's fighting ability by their natural slightness. They had magic on their side, after all. And even if she didn't know a pommel from a blade point, he knew with a sudden, powerful conviction that bit into every fiber of his being that it would be incredibly foolish to underestimate her.

There was something about her. Something . . . else there. Something dark, unnerving.

She darted her head from side to side, continuing to search with a petulant look on her face—softer and more delicate than he'd thought fae typically looked. Wide high set cheekbones. A sharp jaw that tapered into a soft point. Were those her true features? Or had she done something to her face? Magically made herself look more beautiful in the hopes that she would be mistaken for a less competent challenger?

Irritation sizzled in Cedric's chest at the thought.

"*Excuse* me," he snapped, surprising himself with the uncharacteristic brusqueness of his tone as he shoved past her.

Mere moments had passed since she'd nearly ran him down in her hasty pursuit of, well, whatever she was in pursuit of. But the boorish woman clearly had no qualms about her behavior. She barely seemed to register he was there.

Typical fae.

Almond-shaped eyes the color of shining emeralds met Cedric's for a split second. She cocked her head. Ran that jeweled gaze up and down his armor. "You're excused."

Then her eyes flashed, locking onto something behind his head.

Cedric bristled, but before he could even muster the beginnings of a retort, she shouted something unintelligible and took off. She wove through the crowd, chasing a glimmer of moonlit silver that disappeared beyond the castle steps.

It was only after she was gone that Cedric realized the wide-eyed gaze of the two girls he'd thought were whispering about him had followed her. A crease appeared between his brows as he strained to hear their hushed exchange. He could make out only one word.

"Revenant."

CHAPTER 10
TYPICAL HUMAN

Elyria

Two days.

Two fucking days in this stars-forsaken camp, dodging rumors and whispers. The bolder travelers approached her to ask for training tips, begged for a showcase of her magic. Elyria was no stranger to the attention, but she missed the usual endless supply of drink that helped her cope.

Worst of all, Elyria had barely spoken to Kit. Any conversations she began were quickly interrupted, and Kit had taken it upon herself to fulfill every request Elyria denied. It was all, *"I'll train with you!"* and, *"I'm not a wildshaper, but I can show you how I craft a whip from water."* Oh, and, *"Do I have any stories about the Revenant? Do I ever."* Meaning not only did Elyria's past continue to haunt her present, but any hopes

Elyria had of persuading Kit not to take on the Crucible were dying. Being slowly suffocated by Kit's incessant, irritating, and wholly unnecessary congeniality.

Elyria might have been impressed by the way Kit wielded her social graces to evade her attempts to talk, had the circumstances been different.

Had she not been running out of time.

When the aurora vanished overhead, Elyria's heart started beating so loudly and erratically that she wondered if it would burst from her chest. The reality of the situation sank in as she chased after Kit.

She was *just* here. Elyria *just* saw her. She'd rushed forward in an attempt to catch up with her but lost her just as quickly. "Fuck," she said under her breath.

Elyria felt the back of her neck prickle, the weight of judgmental eyes washing over her. She scanned the crowd of travelers making their way toward the castle, half searching for Kit and half trying to determine the source of the daggers she felt currently being stared into her back.

She turned her head a fraction, her eyes darting to a hulking human standing a few paces behind her. She observed him in pieces, trying not to draw attention by staring. Brown hair, tan skin, square jaw. Gleaming armor—a knight. And yes, that was a look of pure, unfiltered contempt on his face.

Elyria sighed, sending a silent curse up to whatever celestial had decided her personal torment was their favorite kind of entertainment. It was moments like this that made her doubt how steadfast the immortal beings were in keeping their vow not to interfere with mortal affairs.

"*Excuse* me," the knight said, the scent of sandalwood and something else—something smoky, like burning embers—assaulting her senses as he lumbered past her. *Shouldered* past, really, as if *she* had been the one doing something wrong. Did he think she hadn't been able to feel the way his eyes burned into her? The judgment oozing from him, despite the fact that they hadn't exchanged a single word?

Her face felt hot thinking about it. As if this entire misguided mission hadn't been disappointing enough, this *man* had the gall to charge past her as if *she* were in *his* way?

Elyria didn't have much experience with humans, not since the war. But she suspected this was typical behavior.

She met the knight's eyes—warm brown with a thin ring of gold encircling his iris.

"You're excused," she said coolly, inwardly grinning at the way his body immediately tensed. She hadn't thought it possible for him to wind himself any tighter.

Who was he to judge her, anyway? He was a *human*. Hardly worth the aggravation she felt simmering in her blood.

She supposed he must have been somewhat important, given the spectators' reactions as he'd plodded past. A champion. And a well-connected one, if the crest welded to the front of his well-maintained armor and the ornate hilt of the sword swinging at his hip were any indication.

As if the sheer size of him wasn't already enough to make him a serious contender beyond the Gate, human or not.

All the more reason to ensure Kit didn't follow him through it.

And maybe the celestials decided to take pity on Elyria after all, because before her standoff with the knight could devolve into anything worse, a flash of moonlight-silver hair flew across her vision. With a final look at the knight, she took off.

"Katerina Ravenswing!" Elyria hollered across the sea of hats and hoods taking their sweet fucking time as they ambled toward Castle Lumin. Heads turned, and Elyria swore she heard a squeak of alarm before Kit darted up the castle steps and out of sight.

Frustration surged within her. She shoved her way forward, ignoring the renewed murmurs and whispers of those around her. She blinked, trying to shake off the sensation that time was slipping away from her too fast.

Kit would not escape her again. Elyria would get to her, finally make her see reason. There was absolutely no way Elyria would sit back and allow Kit to walk to her death.

She would listen. Elyria would make her listen.

That was, if she didn't murder her first.

CHAPTER 11
A FAMILY MATTER

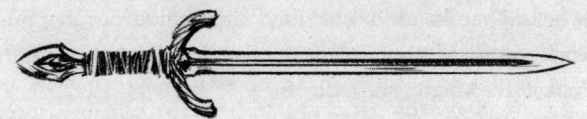

Cedric

The grand hall of Castle Lumin had been, Cedric imagined, quite the impressive sight in its prime. Now the cavernous room where champions and spectators gathered just seemed . . . sad. Thick layers of dust and rot had settled around the space. Painted frescoes crumbled from the walls.

The Gate stood alone in the center of the room, an archway with intricately welded metal doors that sat open, leading to nothing. Beautiful but otherwise unremarkable. A deception, of course, made all the more evident as the Gate began to glow around the edges, like it was readying itself.

Friends, family, and spectators took up spots along the walls as champions began stalking closer to the Gate. Cedric watched each face as they stared down their impending fate. He recognized a few and offered a casual wave to Alden Ashford from across the room. He'd made a point to seek the saint out at camp. Cedric agreed with Lord Church's assessment that allying with a healer wouldn't be the worst idea—at least for the early parts of the trials. Alden waved back, an excited grin on his face. That was good.

He caught the eye of Brandon Cormac, the sage Lord Church had mentioned. Cedric offered the champion a nod. A lock of long blond hair fell into Brandon's face as he nodded back. Cedric took it as a positive sign, even while recognizing that a telepath could make for either the best or worst kind of ally.

A group of three other human champions huddled together to the side of the Gate, their heads popping up in rapid succession to cast dirty looks in the direction of the Arcanian champions. Cedric recognized Leona Blackwood, though he hadn't had the chance to do more than introduce himself briefly to the sorcerer. He didn't know anything about the other two, a man and a woman with matching ginger hair and sharp gray-blue eyes. Siblings—perhaps even twins. Something told Cedric he would have to be vigilant around the trio.

Several Arcanians were spread out on the other side of the hall. A stout dwarven man with a long, intricately braided beard stood with his arms crossed, scanning the room. Cedric noted the fierce-looking hammer leaning against the wall with appreciation, and when the dwarf's blue-eyed gaze fell on him, Cedric gave him a nod to communicate as much.

Cedric thought he saw one side of the dwarf's mouth tip up in a smirk, but it was gone as quickly as it appeared. Unlike most of the Arcanian races, dwarves were well tolerated—respected even—by most of Havensreach. As master weaponsmiths and craftsmen, keeping open trading relationships with the few who crossed into the human kingdom was valuable.

That sentiment did not apply to the other races of Old Arcanis, though, something that Cedric was forced to recognize as his gaze landed on a pair of nocterrians lurking farther down. One spoke animatedly, their crimson hands gesturing toward the Gate. They were being fastidiously ignored by the other, a tall and imposing figure with indigo-hued skin and two crossed batons slung on their back. Their slick black hair was pulled into a bun that sat between two curved horns.

Cedric tried to tamp down on the growing discomfort that rumbled in his stomach the longer he looked at them.

Finally, his eyes drifted to a trio of fae who were deep in conversation. Cedric was taking stock of the builds and weapons of all three, trying to catalog them and discern the level of threat they represented, when Thibault's voice drifted into his ear.

"All good, Ric?" he asked as he sidled up next to Cedric. "We lost track of you for a minute there."

Cedric's eyebrow arched. "Of course. Why would it not be?"

Hargrave came to a stop at Cedric's other side, dark hair slicked back, tied low at the back of his head. "Thought some fae witch might have gotten her claws into you on the way in. Convinced you to enter *her* Sanctum." He gave Cedric a salacious wink as Thibault made a noise of disgust.

Cedric snorted and resisted the urge to smack Hargrave. "Hardly." He knew the guard said it in jest, but while Cedric's reactions were a bit more measured than Thibault's, he couldn't disagree that the very idea was insulting. Perhaps a weaker man might be enthralled by the thought of adding an Arcanian or two to the notches on his belt. He supposed he understood the temptation. The unique circumstances of the Crucible offered an opportunity for fraternization that few humans would ever see again in their lifetime. Not Cedric though. It would take a lot more than a striking face, shimmering green eyes, and pretty purple hair to get him to stray from his mission—and his morals.

He frowned at the specificity of the image that came into his mind. He certainly wasn't referring to anyone in particular.

Hargrave patted Cedric on the back as he turned to continue chatting with Thibault, and as if his previous line of thought had summoned her back into being, Cedric saw her.

She stood on the opposite side of the Gate, perfectly framed by its ethereal glow, the soft light painting the strands of periwinkle around her face silver. Her right hand was wrapped around her carved quarterstaff as she tilted to the side, leaning her weight on it.

Cedric's eyes nearly rolled into the back of his head when he realized that despite her casual pose, she was arguing with the fae woman standing beside her. Their voices rose into the hall, cutting through the quiet conversations happening around them. He didn't think there was a single person present who couldn't hear every word.

The purple-haired hellion did not seem particularly bothered by this. "So that's it? You won't even let me finish saying my piece, Kit?" she screeched.

The one called Kit rolled her eyes. Even from across the hall, Cedric could see they were a fascinating contrast of colors—one of them ocean blue, the other green as new grass. She was of average height and strong body, with rich brown skin and silver-white hair cropped to her chin. A short sword was sheathed at each hip and a pair of silver-and-gold wings were folded behind her back. Not hidden, Cedric noted with interest.

"You've said more than enough," Kit said.

"I haven't even begun to—"

"Look around, Elyria. It's already happening. You need to let it go."

Elyria.

The name was softer and more lyrical than Cedric had expected. He wasn't sure it matched the hellcat currently seething at her . . . friend? Rival? That they knew each other was clear, though he couldn't figure out the nuances of their relationship, nor did he have any notion as to what their quarrel was about.

Cedric recognized Lord Leviathan Church's aggrieved sigh coming from behind him. "As I said before, no discipline, no restraint."

"Indeed, my lord," Cedric agreed, though he didn't tear his eyes from the pair. Until Lord Church's reminder, Cedric hadn't put together that Elyria and Kit were clearly the ones who had been having that . . . family spat . . . when his party arrived. Had they truly been fighting about whatever this was this entire time? He sighed. They would be absolutely insufferable during the Crucible if this kept up.

"I can't let it go," Elyria said through gritted teeth, "if *you* won't let me in. You've spent the past two days avoiding me."

"Can you blame me?" Kit mumbled.

A grin played at the edges of Cedric's mouth. He thought about the way Elyria had been flattened by that burst of water. Kit was a tideweaver, then.

If Elyria heard Kit's sardonic interjection, she didn't let on. "You wanted time to mope; I gave it to you. You wanted to stay distracted; I allowed it—much to my own detriment, I will add. But now we're out of time. I can't let you off the hook anymore."

"You're making a scene," Kit said, her nostrils flaring. She seemed to be looking anywhere but at the many faces now staring at them as she stalked away.

Elyria followed. "I don't care."

"Clearly," someone muttered. Another one of the fae champions—a woman with wine-red hair that cascaded between her orange wings in a smooth wave.

A smattering of snide laughter erupted in response.

"Mind your business, Gael," Elyria sneered, her expression dark. The laughter cut off abruptly.

"I told you when you arrived that you wouldn't change my mind," Kit said, only a few paces from Cedric now. "You haven't. I *will* go through that Gate. I will enter the Sanctum. I will take on the Crucible." Her eyes narrowed. "I will win."

Cedric's mouth was moving before he realized what he was doing. "You mean to keep her from entering the Sanctum?" he asked.

"Cedric." Lord Church's voice was a low warning.

Cedric barely heard it. "Are you so threatened by one of your own kind"—he suppressed the derision in his voice as best he could, but given the way Elyria's eyes narrowed, he must not have done a very good job—"that you would keep her from championing your realm?"

Not that it truly mattered, Cedric supposed, given that *he* had every intention of winning. But there was something in the idea of Elyria trying to prevent Kit from entering that didn't sit right with him. Champions trained for years—decades for the Arcanians, he presumed—to take on the Arcane Crucible. For the champions in this room, today marked the culmination of long-held hopes and dreams. He might have had his moments of trepidation, but it was for Cedric too.

And damn anyone who would actively try to prevent those dreams from being realized. Even for a fae.

Elyria whirled, her eyes narrowing on Cedric. "In what realm is this conversation *any* of your business?"

Cedric jutted his chin. "With the way you've been carrying on, I believe you have made it the business of everyone present."

"Hear, hear!" cheered Gael.

Elyria ignored her. "This is a family matter, human. Stay. Out. Of. It." She punctuated each word with a tap of her staff.

"She's right," Kit said. "It *is* a family matter." Her voice was like ice when she turned to Elyria and added, "So why are you here again?"

The shock that flitted across Elyria's face was quick as a lightning strike, but Cedric saw it. Saw the flash of hurt, the words cutting deep. And then, in the next instant, he saw the way she transformed. How she masked the pain, clawed the raw anger she'd been exuding back into herself.

A chill ran over Cedric as Elyria rolled her shoulders. Cocked her head to one side. Pasted on a caustic smile. "Apologies, *my lady*," she said to Kit, the words dripping with sarcasm. "I misspoke. I meant only that as I was sent here by your mother, I am acting in the best interest of your *remaining* family."

Kit flinched.

Cedric didn't understand the sudden need he felt to move closer, like something was tugging him toward the arguing fae. He took a single step forward before a hand wrapped around his upper arm, keeping him in place.

"Control your emotions," Lord Church hissed in his ear. "Extricate yourself from this mess. This is behavior unbecoming of a champion."

They're champions and look how they're acting, Cedric wanted to say. But he was quiet as he stepped back into place at the nobleman's side.

Elyria was still speaking. "I see now my efforts have been in vain. Do allow me to take my leave." Kit didn't meet her eye as Elyria sketched a mocking bow, slung her staff over her back, and turned toward the entrance doors.

Cedric's brows shot up. Was she truly leaving? The thought shocked him into motion, even as he felt Lord Church's hand tighten on his arm. This was the opposite of controlling his emotions; he knew this.

He just couldn't help himself.

"So, you aren't a champion, then?" he called out, ignoring Lord Church's sharp inhale as he pulled himself free and took off after Elyria.

Her steps slowed. She turned. "Decidedly *not*," she said with a derisive snort.

"Then why—"

"Best of luck with your little game, Sir Knight."

His temper flared, heating his chest. "This is not a game."

"It is the precise definition of a game. We simply aren't the ones making up the rules." She threw her narrowed gaze to the ceiling, as if issuing a dare to the celestials themselves. Her mouth had curved up on one side when her green eyes met Cedric's once more. "Hope you all have fun playing together."

"You're not taking this seriously. People die in the Crucible."

Her smirk faded, replaced by a hard look that she directed at Kit. "I take it all *very* seriously. Now, why don't you go back to sending your futile prayers up to your banished god? You're going to need all the help you can get in there."

"Just fucking go, Elle," Kit said, sounding tired.

Cedric's mouth quirked as he attempted to smother a laugh.

He failed.

Elyria's eyes narrowed to emerald slits. "Was there something else you wished to say?"

"I suppose I'm just surprised that, for all your posturing, you won't be entering the Sanctum." A wave of boldness crested in Cedric's chest, pulled the next words from his mouth. "And perhaps I am a little disappointed that I won't have the opportunity to best you."

"Well, I'm not!" called Gael, humor still scrawled across her face. One of the fae next to her let out a bellowing laugh. "And neither should you be, Sir Knight, given the way you've managed to rile up the Revenant."

Cedric's breath stalled in his lungs. He was sure he'd misheard those gossiping girls outside. He was sure there was no possible way that this fury-filled harpy was . . .

Disbelief carried Cedric forward, closing the distance between Elyria and himself. "*You're* the Revenant?"

CHAPTER 12
GAEL WINTERS, FLAMECALLER

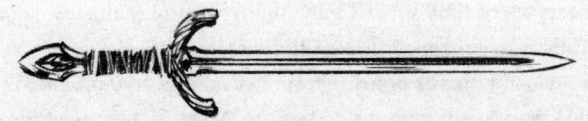

Cedric

Elyria shrugged. "So they call me."

Cedric's vision turned crimson.

Murderer, his brain screamed at him. *Butcher*. His tongue darted over the scar on his lip, his mana token glowing warm against his chest. He suddenly thought he understood how Lord Church had been able to snap that bandit's neck so easily—Cedric's palms itched with the temptation to do the same now. He thought it might be worth risking the celestials' wrath to do it.

Barely six winters at the time, Cedric's memory of the night his parents died was a blur of chaos and fear. He remembered the acrid smell of smoke, the bright blaze of fire. The hard, cold edge of steel pressed to his mouth—a threat to get him to stop crying. The sharp sting of the dagger slicing through his lip when he hadn't been able to.

But through the haze of terror and rage, one part of that night had burned itself into his mind. Two words that had stuck with him through each of the twenty-two years that had passed since: *the Revenant*.

"How *dare* you show your face here?" Cedric was trembling with rage. He clenched his fists at his sides to keep himself from reaching for his sword or token.

Elyria's expression was cold and unyielding. "Do not presume to speak of things you know *nothing* of."

"I know plenty," he snapped, taking another step toward her.

He thought she would match the motion, moving back to maintain the distance between them. But the murderous witch did the opposite.

She stepped *forward*, jutting her chin up defiantly as Cedric stared daggers at her. "And what, exactly, is it you think you know?"

The rich, sweet scent of bitter almonds filled Cedric's nose—sugar and poison. "You killed my family," he spat. "Broke into our home and slaughtered my parents. I should cut you down where you stand."

Elyria blinked. Her brow furrowed slightly, a change in her unyielding demeanor so infinitesimal, Cedric thought he might have imagined it.

And then, as he gaped in disbelief, she *laughed*.

But it wasn't humor pouring from her mouth. It was venom.

"I've killed many humans, to be sure. Most of them were probably someone's father or mother. But breaking into some human hovel to murder your parents in cold blood?" She bit her lip in a farcical show of deliberation. "Yeah, doesn't sound like me. Sorry."

"I was *there*, Revenant. I might have been but a child, but I remember the night my parents were killed. *I heard your name.*"

The cold mask slithered back over Elyria's face. "You heard my name," she repeated blankly.

Cedric stared at her.

"Convenient, isn't it," she said, her tone hard, "how easily a name can be used to disguise the truth?"

A spark of confusion cut through Cedric's anger. "What truth?" he demanded. "That you're not the dark butcher everyone knows you to be?"

Her mouth curved into a cruelly beautiful smile. "Who knows? Maybe it was me. Maybe I've simply forgotten."

"You mock me."

A single shrill laugh pierced the air. "Of course I'm mocking you. When you go flinging around wild accusations without substance or reason, why shouldn't I? Now, I've done many things in my many years in this world. Not all of them pleasant, not all of them right"—her gaze flicked to Kit—"but I can tell you that not once have I had any interest in participating in the slaughter of some inconsequential human family. That said, by all means, Sir Knight, do go ahead and keep believing it was me."

She tracked her eyes up and down his body, and Cedric could have sworn her gaze burned straight through his armor.

"Whatever helps you rest your head at night," she finished, turning away from him in dismissal.

His palms heated, the urge to lash out overwhelming. From the side of his eye, he could see Hargrave and Thibault watching him. He suspected Lord Church was close to them, undoubtedly displeased with Cedric's display.

He found he couldn't bring himself to care.

A commotion drew Cedric's attention. The contemptuous energy had started to spread to the other champions. Leona Blackwood and the ginger twins were heckling Gael and her two companions. One of them, a fae with shock-white hair, spat an insult at the siblings, making Gael laugh.

"You think you're so funny, with your little quips and jokes. But I've had just about enough of you," the ginger-haired sister said, pointing accusingly at Gael.

"It's well past time you shut up, you knife-eared freak," said her brother.

"Knife ears, huh?" Gael snickered. "Come up with that all by yourself, did you?"

"I said, shut . . . up!" Shocked cries rang out around the hall as a bolt of magic shot from the brother's hands. Gael sidestepped it with a casualness that made the attack seem like it was nothing more than a nuisance.

Cedric held his breath, waiting for whatever consequence would befall this man for violating the rule against fighting.

But nothing happened. Perhaps it was more of a warning shot, and he hadn't truly intended to harm her?

Leona groaned. "Save your mana for the Crucible, you idiot!"

The man grimaced from the chastisement. Gael turned away with a dismissive snort.

It was then that Cedric saw the glint of steel as the brother lunged at Gael's back.

Cedric's body moved on instinct. The cowardice he witnessed overrode any disinclination he might've had to bother helping an Arcanian—a fae, at that—and he darted toward Gael in an attempt to block the man's spineless ambush.

He needn't have bothered.

Quicker than lightning, a flash of power burst from the Gate, blasting the redheaded man back. He went flying, hitting the far wall with a *thud*, his dagger clattering to the floor. His sister cried out and raced to his side.

Jaw slack, Cedric looked from the man's crumpled form to the Gate, which had already returned to its prior state. If he hadn't witnessed it with his own eyes, he wasn't sure he would have believed it. But it turned out the Crucible had meted out punishment after all. And with the speed and intensity of that magical lash, Cedric understood why everyone took the rule so seriously.

His attention thoroughly seized by what had just happened, Cedric realized too late that he was still in motion—and that Elyria was moving in the same direction he was.

His solid frame collided with hers, her body a sudden, unyielding wall. Four hells, she was a lot stronger than she looked. The impact sent a jolt through him—electric and hot—as he stumbled back. He reached out reflexively to steady himself, and the next thing he knew, his hands were wrapped around her forearms.

Stunned, their eyes locked—silver-streaked green meeting warm golden brown. Confusion and revulsion twisted in Cedric's gut. He jerked away at the exact same moment Elyria yanked her arms back, clutching them to her chest as if the contact had burned her.

"What the quartered hell are you doing?" Cedric spat.

"What are *you* doing?" Elyria snapped back, caustic bewilderment on her face. "Get out of the way before you hurt yourself."

"Hurt myself? I was trying to *help*."

She snorted. "Take a look around, Sir Knight. Nobody needs your help."

Cedric lifted his eyes to where Gael now stood over the ginger twins, the sister braced protectively over her brother, who remained prostrate on the ground. A single flame burned above Gael's pointer finger as she wagged it at her would-be assailants.

"Tsk, tsk. Do they not teach the rules of conduct over on your side of the continent?" Gael taunted.

"They're *humans*, Winters," her white-haired fae companion said. The way he said the word rankled Cedric's nerves. "What do you expect?"

"True enough, Paelin," Gael replied. She stared at the siblings sprawled on the ground with a contemplative look. After a moment, she extinguished the flame on her finger with a sigh, as casually as if she were blowing out a candle. "Well, hopefully they've learned their lesson."

Leona Blackwood approached the group, dropping to one knee in order to help the brother sit up. "We've certainly learned something," she said, her voice dripping with disdain.

Gael smirked. "And what's that?"

Challenge flashed in Leona's eyes. "Who we'll look for first once we're on the other side of the Gate."

Murmurs rippled through the hall. For the first time since the confrontations had begun, Cedric locked eyes with Lord Church. The nobleman gave Cedric a subtle nod, confirming what he'd been thinking. If his fellow champions wanted to settle their debts inside the Crucible, let them. All the better for him if they stayed distracted, fighting among themselves while he raced through the trials alone. He would yet win the crown.

Cedric's eyes darted to Elyria, but her gaze was still on Gael.

"Winters?" she asked, her head tilting to the side as if struck with a sudden realization.

"My surname," Gael explained, her flame-red eyebrows drawing together. "What of it?"

A spark lit in Elyria's emerald eyes. "Your name is Gael Winters. But you're a flamecaller?"

Someone huffed a quiet laugh. Someone else *guffawed*. Despite the rage that still simmered in the back of his mind, Cedric felt the corner of his mouth twitch.

"Yes, yes, *hilarious*," Gael said, the humor in her tone betraying the annoyed expression she wore.

A grin played on Elyria's lips. She looked like she was about to toss another jibe in Gael's direction when a cold voice suddenly cut back in.

"Were you not leaving?" Kit said.

Elyria flinched, but before she could respond, a clangorous gong suddenly reverberated through the hall.

The champions turned in unison toward the source of the sound. A hush fell over the crowd. The ethereal light of the Gate shimmered. Then, as if it were some solid, tangible thing, it started to shake. Threads of light vibrated until they combined into a seemingly solid mass of luminance—an incandescent curtain.

The Gate was open.

From behind the curtain, a white-cloaked figure emerged.

"Champions." The voice was somehow many voices at once—thunderous and tranquil, rasping and smooth. "I am the Arbiter."

Whispers echoed through the crowd of spectators. Every champion's mouth was clamped tight, all eyes locked on the Arbiter.

"Tell me," said that multifaceted voice, "who desires to enter the Arcane Crucible?"

CHAPTER 13
GET TO THE GATE

Elyria

"Who will commit themselves to the celestial sanctum? Who will test themselves in the Crucible?"

The Arbiter's face was obscured by a gleaming white hood and the shadows it cast, but Elyria thought she could *feel* the being beneath the billowing robes smile as they surveyed the gathered champions.

She had a vague recollection of seeing the Arbiter when she had accompanied Evander here last time. She grasped at the threads of her memory, trying to discern what had occurred, the words that were said, but they slipped through her fingers. All she could recall was how Evander had looked—so confident, so beautiful. How the last thing he'd done before stepping through the Gate was look back at her.

"I commit myself." Paelin's voice cut through Elyria's reverie. He took a step toward the Arbiter before falling to one knee, his fist clasped over his heart. "I desire to enter the Crucible and prove my worth to the realm."

"Then so you shall," said the Arbiter, their multi-tonal voice echoing in Elyria's ears. "But before your trials begin, know this. The Arcane Crucible offers deadly tests of strength and power, yes. It will test your resolve, the depth of your spirit. But most importantly, it tests your propensity for harmony—for unity."

Elyria balked. She did not remember anything like this from last time.

Looking to the side, she tried to catch Kit's eye, as if perhaps she'd be able to speak to whether this was some new revelation, or if Elyria had just blocked everything out from before. Kit's gaze was unwavering, fixed on the Arbiter, her expression unreadable.

"Unity?" The voice that came from the shadows was strangely familiar. Soft and hard, masculine and feminine. The midnight-skinned nocterrian stepped out of the shadows along the far wall, and Elyria gaped at them. Black hair. Curved horns. The same one from the jail.

Their red-black eyes flicked to Elyria's for the briefest moment as they passed. "What does that mean?" asked the nocterrian. "That the crown cannot be won by a single champion? That we have to work together?"

"And harmony between who?" asked Gael. "Are we to choose allies inside the Sanctum? You cannot possibly mean to say"—she ran her eyes over the trio of human champions huddled together on the floor and let out a derisive snort—"we are *all* expected to work together."

The Arbiter did not respond. Uneasy murmurs ran through the crowd. Several champions openly scoffed.

"Surely you cannot be serious," said one of the humans. Not one of the ridiculous, short-tempered twins, but the third—a woman with dull brown hair, an upturned nose, and hazel eyes that were set too far apart. Their leader, it seemed, and the one who had just declared her intent to do whatever the *opposite* of harmony was once the Crucible officially began.

"I'm not usually one to turn down multiple partners." A fae with long, straight cobalt hair, parted deeply on one side and shaved underneath, stood between Gael and Paelin. Cyren, if she recalled correctly. "But this is asking a lot, even for me." He tossed a wink in Elyria's direction.

The discontented murmurings grew into a symphony of complaints.

"I'll travel to the fourth quarter of hell before I trust one of *them*," spat the leader of the human trio.

"And what does this mean for the crown?" cried someone else.

"Yes! What have we been training for if not to win the crown for our people—for glory?" asked Paelin.

"This is absurd," said the dwarven champion, his eyes briefly falling on the chestnut-haired knight, his jaw tight as he quietly observed the others.

"Have you forgotten about the Great Betrayal? You would have us work with the cretins responsible for sundering the realm?" shouted Gael.

"It was not *our* kind who carved up the continent in a fit of rage," hissed the ginger-haired human woman.

"Fae scum," added her brother.

Elyria rolled her eyes. *Helpful contribution.*

"True, you're certainly not powerful enough for that. Your kind just committed an act so heinous that it launched a war," said Cyren.

"The war that led to the Shattering," Gael added.

The cries of dissent grew louder.

"We didn't train like this. We're not prepared for this!"

"And why have we never heard of such a thing before?"

Yes, why hadn't they? Elyria wondered. It was a fair question. Elyria had only ever known the Crucible to be an individual competition—one where champions entered knowing they would win or they would die. Was this just another part of the Crucible's strange magic?

She pursed her lips, looking around the room at the furious, confused faces of the champions and their entourages. Even as someone who thoroughly disagreed with the entire stars-damned concept, she had to admit it hardly seemed fair that the Crucible would keep its champions ignorant as to the true nature of the trials.

Unless it hadn't.

She thought back to Ollie's recitation of the prophecy back in Coralith, regretting the way she cut him off before he finished. The prophecy might have been common enough knowledge throughout Nyrundelle, but having made a distinct point to avoid all Crucible-related topics for the past twenty-five years, Elyria's recollection was rather rusty.

From shadow and fire, champions rise, she thought, trying to remember. *Forged in the Crucible of fate.*

That part seemed simple enough. A rather dramatic beginning, but here they were—a room full of champions about to take on the Crucible.

Strength, spirit, magic, and concord test the trials beyond the Gate. Again, easy.

But what was the next part? "From bitterest rivals to . . . bitterest rivals . . ." she murmured, thinking aloud as the cacophony of complaints around her continued to swell.

"To heartbreaking ends." A low voice cut through the noise as smooth as a knife through butter.

Elyria looked up to find the brown-haired knight eyeing her with bemusement. "What?" she snapped.

"From bitterest rivals to heartbreaking ends," he said. "The prophecy, yes?"

She rubbed her jaw, grinding her teeth as she wondered just how long he'd been watching her.

Her reaction certainly didn't seem to bother him as he continued to speak, however. *"From shadow and fire, champions rise, forged in the Crucible of fate. Strength, spirit, magic, and concord test the trials beyond the Gate. From bitterest rivals to heartbreaking ends, blood shall find a way. With mettle and promise, darkness and light, so dawn brings a new day."*

Elyria felt the skin tighten around her eyes as she listened to the knight—whose input she most definitely had not asked for—complete his recitation with an ostentatious flourish, a smug look in place. She wanted to wipe it right off his chiseled face. She bit down on the impulse, though, supposing she couldn't be *too* annoyed with him. As obnoxious as it was, the knight had been . . . helpful. She'd clearly forgotten more than she realized.

Although she could have sworn she remembered the prophecy being much longer. And that last line in particular felt foreign, like she was hearing it for the first time only now.

She also had absolutely no idea what it meant. Perhaps there was a touch of what the Arbiter had proclaimed hidden within the prophecy—wasn't concord just another word for unity?—but it was so subtle that Elyria couldn't blame the champions for not recognizing it ahead of time.

"Cryptic celestial bullshit," she muttered, and the knight's accomplished expression morphed into a glower.

"Don't say things like—"

"This must be a test!" cried one of the champions, cutting off what Elyria presumed was some protestation at her obvious sacrilege. "It's meant to throw us off-kilter, have us distracted, fretting over alliances instead of focusing on the challenges ahead."

"All I know is I'd rather face the Crucible alone and die with honor than debase myself with one of *them*," said someone else.

"Silence," commanded the Arbiter. They did not yell. They did not scream. But the word reverberated through Elyria's very being, as if spoken directly into her mind.

The grand hall fell silent.

"You will have many decisions to make inside the Sanctum," the Arbiter said. "No longer will the Crucible's magic dissuade you from fighting one another. The choice to progress alone or together belongs to each of you." They paused, allowing the weight of those words to sink in. "But know this simple truth, champions: Without unity, you will fail."

"I shall take my chances," said Paelin.

"So be it," replied the Arbiter, and Elyria thought the layered voice sounded disappointed. "Paelin Saltwillow, do you commit yourself to the Arcane Crucible, to pursuing the truths and challenges held within?"

"I do."

"Do you consent to be marked by the celestials, binding yourself to the Celestial Sanctum?"

"I do."

"And do you do this, knowing that once you step through the Gate, you shall not return until the Crucible is complete and its prize claimed?"

"I do."

The Arbiter raised their arm, their hand remaining hidden within the billowing sleeves of their robe as they touched Paelin's forehead. "Then I crown you a champion of the realm. Go forth and enter the first trial with the blessing of the celestials."

Cheers rang out from the crowd of spectators. Paelin didn't glance back as he strode toward the Gate and walked straight through. The Gate glowed, the curtain of light within blowing on some otherworldly breeze, and he was gone.

Gael went next. "See you on the other side," she said to no one in particular before stepping through the curtain.

One by one, the champions came forward. One by one, the Arbiter called their names and branded them with the magical contract that bound them to the Celestial Sanctum.

The dwarf, Thraigg Ironfist.

Cyren Tenrider, the blue-haired fae, though not before sending a sinful grin in Elyria's direction.

Leona Blackwood, the human trio's leader, followed by those miserable redheaded siblings, Belis and Belien Larkin.

Tenebris Nox, the nocterrian from the jail, and their crimson-skinned compatriot, Dissidua Pyr.

Elyria's brow shot up when a sylvan woman who had been tucked against the far wall approached. Zephyr, the Arbiter called her. No surname. She was petite, equipped only with a small dagger sheathed to her thigh and a belt full of pouches and pockets and clinking vials.

No cheers or sobs rang out from the crowd as she met the Arbiter. She'd come alone, and Elyria couldn't help but wonder what she was doing here. Was the lure of glory so great it reached even the sylvans in their forests? Zephyr bit her lip as the Arbiter branded her forehead, but that was the only sign of any potential hesitance before she stepped through, and Elyria had to admire her gentle confidence.

It was a quality that could *not* be ascribed to the two human champions who went through next, hooting and hollering as they waltzed through the Gate.

Then, finally, it was that obnoxious, judgmental knight's turn. He finished conversing with the nobleman Elyria had noticed watching their earlier confrontation. The noble clapped the knight on the back before leaning close and whispering something in his ear. The knight nodded, and there was a vulnerability in the expression on his face that, against all reason, made Elyria's heart clench.

"Cedric Thorne," called the Arbiter as he approached, and that heart-clenching feeling was quickly snuffed out as Elyria stifled a snort. How a name so plain could simultaneously sound so pretentious, she wasn't sure. She supposed it fit him.

"Convenient, isn't it, how easily a name can be used to disguise the truth?" Her own words from earlier came back to her, rattling around in her mind. She wasn't sure why. She grinned to herself as she recalled what the knight—what *Cedric*—had said back.

"What truth? That you're not the dark butcher everyone knows you to be?"

Dark butcher. Now *that* was an epithet Elyria could get behind. No more of this Revenant shit. It was all too clear that moniker had taken on a life of its own.

"Best of luck, Sir Thorne," Elyria said smoothly as the knight stepped away from the Arbiter. "Do try not to die in there."

He looked at her with the strangest expression, somewhere between murderous and astonished. But Cedric Thorne said nothing as he walked through the Gate.

Elyria took a trembling breath. Only Kit remained now.

She had lingered, Elyria noticed. Hung back. Elyria's chest felt tight. Had her pleas finally gotten through to her? Or perhaps the change in plans, the Arbiter's declaration—warning?—had thrown her?

Kit's stunning, mismatched eyes met Elyria's. There was pain in them.

The hope squeezing Elyria's heart turned into a cold iron vise.

She hadn't changed her mind.

"Katerina Ravenswing."

Kit's face was set with determination as she came to a stop before the Arbiter.

Elyria rushed to her side. "Kit, no," she begged, pulling Kit's arm to force her away from the Arbiter. To face Elyria instead. "Please."

"I have to do this, Ellie." She placed a gentle hand on top of Elyria's, still gripping her forearm.

"You don't."

Kit's eyes filled with a mix of emotions that Elyria didn't understand. "I think he would be really happy that you tried so hard, you know. Perhaps even if I don't come out on top in there, just knowing how hard you worked to save me will bring him some peace."

Elyria's eyes burned.

"Don't worry, though," Kit added, scrunching her nose. "I still have absolutely every intention of winning."

And with that, she wrenched her arm out of Elyria's grasp and waved her hand. Gasps rang out from the surrounding spectators as a wall of ice cut across the room. It happened so fast, Elyria barely had time to step out of the way as the frozen barrier grew higher and higher, not stopping until it spanned the entire room, floor to ceiling. Completely cutting Elyria off from Kit and the Arbiter.

It was an extraordinary display of magic, and Elyria might have been proud of Kit if she wasn't so thoroughly pissed off.

Elyria pounded on the ice, each blow a frigid sting against her naked palm. A shadow crossed behind the opaque barrier, and Elyria thought she could make out the outline of a hand being held against it.

"I'm sorry, Ellie," Kit said, her voice muffled. "This is how it has to be."

"Kit!" Elyria cried, beating her fist against the wall harder, but anything else she might have said was interrupted by the blistering cold suddenly traveling up her arm. With a jolt, she jumped back, cradling her frostbitten hand, powerless to do anything but watch as Kit's shadow turned away.

"I am ready," Kit said.

The Arbiter's voice was still clear as a bell as it rang in Elyria's mind. "Do you commit yourself to the Arcane Crucible, to pursuing the truths and challenges held within?"

A frustrated cry ripped from Elyria as Kit said, "I do."

"Do you consent to be marked by the celestials, binding yourself to the Celestial Sanctum?"

"I do."

"And do you do this, knowing that once you step through the Gate, you shall not return until the Crucible is complete and its prize claimed?"

There was a moment of hesitation, and despite the frosty barrier between them, Elyria felt Kit's gaze find her through the ice.

"I do," said Kit.

Elyria's scream was caught in her throat.

And then she was gone.

The instant Kit stepped through the Gate, the wall melted away, drenching Elyria's legs with ice-cold water as it puddled to the floor in a massive sheet. Still, she stood there. Stunned. Helpless.

The crowd of spectators had been steadily thinning as their respective champions entered the Sanctum. What few folks remained started to shuffle toward the exit. The show was over. The Crucible had begun.

Fourteen champions now fought for their lives in the Celestial Sanctum.

Feeling returned to Elyria's numbed skin in a sudden rush, a thousand painful pinpricks fluttering up her arm at once. The shock caused her to bolt forward, her body uncontrolled as she stumbled directly into the Arbiter.

With a sneer, Elyria shoved the white-cloaked being away. She didn't know what kind of celestial smiting might befall her for doing so, but she shoved, nonetheless. It was like pushing on air. Yet when an ethereal, glowing hand emerged from the Arbiter's oversized sleeve and grabbed Elyria's arm, it was solid as steel.

"Your quarrel is not with me," said the Arbiter's many voices, their grip crushing.

"I beg to differ," Elyria spat.

The Arbiter's head tipped back, and for a moment, Elyria thought she might glimpse the face hidden beneath the voluminous hood. But it stayed in place, the being's face still masked in shadow as the Arbiter started to tremble. Then shake.

Elyria's arm ached under the Arbiter's iron grip as they convulsed, their layered voice strained and eerie as words tumbled forth.

"From bitterest rivals to heartbreaking ends, two bloods shall find their way. Through sacrifice, darkness, and friendship betrayed, as dawn brings a new day."

Almost as quickly as it had begun, it was over.

"What the fuck was that?" Elyria yelled as she wrenched her arm from the Arbiter's grasp. The being swayed on their feet, dazed.

"The prophecy!" called a lingering spectator, awestruck. "Praise to Lunara!"

"The Revenant is celestial-blessed!" called another.

Elyria spun, half prepared to violently correct whoever had spoken and half determined to demand the Arbiter explain. Why were they spewing this prophetic nonsense at Elyria, of all people? And why did it seem different from the version Cedric had recited only minutes before?

A scream pierced the air before she got the chance to ask.

Elyria whipped around, her eyes wide with shock as someone burst back through the Gate, clutching his shoulder. Brandon Cormac, one of the human champions. His face was contorted in terror, blood gushing from a deep wound that started on his upper arm and cut across his chest. Elyria thought she glimpsed a flash of white bone amidst the jagged, torn flesh.

He staggered forward, collapsing onto his knees in front of Elyria. "The t-trial," he garbled, his mouth full of blood. He tried to speak again. He couldn't. Not aloud.

"The beasts. They're savage. They're everywhere. Get to the gate." The words echoed in Elyria's head, and she trembled at the realization that Cormac was a mindwielder. *"You have to get to the gate. But you can't—they don't—they won't allow—"*

He shuddered. Clutched his forehead with a red-stained hand and then let out a scream so agonizing, so harrowing, Elyria knew she would hear it in her nightmares for a long, long time.

The celestial mark on Cormac's forehead glowed brightly, even as his body crumpled. Elyria reacted quickly, crouching to catch him before he hit the floor. She rolled him onto his back. But there was nothing she could do—nothing to be done.

His eyes were frozen open, unseeing.

The man was dead.

A piercing wail sounded from somewhere behind her. A horror-stricken gasp. Someone was sobbing. Other voices began to mix in Elyria's ears, gossiping whispers and words of comfort alike.

A voice pierced the din. Many voices, speaking as one. "He was marked. He was bound to the Sanctum." The Arbiter bowed their head, still swaying unevenly. "He left the Sanctum."

Brandon Cormac's body erupted in blue flame.

And as he burned, as the flames reduced his body to ash, Elyria could think of only one thing: Kit.

Her eyes met the shadowed void where the Arbiter's face should be. She sensed an infinitesimal nod from beneath the hood.

Elyria shivered, colder now than when Kit's magic had nearly frozen her in place. Kit could have already fallen. Could have been clawed apart by whatever vile creature had left Cormac so wounded and so terrified that he'd risked the celestials' wrath by running back through the Gate rather than face it. The thought stole the breath from Elyria's lungs.

The curtain of light within the Gate wafted in a phantom breeze, as if beckoning her forth. Did it simply want someone to replace the champion the Sanctum had lost? And was Elyria absolutely insane for considering it?

"This is madness," she said to herself.

The Arbiter responded anyway. "Perhaps."

Elyria stood.

"Should you do this, you must know there is no turning back. Not for you, Elyria Lightbreaker."

Elyria clenched her fist, her fingernails biting into the skin of her palms. She couldn't just stand by knowing the horrors Kit was likely facing at this exact moment. She certainly couldn't simply *leave*.

What did she have to go back to anyway?

She took a deep breath. Tightened the straps of the dagger sheaths on her thighs. Made the mistake of looking toward what remained of the crowd of spectators, many of them staring at her in awe.

The Revenant is celestial-blessed!

Elyria snorted. Then, recalling the prophecy, she took a deep, slow breath. "Forged in the Crucible of fate, right? Champions rise?"

The Arbiter nodded.

"Well, then. What have I got to lose?"

PART II
FRAY

CHAPTER 14
THE FIRST TRIAL

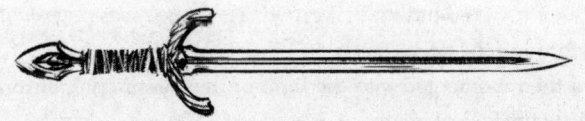

Cedric

The world shifted around Cedric—a vortex of light and shadow. The ground disappeared from beneath his feet, and for a moment he felt as though he would never stop falling. Then he was back on solid ground, the air thick with the heady spice of magic.

It took him a moment to get his bearings. At his back, the Gate he'd stepped through was embedded in a wall of jagged stone that reached toward a starry, aurora-filled sky. The wall stretched out on both sides, curving as it formed the perimeter of an enormous circular arena.

The loamy scent of earth filled Cedric's nostrils. Under his feet, the ground was uneven—a mix of packed soil and soft, slippery clay. The aurora overhead illuminated towering mounds of earth and craggy rock formations that jutted up from the ground at irregular intervals.

Leafless trees, thickets of barbed bushes, and dark, yawning caverns dotted the terrain.

Cedric squinted. At the far end of the bleak landscape in front of him, he could make out a glowing archway. It did not look entirely dissimilar to the Gate he'd just come through, but he knew that it was different. Knew, somehow, that it was important. That no matter what this trial threw at him, no matter what happened next, he *needed* to make it to this new archway.

And, apparently, he would be doing so alone. Not a single one of his fellow champions was anywhere in sight. Had they truly been so quick to fly into the arena? Taken off immediately? Or had the Gate dropped each champion in a different place? Either way, so much for the Arbiter's claims that they needed to work together.

Sucking in a steadying breath, Cedric took his first steps into the arena. He made it fewer than twenty paces before a feral snarl echoed out from a nearby cavern. He whipped his head toward the sound, his hand immediately moving to his sword.

He heard it before he saw it. Claws scraping against rock. A rattling breath, as if it were holding in a growl. The *swish, swish, swish* of a tail cutting through the dark.

And then it emerged into the light of the shimmering aurora, and Cedric saw the face of death.

Pitch-black skin stretched tight over a skeletal face. Eyes like red embers, burning with predatory focus. Streaks of white ran down each side of its back. It stalked forward on all fours, razor-sharp talons protruding from each paw. And there, at the tip of its scaly tail, a scythe-like barb larger than Cedric's hand.

It suddenly became all too clear what the purpose of this trial was. This was an arena of death.

The beast prowled toward Cedric, its lip curling up over fangs that dripped with something black and viscous. With his sword securely clutched in one hand, Cedric wrapped the other around his mana token protectively. He hadn't wanted to risk draining his token this early, but neither had he thought he'd be facing down a creature from the fourth quarter of hell within the first five minutes of entering the Crucible.

Maybe Elyria hadn't been *completely* wrong in trying to prevent Kit from entering. If there was someone Cedric cared about—or had been charged with protecting, as seemed to be the case for the two fae—he certainly wouldn't have wanted them facing this.

And he especially wouldn't have wanted them facing it without the use of their magic, something Cedric realized with a spike of alarm that he *would* be doing. A lightning-quick glance at his token showed there was still mana inside; the emerald embedded in the stone still glowed.

He just couldn't reach it. Couldn't touch it.

Cedric swore he heard the creature huff in amusement as the realization sank in.

He couldn't use magic here.

The beast was little more than a blur of shadow as it lunged. Cedric lifted his sword, swinging it in a wide arc that connected with the beast's leathery hide. It fell to the side with a yowl of pain but scrambled back to its feet a moment later, its ember eyes narrowed. Cedric set his feet in a defensive stance, the tip of his sword pointed at the thrumming vein in the beast's neck.

The creature pounced.

Knife-tipped claws collided with Cedric's sword, knocking it from his grasp. The force of the blow sent him sprawling backward. He landed on his back. A pained grunt was forced from his lungs as the beast's heavy paws pressed on his chestplate, pinning him with crushing force. Its nails screeched against Cedric's armor. Rancid breath washed over him as the monster leaned closer, fangs bared.

Cedric refused to believe this was how it would end. His fingers fumbled at his side, blindly searching for the dagger sheathed at his waist. Finally, they brushed against the cool metal of the hilt. A flicker of triumph ignited in Cedric's chest . . .

Just as the creature collapsed onto him. And did not move again.

Groaning, Cedric rocked under the monster's crushing weight until he got enough momentum to roll the body off himself. His brows shot up when he realized someone else's sword was buried in its side. A pair of worn black boots stepped into the periphery of Cedric's vision. He followed them up, taking in their owner's crimson skin, a leather cuirass that was slightly too large, and finally the pair of short horns, half-hidden under sleek black hair.

One of the nocterrian champions, Dissidua Pyr.

"You have my gratitude." Panting, Cedric rose to his feet, his eyes pinned on the fallen beast as he retrieved his sword. He turned to Dissidua, his hand extended in thanks.

The nocterrian eyed Cedric's hand as they used the creature's lifeless body to wipe black blood from their blade. "Keep it."

Cedric barely had time to react before Dissidua's blade was slicing down at him. He threw his own sword up just in time to block the blow. "What are you doing?"

"What does it look like, human?"

Cedric gritted his teeth as he threw his weight into his sword and pushed Dissidua back. So much for unity. That didn't take long.

The nocterrian released an irritated noise as they spun their sword back toward Cedric in another attempted strike.

Prepared this time, Cedric parried it easily. "I am not your enemy in here."

"You are my enemy everywhere."

Another strike, another clash of steel on steel. Only now the nocterrian suddenly had a long dagger in their other hand, crossing it with their sword to form an X as they bore down on Cedric. Cedric cursed as he felt his knee quiver. He was still recovering from being crushed by that beast. But he knew if he let Dissidua get him on his knees, it was over.

Mustering his remaining scraps of strength, Cedric dug his heel into the dirt and *shoved*. Dissidua was forced to retreat several steps.

The reprieve could barely be called as much. Mere seconds passed before Dissidua was launching themselves at Cedric again, fast, vicious— a wolf lunging for its prey.

Cedric blocked one relentless blow after another, muscles screaming in protest. "Why are you doing this? You save me just to kill me? This is madness!" he shouted.

Dissidua's crimson lips twisted into a humorless smile as they pulled back. "You misunderstand," they said. "I didn't save you. I took your kill. Now I get to add you to my tally and cut down another champion standing between me and the prize."

Another? Cedric held his sword aloft, its sharp tip pointing at the nocterrian's throat. "This isn't that kind of competition."

"Isn't it? Only one of us will walk away with the power of the crown. Do you truly expect us all to hold hands and waltz through this Crucible *together*? Noctis take me, humans are even stupider than I thought."

"Yet I am not the one picking needless fights with my fellow champions." Cedric gritted his teeth. "I don't want to hurt you."

Dissidua snorted, lunging forward with weapons raised, aiming for the tender flesh above Cedric's chestplate, where his neck met his shoulder. The nocterrian's mouth curved with what Cedric was sure was another acerbic retort poised at the tip of their tongue.

He would never find out.

A savage growl was their only warning as another blur pounced from the shadows—a second beast, slightly smaller than the first but just as fierce. Just as deadly. It sprang upon Dissidua, who screamed as its claws shredded their leather armor like it was made of paper.

Cedric hesitated for less than a heartbeat, slashing his sword down against the new beast, its leathery hide tinted green by the aurora's light. Despite everything, he couldn't just leave the nocterrian to die.

The beast's roar was bloodcurdling as Cedric's sword connected, its barbed tail thrashing, eyes wild as it looked for the source of its pain. It twisted as it leapt into the air, landing deftly to Cedric's left. He readied himself to take another swing at the creature, but with a howl, it loped off.

The air was laced with the scent and taste of copper as Cedric sucked in several panting breaths. A nauseating gurgle filled the air. He looked down at the prone body of Dissidua Pyr, their hands clutching at their throat, torn and gushing a river of maroon. The nocterrian's eyes were pinned open in fear and pain as they exhaled a final, wet breath.

Cedric sheathed his sword, hands shaking. His heart beat a thunderous tempo behind his armor.

It was so needless. If Dissidua hadn't wasted their time fighting Cedric, they never would have been caught off guard by the second creature. It's not as though Cedric *liked* the Arbiter's pronouncement. He didn't relish the concept of being forced to work with the Arcanians any more than the next champion. But he certainly didn't see the point in killing one another, either.

Not when it was clear the Crucible would do that for them.

A high-pitched scream rent the air. Cedric raced down a sloping dirt hill toward the source of the sound, adrenaline pumping through his veins. He didn't think he was too far from the archway now, but he couldn't ignore the sound of distress.

Pushing through a thicket of thorny bushes, he burst into a small clearing with a rocky spire jutting out from its center and found himself staring at a pack of truly gruesome creatures.

Smaller than the lethal monsters he had initially encountered, the nightmarish makeup of these new beasts caused Cedric's stomach to turn. They looked as if whatever malevolent magic had created them had gone wrong. Four black eyes peered out from flat faces—their features were squished, as if someone had smashed them in. Six thin, spindly legs jutted out from squat, scaly bodies. Tiny wings protruded from their backs, twisted and mangled, though he doubted very much that they could fly.

A good thing, Cedric supposed as his gaze drifted up the spire and locked onto the petite sylvan woman hanging from it.

Zephyr had surprised everyone when she strode forward to claim her place in the Crucible. From what Cedric knew, sylvans weren't well regarded for their fighting prowess, nor did they seem to carry a predilection toward violence at all. They were better known for their propensity for curative magic and herbalism. Healers and apothecaries. Not fighters.

Something that seemed to hold true as Cedric observed the sylvan, panting as she desperately clung to the column, her gaze never leaving the beasts below. There were half a dozen of them, all leaping and crawling over one another in an attempt to get to her.

Zephyr kept one arm wrapped around the stone pillar as she balanced on a small ledge. Her other hand was pressed to her leg, trying to stanch the flow of viscous green blood from a wound below her knee. A glint of light reflected off a dagger on the ground nearby—she was disarmed.

I could leave her, he thought. There was nothing that said he had to help, had to rush to aid this person who had gotten so far in over her head, she was but a heartbeat away from failure. She was a champion—a challenger, a *rival*. More than that, she was an Arcanian. He could very well leave the sylvan to her fate and go on as though he'd never seen a thing. It was what Lord Church would expect of him.

Nobody would know.

Except . . . he would.

And hadn't he come just as close to being wiped from the Crucible due to an unexpected encounter with some cruel, netherworldly beast? If Dissidua had not turned around and immediately tried to kill him himself . . . Perhaps this was a blessing from Aurelia, another chance for Cedric to secure an ally.

Zephyr whimpered, her grip on the stone pillar slipping. Cedric let out a long sigh. Pushing past his hesitation, he charged forward, his sword slashing into the first creature he could reach. It cut easily through the beast's scaly skin, severing bone and sinew. Dead in an instant.

It took a moment for the remaining five beasts to realize that they were under attack. Cedric took advantage of their confusion, withdrawing several paces. By the time the beasts noticed their slain pack member, he'd managed to back up a fair amount.

Two of the creatures turned, scuttling on those disturbing, spider-like legs to close the distance between themselves and Cedric. Lips peeled back over sharp fangs as one of the beasts leapt forward.

Cedric spun to the right. The creature yelped as it flew past him, uncontrolled. It slammed into a row of thorny bushes, immediately getting tangled in the sharp brambles.

"Ha!" Cedric released a triumphant laugh.

It was premature.

Pain erupted at his back as the second beast slashed at a gap in his armor. That was how Cedric learned that a massive, hooked claw was attached to the end of each spindly leg. Gritting his teeth against his stinging back, he slashed out and neatly hacked two of those legs off the nearest beast.

The noises that came from the creature were . . . unsettling. Even as the wounded beast scuttled away, leaving a trail of black blood in its wake, the other three converged on Cedric—as if their brethren's screeches were a rallying cry. A din of shrieks and growls echoed in the distance. Cedric groaned. The last thing he needed was more of these things coming for them.

With Cedric's attention split between the creatures prowling at his front and the feral cacophony—still distant but growing closer much too quickly for his liking—he didn't notice when one of the remaining three beasts moved out of sight. Didn't notice when it stalked behind him. Didn't notice it rearing up on its back four legs until it was nearly face-height.

He didn't notice. Not until he felt the creature's hot, rank breath on the back of his neck.

Cedric spun, bringing his sword up just in time to defend against its razor-taloned front legs. But the quarters were too close, and Cedric couldn't get the leverage he needed to push the creature back. All he could do was brace the edge of his sword against the beast's claws, keeping himself just out of reach of its snapping jaws.

Sweat rained from Cedric's brow, his muscles tensing with effort as he held, held, held—

And then the creature was collapsing in on itself, its legs curving inward as it crumpled to the ground. A crown of closely shorn hair, green as the forest, popped up from behind the beast's body.

"Behind you!" Zephyr yelled, plucking her dagger from the dead beast's ribs.

Cedric whirled, his sword plunging forward into the abdomen of another creature. It died with a pitiful whine. But when Cedric tried to pull his weapon back out, it was stuck.

The final beast was on top of him instantly, fangs bared, its many beady eyes pinned to Cedric's throat. Time stretched, a miniature eternity as the knight evaluated his options. Then the creature was rearing back, readying itself to leap, to bite, to kill.

Cedric swung into action.

Abandoning his sword, he dropped to his knees, spinning as he swiped the dagger from his waist and thrust it upward, just as something whistled past his ear.

Zephyr's thrown dagger sank into the creature's forehead, Cedric's own weapon piercing its ribs at the same time. It never even got the chance to howl.

For a few excruciating moments, neither Cedric nor Zephyr moved. Their breaths were ragged, heavy, but they remained still as they took in the carnage around them. Hot, black blood soaked Cedric's hand, still clutching the hilt of the dagger buried deep in the creature's chest.

And then Zephyr was standing on shaking legs, offering a hand to him. "Thank you."

Her voice was high and bright, even as she gasped and panted, attempting to catch her breath. It made her sound very young, though Cedric knew that meant nothing. She could be a girl, or she could be older than Cedric's great-grandparents. It was impossible to tell when it came to Arcanians.

"Thought I was done for," she said.

There was a wet squelch as Cedric pulled his dagger out of the dead monster. He used his other, slightly-less-bloody, hand to retrieve Zephyr's from between the creature's eyes. "I could say the same," he said as he handed the weapon back to her. "Loathe though I am to admit it, I was in a bit over my head at the end there."

"You wouldn't have been if you hadn't had to help me fight off those gnarlings," argued the sylvan, her lower lip sticking out in a pout.

Against all logic, Cedric found one side of his mouth curving up in a grin. "Gnarlings?"

Zephyr pointed her dagger at the fallen creature before tucking it into the sheath at her hip. "That's what we call them back in Verdentia, anyway. I've never seen one outside the forests there myself, but . . ." She shrugged.

"Gnarlings," Cedric said again, testing the word. He gave a casual wave of his hand. "Well, I've learned something new. Let us call it even."

One side of her mouth tipped up in a small grin. "Do you think more of them will come?"

Cedric paused, listened. "I do not know," he admitted. "But the growling seems to have faded."

"Two of them got away." Her gaze fell to the weeping trail of black blood that carved a path away from the clearing.

"Perhaps they warned off their brethren."

Her grin widened. "Understandable. We are quite the formidable pair."

The corner of Cedric's lip quirked. "Indeed. Regardless, I would rather not find out if more of those things are on their way. We should move on."

Zephyr hesitated. "You—you would have us move on . . . together?"

Cedric appraised the petite champion. She would hardly have been his first choice as an ally. Too small and too weak to fight off beast and brute, especially given the distinct lack of magic usage in here. He supposed he had to give her credit for being quick enough to outrun the gnarlings, at least. Glancing at the beast she'd felled, he had to admit her aim with that dagger wasn't too bad either. And though she could easily have run away the moment Cedric drew the gnarlings' attention, she had chosen to stay and fight—a sign of grit and determination that Cedric found . . . admirable.

Plus, there was something vulnerable in the way she asked that pulled at Cedric's heartstrings.

You're so fucking soft. Once again, Cedric could hear Tristan's voice ring in his ears. His friend was always on his case about his bleeding heart.

Cedric cleared his throat. "I will admit, you are the first sylvan I have ever met," he said. "But as you did not take the opportunity to plunge that dagger of yours into my back at the first chance, I think we will get along just fine. And is that not what the Arbiter asked of us?"

Zephyr nodded, but her face was still lined with worry. She sucked her dark green bottom lip behind her teeth. Cedric decided he'd give her a moment to consider and bent to retrieve his stuck sword from the chest cavity of the dead monster that was determined to keep it.

The motion pulled on the wound at his back. Cedric hissed his discomfort. He'd forgotten about it entirely in the adrenaline-fueled battle.

"You're hurt!" Zephyr exclaimed.

Cedric attempted a shrug, though it only served to make the wound pulse with further pain. "So are you."

Zephyr shook her head. "Just barely now."

"Now?"

She pointed to her leg, where she'd wrapped the wound below her knee with some kind of botanical bandage. "Not trying to sound pompous about it, but I've a talent for healing minor to moderate injuries," she said with a shrug.

Cedric touched his token. "But our magic—"

Vials clinked as she tapped the leather belt slung around her hips. "Granted, it would be much easier if I had my powers, but in this case, they're not strictly necessary. May I take a look?"

"Fine, but not here. Let's find somewhere less . . ."

"Carnage-y?" Zephyr offered.

Cedric huffed a laugh. "Yes. Carnage-y. Precisely the word I would have chosen."

CHAPTER 15
DRAGONFYRE

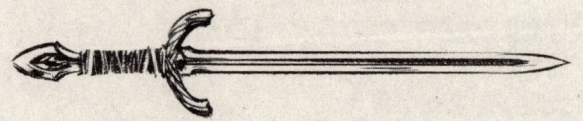

Cedric

A thunderous roar shook the ground beneath their feet as the two champions raced on. Zephyr skidded to a halt, a cloud of earth rising at her ankles, and Cedric stopped short to avoid ramming into her.

"Four hells, watch it!" Cedric shook his head. "Your little healing salve might have worked a miracle on the cut on my back, but I don't imagine it'll do much good if I twist an ankle."

The sylvan shot him a sheepish look. "Sorry, but . . . you heard that, right?" Her voice was wary.

"I did," Cedric replied. "Stay alert."

Zephyr nodded, her expression solemn. Cedric had to admit, her company had been welcome as they dashed through the arena, avoiding beasts when they could, cutting them down when they couldn't. Her sense of direction was keen—as was her hearing. Had he been alone, Cedric was quite sure it would have taken him at least twice as long to get across the arena . . . and he likely would have attracted quite a few more dark beasties along the way. Perhaps there was something to this teamwork concept, after all.

The archway was nearby. Cedric could not see it at present, hidden as it was by the craggy cliffs overhead as they trudged through a sunken valley. But he could feel it. It called to him, beckoned him.

Cedric offered his hand to Zephyr as they climbed onto a flat mesa that overlooked the far end of the arena.

"There." She pointed ahead as she fought to catch her breath. The archway stood a mere hundred feet or so away, glowing invitingly.

Another roar shook the earth, enough so that Zephyr stumbled. Cedric's gaze shot to the sky, squinting as he tried to determine the source of the sound. Then he leapt back in surprise as a massive beast soared over their heads.

His eyes widened as the monstrous creature landed in front of them—directly barring their path to the archway. Row after row of glistening black scales reflected the aurora, causing them to shine in shades of purple and green. At one end, a long sharp snout. A much longer clubbed tail at the other.

The breath whooshed from Cedric's chest as the mighty beast flapped its colossal wings once more, before folding them at its sides with a snap.

"Dragon." Zephyr's voice was nothing more than a whisper. Reverent. Terrified.

Thin black pupils set in golden starburst eyes burned with something primal as Cedric met the dragon's stare. He knew he should avert his gaze. He should look away. He should do literally anything other than continue staring at the incredible, terrifying beast, something the dragon would surely take as a challenge.

But Cedric could do nothing but watch as smoke curled from two slanted nostrils. As the dragon's gaze seemed to peer right into the very depths of his soul. As the beast reared back to full height before loosing another ground-shaking, earsplitting roar.

Zephyr took a step closer to Cedric, out of fear or some wildly misguided instinct to protect, he didn't know. He, in turn, was moving to push the small sylvan behind himself when another voice filtered into his ears.

"Oi! Come on then, ye foul beastie!" The dwarven champion, Thraigg, stood alone on the dragon's other side, his piercing blue eyes narrowed in defiance as he waved his mammoth-sized hammer. "Do yer worst. I've a taste for dragonblood tonight!"

Cedric wasn't sure what Thraigg was playing at, trying to draw the beast's attention when the dwarf had a clear path to the archway. But he certainly would not complain about the unexpected distraction. Not as the beast tilted its head—a feline movement that made Cedric feel certain it was calculating whether to abandon the snack in front of it for the smaller, noisier one at its back.

Unfortunately, the calculation did not end in Cedric's favor.

He barely had time to shove Zephyr out of the way before the dragon's massive maw descended upon him. Spinning to the side, Cedric drew his sword just in time for it to crash against ivory fangs—each tooth the length of his hand. The creature's breath was scorching, laced with the sulfurous stench of burning earth.

"Get to the archway, Zephyr!" he shouted, voice strained. He pushed back against the dragon's might, his heels digging into the earth. "Go!"

"I can't leave you here!" Her response was barely audible over the gritty clash of steel and teeth.

"Listen to him, girlie," hollered Thraigg as he leapt forward, swinging his hammer. "I'll get yer knight past this vicious beastie yet."

The dragon pulled back, snorting as if amused by the thought of being bested. Its tail lashed out with breakneck speed, the air shuddering as it passed over Thraigg and whipped toward Cedric. The knight saw it coming a second too late, and though he moved in time to avoid the massive club at the end, the heft of the tail connected with Cedric's midsection, sending him flying backward. He slammed into a nearby rock formation with a *thud*, his sword skittering away.

Pain blossomed across his ribs, white creeping in at the edges of his vision. He thought he felt something warm and wet bloom at the back of his head.

There was no time to determine if that was true, however, as the dragon's fiery gaze locked on Cedric, crumpled at the base of the rock. Behind the wicked beast, Zephyr was creeping forward as if she meant to help him, and his eyes widened in warning. What was she doing? None of them were a match for this creature—that much was clear. It was dumb luck that Cedric's chest hadn't been caved in by the force of that tail. Zephyr needed to take advantage of its fixation on Cedric and get her ass through the archway.

Thraigg chose that moment to charge, his hammer raised high as he hollered, "Try ignoring me now, ye ugly lizard!"

The dragon yowled as the dwarf brought his weapon down on the beast's hind leg. It whipped its head toward the source of its pain, affording Cedric the distraction he needed to get away.

He seized the opening, ignoring the stars blurring his vision, and darted toward the spot where his sword had fallen. He wrapped his fingers around the hilt just as the dragon's tail lashed out, sweeping Thraigg off his feet and sending him careening into Zephyr. The two of them collapsed in a heap of tangled limbs and weapons.

Then it turned to Cedric once more, chuffing in a way that sounded suspiciously like a taunt.

Cedric set his stance, lifting his sword. The beast lunged at him, claws raking the air. Ribs screaming in protest, Cedric pivoted and brought his blade up to meet the strike. Steel screeched against scale, sparks lighting up the night as he deflected the blow.

Snarling, the dragon reared up, forcing Cedric back to avoid being crushed as its legs met the earth with a thunderous shake. The moment it touched back down, Cedric rolled forward and drove his sword up into the soft flesh of its underbelly.

A bellow of pain erupted from the beast, and for a single victorious moment it seemed like it might slink back, retreat.

It did not.

It swung. And before Cedric could even make sense of what was happening, he was being smashed back against the rock, the dragon's heavy claw pinning him across his chest. He gasped as the pressure forced the air from his lungs. The edges of his vision darkened. His sword fell from his grip.

Cedric was certain someone—Thraigg? Zephyr? Both of them?—was shouting, but the sound was distant, muted. And it was all he could do to continue breathing.

Hot, pungent air blasted his skin as the dragon drew its head close enough for Cedric to see his reflection in its shining black scales. Blood ran down the side of his neck, staining the collar of his doublet crimson beneath his armor. His eyes were dark, his cheeks hollow.

The first trial. He hadn't even been able to make it past the first trial. Some champion he was.

The dragon tipped its head back, and Cedric heard the distinct sound of something sparking in the back of its throat. He nearly laughed. He supposed that of all the ways this monster could end his life, being roasted by dragonfyre wasn't the worst one. At least it would be quick. Better this than being eaten alive and drowning in the beast's belly or being slowly torn apart by tooth and claw. And maybe Zephyr and Thraigg would still get to the gate while the dragon was busy with its knightly meal.

Admittedly, the thought didn't bring him much relief.

Tossing a silent prayer to Aurelia into the ether, Cedric steeled his nerves and glared at the dragon, even as the glow of fire built in the back of its throat. He hoped Lord Church would understand that he had tried. And he hoped that the fact he was willing to meet his death head-on would count for something in the Hereafter.

But before the flames could erupt from the dragon's mouth, something swept past Cedric's vision. Bits of stone and sediment buffeted the side of his face as a staff dug into the rock by his head. A figure vaulted from behind him. A booted foot connected with the dragon's jaw. Its head jerked to the side.

A pained roar tore from the beast's throat, even as flames shot from its open mouth. Heat singed the tip of Cedric's ear as orange dragonfyre spewed past, just a few footspans from roasting him whole.

The dragon stumbled back with a yelp, releasing its hold on Cedric as its flame sputtered out, a dagger suddenly protruding from the massive beast's snout. Cedric fell forward as his mysterious savior landed in a crouch directly in front of him.

His breath caught in his throat.

Dazzling wings that matched the aurora overhead beat once before folding against her back. Periwinkle hair blew in the wind, that faint almond scent cutting through the brimstone-laced air.

Elyria.

The Revenant had come.

CHAPTER 16
AS YOU WERE, DRAGON

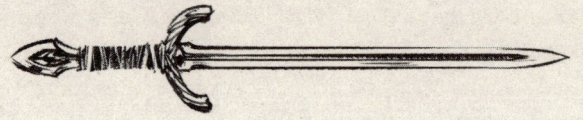

Cedric

She didn't pause. Didn't look back as she sprang forward, her staff spinning in a flash of wood and metal. With a leap, Elyria was parallel to the dragon's snout, ripping her dagger back out as the creature howled. Fangs dripping, it snapped at her in retaliation, but she was little more than a blur as she darted out of the way.

The fae warrior's movements were fluid, graceful. She danced around its whipping tail and avoided its slashing claws. She wielded her wings like fins—flaring them one at a time when she needed to make a sharp turn, using a quick flap to boost the height of her jumps. She struck with precision, the hard metal end of her staff finding points of weakness in the dragon's armor-like scales as if she could see straight through them.

It was a miraculous and terrifying sight.

Cedric tore his eyes from the beautiful onslaught and stumbled over to his sword, though he hardly needed it anymore. Not as Elyria's calculated barrage of blows had the beast retreating by the time he wrapped his hand around the hilt.

"Stop showboating!" called a voice, somewhat familiar. Kit stood a short distance away, her silver hair glowing in the aurora's light, golden wings fluttering with agitation.

Elyria rolled her eyes but pulled back. With a single pump of its massive wings, the dragon was in the sky, soaring away with a forceful blast of air that pushed Cedric back down to one knee. He planted his sword in the ground to keep himself from being knocked over completely.

"Just doing my civic duty," drawled Elyria at the same time her gaze landed on Cedric. "Oh. It's you." Her lip curled, her wings folding in closer to her body. "Hey! Dragon!" she called, her eyes darting to the sky. "You can come back. As you were and all that."

"Hilarious," Cedric grumbled as he got to his feet again. He couldn't begrudge the fact that she'd clearly saved him from a rather . . . chargrilled . . . fate, but did it have to be *her*? The idea of owing his life to her twisted something deep in his chest, a knot of conflicting emotions that made his armor feel too tight.

He wanted to snap at her, to brush off her aid as wholly unnecessary, to prove he wasn't some helpless fool in need of her rescue. But, of course, that wasn't true. Not even in the slightest. Cedric's cheeks warmed as he had to begrudgingly admit to himself that she had not only saved him but had done so with a level of skill and precision that left him feeling . . . small.

And that made him hate her even more than he already did.

"I certainly thought so," Elyria said with a smirk. "Next time, I'd recommend *not* getting nearly roasted by dragonfyre, by the way."

Cedric clenched his jaw, forcing himself to meet her emerald gaze. "What are you doing here? I thought you were above *games* such as these," he said, grunting as he freed his sword from the rocky soil.

She arched a brow. "That's an interesting way of saying 'thank you.'"

Cedric opened his mouth, an entirely different set of words on the tip of his tongue, but Thraigg's rough voice interrupted him before he had a chance to retort.

"Oi." The dwarf wheezed a bit as he helped Zephyr to her feet. "You two want to finish this later? Dunno about ye, but I'm ready to get the hells out of here." He pointed his hammer at the glowing archway.

"Right," said Cedric, striding over to the pair. "All right there, Zephyr?"

The sylvan nodded. "You?"

Cedric prodded gingerly at the back of his head and grimaced. "Nothing you can't help fix, I'm sure."

Elyria snorted as she walked past, her almond scent hitting him again. It reminded Cedric of fresh marzipan—sugary and nutty, with a note of tart cherry . . . and the barest hint of something floral. But there was something dangerous there too. After all, too much bitter almond could kill a man.

Heart pounding, he refocused on the glowing archway ahead. Elyria, Kit, and Thraigg were already moving toward it—only Zephyr stayed back, a worried expression on her face as she looked at Cedric.

"I truly am fine," he told her, his eyes still on the trio as he started after them. The dwarf said something that made the two fae women laugh, and a sour taste crept into Cedric's mouth. "How can they act as if we weren't—"

"A few seconds from being dragon fodder?" Zephyr offered.

"Precisely."

She shrugged. "Perhaps they are used to this sort of thing."

Cedric frowned. What kind of life must one have lived to be able to act so nonchalant after such a harrowing experience? He'd trained the majority of his life to enter the Crucible, yet he'd nearly met his death how many times already?

He found himself wishing Lord Church had assigned him more missions that took him outside of Kingshelm, had bade him take on more dangerous quests. His world experience felt significantly lacking all of a sudden.

Cedric shuffled forward, Zephyr trailing a few steps behind. He was so lost in thought he didn't hear the beat of wings, didn't feel the whoosh of air. But he did hear the dragon's bone-chilling screech—they all did—as it returned, membranous wings spread wide, nearly blotting out the aurora.

Cedric quickened his step, heart pounding in his ears. "Go!" he yelled. "Go through!"

Elyria and Kit ran for the archway. Nonsensically, Thraigg slowed to a stop, turning back to face Cedric and Zephyr. "Faster, ye ninnies!" he bellowed, waving his hammer wildly as he urged them on.

Cedric issued a strangled yell for Thraigg to hurry up as he rushed past, but the dwarf appeared to have other plans. With a defiant cry, he drew a hatchet from his belt and released it into the sky. It spun toward the dragon before lodging itself squarely in the fleshy underside of the joint where the creature's wing connected to its body.

The resulting shriek of shock and pain nearly shattered Cedric's eardrums. The dragon floundered in the air, then twisted toward the ground, one wing flapping uselessly.

"I told ye not to ignore—" Thraigg's victorious shout was cut short as the flailing dragon plummeted toward the exact spot where the dwarf stood, stunned.

Without thinking, Cedric doubled back, hooking Thraigg under the arm and pulling him aside. The dwarf barely missed being crushed by the creature's massive tail as it met the ground, sending rock and debris flying.

"Move!" Cedric barked, pushing Thraigg toward the archway. Elyria and Kit were almost through, Zephyr not far behind.

A furious roar lit up Cedric's nerves. He spun to see the limping dragon, its eyes wide and wild, flaring with rage, with pain.

Its head tipped back.

"No!" Cedric rolled diagonally so he was no longer in line with the other champions, an attempt to keep them out of the path of the dragonfyre he knew was coming his way. The heat of the dragon's breath grazed his skin once more, and he felt a sickening certainty that he would not be lucky enough to escape a second time. The dragon was too close, too fast—

A blur of motion caught his eye. Not a person this time, but a weapon.

Thraigg's massive hammer flew through the air, striking the

underside of the dragon's jaw with a furious crunch that forced the beast's mouth shut before returning to the dwarf's outstretched hand.

Cedric wasted no time scrambling back to his feet. "Handy trick!" he shouted, nodding at the hammer as he sprinted for the exit. Just twenty feet away now. Ten. Five. Thraigg grinned toothily as he matched Cedric's steps, and the two threw themselves into the glowing archway with a final burst of speed.

The world tilted, the familiar sensation of being pulled through space washing over Cedric. And then they were through, the ground solid beneath their feet once more.

"They made it!" shouted someone as Cedric stumbled forward, catching himself before he fell. Thraigg burst forth just a few paces behind.

Zephyr approached Cedric first, her face pale. "You did it," she whispered, her gaze darting between him and the archway as if she couldn't quite believe her eyes.

Cedric could only nod, his heart pounding too fast and fiercely for his tongue to form words. He surveyed his new surroundings between gulps of labored breath. Zephyr, Elyria, Kit, and a handful of other champions were strewn about a stone antechamber. Most didn't look much better off than Cedric felt—he noted the blood and grime covering the majority of them, though spirits seemed to vary. Gael Winters was clapping her friend Paelin on his shoulder with a hearty, disbelieving laugh. Alden Ashford's sandy head was bent as he muttered prayers of gratitude to Aurelia. The remaining nocterrian champion, Tenebris Nox, simply leaned against a wall, silent and still as a statue.

Cedric managed to slow his breathing. His heart started to beat more evenly. Then it stuttered as he caught Elyria's eye for the briefest moment, her expression utterly bewildering. It was fleeting, gone too fast for Cedric to make sense of the emotions he thought he saw flicker across her face. Was she . . . relieved to see he'd made it through?

He looked back at the archway and thought of the way she had saved him—about all the ways he'd already escaped death by a hairsbreadth. Cedric's heart sank with the knowledge that this was only the beginning.

And much worse was yet to come.

CHAPTER 17
HERBWITCH SHIT

Elyria

Elyria's breath came in sharp, ragged bursts as she stepped through the archway, her boots striking solid ground with a finality that felt a lot like relief. The searing heat of the dragon's breath clung to her skin, but it was only one of many things that would haunt her. The first trial had been far more than she'd expected—unsurprising, she supposed, since she hadn't really known what to expect at all.

Perhaps being endlessly hunted by shadowy beasts—claws like obsidian, eyes like embers—was a fitting comeuppance for Elyria's sheer stupidity in following Kit through the Gate. They'd been relentless, and Elyria had fought through them with a single-minded focus. There was only one thing that mattered, one goal: reaching Kit.

And so, Elyria had cut them down, her staff spinning in deadly arcs, her daggers cutting through flesh and sinew and bone. And there had been moments—brief but terrifying—when she hadn't been sure she'd make it.

If Elyria made it through the rest of the Crucible alive, she would figure out a way to have words with the Arbiter about whatever that no-magic bullshit was.

Fighting to steady her breathing, Elyria ran her gaze around the dim stone chamber. Some of the other champions had made it through ahead of her. They were strewn around the room, still catching their breath, regrouping after whatever brutal encounters they'd faced during the trial. Most importantly, Kit was there, intact and unharmed. And that was all that mattered.

Even if Elyria still couldn't make sense of the look that had been in Kit's eyes when she'd finally caught up with her in the arena. So many overlapping emotions—relief and gratitude, obstinance and willfulness. Kit knew that Elyria was only here for her, and Elyria thought she might just love her for it . . . and loathe her for it at the same time.

Because Kit was in this to win—for Evander, for herself—and nobody was going to stand in her way.

Elyria wasn't sure whether she was proud or terrified. Likely a little of both.

The rush of adrenaline had barely faded when the other champions began shouting. Two more had just come through the archway.

It was *him*.

Elyria clenched her fists at her sides, trying to shake off the tangle of emotions twisting in her chest. Saving Cedric had been a reflex, the kind of instinct honed through years of combat—one she couldn't just forget. For Solaris's sake, she hadn't even known whose fiery fate she was preventing.

But the look on his face after—the disbelief, the *resentment*—unsettled her. The frustration in his eyes when he realized who she was, the way his jaw had clenched with something like . . . shame? And there had been . . . something else there too. Something she couldn't quite place.

Why did it bother her so much? Why did she care? At best, he was just some human, some rival from across the Chasms. At worst, he was an *enemy*. Another champion standing between Kit and the prize at the end of this deadly game. And thus, standing between Elyria and her ability to get her friend out alive.

On the other hand, he was clearly an idiot. What other reason could there have been for him to rush headlong into danger with no plan?

And yet . . . Seeing him pinned there, nearly broken under the weight of the dragon's claws, had sparked something in her. Stirred some protective instinct she'd thought long buried.

Then there was the way he'd thrust himself back into the fray when the dragon returned, wounded and with no reason to risk his life further. She saw the way he rolled aside as the creature prepared to release another bout of vicious dragonfyre, drawing its aim away from the rest of them. Away from her.

Admirable fool.

He was going to get himself killed sooner rather than later if he kept acting like that.

Which, of course, didn't matter in the slightest. She certainly didn't care if he died.

Unfortunately, she also couldn't explain why the knot in her chest tightened at the notion.

Elyria pushed the thought away. She had to focus on her present situation. On whatever was coming *next*.

The chamber she'd been thrown into was large and spacious. Thick stone bricks etched with intricate carvings made up the walls around them, which were dotted with high, small windows before curving up to form a large domed ceiling that loomed overhead. Wide stone benches and large floor cushions were strewn throughout the space. Tables laden with pitchers of water, bowls of fruit, and plates piled high with cheeses and dried meats dotted the room.

This was a space for recovery. A reward for having survived the harrows of the first trial.

The archway she'd entered from was affixed to the wall on one side, while multiple doors lined the opposite wall. She watched a couple of curious champions try and fail to open all twelve of them.

The air was thick with ancient magic. Eager to test whether the rules from the arena were still in effect, Elyria drew forth the usual magic she used to cloak her wings, shuddering in relief when she found herself able to hide them with ease.

A heavy silence swept through the chamber as the other champions soon followed suit—flopping onto cushions or perching on benches to heal, to replenish, to refuel. She tried not to let her vision linger on Cedric and the sylvan woman—Zephyr—in the corner. His gauntlets and vambraces lay in a heap on the bench next to him as she wove some sort of healing magic over the knight's head.

Kit was close by, scanning the chamber with the same sharp awareness Elyria was wielding. Elyria felt a prickle of pride, then a pang of guilt as she thought of their earlier confrontation—er, make that *confrontations*—and the harsh words they'd exchanged in Castle Lumin.

Now was not the time for regrets though. Not here. Not with whatever the hells the Arbiter, or the celestials, or whoever designed this stars-damned game had lurking around the next corner.

The next trial. The next danger. That needed to be Elyria's sole focus—making sure that when the dust finally settled, Kit would still be standing.

Even if Elyria herself wasn't.

"Still breathing?" Elyria's voice was rougher than she intended as she stepped closer to Kit.

"For now," Kit said.

"Good. Let's try to keep it that way, shall we?"

A sudden tension filled the room. "So . . . is nobody really going to say it?" Gael said, waving her arms in a wide gesticulation, as if calling the champions to attention. "Fine, I'll say it. What the *fuck* was that?"

"To what, precisely, do you refer?" The nocterrian, Tenebris Nox, was half-buried in shadows as they leaned against the left wall. "The onslaught of fangs and claws? The trek across mountain and valley just to get to another gate?"

"For me, it was the stars-damned dragon at the end," Thraigg chimed in gruffly.

"And the lack of absolutely *any* information whatsoever," groused the rodent-faced human with sand-colored hair, Alden. During the rundown Kit gave Elyria in the arena, she'd learned he was a "saint," a title for his talent for healing magic that would have had Elyria snorting with laughter had an enormous cockroach-like creature not decided to attack at that very moment. She'd long thought human naming conventions for their magic wielders were pointless. They called their mindwielders "sages" and their oracles "seers," seemingly for no other reason than a desire to distance themselves as far as possible from the Arcanian terms—even if they meant the exact same damned thing.

"Precisely! They throw us into a literal lion's den and expect us to figure out what to do, where to go?" Leona Blackwood's voice hovered somewhere between snide and shrill, and it had Elyria cringing.

It also had her begrudgingly concurring, and she didn't like that. Because she *really* didn't like Leona.

"We all knew the risks coming in here," said Cedric, though there was the slightest tremor in his voice.

"We had *no magic*!" Leona cried.

Paelin pursed his lips. "Yes, that was a bit surprising, to be sure."

"Oh, was it?" Leona spat. "I noticed your wings weren't affected. You could have simply soared across the entire arena. How is that fair?"

"If only," Paelin said with a snort. "Would have been nice. Too bad the volacarnii made doing so *just a little* tricky."

Kit tensed at the mention of the creatures. Elyria knew what she was thinking and was suddenly incredibly grateful that the two of them hadn't encountered the vicious flying monsters in the arena. They really were nasty pieces of work.

"Could barely get off the ground before they descended," Paelin continued, pinching his tunic at his waist and holding it out to showcase a large rip in the fabric. "One of them nearly got me."

"If only," Leona repeated, sneering.

Gael rolled her eyes. "And anyway, our wings are not part of our magic; they're part of *us*. Taking them would be like chopping off one of your arms, human. Is it our fault the Crucible did not hinder our natural capabilities during the trial? We were still without our powers, same as you."

Zephyr let out a squeak of agreement. "Felt like part of myself was missing."

Elyria couldn't disagree with that. It had been disconcerting not to feel the magic that constantly simmered in her veins. Downright dangerous. But if she was being honest, it was also . . . peaceful? That shadowy presence in the pit of her belly was quiet for the first time since . . .

"So, what *are* we supposed to do now?" Paelin asked.

"What we're already doing, asshole," muttered one of the other pot-stirring humans from earlier. The redheaded brother—Belien. "We breathe. We heal. We wait for the rest." While Leona sat nearby, chuckling at his response, Elyria realized his sister was nowhere to be seen. And she wasn't the only one who noticed.

"Speaking of the rest, where's your other half, ginger prince?" quipped Gael, limping slightly as she moved to a nearby bench.

"We were separated in the arena," he said darkly.

"She didn't make it? You have my deepest sympathies," Gael said, sounding anything but sympathetic.

The murderous look on Belien's face had Elyria bracing for the human to lob another ill-fated attack at Gael. The Arbiter said the rule barring violence against one another was no longer in effect, but they were all injured, all exhausted. Elyria had hoped they'd get at least a little reprieve before the fighting started anew.

To her great surprise, the humans seemed to agree. With a sigh, Belien leaned back and scrubbed a hand down his face.

"Belis will come through any minute," said Leona, placing a reassuring hand on his knee.

"We will pray it is so." An irritatingly earnest voice came from behind Elyria, so close it made her shiver. That charred sandalwood scent drifted over her as Cedric Thorne walked past, Zephyr close on his heels, and took a seat with the other humans—Belien and Leona on one side, Alden on the other. He shook hands with the saint before turning to engage the other two in conversation, gesticulating animatedly.

Elyria bit back a huff of annoyance. So much for whatever shamble of an alliance they had formed during those last moments in the arena. If Cedric wanted to associate himself with human trash who handed out slurs against Arcanians like they were candy, so be it.

But as Elyria wandered back to the other side of the room, taking her own seat beside Kit, a pang of pity ran through her on Zephyr's behalf. The sylvan stood awkwardly behind Cedric, shifting on her feet as Leona, Belien, and Alden vacillated between exchanging knowing looks with one another and shooting highly obvious sneers at Zephyr.

Elyria didn't know if Cedric didn't realize his compatriots were being openly derisive toward the sylvan, or if he didn't care. And she didn't know which was worse. She also didn't know why Zephyr was subjecting herself to this. Whatever reasons the sylvan had for aligning herself with Cedric, she couldn't possibly have known Leona and Belien would be part of the deal.

Elyria's irritation rose, starting to meld with a rage that, logically, she knew didn't belong to this situation. It's not as if anything had happened yet, after all. But "yet" was, in fact, the key. Elyria had heard too many stories over the ages of what humans did to the innocent Arcanians found in their lands. Did the knight not realize what he was potentially subjecting Zephyr to by association?

Thoughtless fool.

"You all right, Ellie?" Kit's voice broke through Elyria's indignation, her casual use of the nickname calming the thrumming shadow that had started to stir in her core.

"Sure," Elyria replied, tearing her glare from Cedric as she leaned back. "Just anxious for whatever comes next."

Kit nodded. "Aren't we all."

In the end, only one more champion came through the archway. It was not Belis. And the keening cry that came from Belien when a bloodied and battered Cyren Tenrider stepped through the archway and it finally stopped glowing, the magic inside stilling, was haunting. The quiet sobbing that followed as the archway disappeared entirely, leaving only a blank expanse of stone along the wall in its wake, was worse.

Elyria might have felt bad for the man had he and his sister not proven themselves to be terrible people. She would be lying if she said she felt the world of Arcanis was worse off with one less prejudiced asshole in it. And thankfully, she didn't have to listen to his wailing for long. Not when a sudden, booming voice resounded through the chamber.

Many voices, speaking as one, in fact.

"Congratulations, champions," said the Arbiter's voice. "You have bested the Trial of Strength."

Elyria searched for the source of the sound, but there was no sign of the white-hooded figure.

"Only those willing to bleed for the crown dare dream to hold it. You have fought. You have bled. You have experienced loss," the voice echoed in her head. A strangled sob escaped from Belien. "You have proven your strength. Now you will take the time to heal."

Murmurs rippled through the champions.

"Welcome to the Celestial Sanctum. The doors before you lead to rooms where you may rest, bathe, and continue tending your injuries. Use this time wisely. Tomorrow, the second trial begins."

The voice faded, uneasy glances suddenly replacing the unfocused wonder that adorned most of the champions' faces. They might be receiving a night of respite, but that did nothing to relieve the palpable tension stretching throughout the chamber.

Zephyr, ever the healer, seemed to take the Arbiter's words as decree. She immediately set to work, moving from champion to champion with quiet efficiency as she offered to tend to their wounds. Leona waved her away with a shrill laugh—*idiot*—but Elyria accepted the assistance with gratitude.

"How did this happen?" Zephyr asked in a soft voice, prodding at a gash on Elyria's lower back that she hadn't been able to reach.

"Same story as everyone here, I'd imagine," Elyria replied, relief sweeping through her as she felt her skin knit back together. "Some little monster caught me by surprise."

Next to Elyria, Kit rolled her mismatched eyes. "It happened because she was too busy pushing me out of the way to watch her own back," she said with a rough laugh. "Because she has apparently forgotten I am a fully grown fae, more than capable of defending myself."

"I just don't like you having all the fun," Elyria replied, trying her best to keep her tone light.

Kit's gaze softened. They hadn't really spoken about the fact that Elyria was here. Hadn't had a chance to. But had they been alone, Elyria thought Kit might actually admit she was grateful Elyria had entered the Crucible for her.

Then Kit's expression hardened, and Elyria immediately second-guessed that thought.

"You don't need to protect me, Ellie. I can handle myself."

"I know you can." Elyria struggled to keep her voice even. "But that doesn't mean I'm not going to keep trying." She waved her arm, gesturing to their general surroundings. "Clearly."

The corners of Kit's mouth twitched upward—a small smile. "You're impossible."

Elyria shrugged, feigning nonchalance, even as warmth spread through her chest at Kit's thawing toward her. She supposed that fighting their way through an arena of death together was as good a way to work through their issues as any. She wondered whether she should say more—or if it would push Kit away again, reigniting their fight.

And then she thought, *Fuck it*.

Chances were high she would die in this stars-damned Crucible anyway. The rules were different now. Might as well say what she wanted. Might as well tell the truth.

"I know I have a lot of lost time to make up for," Elyria said, her voice soft. "I hope this shows you how serious I am about doing so."

Kit's eyes glistened, but she just nodded, an acceptance that lifted a weight from Elyria's shoulders. They fell into a comfortable silence as Zephyr finished healing the wound on Elyria's back and made quick work of the numerous shallow cuts and scrapes decorating Kit's limbs.

"Oh." Zephyr halted Elyria as she was getting ready to move on. "Did you also want me to . . . ?"

Elyria followed her gaze and saw that her pant leg had ripped, exposing a sizable section of her left thigh.

Shit.

"What the fuck is that?" Kit asked sharply, her gaze narrowed on the grotesque checkerboard of scars that were now visible.

"It's nothing." Elyria hastily pinned the torn flap of her pants back in place with a tendril of magic.

Kit knocked her hand away. "That's not fucking nothing, Elle. What the quartered hell happened to you? Is your entire leg like that?"

"I don't want to talk about it," Elyria snapped, her tone sharper than she intended.

She turned her head, and warm brown eyes met her own for a split second before they darted away. Had Cedric been watching their exchange? A flush of embarrassment crept up Elyria's neck. The idea of him seeing the evidence of her at her most vulnerable, most exposed, tied her insides in knots. She hated the feeling.

How much had he seen? How much had he heard? He was a fair distance across the room, so chances were he couldn't see much, but the last thing she wanted was for those eyes to fill with pity. She didn't need any more of his judgment. She didn't need him thinking she was weak. And she certainly didn't need him knowing about her past—anything more than he already thought he knew. Least of all, anything *true*.

"Ellie?" Kit's voice pulled her back, though Elyria could still feel the burn of Cedric's lingering gaze.

"It's nothing, truly. An old wound," she lied. "Nothing Zephyr can do about it anyway."

"Well, that's not—" Zephyr cut herself off. "I mean, that is . . . I don't mean to be presumptuous," she said meekly.

"No, go ahead. What were you going to say?" Elyria prodded.

"I just . . . I have a poultice that I think will help with the scarring, if you would like."

"Stars above," Elyria exclaimed, a beaming smile erupting on her face. "Yes, yes, I would like. I would like very much."

Kit pursed her lips at Elyria's overeager reaction, but Zephyr only laughed. The sylvan healer fished a tin from one of the many pouches hanging from her belt. "Given where we are and what we're doing, perhaps there's no point . . . but here, give this a try. Layer it over the worst of the scars before you go to sleep each night. I warn you it doesn't smell amazing . . ."

She popped the top off the tin, and Elyria took a tentative sniff. She immediately regretted it.

Zephyr took in the look on Elyria's face and was quick to add, "But the smell doesn't linger, I promise. And you should see a marked improvement in both appearance and texture within a few days. Is there pain?"

A mock-gagging sound came from nearby before Elyria could answer. "Four fucking hells, cap that foul shit, greenie," sneered Belien, crouched on a pillow a few feet over while Alden wrapped his ankle.

The word might've been a derogatory term for Zephyr's people, but it was Elyria who saw red. "Why?" she spat. "I'd think your tear ducts would appreciate the reprieve."

"What was that, fae scum?" Belien hissed.

Elyria sighed at the distinct lack of creativity in his insults. "Just that if you're busy protecting your delicate sensibilities from a smelly bit of medicine, at least you're probably too busy to keep crying. I imagine your eyes could use the break."

Belien stood abruptly, a movement designed to intimidate. The effect was rather lessened by the way he wobbled on his good ankle, however. "Watch that smart tongue, pixie, lest I be tempted to tear it out."

Elyria rolled her eyes. So much for choosing the path of unity. "Didn't you learn your lesson about threatening us back at the castle?"

His eyes narrowed. "There's no celestial magic to stop me now that we're in here."

Her mouth pulled up in a lazy grin. "Shall we put that to the test?"

"Don't waste your energy on him, gorgeous," called Cyren from across the room. "Though I can't say I wouldn't enjoy the show." He shot yet another wink at Elyria, and she raised an eyebrow in response. She was starting to suspect it was his signature move.

"The man has a point," Kit said. "Just because we *can* fight each other doesn't mean we should. Not when the Crucible seems more than happy to do the deed itself."

Elyria was readying another cutting remark to direct at Belien when a petite, green hand touched her forearm.

"It's all right, Elyria," Zephyr cut in, her tone pleading. "Please don't trouble yourself with him. I'm fine."

Belien snorted as if he'd won something and sat back down with a smug grin. Alden snickered, and Elyria could've sworn she heard the saint mutter something that sounded like "herbwitch shit" under his breath.

She wasn't familiar with the term, but it was clear from the way Zephyr's face fell further that it was just as unwelcome as the slur Belien had used.

Zephyr hastily crammed the cap back on the tin before handing it over. "Each night before bed," she reminded Elyria, her voice timid.

Fury burrowed deeper in Elyria's chest. But Zephyr had asked Elyria to back off, not wanting to cause a further scene. So, instead of taking out her ire on the bigots who deserved it, Elyria's dagger-filled gaze sought someone else.

CHAPTER 18
ON WITH IT, BOYO

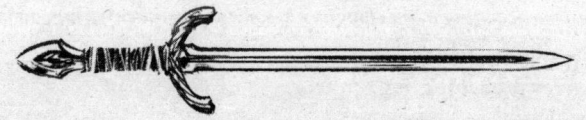

Cedric

Cedric did his best to remain unobtrusive, observing the various interactions unfolding around the chamber. He had no intention of getting involved in the bickering and posturing that had ensnared the other champions—least of all whatever Elyria was engaged with. After that embarrassing display in the arena, Cedric was keen to put some space between the fae warrior and himself.

So why did his eyes keep wandering over to where she and Kit sat? And why did something twist in his gut when he saw Zephyr working her healing touch on a deep gash that cut across the Revenant's back?

Observing the way Elyria fought in the arena, how she'd danced with that dragon, had made it clearer than ever how she earned her moniker—and that she deserved it. And that was *without* her magic.

Cedric shuddered at the thought of what it would be like to meet the Revenant in battle at full power. He hoped he never had to find out.

And yet, for a reason he could not possibly begin to explain, he also hoped he did?

Learning—or, at least, being told—that the figure he'd long thought responsible for his parents' murder was, perhaps, not quite the monster he had imagined was really fucking with his head.

He'd gone most of his life nursing a visceral hatred for the Revenant. The name was seared into his memory as deeply as his own. It had pushed him toward a desire for retribution against the Arcanians for as long as he could remember. A justice he'd thought he could attain by beating the Crucible and securing the crown for his own people.

He hated the Revenant. *Hated* her.

But when Elyria looked at Kit, it was like she was a different person—someone Cedric had never imagined the Revenant capable of being. Was this truly the same person he'd sworn vengeance against?

"I've done many things in my many years in this world. Not all of them pleasant, not all of them right. But I can tell you that not once have I had any interest in participating in the slaughter of some inconsequential human family."

She could have been lying.

She was probably lying.

But what if she wasn't?

Cedric touched a knuckle to the scar at his lip, struggling to keep his expression neutral as his thoughts churned. So what if she *was* telling the truth? It didn't change anything. Didn't change the fact that he was who he was, and she was one of *them*. All it did was confuse him.

The Revenant as the figurehead he could blame for his pain made sense. Elyria was something else entirely. And that unsettled him deeply.

Despite his best efforts, Cedric's gaze drifted back to Elyria, Kit, and Zephyr. The sylvan had finished sealing the gash on Elyria's back and had even healed some of the small wounds he'd noticed on Kit. But from the way the three of them were suddenly radiating tension so thick he could have cut through it with his sword, you would have thought the healing had just begun.

Elyria's head snapped up, and he wasn't quick enough to look away before her eyes locked with his. She scowled, scrabbling at her pants in a way that made Cedric suddenly feel like he was intruding on something private. And if the defiance, anger, and something Cedric couldn't place—pain, maybe?—flowing from the fae wasn't confirmation enough, the blush of embarrassment that began coloring her pale cheeks certainly was.

Cedric felt an unexpected pang of guilt burst in his chest. He averted his eyes, his gaze landing on a crack in the stone wall beside him that was suddenly the most interesting thing he'd ever seen.

His attention could only be deflected for so long, however, and a minute later he found his gaze wandering back to the trio.

The tension in the room ebbed as Kit murmured something to Elyria. Zephyr joined back in their conversation and was showing the two of them some tin she'd pulled from her belt of magical healing tricks. A genuine smile broke out on Elyria's face as she nodded, transforming it into a somehow even more exquisite version of itself.

The change was so unexpected, Cedric nearly choked on his own breath.

His face screwed up—lips pursing, breath quickening—as warmth blossomed in his chest. Pride. Surely that was what he was feeling. Pride over whatever Zephyr had done to elicit Elyria's radiant reaction.

He most certainly was *not* reacting to her smile itself.

That was the only thing that made sense. Stopping to help the sylvan healer in the arena had indeed been one of Cedric's better decisions of late, after all. She really was very good.

Yes, pride. That definitely explained the warm feeling stretching over his ribs. It made absolute sense that pride in his new ally's healing mastery would strike Cedric utterly senseless.

He refused to dissect the thought further.

And that was fine, because when Cedric tried to locate that beaming smile and the fiery fae it belonged to again, it was nowhere to be seen.

Instead, Elyria's face was arranged into a sneer so chilling, he thought the temperature in the room might have actually dropped.

What the fuck just happened?

Cedric missed the impetus for the rapid change in her countenance— the woman was bound to give him whiplash—but he didn't miss the smug look on Belien Larkin's face as he stared down Elyria. Nor did he miss the low snickers coming from Alden Ashford. And he certainly didn't miss the way Zephyr seemed to have suddenly retreated into herself, all traces of the calm confidence she'd exuded while healing Elyria and Kit erased.

Fucking Alden. Something itched at the back of Cedric's mind, and he suspected he'd made a mistake in sitting with the saint earlier. He'd had hopes of building upon the groundwork of allyship he'd lain back in the camp. But if Alden was aligning with Belien and Leona, he was a lost cause. Cedric would rather take on the rest of the trials alone than get looped in further with that miserable lot.

Bolstered with new resolve, Cedric looked up to see a storm of periwinkle hair stalking toward him.

"You," Elyria growled, stopping just short of him.

"Me?" Cedric replied. Her fury was nearly as hot as the dragonfyre had been, and he didn't understand why she aimed it so viciously at him.

"What the quartered hell is your problem?" she demanded.

Cedric's brow furrowed. "Excuse me?"

"You know exactly what I'm talking about."

It took every ounce of will in Cedric's exhausted body not to roll his eyes. "I promise you, I do not."

"Then you are a bigger fool than I thought. Hard though that is to imagine."

"Now, wait just a—"

"Arcanians are not tools to be used and tossed aside. We are *people*. You do not get to use Zephyr to watch your back and heal your injuries, only to discard her at your earliest convenience."

"I did no such thing. I would nev—"

"And aligning yourself with other *humans*"—the word dripped with disdain—"with little regard for how their attitudes and actions might affect those of us who might've been otherwise predisposed to ally with you is just shit decision-making. Ergo, fool." She seemed to consider what she'd said before clarifying, "And by 'us,' I mean Arcanians as a whole, of course. Not 'us' as in me, specifically."

"I never would have presumed otherwise," Cedric said, his pulse ticking in his jaw from how hard he clenched his teeth. He wanted to argue, wanted to tell her she was *wrong*. But her words were a confirmation of the thoughts he'd already begun to form on his own.

Whatever vestiges of warmth might have lingered in Cedric's chest evaporated like water in a too-hot pan.

"Zephyr can handle herself," he said, though the words sounded weak even in his own ears.

Elyria scoffed. "Can she? A talented healer, she may be. But she's hardly a warrior like you or me. And she shouldn't have to be. Lunara only knows why she's even here in the first place. And now you've aligned with those who would make her a target. I don't know what the rest of this stars-forsaken Crucible may hold, but what happens when they turn on her? Will you turn as well?"

Cedric tried to ignore how his pulse stuttered at the way she'd casually equated the two of them. Warriors like her, aside from her, didn't exist. Of that, he felt sure. And after the way the Trial of Strength had ended . . . Was she being sarcastic?

"I've aligned with no one," he said, crossing his arms. "I'm not the same as—"

Elyria cut him off with a noncommittal noise. "You really think you're different, don't you? You're not." She raked her eyes up and down his body, lingering for the briefest moment at the token hanging against his chestplate. "You're just like the rest of *your kind*—using the land for its magic. Using its people like we're nothing. And I'm . . . You know what? I don't care." And before he could say anything else, she spun on her heel and strode away.

Cedric stood there, gaping at Elyria's retreating back, the sting of her words lingering on his skin like a bruise. He hated the look on her face as she walked away, so assured that she was right.

He hated that she *was* right.

He cast his gaze about the room, looking for Zephyr. The sylvan healer had slunk into a corner, busying herself with the pouches and herbs in her belt. Cedric's mind was noisy—a confusing mix of overlapping emotions. Guilt. Gratitude. Irritation. That one was solely directed at Elyria.

He *was* grateful, not only for Zephyr's help in the arena but for her calming aura. For the way she'd pushed past her own reticence to ally with him. Perhaps he should have been more guarded about the alliance, but there was something about the sylvan that made Cedric feel at ease. Not once had the thought crossed his mind to discard her.

But he also hadn't thought through the implications of what his association with her meant for his original plans to establish alliances with the other human champions. That they might hold his willingness to adhere to the Arbiter's guidance against him. Or rather, that they'd hold it against her.

A fool, Elyria called him. He certainly felt like one. He'd thought he could remain steadfast, focused. Unbothered by the more trivial side of these human-Arcanian interactions. Cedric's goal was the crown, by whatever means necessary. But just one trial in, and already the Crucible was changing so much for him.

Was changing . . . him.

Drawing a deep breath, Cedric turned away . . . only to find himself standing chest-to-face with Thraigg. The dwarf had his thick arms crossed over his broad chest, studying Cedric with a calculating look in his steely blue eyes.

Cedric tensed, unsure how to react. He supposed he should thank the man—he had aided him not once, but twice against the dragon. On the other hand, there was still the question of why he had done so.

"On with it, boyo," Thraigg rumbled, his voice as gravelly as the stone beneath their feet.

"Pardon me?"

"Ye've got the look of a man with questions. Ask them."

Cedric blinked. The dwarf was direct, he'd give him that. Perceptive and direct. "I'm just . . . surprised," he said. "About what you did back there. In the arena."

"Aye," Thraigg said warily. "What about it?"

"You had a clear path to the archway. You didn't need to fight. Didn't need to get involved with the dragon at all."

"Yer point?"

"So . . . why did you?"

Thraigg's beard shook as his lips curled into a knowing smile, the coins and metal beads braided into his hair jangling jovially. "Ye'd be right in thinking I've no love for reckless knights, let alone human ones," he said. "But far be it from me to question the commands of the Divine."

"The Divine?"

Thraigg's beard jingled again as his chest rose and fell with low laughter. "Who do ye think runs this show, boyo? The celestials might say they're not able to interfere in the affairs of us wee mortals, but their touch is all over the Crucible. And if their mouthpiece says unity is the name of this game, well, then, slap my arse and call me 'brother.'"

Cedric didn't know whether to laugh or scowl at the dwarf's crassness. "Their mouthpiece? You mean the Arbiter."

"Aye. So, when I saw ye and yer little green friend in the arena, cowering like daisies in a rioting wind—"

"I didn't cower," Cedric mumbled under his breath.

"—the Arbiter's voice was an avalanche in my head. 'Unity, unity, unity,' it chanted. And I went ahead and *unified* my hammer with some dragon scales." He chortled at his joke.

Brow furrowed, Cedric considered Thraigg's words. "That's it, then? You felt *called* to help me? Forgive my skepticism, but you simply do not seem the humanitarian type."

"Ain't charity, lad. I've no patience for that kind of nonsense. I've my own reasons, and none of them involve seeing ye roasted alive. But I don't play games 'less I plan on winning. Aye, I did what I did back there. Don't make me regret it." With that, the dwarf moseyed off, snatching a pitcher from one of the nearby tables as he ambled toward the doors.

"Duly noted," Cedric muttered at his back, unable to hold in a smirk. For some reason, the exchange left him feeling strangely grounded—like some part of him was beginning to settle, like he'd found an anchor amidst this sea of uncertainty.

Everyone in here was playing the game. They were in it to win, but if they had to go by the Arbiter's rules—had to hold hands and skip merrily until the Crucible called for them to show their teeth to one another—they would.

He looked at his fellow human champions, strategizing together in one corner of the room, and frowned. Perhaps not everyone was so willing to play together.

Elyria was a study in tension when Cedric's gaze found her again, hauling Kit to her feet and ushering her toward one of the doors at the back of the chamber. Her scowl had softened, but the anger in her eyes had yet to fade. Cedric could still see the hard set of her jaw, the way her fingers twitched as if itching for a fight. Part of him hoped that Belien or Leona—or hells, Alden—would say something to her again, just to see what she'd do.

Alas, she and Kit disappeared behind one of the doors without incident.

Cedric approached Zephyr, whose earlier warmth was already replaced with guarded caution. Guilt churned in Cedric's belly.

"Zephyr," he began, doing his best to keep his voice soft. "I . . . I feel as though I owe you an apology."

Her eyes widened, clearly caught off guard. "Why? For what?"

"For earlier. I put you in a position you didn't ask for by making moves to link up with Alden. I didn't realize he had already formed some kind of alliance with Belien. And I . . . I should have talked to you first. Should have understood you might be unlikely to want to associate with the most vocally bigoted champions in here." He offered a lopsided grin—an attempt to ease the tension.

"There is nothing to apologize for," she protested, but Cedric noted the way her shoulders relaxed—just a fraction. "It's not as if you and I had entered into some kind of formal alliance ourselves. We were more of a wrong place, wrong time kind of matchup." She grinned, though it was fleeting as she went on to add, "I understand if you'd want to part ways."

"Preposterous," Cedric said. "We're a formidable pair, remember?"

She visibly brightened. "Right."

Cedric breathed a sigh of relief. It felt like a step in the right direction, though he couldn't shake the feeling that he was still missing something.

The many voices of the Arbiter echoed in his head. *"Without unity, you will fail."*

Was this unity? Was this enough? As hate-filled emerald eyes blanketed his vision, Cedric didn't think it was.

Almost as if being pulled by a force outside of himself, his head tilted in the direction of the door Elyria had just walked through.

"You two . . . you have some kind of history?" Zephyr asked, following his gaze. Her voice was soft, tentative, like she knew she was touching on something fragile. Cedric wasn't sure how to respond. Could it be considered history if one of the parties had been utterly unaware of the other's existence until today? Was it history if everything he thought he knew was crumbling around him?

He settled for a shrug, doing his best to seem indifferent.

Zephyr pressed her lips together, like she was trying to contain a grin. "Looks like everyone's retiring. Shall we head off for the night then, partner?"

Cedric nodded. Tomorrow would bring the next trial and a whole new set of crises. So tonight . . . Tonight, he would rest. He would think. And he would try to figure out what he was truly fighting for.

CHAPTER 19
WOULD'VE, COULD'VE, SHOULD'VE

Elyria

"And then there were twelve."

"Could've been eleven," Kit tutted, casting a sidelong glance at Elyria as they settled into their respective beds.

The room was plainly appointed, just large enough for the two beds that had magically appeared when they stepped through the door. After nights spent in cramped tents and cold jail cells—Elyria's bones ached just thinking about it—it was nothing short of luxury.

"Could've, would've," Elyria sighed. "Had only I known it was Sir Stick Up His Ass that I was saving, I would have let that dragon finish what it started."

"Whatever you say." The knowing taunt in Kit's voice rankled

Elyria. "Now that I think about it, it should've been ten, actually. If you hadn't charged in after me, the knight would have been dragon food, *and* you wouldn't have filled Cormac's spot. You really are trying to make this as difficult as possible for me, aren't you?" she teased.

Elyria stuck out her tongue. "The knight is reckless. He's already nearly gotten himself killed several times. I'm sure your odds will even out again before you know it."

Kit smirked, her blue and green eyes glinting. "And how would you feel about that?"

Elyria stiffened. "I'd be glad for it, of course. One less champion in your way."

"Mm-hmm," Kit murmured, her tone making it clear she didn't believe Elyria for a second.

Swallowing her indignation, Elyria opted to change the subject. "I feel like a new woman," she said as she braided the wet length of her hair over her shoulder. "Clean sleeping gown, soft bed, hot bath . . ." She waved a hand, first at the doorway between their beds, which led to a cozy bathing room, then to the dresser on the other side of the room. Inside, they'd found a myriad of clothing options, sized and styled as if they'd been selected just for them. "A *champion* could get used to this shit."

A contented breath left her lungs as she leaned back. Even knowing this was only a temporary lull, a false comfort before the storm of additional trials that would follow, Elyria was grateful. Her stomach was full. Her body was mended. And, sneaking a surreptitious glance at Kit as she fluffed her pillow, Elyria thought some of her older, less visible wounds might be starting to heal as well.

Kit was undeterred by the attempted topic change. "Cormac was out in minutes, and we know Belis never made it through the arena. Who was the last one?"

"That other nocterrian, I think. I don't remember their name."

"Ah, yes, Dissidua. For the best, I think. I didn't trust them. Don't trust the other one, either."

"Tenebris Nox? Careful there, Kitty Kat. You're starting to sound eerily similar to our bigoted human friends out there."

Kit scowled and launched one of her fluffy pillows neatly at Elyria's head. "Not because I have anything against nocterrians, you lout."

Elyria grinned as she caught the pillow and tucked it between her legs.

"I only meant . . . Honestly, I don't even know. There's just something off about them." She paused. "They've been watching you."

Elyria frowned. "Watching me?"

"I first noticed it in Castle Lumin. The two of them were hanging back, keeping to the shadows, and I was too mad at you to think much of it at the time. But now . . . I feel certain Nox has been keeping an eye on you."

"I saw them back in Coralith," Elyria admitted. "They were being held in the same jail as me."

Kit's eyebrows shot up at the mention of jail, but she said nothing.

"Perhaps they are simply eager to know my motivations for being here," Elyria continued. "I confess I'm curious to know the same about them. I didn't think nocterrians had much reason to brave the Arcane Crucible." Her brow furrowed. Nocterrum wasn't even part of the realm during Queen Daephinia's rule. The mysterious island and its shadow-born people were barely impacted by the Shattering.

"Power is power," Kit said. "It lures everyone."

"Except you." Elyria smiled at her. "Unlike the rest of these so-called champions, you're not here because you dream of glory or long for the power of the crown. You're here for Evander. And I'm here for you. Let the king decide what to do with the crown after you've won it."

"After *we've* won it, you mean, right?" Kit bit her bottom lip anxiously, and Elyria found herself longing to soothe away her worry. She hadn't entered the Crucible only to become a source of angst for her friend. The last thing she wanted was to be a distraction.

"Right. And regarding our nocterrian friend, I'll be careful," she said, injecting confidence into the words even as she knew they were hollow. Careful didn't exist in a place like this.

Kit simply nodded.

Elyria cleared her throat. "Any theories on what tomorrow might bring?"

"The next trial? Not a clue," Kit replied. "Just that we're one down, three to go."

"How do you figure?"

"You heard the Arbiter. Strength and power. Resolve and 'depth of spirit,' whatever that means. We just completed the Trial of Strength. So, three more await."

"Technically, the Arbiter never said that those *were* the trials. Only that the trials would *demand* strength and power, and that they would test our resolve and spirit."

"Semantics." Kit waved a hand, and the candles lit in sconces were extinguished with a wet hiss, thrusting the room into peaceful darkness.

Something sharp nettled Elyria at the mention of the Arbiter's words. Their final proclamation rang over and over in her mind.

From bitterest rivals to heartbreaking ends, two bloods shall find their way. Through sacrifice, darkness, and friendship betrayed, as dawn brings a new day.

She had many questions about why the Arbiter had decided to remind Elyria of the final lines of the prophecy, but her mind was caught on one part in particular.

Friendship betrayed.

She tilted her head toward Kit's bed, squinting as though she might see her friend in the darkness. Surely, this was but cryptic nonsense. Some error, brought on by the Arbiter's shock at Elyria stumbling into them. It might not have even been officially tied to the Crucible—no other champions heard the words, after all. And with multiple versions of the prophecy apparently floating around, who was to say what was the truth?

With mettle and promise, darkness and light, as dawn brings a new day.

Elyria had to admit, she vastly preferred Cedric's version of the final line. None of this betrayal shit. Unfortunately, she also felt rather convinced that, were she forced to choose which version was likely the correct one, it would be the one that came from the mysterious glowing being who reigned over the Arcane Crucible.

Resolving to put it out of her mind, Elyria wiggled further down into her bed. Her eyelids were heavy. Had they really been at Castle Lumin only that morning? This might very well have been the longest day of Elyria's considerable life.

"Ellie?" Kit's voice pierced the quiet.

"Yeah?"

"Do you . . . do you think that Ev at least got this far?"

Elyria swallowed. "Without a doubt."

Kit was silent.

"You knew your brother," Elyria continued, her throat tight. "I'm sure his stubborn ass made it all the way to the very end before . . . well, before."

A huff filled the dark room. "Yeah. Maybe," Kit said.

Elyria wanted to say more—do more. Wanted to reassure Kit. But her eyes closed, and before she could say another word, sleep pulled her into its embrace.

Elyria woke the next morning to a loud chime ringing through the bedroom. Groaning, she shielded her eyes from the golden light that spilled into the room through slats in the stone walls. Kit was already awake, stretching her long arms over her head with a frown etched into her brow.

"Rise and shine, I guess," Kit mumbled sleepily.

Before Elyria could respond, the chamber door swung open with a soft creak. Was the room *kicking them out*?

"Four fucking hells," Elyria muttered to no one in particular. "Give a girl the chance to wake up, will you?"

They made quick work of popping into the bathing room and exchanging yesterday's torn and bloodied clothing for fresh, clean outfits. After gathering their weapons, they stepped back into the Sanctum's main chamber, Kit jumping as the door to their erstwhile bedroom slammed shut behind them. *Rude.*

Steps still somewhat sluggish, they ambled toward the center of the chamber, where most of the other champions had already gathered. Yesterday's haphazardly strewn floor cushions and benches had vanished, leaving a long table laden with bowls of steaming pottage and plates piled high with bread and fruit in their stead. Elyria exchanged a ravenous grin with Kit before darting forward to claim her breakfast.

"Ahem." A low voice let out a light cough behind Elyria's head.

She looked up, her cheeks bulging with the bites of breakfast she'd hastily shoveled into her mouth and met the amused stare of Cedric Thorne.

"Caahelloo?" she garbled through mouthfuls of bread.

"Er, what?" he replied, his eyebrow arched mirthfully. The scraping sound of his armor grated against Elyria's ears as he shifted in place.

She swallowed, grimacing as she forced the too-large bite down her gullet. "I *said*, 'Can I help you?'"

"Ah," said the knight, dragging his eyes from where they tracked the bob of Elyria's throat with rapt attention. A flush threatened in her cheeks. "Well, yes, in fact," he said. "You're blocking the bacon."

"There's bacon?" Elyria's voice jumped an octave as she whirled back to the table and grabbed the entire platter of glistening meat. The salty scent wafted into her nostrils and her mouth flooded.

Cedric coughed once more, and Elyria thought this time he might be covering a laugh. "May I?" he tried again, reaching for a slice.

Elyria tightened her hold on the platter and shuffled back a step.

"Stars above, woman." He shook his head with a sigh. "You cannot possibly think yourself capable of eating that entire thing."

Elyria's skin prickled at the challenge. "I thought it was made clear yesterday that you have no idea what I'm capable of." She didn't understand the emotion that flashed across Cedric's face in response.

"I wouldn't mind seeing her try," Cyren called unhelpfully from the other side of the table. Next to him, Gael smacked the blue-haired fae on the shoulder and he laughed.

"Oh, stop hogging it, you fairy freak," Leona Blackwood's nasal voice cut in.

Elyria turned slowly toward the source of the insult. "I see what you did there. 'Hogging it.' Clever." She popped a slice of dripping bacon between her lips, slurping as she sucked it into her mouth and resisting the urge to moan at the taste.

Leona's brown eyes narrowed before she turned to Cedric. "What interesting company you keep, Sir Thorne."

"Indeed," rumbled Belien as he came up from behind. "This is who the *great champion of Kingshelm* deigns to ally with?"

"Ahmnoh—" Elyria began to protest, her mouth again full.

"We're not allies," Cedric finished for her. Elyria grunted in confirmation.

"Still." Leona's nose tipped up as her scornful gaze fell on Zephyr, standing at the other end of the table, plucking a few grapes from a bowl.

Belien's mouth twisted into a leer, his gaze flicking to Leona, who gave him an encouraging nod. "It's just funny, isn't it? The famed Sir Cedric Thorne, darling of Lord Leviathan Church, standing shoulder to shoulder with a bunch of freaks. If it's not some knife-eared pixie, then it's some herbwitch greenie. Guess the great knight has a thing for strays."

Some knife-eared pixie? Elyria thought with irritation. Where was the fear of the Revenant when she needed it? Alas, she'd certainly heard worse. And had she been the only target of Belien and Leona's ire, Elyria might have let the comment slide. But when she heard Zephyr's sharp inhale, as if the sylvan had been struck clear across the face, it was all Elyria could do to keep herself from cracking the platter in her hands over Belien's ginger head.

Cedric straightened beside her. "Such ugly words you spew, Larkin," he said. "I would have thought losing Belis might inspire a kinder touch."

Belien's mouth twisted. "You will keep my sister's name out of your mouth." He leaned in closer. "Or you'll find out soon enough, Thorne, what becomes of all the self-righteous fools who attempt the Crucible."

Elyria finally set down the platter of bacon. "Four hells. Humans are so petty." She huffed a dramatic sigh. "Did you forget where you are? You're a champion bound to these stars-forsaken trials too. Exactly the same as him."

"I'm not like him!" Cedric and Belien exclaimed simultaneously.

She ignored them both. "The fact that either of you is acting like we're getting out of this alive is—"

"Nobody asked you, fairy bitch," Belien interrupted. The words were laced with venom, and Cedric's hand twitched toward his sword hilt.

For a moment, Elyria wondered if the knight would strike out.

For a moment, she almost hoped he would.

"Enough." Elyria's voice was an icy whip as she stepped between Cedric and Belien.

Belien scoffed but took a step back, his bravado faltering. "Your pixie guardian here won't always be around to fight your battles for you, Thorne," he said, the threat clear in his voice.

"You're welcome to try again anytime," Cedric snapped back, voice low and menacing. It stirred something in Elyria's core that she dutifully ignored.

Then Leona was tugging on Belien's arm, pulling him away with a disdainful look cast in Elyria's direction.

"Well, I never," said Elyria, her hand draped dramatically over her forehead as if her delicate sensitivities couldn't handle the words that had just been exchanged. Then she grinned at Cedric before snagging another piece of bacon from the table and taking a large bite.

"I had that handled," Cedric muttered.

"I'm sure you did," Elyria replied coolly.

His mouth opened. It closed. And then the knight snatched up the platter of bacon with a petulant huff and stormed off toward Zephyr.

Kit sidled up to Elyria as soon as he left, a bowl of berries clasped in her hands. "You really just can't help yourself, can you?"

"What?" Elyria fished a plump raspberry out of the bowl and popped it in her mouth, savoring the way the tart sweetness washed over her tongue, cutting through the lingering flavor of salt and fat.

"Can't stop yourself from saving him."

Elyria shot her a glare. "I'm not in the mood, Katerina."

Kit shrugged. "Just calling it like I see it."

A series of chimes interrupted whatever retort Elyria might've thrown back at her friend, drawing all attention to the doors along the far wall. Silver light pulsed behind their frames, and she noted that where yesterday twelve doors had stood, only six remained now. Was this the Sanctum's way of pushing them into alliances? Elyria felt a spark of gratitude in her chest that she already had Kit on her side. Or rather, that she was on Kit's.

"Champions who have fought with steel and claw," boomed the Arbiter's resonant voice, "the Trial of Spirit awaits."

Kit nudged Elyria's shoulder—an obnoxious, silent *I told you so*.

"Behind each door lies a test of truth. Behind each door lies a challenge of will. Choose your path."

Tension rippled through the gathered champions. Eyes flicked to each door, then to each other. Calculating. Considering.

"Trust your strength. Trust your resolve. Trust each other," finished the Arbiter, before the voice dissipated into the ether.

Elyria's eyes narrowed. *Trust each other.* How convenient that the Arbiter's parting words should be another call for unity, given the alliances here were fragile as spun glass.

A jolt of anticipation coursed through Elyria's veins as the doors began to glow more brightly. The magic within whatever lay beyond shimmered like a mirage. Elyria knew better than to think the bedroom where she'd lain her head last night was still behind any of them.

Kit was already moving toward one of the doors, determination emblazoned upon her face. Elyria trailed a few paces behind, confident that whatever came of this rekindled friendship, it was at least strong enough to get them past the challenge that lay beyond whatever door Kit chose.

The doors flung open in a burst of light, and chaos erupted. The chamber was a flurry of movement as champions darted forward in a frenzy. Someone jostled Elyria's shoulder, causing her to turn out of reflex—just for a second.

It was enough. She lost sight of Kit.

Shit. Elyria pushed through the crowd. Panic spiked in her chest as she shoved past Gael and Tenebris Nox, both making a beeline for the same doorway before the latter changed their mind, leaping into a different pool of silver light.

Shit, shit, shit, shit.

Champions disappeared one by one, and Elyria's heart dropped into her stomach as she realized Kit had already gone through. But which one?

Soon, Elyria was the only champion left. She stared at the glowing doorways, clawing at her memory, parsing through the moments that had preceded this as if she might suddenly understand where Kit had gone, where Elyria was to follow.

Something flickered in her chest. A stirring. But it wasn't the same dark, swirly feeling she'd come to understand as her inner shadow rousing. It was more like . . . a *tug*. A pull, subtle but insistent.

It coaxed her toward one of the glowing doorways, called her to it. Elyria could only pray it was pointing her down the same path as Kit.

"Intuition, don't fail me now," she muttered to herself before striding forward. With each step, the pull grew stronger, stronger,

stronger—until Elyria was pushing through silver light and that familiar, world-tilting feeling coursed through her.

She found herself standing in a squat, square room. It was dark, the features of the room only made visible by the ambient glow of torches lining the walls to her left and right. There were no windows. No doors—not even the one she had presumably just come through. Just a painted arch on the far wall, golden swirls and vines drawn onto the stone, framing nothing.

Her stomach lurched. What was this?

A scraping noise came from behind her. She turned, her pulse quickening to a frightening beat.

Then it slowed. Nearly stopped.

And Elyria heard her heart beating in her ears when it started to pump again.

"Oh, for fuck's sake," she said.

Because there, armored arms crossed tight over his chest, lips pressed into a hard line, was Sir Cedric Thorne.

CHAPTER 20
THE SECOND TRIAL

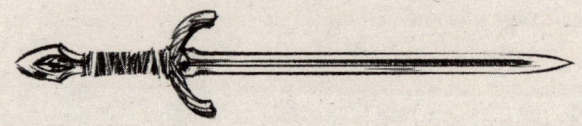

Cedric

"You're not Zephyr." The room was unnervingly silent as Cedric and the Revenant gaped at each other. She blinked at him, her green eyes lit with streaks of silver that danced in the light seeping from the torches along the walls.

The Arbiter's announcement had brought chaos, to be sure, but hadn't Zephyr been right behind him? He'd presumed their conversation yesterday meant they'd be pairing up to tackle this next trial—she had called him "partner"—but perhaps the sylvan had chosen a different door? Or was this some new, cruel trick of the Crucible—instructing the champions to trust each other, only to pair up those least inclined to do so? Why did it have to be *her*?

You're not Zephyr. Mentally, Cedric smacked himself upside the head. Maybe Elyria didn't notice just how stupid that sounded.

She noticed.

"Is that your power?" She inclined her head at the token hanging from Cedric's neck. "The magic of stating the obvious?"

He scowled. "You should save some of that quick wit for the trial itself. And speaking of . . ."

Elyria arched a brow. "What, no time for pleasantries?"

"Do illuminate me as to what part of this could possibly be construed as pleasant."

Something zipped through Cedric's center at the sight of Elyria's pursed mouth quivering, as if she fought a grin.

He cleared his throat. "The sooner we get through this trial, the sooner we cease being . . . together. Might as well get on with it."

"Get on with what?" She waved her arms animatedly, gesturing to the empty room. "There's nothing here."

Cedric looked pointedly over Elyria's head, where the painted vines on the wall had started to glow.

"For fuck's sake. Another archway, another gate?" she muttered. "Can they truly not come up with anything more creative?" A shimmer rippled across the wall as Elyria neared it.

Something about it made Cedric shudder. "I don't think this is the same kind of gate." Instead of glowing with the ethereal, inviting light Cedric had already become accustomed to, the section of flat wall *transformed*. Like alchemy, the stone between the edges of the painted frame melted into liquid gold.

"Well, this is new." Elyria's reflection stared back at the two champions—a golden mirror. She studied it, a soft melody falling from her lips, almost absentmindedly. She drew her staff from her back.

"I wouldn't"—Cedric began, just as the end of her staff tapped the mirror—"touch that." He sighed. "What is wrong with you?"

Elyria shot him an unimpressed look. "It's called curiosity. I know it may be difficult for you to imagine with that stick up your ass, but it's a perfectly normal—"

"Riiiiiight," he cut her off, drawing out the vowel. "What part of this entire thing is normal, again?"

She leaned closer to the mirror, inspecting her warped reflection for a moment before turning to face Cedric. "You tell me. Word around the

Sanctum is that you've been preparing for the Crucible since you were knee-high to a gryphon. You *are* the *darling of Lord Leviathan Church*, are you not?" She grinned, a glint in her eye that made the air in the room seem suddenly thin.

He didn't like that teasing twinkle. Didn't like the way it made him feel—warm and a little bit itchy. He also didn't like hearing Lord Church's name come out of her mouth, how it made the world that existed outside the Sanctum come crashing in on them here. The knowledge that he was in here, forced to work with *her*, while Lord Church waited for him out there made Cedric's stomach twist uncomfortably.

It took him a moment to realize Elyria was waiting for his response.

"Something like that," he muttered. "But that doesn't mean I can speak to whether this qualifies as a typical experience."

"Why not?"

"You know why not." The air between them grew suddenly very still.

"Because anyone who might have made it here before is dead," she said, her voice low. A moment passed. Her eyes turned glassy. Then she made a jerking motion with her head, as if she was trying to shake some thought loose.

Cedric's brow creased. Had she lost someone to a previous Crucible? He thought back to the argument he'd witnessed between Elyria and Kit in Castle Lumin. Well, the argument he'd inserted himself into.

"I am acting in the best interest of your remaining *family,"* Elyria had said.

It made sense, he supposed. The desperation Elyria had exuded, trying to convince Kit not to enter the Sanctum. The deep hurt she'd covered up at Kit's implication that Elyria wasn't part of that aforementioned family.

"Did you—"

"Still," she cut him off, "you might use a little imagination here. Or is that beyond the abilities of the great Sir Cedric Thorne, champion of Kingshelm?"

"Imagination?"

She rolled her eyes, all signs of whatever thought or memory that had trapped her moments before now gone. Her icy, indifferent mask had slid right back into place. "Yes. Imagination. The ability of the mind to be creative or resourceful? Ring any bells?"

"I know what the word means," he said drily. "Just not my strong suit, I'm afraid."

"*Imagine* that," she said. "Ah, well. I suppose I'll just have to be creative enough for the both of us." She rapped on the surface of the mirror with her staff again, inspecting her reflection.

"Stop doing that," he chastised. "I thought the Revenant was supposed to be this legendary warrior, not an impulsive fool."

She tensed. "And I thought you were supposed to be a knight, not some humorless prick."

"Humorless?" he echoed, affecting the tone of mock offense Tristan so often used around him. "I'll have you know I'm considered by many to be positively delightful."

Elyria's answering laugh rang through the small room like a bell. It was an infuriatingly beautiful sound. "Is that so?" she said, eyes sparkling, smile beaming.

He forced his gaze anywhere but that transformed, beatific face. "When I'm not stuck with reckless fae who think poking strange, magical, golden wall-mirrors out of *curiosity* is a good idea."

"And here I thought being stuck with me would be the highlight of your day." She turned back to the mirror with a shrug. "Admit it, Sir Grumpypants. You'd be bored to tears without me."

A short, incredulous laugh left Cedric's lips. "Quite the opposite, I assure you. I'd be thrilled not having to babysit someone who treats every challenge like it's—"

"You? Babysitting *me*?" She cut him off with another bout of pealing laughter. "Now, that's the funniest thing I've heard in, well, in a very long time. How old are you, human? You can't be more than, what, twenty-nine? Thirty years of age?"

Cedric mumbled a response.

She cupped her hand around her ear. "Sorry, didn't catch that."

"Twenty-eight," he said.

"Even better."

Cedric's face screwed up in a scowl. "And just how old are you?"

Elyria let out a melodramatic gasp. "How dare you? Don't you know how rude it is to ask that of a lady?"

"I'm not being rude," he said with a frown. *And I don't see any ladies around here,* he wanted to add. He held his tongue. It was too easy.

Elyria tutted. "I'm two hundred and sixty-one, if you must know."

Cedric did a quick calculation in his head, based on what he knew of the fae life cycle. They regularly lived to nine hundred years or more. "Wouldn't that make you . . . essentially the same age as me?"

"That's a bit reductive, but sure. As long as you disregard the extra centuries of life experience entirely."

Cedric bit the inside of his lip to keep himself from smiling. "If only you directed even a fraction of that worldly experience toward figuring out what we're supposed to be doing here, rather than toying with me."

Mischief danced in her emerald eyes. "I'll make you a deal, then. You loosen up a little when the occasion calls for it, and I'll do just that."

"That sounds like a losing proposition for us both."

"On the contrary," she said, slinging her staff over her shoulder and raising a delicate, pale finger toward the mirror. "*That* is what we call a win-win situ—"

She brought her finger to the mirror, just the barest touch. It was enough. The surface turned liquid again, gold rippling out from where she made contact.

Cedric heard her sharp intake of breath too late.

Molten gold slid up her wrist, wrapped around her arm, *took hold* of her.

He lunged, his hand outstretched, trying to grab her, trying to pull her back. He missed her by a heartbeat. His fingers snagged a few long strands of periwinkle hair as the Revenant was sucked into the gilded depths. All that remained were the sharp sounds of wood and metal rattling against rock as Elyria's staff and daggers bounced against the floor, discarded.

The rippling gold stilled, hardening back into unyielding stone.

Shit.

Panic gnawed at him. Where had she gone? This couldn't be how it was supposed to go.

Could it?

It struck him then that perhaps this wasn't the most terrible thing that could have happened. Was he not just lamenting their being stuck here together? So why was his pulse racing? Why did his armor suddenly feel too tight?

Cedric slammed his gauntlet-clad fist upon the wall—once, twice. The stone shook. He drew back. "This is your idea of unity, is it?" he yelled into the empty room.

As if in answer, the wall shimmered again, gold light dancing between the intricate swirls of paint.

"Let me in," he said.

"Are you certain?" a voice replied, echoing in his head. Not the ominous, multi-tonal voice of the Arbiter, but someone else. High pitched. Young. Eerily familiar.

A chill crawled up Cedric's spine. He shook it off. "Yes," he said, laying his palm against the stone.

"Even knowing the darkness you must face?"

He swallowed. "I will face whatever the trial demands."

The voice in his mind hummed with approval as the liquid gold rippled. He held his breath, waiting for the mirror to envelop him the same way it had Elyria.

Nothing happened.

His jaw tightened. He poked at the mirror, rapping his gauntlet against it. It felt as if he was tapping on glass.

"What is this?" he asked aloud.

"When defenses are raised, the path cannot open. Shed your shields," crooned the voice in his head, *"that you may reveal your truth."*

"What does that—" He looked at himself in the mirror, at the gleaming armor upon his chest, the pauldrons sitting heavy on his shoulders. "You mean that literally, don't you?"

Cedric could've sworn he heard the equivalent of a *shrug* inside his head.

He chewed the inside of his cheek. Elyria hadn't had to remove any protections. The trial had taken the fae as she was. Granted, the supple leather bodice and breeches that clung to her lithe frame—not that he'd been looking, of course—were certainly not the same as a knight's armor. But was he supposed to believe that the world's most defensive, sarcastic woman didn't have her own kind of shield up?

The gold began to roil—agitated, impatient. Finally, the knight began removing his armor. He slipped off his gauntlets first, flexing his fingers. His cuirass clanged as it hit the ground, an echo of the hollow thud that seemed to beat in Cedric's chest. He was used to the comforting weight of steel pressed against his heart.

Piece by piece, his armor fell away, and as he unbuckled the final item, a strange lightness settled over him. Not just the physical relief that came with unburdening his body of its heavy protection. Not a sense of freedom, either.

The disquiet of being . . . untethered.

He looked at his golden reflection in the mirror again. No longer was he Sir Cedric Thorne, champion of Kingshelm, ward and vassal of Lord Leviathan Church. He was just . . . Cedric.

The thought scared him so much that for a moment, he considered turning back. Retreating into the safety of the version of himself he knew, figuring out some other way—any other way—to move forward.

Leaving his armor behind meant leaving behind the parts of himself that he understood. Forging ahead undefended and unarmed.

Naked.

Vulnerable.

He hated it.

But the trial demanded truth, and truth could no longer hide behind steel.

Clad in only his arming doublet, breeches, and boots, Cedric placed his sword and dagger next to Elyria's weapons, which he'd already propped neatly against the wall next to his armor. He tucked his mana token beneath the collar of his doublet, shuddering at the thought of that being taken from him too.

He tried to ignore the way the voice in his head once again radiated approval as he faced his reflection in the gilded mirror.

"Now we see you," whispered the voice, curling through his mind like smoke. *"Now you are ready."*

The gold shimmered—beckoning him. With a steadying breath, Cedric pressed his palm against the wall once more. This time, the liquid gold flowed out, lacing over his hand, his wrist, roaming up his arm.

Cold as ice. Burning, on fire. Wet and dripping. Dry and rough. Cedric's nerves lit up with an onslaught of conflicting sensations. Then he plunged into a disorienting void.

It was dark. So dark. And for a moment, Cedric feared he would be trapped in this abyss, without light, without warmth, forever. But then the darkness lifted, and blue-green light filtered over the world around him.

He was on a bridge. A narrow wooden bridge, strung together with rope, suspended over . . . nothing. A bolt of terror raced through Cedric. Like a reflex, he pressed his palm to his chest, feeling the hard edges of his token dig into his skin. It eased his worry infinitesimally.

Above him, the aurora blazed, the faintest rivulets of blue, green, and purple carving through the sunlit sky. But below him? That void, that darkness he'd crossed through? He swayed over it now—a grim pit of swirling nothingness.

It stretched out around him, not just under the bridge, but to his left and to his right—an infinity of nonexistence. This was a thousand times worse than crossing the Chasm. What a fool he'd been for being nervous then. What he wouldn't give for the firm stone and brick, the security of the wagon, rather than standing alone amidst rotting planks and fraying rope.

And he was alone.

The voice in his head had gone quiet—disappeared. Elyria was nowhere to be seen. Where was she? Where was *he*? What was this?

Sweat gathered on Cedric's forehead as he took a single, tentative step forward. The wood groaned under his weight. He immediately grabbed the rope on either side of him, holding on with a white-knuckled grip. The coarse edges of the rope bit into his palms.

A sound caught his attention. He squinted ahead—some fifty, sixty feet in front of him, there was . . . something. Some . . . one? The figure waved their arms wildly, jumping up and down on a platform of rock and dirt that materialized before Cedric's eyes.

"Help!" the figure called. A woman, the desperation in her voice clear as day. Frantic. "Help us, please!"

Cedric swallowed hard and tried to slow his rapid intake of breath. Someone was in trouble. Someone needed help. And regardless of whatever this trial thought it was testing—his ability to overcome his irrational fear of heights, it would seem—he knew he had to move.

So, without looking down, without looking anywhere but at the lone, waving woman on the platform ahead of him, Cedric took his first step.

It felt like an eternity had passed before his feet finally touched solid ground, but touch it, they did.

"Thank Aurelia!" cried the woman, her weathered face visibly relieved as Cedric approached. She tucked a strand of loose gray hair back into the bun sitting at the nape of her neck before motioning for Cedric to follow her. "Come quickly, please! I don't know how much longer they have."

"Who?" he asked, though he did not hesitate to fall in step with the old woman.

"Just hurry," she said. Trees seemed to sprout in the corners of Cedric's vision as they rushed forward—what he'd thought was a small platform connected to that stars-forsaken bridge was rocky land that stretched for miles, as real as what had been in the arena during the first trial.

Real. Was this real? It felt real. It felt . . . important. Like he was headed toward something crucial.

"My name is Cedric, ma'am," he said to the woman, breathing heavily. They had already been pushing forward at a hard pace for some time.

She gave him an odd look but did not slow her stride. "Alouette," she replied between gulps of air. A pretty name. He thought it might be familiar, though he couldn't place it. The trees grew thicker, denser. Worry began to crease Cedric's brow. Where was she taking him? He heard nothing, saw nothing, other than the landscape around him, seemingly becoming more detailed, more lush as they walked.

The path they were on forked suddenly. "This way," Alouette said, her voice a harsh whisper. "We must be quiet now. We're very nearly there."

Unease prickled at the back of Cedric's neck. He opened his mouth, ready to ask—to demand—that Alouette tell him what was happening.

Then he saw it.

Thatched roof. Vine-covered white walls. Blue door. A single tall cherry tree growing in front, a low swing hanging from its branches.

A panicked breath caught in Cedric's throat. This place . . . He knew this place.

Alouette went still at his side. "Welcome home, Cedric."

CHAPTER 21
BLOOD & IRON

Elyria

The entire world was darkness.

Not the comfortable, starlit dark of night.

Not the warm black that graces one's vision from behind closed eyelids.

An endless void that crawled into Elyria's skin, through her bones, permeating every inch of her being.

Her darkness.

She strained her senses, trying to get a feel for, well, anything. She felt solid ground beneath her feet. Smelled iron and smoke in the air. Heard the soft patter of rain hitting dirt.

Where had the Crucible sent her?

And where was *he*?

She pushed that thought away as quickly as it came, refusing to give the nagging sense of worry any more space in her mind. Cedric was likely back in that stony chamber, gloating over how right he'd been to discourage her from touching the mirror. Or perhaps he was stewing with annoyance, irate that she'd figured out how to move into the next phase of the trial—even if it was by accident.

The thought very nearly brought a smile to her lips.

But the suffocating blackness would not allow even that small comfort. Shadows closed in tighter. They gripped her, clung to her, held her, tore at her. She couldn't move, couldn't breathe, couldn't—

The dark shattered. And she was no longer in a lightless prison but standing in an all-too-familiar place.

Her stomach twisted as the acrid scent of smoke, sweat, and iron grew stronger, filling her nostrils, burning her eyes.

No. Not here.

Castle Lumin towered over her, a sentinel at Elyria's back as she stood in front of the gatehouse, rain falling in sheets, slicking down the loose strands of periwinkle that had come free from her braid. It dripped into her eyes as she stared straight ahead, refusing to turn, refusing to look. She didn't want to see what she already knew was there.

The rest of the castle garrison, brave men and women—her friends, her comrades—littered the blood-soaked earth in front of her, at her back, at her side.

Not again.

Some of the soldiers groaned, tried to move, tried to stand. Others clutched at the blood-red crystal arrows jutting from their chests and thighs, trying to stem the bleeding from the *sanguinagi* weapons. More of them were utterly still, expressions vacant, eyes unseeing.

This isn't real. This is a memory, she told herself. *Just a memory.*

Pain lanced her side—sharp, searing. She looked down to see the red shaft of an arrow protruding from her hip. Felt the wet warmth blooming, sticky on her fingers as she drew her hand away from the wound.

It felt real.

A memory shouldn't bleed, she thought.

This was something more.

Every nerve in her body screamed at her to run, to leave, to get out.

But she couldn't.

Not then.

Not now.

Like then, there was just Elyria and the last flickering embers of her wild magic. She was all that stood between Malakar's dark army and the castle behind her. Between them and the queen.

Shouts cleaved the air. They were coming.

The ground rumbled as she clenched her fists, summoning the dregs of her power to the surface.

She was going to lose. She knew this. She'd already lost once.

But just like last time, she also knew she would fight to keep the enemy from breaching the castle. She would fight to her last breath.

Elyria raced forward to meet the cultists before they could swarm the injured garrison. Crossing her forearms, she conjured a shield of vines and roots to hold at her side. It immediately met a wave of crystal arrows.

Gritting her teeth, she dug her heels into the ground, holding herself steady against the onslaught of blood magic. She waved her free arm. Rocks flew through the air, crashing into cultists' heads, hands, chests. Vines snaked out of the ground, wrapping around legs, snapping ankles, buckling knees.

But there were too many of them.

And her magic was . . . it was nearly gone. A kind of coldness crept through her veins, chasing the wild light of her power. She had used too much.

Elyria screamed as a red blade skewered her shoulder, the dark grin of a *sanguinagi* cultist rising over her. The wolven face of Malakar's sigil on his chest glinted as he shoved the sword in deeper, further. It burned. It tore at her insides, her own blood fueling the dark magic of the conjured weapon—strengthening it.

She fell to her knees. The *sanguinagi* laughed, a low, menacing sound. He twisted the blade. The cold spread to Elyria's chest.

Unable to maintain the magic that cloaked them, her wings rematerialized. Just in time for Elyria to fall on top of them, too weak to adjust, to avoid crushing one at a terrible angle.

And even though she *knew*—knew that this was what really happened, that this was how it ended, that she was reliving the inevitable—Elyria Lightbreaker did not want to die.

It was the last thought she had before she did.

Light.

Blinding, white light washed over Elyria. It burst across the battlefield—a tidal wave of brilliant energy that rolled over buildings and soldiers and cultists alike.

Elyria knew this light. Recognized it. Remembered it. Floating above her own body like a specter, she watched the Shattering happen all over again.

Queen Daephinia sacrificed herself in a final bid to rid the world of Malakar's evil once and for all, shattering the Crown of Concord and unleashing its power across Luminaria. A power so pure, so mighty, so explosive that, for a moment, it felt like hope.

It wasn't.

Elyria had failed to protect her queen.

And as quickly as the light had appeared, it was suddenly sucked back into the castle, as if it had never been there at all.

But it had touched her. And in the singular heartbeat after Elyria breathed her final breath, that light doused her wings, seeped into her wounds, crawled into her veins. It expelled the *sanguinagi's* poisonous magic, erased its touch. It healed her injuries, cast out *death*.

One moment, Elyria was a wraith—watching, listening, waiting. The next, she was yanked back into her body, flesh and blood once more. The air was thick with ash as she gasped, struggling to breathe anew, to swallow the life-giving breaths she'd just been without.

It wasn't raining anymore.

Elyria bolted to her feet, eyes wild. She hadn't remembered what it felt like when she came back to her body. Hadn't remembered the thrum of energy in her fingertips, the racing beat of her heart. It was all foreign. She'd disconnected from herself, even if just for a few moments, and now everything felt discordant. Strange. New.

A battle cry came from Elyria's back. She turned, eyes widening as members of her garrison were getting to their feet, the enemy's crystal arrows crumbling into pieces.

She gasped, realization barreling into her. The power of the crown had washed over every injury on the battlefield. The soldiers had been healed too.

Still, not everyone rose. Save for Elyria, those who had died remained dead. She didn't know why she was the exception. The timing of her death? Was she just that lucky?

Or perhaps she was very, very unlucky.

Because that's when she saw it. The shadow. The darkness. The silky, smoky wisp that came from the castle, from the same place where that healing light had originated. It slithered between Arcanians and cultists, newly engaged in battle, unaware that the war was already over. Daephinia and Malakar were both gone. Their soldiers fought over ghosts.

"Stop!" she tried to yell. Her voice and body didn't cooperate. She didn't quite know who she was trying to stop anyway. The soldiers, immediately back to bloodying each other even after being given a second chance? Or the darkness, which continued sliding between bodies and over the damp earth. Searching. *Hunting*.

For her.

Elyria gasped as it latched on to her. As black tendrils coiled around her legs, her arms, up her neck, and finally, dove into her mouth. She felt them slide down her throat, spread through her insides. It was like drowning in ice. Suffocating in tar.

Shadows poured into her, filling her with a grim, heady power. It was all wrong. The darkness seeping into her veins with whispered vows of strength and greatness—*wrong*. The way it gnawed at the edges of her resolve, promising vengeance—*wrong*. The way somewhere, deep inside, a part of her relished it—*wrong*.

Elyria—past and present—screamed inside her head, helpless as the shadows smothered her, buried her. She watched in horror as her limbs moved of their own accord, dark magic swirling in her open palms. She stalked through sets of battling soldiers, shadows pushing them aside until she found him.

The one who killed her.

He was fighting one of the soldiers from her garrison now. Elyria recognized the girl—a fellow fae she'd bunked next to for a short time. A new, bloody weapon glowed in the *sanguinagi's* hands as he brought it down against the soldier's shield.

Elyria cried out in her mind again, but it did nothing to stop the shadows from shooting out of her hands. Did nothing as they wrapped around the Arcanian soldier, flinging her aside. Did nothing to prevent the gruesome crunch as the soldier collided with the gatehouse wall.

The darkness didn't care. It narrowed its focus on the cultist, whose eyes were wide with shock. Like he didn't know whether he should be grateful for the assistance or run as far and fast as he could from the dark creature in front of him.

He chose wrong.

And as the cultist approached Elyria with a cautious expression, she felt the shadows swirling around her arms tighten and condense, solidifying into a gruesome black sword.

Raw, jagged edges ripped through the cultist's flesh and muscle like butter as she thrust it into his chest.

He fell limply to the ground, still impaled on Elyria's blade. She planted her boot on his shoulder and shoved him off with a kick.

It wasn't enough. The darkness was not satisfied.

Elyria was a passenger in her own body as she charged, wings flaring, into the thick of the battle. She slashed, she squeezed, she raged.

She killed.

A dark tendril wrapped around the throat of a *sanguinagi* who was accosting a soldier. Elyria clenched her fist, cinching the shadow tight. The soldier cried out in shock as the cultist's head fell from his body.

With a flap of her wings, Elyria was in the sky. The shadows took the shape of barbed spears. She hurled them into the battlefield below.

As if somehow the darkness knew which side of the war it had latched on to, it focused on the cultists. But it wasn't careful. It was imprecise.

And it was merciless.

Elyria could do nothing but watch as innocent soldiers were caught up in her bloodlust.

Screams sounded—some in defiance, others in surrender—but the darkness did not care.

She couldn't stop.

She didn't want to stop.

"What . . . are . . . you . . . ?" The cultist's words were wet, barely audible through the blood that gushed from his mouth.

The voice that answered was not hers. "I am death and retribution, reborn." She twisted the shadow blade piercing his chest. "I am the Revenant."

CHAPTER 22
EMBERS & ASH

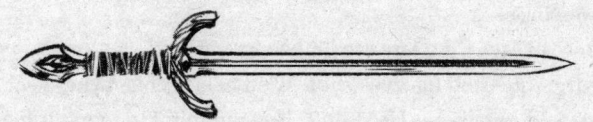

Cedric

"Welcome home, Cedric."

The words wrapped around him like iron chains, pinning him in place as he stared at the cottage. It had been more than two decades since Cedric had looked upon the straw-colored roof, the twining green vines that framed a dusty blue door. It looked exactly as he remembered.

And he did remember.

No matter how hard he tried, he'd never be able to forget.

"Impossible . . . ," he whispered. A breeze caressed his face, making the branches of the cherry tree in front of the cottage sway. Tiny white-pink petals drifted through the air, a fragrant snow that settled in Cedric's hair, stuck to his cheeks. His wet cheeks.

He roughly wiped away the tears with the back of his hand, then took a step back. A firm hand grabbed his forearm, gnarled fingers digging into his flesh. Alouette was surprisingly strong for her age. Cedric remembered that. He remembered *her* now too. Shame crept up from his gut for not recognizing her at first. His family's loyal housemaid, the nanny who'd helped raise him, who'd been with them until—

"This isn't real," he said, shaking his head. It couldn't be.

"Is that which shapes us not real?" she asked, releasing his arm. His skin tingled where she had gripped him. "Go on, child. They're waiting for you."

"No one waits for me," he said, voice thick. Cedric glared at the door, half-expecting it to burst open, for his parents to run out, for the Crucible to reveal some new twisted manipulation of his memory.

Half hoping it would.

His chest filled with something that felt like dread.

But nothing happened. Nothing moved. The cottage was still, serene. Just as it had been that night.

The air tightened around him. Cedric suddenly fought for breath. Pressure built in his chest. It was tight—too tight. His armor must have been pressing—

He wasn't wearing any armor, he remembered.

Cedric squeezed his eyes shut. Tried to slow his racing heart, ease his panicked breathing. He didn't. He couldn't. He thought his heart might burst clear of his chest for how hard it was beating.

He wanted to laugh. Turns out, it wasn't a dark beast or a dragon or a horde of gnarlings that would do him in. It was his own traitorous body. The *great champion* was going to die of a heart attack, right here, with only a ghost to witness it.

A warm voice filtered into his ears. Melodious, soft, full of life. Cedric knew it immediately. It filled every haunted corner of his mind, his soul.

He never thought he'd hear it again.

And as that beautiful voice hummed a sweet, gentle song, his heartbeat finally slowed. His shoulders sagged. His breathing evened.

When he finally opened his eyes again, the door had swung open on silent hinges. Golden light spilled into the night. Laughter echoed faintly. And from somewhere within, Cedric's mother continued humming a sweet lullaby.

Cedric's past crashed over him, wave after wave of heart-clenching memories. He could see it, smell it, taste it. Fresh bread cooling on the windowsill. His father's strong hand gripping his shoulder, ruffling his hair. His mother's flaxen locks spilling down her back as he chased her round and round the cherry tree.

"Go on," Alouette encouraged, her voice drawing Cedric back to the present. The illusion was so vivid, the memories so tantalizing, that for a moment, he almost said yes. He almost went through that door.

But the truth of what lay beyond it lingered just beneath the surface, a shard of glass waiting to cut him open. He couldn't go in, couldn't face what he knew awaited him inside that house.

The end of his world.

"I can't do this," he snarled, stumbling back from Alouette. Pulling his token from beneath his collar, he murmured an ancient command in his mind and waved his arm at the house. Blue paint chips shuddered off the door as it connected with the frame, slamming shut.

He turned toward the trees, desperate to locate the path they had taken to get here. He would go back. Surely the other side of that golden mirror lay somewhere at the end of the bridge. Better to face an endless void than this madness.

But no matter which direction he turned, no matter how many steps he took, Cedric found himself facing the cottage again.

The door opened wider, beckoning him. Calling him.

"You cannot run from this, my child," Alouette said, her voice cold as winter frost. "Face what broke you. Face your truth."

Truth. The words cut through Cedric's fear.

"Shed your shields, that you may reveal your truth."

This was still a trial. The Trial of Spirit, the Arbiter called it. A test of truth, a challenge of will.

He had not survived this long—he had not survived this *night*—to fail now.

His heartbeat was a war drum in his ears as he moved toward the house. He glanced into an ivy-framed windowpane as he passed. The face of a boy stared at Cedric from inside—scared, tear-stricken. Fear radiated from wide, golden-brown eyes.

And then, with a sickening lurch, Cedric wasn't looking in through the window anymore. He was staring *out* of it.

A warm glow washed over the room. Fire crackled in the hearth, two worn, comfortable chairs propped in front. The scent of roasted meat and yeasty bread filled Cedric's nostrils, and his little belly rumbled.

"Cedric!" called his mother, her voice light, musical. It wrapped around Cedric's lungs, squeezing all the air from his chest. "Come, my love. We're just about to start supper."

He turned. Saw those bright, beaming sea-blue eyes. Just like Cedric, a slim golden ring bordered her irises. And for a moment, he didn't know what to do. Didn't know whether to run again, to try to carve himself out of this living memory—before it became a nightmare—or whether to embrace it. Embrace *her*.

His footsteps pitter-pattered against the wooden floor as Cedric flung himself into his mother's arms.

"Oh, my!" she exclaimed, grabbing the kitchen table for support as Cedric barrelled into her, nearly knocking her back. "What's gotten into you, my little phoenix?"

He mumbled something unintelligible into her stomach. Several moments passed before he finally lifted his head. His mother shone down at him with a kind, knowing smile on her lips—the one she always seemed to have reserved just for him.

She was exactly as he remembered. The straw-colored hair that flowed loosely over her shoulders. The golden locket she never took off hanging from her neck. Her faint lavender scent. The way she tied her apron—crisscrossing her frock, the bow tied in front.

But then, there were some things he didn't remember too. Or, perhaps, they were things that he had simply never noticed as a child. That didn't mean anything to him at the time. Like the dark circles under her ocean eyes. Like the dagger she wore at her hip—that she *always* wore, he realized.

Cedric didn't know what it all meant.

What he did know was that his mother's arms were warm as they wrapped around his small body. She was warm. She was *alive*.

And she was clearly concerned as to why Cedric still clung to her.

"What's wrong, my darling?" she asked, her smile turning down at the corners.

He wanted to shake his head. He didn't want to say anything that would jeopardize this moment, that would cause his mother to pull back or pull away. He wanted to stay in her arms, here and now—past, present, or whatever this was—forever.

But his small head nodded, tears lining his eyes, and Cedric realized he wasn't in control of his body like this. "I was frightened," he said, his voice high, young. "I thought I saw someone outside."

Every muscle in his mother's body tightened in response to his words. Her gaze fell somewhere behind Cedric's head, all vestiges of that smile flattened. But then she brushed a lock of hair from his face and took his chin between her thumb and forefinger. "I'm sure there's nothing there. But if there were, surely they got one glimpse of my brave, strong boy standing watch at the window and took off running."

Boots thudded softly behind him, and a large, strong hand clapped down on Cedric's shoulder. "Why don't I go take a look, just to be sure?" His father shot him a wink as Cedric caught his eye—the richest, warmest brown. The mirror of Cedric's own.

The surge of emotion welling in Cedric's chest threatened to break him. He wanted to shout. Wanted to scream, "No! Don't go out there!"

But he couldn't.

Instead, the boy sniffled. Nodded. And watched his father walk out the door for the final time—again.

Cedric's mother cleared her throat. "Now, about that supper," she said, gently unwrapping his arms from around her waist. "I hope you're hungry. Alouette prepared your favorite."

Something pounded against the door, and it was like all the warmth was suddenly sucked from the room. Shouts sounded from outside. Cedric's mother froze midstep.

"Lysander?" she called. "What's—"

"Go, Lennie!" came his father's muffled voice. "Take the boy and—"

The words cut off as the front door burst open. The wood groaned and splintered as it smashed into the wall. Screams sounded—Cedric's?—as his father soared back through the open doorway.

His body hit one of the chairs in front of the fire, toppling it.

"Cedric, don't!" cried his mother. But Cedric was not in charge of his young body as he darted forward to where his father had fallen.

The boy dropped to his knees with a wet, squelching sound, landing in the pool of crimson seeping from his father's body. Cedric felt his mother rush to his side, felt her hands grabbing at him, scrabbling to draw him to her—urging him to safety. But he couldn't move. Couldn't break his gaze from the gaping wound in his father's chest.

A chest that no longer rose, nor fell.

Three shadowy figures stormed in through the doorway, the firelight glinting off the wolven medallions hanging from their chests. Cedric couldn't make out their faces. It was as if the memory—the nightmare—obscured their features. Or perhaps this was truly how they had looked that night, their identities somehow masked, and Cedric had simply forgotten. Just as he'd forgotten what happened next.

His mother's forearm wrapped around his chest. "You cannot have it," she said, her voice like stone as she dragged Cedric against her. Her dagger was in her other hand. "You'll have to kill me first."

One of the figures laughed—a low, menacing sound. "You act as if that would be a problem for us, my lady," he said, tipping his head at Cedric's father's body. "But I've never been one to waste a good thing."

He nodded at his companions. They tore into the cottage, yanking drawers open, overturning furniture. They were searching for something. Cedric didn't know what. He didn't remember any of this. His ears were filled with nothing but crashing, slamming, scraping, and the desperate pounding of his own heart.

The companions returned. Whispered something in the first man's ear.

"Where is it?" he demanded.

Cedric's mother's mouth curved into a scornful smile, even as thick tears ran down her cheeks. "You'll never know."

Ribbons of darkest red shot from the man's hands, wrapping around Cedric's body, his arms, his legs—binding him. His mother cried out as he was yanked from her, the man drawing him to his side.

She moved quickly—quicker than Cedric ever knew her to be capable of moving. She raised her dagger, aimed it . . .

. . . and froze dead in her tracks.

Cedric felt the cold bite of steel against his face.

Now this—this he remembered.

The boy began to cry.

"Shh, little lordling," the man hissed. "You need to be quiet, or I won't be able to hear what your pretty mama says."

"Let him go," she begged, pressing a hand to her chest. "Let him go, and I'll tell you. Just let him go. Take me instead."

The broken look on her face made Cedric cry harder.

"What did I just tell you, boy?"

"Stop!" His mother's shout pierced the air as the knife sliced down, carving the scar Cedric would carry the rest of his life into his lip.

And this, he knew, must be the end. This was where his nightmares always ended. With screaming. With blood. His mother would die, and then Cedric would see and hear and feel nothing but the sweet relief of darkness as he passed out from the pain.

Not this time.

His bindings released as he crumpled to the floor, both hands covering his face. His blood was warm as it ran in rivulets down his chin and neck.

Too warm.

Hot.

Burning.

His face burned—burned like it was on fire.

No. Not his face. The floor. The air. The house.

The cottage was on fire.

Cedric peeked through his fingers, his palms still pressed to his mouth, trying to stem the bleeding, cushion the wound.

The cottage *was* on fire.

And so were the men.

They were screaming. Screaming and thrashing and writhing, clawing at flames that ate through their flesh with relentless hunger. It burned away their clothing, melted the medallions on their chests.

Movement caught Cedric's eye.

Through the flames, he saw her. Standing near the threshold, silhouetted by the roaring inferno, the locket hanging from her neck glinting in the firelight. He caught a glimpse of her face as she turned—fury and determination at war in her brilliant eyes. And something else, too. Something like . . . resignation?

Her dagger was still in her hand, the blade reflecting the flames like it was made of molten gold. She pointed it at the man, the leader of the trio. The one who'd given him his scar. The one who, though doubled over in pain, wasn't on fire anymore.

That wasn't what caught Cedric's attention.

It was the shadow coiling around his mother's feet. The tendrils of black smoke that wound up her legs, curled around her waist like the darkest embrace. The air rippled with power—achingly familiar, a ghost from some half-remembered dream.

Beyond the open doorway, a figure loomed—cloaked, clouded, covered in shadows. A fourth member of this group who'd managed to shatter Cedric's entire existence in a single night.

Unbidden, the words fell from Cedric's own young lips: "The Revenant."

He'd had it wrong all this time. He hadn't *heard* the name that night. He'd *said* it.

Cedric saw the shape of evil approaching his mother as she stood tall, ignorant of the threat at her back even as she readied herself to fight the one to her front. He saw the darkness, and his child's mind told him it was the Revenant, the boogeyman, the shadow-born legend from the cautionary tales he'd been told.

And now Cedric could do nothing but watch as those shadows crept up his mother's body, circling closer and closer to her heart.

She hurled the dagger at the man in front of her. He screamed in pain as it lodged in his thigh. Her gaze met Cedric's again. She said something he couldn't hear, couldn't make out. Then she mouthed three little words.

Those, he did understand.

She smiled that knowing smile, meant only for him.

Behind her, the figure clenched a fist, and the shadows tore his mother apart.

"No!" Cedric—past and present, child and adult—cried out. And then darkness surged, and finally, finally, he felt nothing more.

CHAPTER 23
INTO DARKNESS

Elyria

Elyria didn't know how long she fought. Didn't know how many lives she took.

The world was a haze of chaos, flickering flames, and the metallic tang of blood. Shadows swirled around her—intoxicating, maddening. Her thoughts were muddled, fragmented as they blurred together—the faces of the cultists she continued cutting through on the battlefield, the cries of the dying, the pulse of twisted power thrumming in her veins.

She swung the shadow-forged blade in a wide arc, cleaving through another enemy. They evaporated into mist. Confusion stole Elyria's breath as the slain bodies and battling soldiers surrounding her dissipated—dust on the wind.

And then Elyria was alone.

Utterly, completely alone.

Darkness descended once more, that endless void curling around her, surrounding her, enveloping her.

This is who you are, the darkness whispered in her ear.

This isn't real, she tried to say back.

It's who you've always been. A monster. A creature of vengeance. Darkness infinite.

"Get out of my head!" she screamed—in her mind, outside of it, the past bleeding into the present.

Elyria fell to her knees, head clutched in her bloody hands, shadows coiling tight around her torso. The images in her mind warped and melded together. Two hundred years of constant vigilance. Of doing everything—anything—she could to keep the darkness under control, keep it chained, keep it buried. Two centuries of fear over slipping, over what would happen if she ever let it out again.

Two centuries filled with regret and sorrow over the few times she had.

Hardly anyone knew. Not even Kit. There were whispers, to be sure. Rumors of what happened on the battlefield outside Castle Lumin. But that's all they were. Elyria had kept the truth locked away—entombed so deep inside her that it only surfaced in her darkest moments. No, her weakest ones.

Except for him.

Evander had known. Had been there the first time she slipped. The first time since the Battle of Luminaria that shadows tore out of her, seeking blood and vengeance. It wasn't a lapse born of malice; she knew that. It had been a reflex. A defense. The outpost where she was stationed was nearly overwhelmed, one of the remaining cells of Malakar's cultists having infiltrated in the night. The chaos was unbearable—soldiers falling all around her, crystal arrows piercing wings, puncturing armor.

Elyria was already bloodied, weary after fighting to push the enemy back, to force them past the boundaries of the outpost so the wards could be reinforced. She couldn't get them all out. And she'd been so busy battling another wave of cultists that she hadn't noticed the single *sanguinagi* advancing on a trio of young soldiers—barely more than recruits—who were scrambling to hold the line.

They didn't stand a chance. She could see it in their eyes—could *feel* their terror as the blood mage stalked toward them, a glowing crystal sword materializing in his hands. Their fear, their desperation, their hopelessness. It cracked something inside her.

She felt the darkness claw its way to the surface. It whispered such sweet promises. She could save them. She could stop this. Stop it all. All she had to do was let go.

So, she did.

And when the darkness finally receded, when the shadows slithered back into the depths of her soul, there was nothing left.

Not of the *sanguinagi* she meant to stop.

Not of the young soldiers she meant to save.

She'd killed them all.

Evander found her afterward, huddled in a corner of the ruined courtyard. Shaking, frayed, broken.

He hadn't flinched.

Hadn't recoiled from the monster she was.

He'd held her close. Told her she wasn't alone. That he would stay with her, would help her, would *fix* this.

Elyria knew better. Knew there was no fixing this. There was no going back from what she'd done.

It didn't stop Evander from trying. And twenty-five years ago, when he declared to Elyria and Kit and his mother and the entirety of the Ravenswing estate that he would be entering the Arcane Crucible to win the Crown of Concord—for glory and country, for their people—she knew.

She knew he was doing it for her.

Elyria's breath hitched. It was her fault he'd entered the Crucible. Her fault he'd gotten tangled up in this mad quest for an unwinnable prize. Did the Crown of Concord even exist anymore? For all anyone knew, Daephinia could have shattered it into a thousand pieces. The prize at the end of this endless trial could be nothing more than a few fragments of power. Hardly worth dying over.

But that's what Evander was. Dead.

Because of her.

Guilt weighed Elyria down. It crushed her, flattened her to the ground. The shadows curled closer, chains that tightened around her.

You see your power. You know what you are capable of, said the darkness, almost lovingly. Like what she was *capable of* was in any way a good thing. Something she should be proud of. Something she should *want*.

Embrace us, it crooned. *Let us make you what you were always meant to be. Our dark weapon. Our queen of shadow.*

For a moment, Elyria's resolve wavered. Part of her—some small, terrified part—wanted to believe the darkness. Wanted to stop fighting, stop trying. The darkness would give her strength. It would take away this fear, this guilt. It would be a buoy in the sea of loneliness constantly threatening to drown her.

Only power would remain.

No, she thought. The word was quiet, just a whisper in her mind. She needed to get out, needed to be free of this. The ground trembled beneath her as her wild magic fought to cut through the darkness, roots bursting forth, thrashing wildly. But the shadows only constricted, and she let out a cry of pain as they cut into her skin.

The darkness laughed. *You've been hiding for so, so long. Cowering in the light. Weak. Afraid of who you really are.*

Elyria shuddered. Her hands shook as the shadows slid through her fingers—ice-cold, unyielding. Her limbs went numb, the cold seeping into her bones. She *was* weak. She *was* afraid. And she was so tired of fighting.

Come. Come now and embrace the dark.

The shadows crept up her body, both smothering and sheltering. They offered power. They threatened to consume her.

Her blood pulsed in rhythm with her heartbeat—erratic, frenzied. Her breath hitched as she teetered on the edge of surrender.

And then a voice broke through her mind. A voice filled with warmth, conjuring a memory of black hair and golden eyes.

"You're the strongest person I know, Elle," Evander said. "You bend, you bleed, but you always rise. Don't run from yourself. You don't have to hide."

The corners of Elyria's eyes prickled at the memory. Evander had believed her worth saving. How would it honor his memory—his sacrifice—if she gave up now?

It wouldn't.

She couldn't.

But Elyria didn't know if she had it in her to continue the fight. For years, for *centuries*, she had struggled to keep the shadow inside her at bay. Rejected it. Denied it. Hidden it.

And what had that accomplished? It was still here. She was still drowning in it. Haunted by it.

It would never go away. It was part of her.

Something shifted. Warmth—the smallest spark—ignited in Elyria's blood, spread through her veins in a slow, deliberate wave. It banished the chill that had taken root in her, replacing it with a new kind of fire.

The constricting bind of the shadows loosened.

Realization bloomed within her—a seedling pushing through cracked stone.

The darkness was not just part of her.

It *was* her.

It was *hers*.

Elyria's heartbeat steadied. She let out a long breath. The thrashing roots surrounding her calmed. The blackness that held her vision hostage dissipated.

"You're mine," she whispered. "You're me."

The shadows coiled around her, a thick smoke that settled on her shoulders, wisps trailing down her arms. Watching. Waiting.

A flicker of doubt gnawed at the edges of Elyria's mind. What if she was wrong? What if this would cement her as the very monster she feared becoming?

She shook her head, Evander's words ringing in her ears. She'd already spent a lifetime fearing her inner darkness. She feared what it would make her do, what it would force her to become. But that was never her truth. She was the one doing the forcing. She never tried to control it, not really. All she ever did was shove it away, locking her power behind a dam that was always bound to crack.

The shadows didn't define her.

She defined them.

Tell us who you are, demanded the darkness.

Tears blurred her vision. Her voice strengthened. "I am Elyria

Lightbreaker. The Revenant. And I may have been left broken, but I am not so easily shattered."

She flexed her hands. The shadows stilled. Then they flowed back into her, the chaos settling, melding with the wild magic in her blood. Her fingertips tingled. The luminous warmth of her magic mingled with the cool tendrils of shadow . . . and something new emerged.

New, and yet also, somehow, familiar.

Something balanced.

The darkness wasn't gone. She could still feel it there, in that pit deep inside her. But it was no longer a suffocating weight. It was no longer some feral, sleeping beast she feared waking. It no longer felt like an enemy.

It felt like power. No longer divided, but whole.

Her power.

Strength flowed through Elyria's veins like wildfire, raw and unfiltered.

Hers to wield. Hers to shape. Hers to command.

The blood-soaked battlefield around her began to flicker, the illusion unraveling. Elyria stood tall, her wings unfurling in a blaze of shimmering color that matched the aurora dancing overhead. The twisted landscape of smoke and death dissolved into mist. And she was left standing alone in the void once more, whole and steady.

That was the moment she felt it. A pulse of fear. A distant *tug*.

A voice called to her through the endless nothing.

And then she was falling—through the void, through memories, through illusions.

Her nose stung with the acrid scent of smoke. The crackle of burning wood filled her ears. Elyria stood facing a blazing cottage, the entire front wall collapsed. Amidst the flames, she could make out a small table, some overturned chairs. And there, in the center of the open room, curled up in a ball on the floor as fire danced around him, was Cedric Thorne.

CHAPTER 24
THROUGH THE FIRE

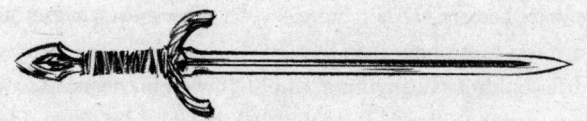

Cedric

Cold.

He was so cold.

And yet heat was everywhere. Cedric could feel the flames licking his skin as the cottage burned. He didn't know where the man had gone, the wielder of shadow and blood. The one who'd torn his beautiful, kind mother from this life. There were no bodies. Not the mangled, charred intruders. Not Cedric's father, bloody and brutalized on the floor.

Cedric wasn't even sure his own body was there. If it was, it was no longer the six-year-old frame he'd been trapped inside, unable to speak his thoughts or move of his own accord as he relived the worst night of his existence.

Cedric was alone.

Cold and so, so alone.

And then, suddenly, he wasn't.

A voice stretched through the haze—soft, lyrical. It wove between the crackling flames and wisps of smoke. Familiar. Comforting in a way that made Cedric's raw nerves settle for the first time since this nightmare began.

"You're all right," the voice murmured. "You're safe. I've got you."

Cedric's head throbbed. He closed his eyes, but the images of what he'd just seen—the memories—were seared behind his eyelids.

Soft singing filled his ears, cutting through the phantom screams in his head. He didn't know the song, but as he felt a hand on his back, moving in slow, concentric circles, Cedric's thudding heart calmed ever so slightly.

"We need to move," said the voice. "Can you get up?"

He pulled at the edges of his thoughts, trying to weave them together into some sort of sensible mass. Each time he thought he might have pinned one down, it slipped away.

The voice became sterner, more severe. "Come back to me," it commanded. "You're stronger than this."

Cedric couldn't say anything. Couldn't even lift his head to look in the direction of the voice. He was worried that if he did, it would disappear too. He didn't want it to. There was something about it. It *tugged* at him, a golden thread tied to something deep in his chest.

Something else was tugging at him too. Not in his chest but at his arm. Both arms. Someone was pulling at them, yanking them up. "By the stars, get your ass up and *move*, Cedric!"

Oh, the voice was mad now.

Cedric's heart pounded in his chest as he slowly lifted his head, blinking away the sting of smoke. His blurred vision took in the figure attempting to lug his heavy body across the smoldering cottage floor. Small, strong hands gripping his wrists. His eyes traveled up slender arms to the waves of golden hair draped over each shoulder.

For a moment, he dared to hope. Dared to believe that somehow, impossibly, his mother had survived. That she was here, now, calling to him, pulling him from this nightmare.

And then a sweet almond scent cut through the noxious smell of embers and ash, and Cedric jolted up.

Because those weren't his mother's golden waves. It was the firelight reflecting off the hair cascading down the figure's shoulders. And those were *wings* looming behind her head.

His vision clearing, reality slammed into Cedric with a cold, hard edge. It wasn't her. Of course it wasn't her.

It was Elyria.

Relief surged through him, dizzying and disorienting—a wave that hit him so suddenly he barely had time to take a breath. She was here. She was okay. And for one bewildering, baffling moment, that was all that mattered.

Something between a gasp and a laugh escaped Cedric's mouth as he lurched to his feet. She dropped his wrists, a small sound of surprise slipping from her lips as she backed up until she was outside the cottage. Cedric followed, his fingers outstretched, reaching out as if he needed to confirm that she was really here.

The Revenant was here.

Jagged, raw mistrust suddenly clawed its way up from deep in Cedric's gut. *Why* was she here? How did she find him? Was this another trick of the Crucible, another part of this hellscape? Had this stars-forsaken trial not broken him enough already?

The hand he'd reached toward Elyria clenched into a fist. His pulse spiked. His mind reeled. The whats and hows and whys all ran together in a muddy, thorny mess. And at the center of it all—*her*.

Cedric's gaze snapped to her. "You," he hissed. "This was you, wasn't it? You did this."

Elyria's green eyes widened, something Cedric thought looked strangely like hurt flashing across her face. It lasted only a fraction of a second, however, and her typical cool, defensive mask was back on before Cedric could be certain of what he saw.

"What in the deepest quarter of hell are you on about?" she said, her mouth twisted in a scowl.

"I—" Cedric's voice trembled with the weight of his confusion. Was it the Revenant he'd seen? Was it *her*? "I heard your name."

"So you've mentioned," she said drily, though her eyes went to their surroundings as if trying to piece together where they were, what she was missing.

"Don't play innocent," he snarled, moving further into her space.

She compensated with an immediate step back, her wings vanishing with a wisp of magic as she narrowed her eyes at Cedric. Like she didn't want him getting too close to them.

"You think I'm involved in *this*?" She waved an arm at the smoldering cottage behind Cedric. "That whatever twisted nightmare you've been living is my fault?" Her voice was like ice. "I just fought through my own trial—quite literally. Even if I had the energy or the inclination, how in the four hells would I be able to mess with yours?"

Cedric wasn't listening. His mind was spiraling, pieces of the nightmare still bleeding into reality. He touched his hand to the scar on his lip, and when he drew it back, blood stained his fingertips.

Everything hurt. His lip, his mind, his heart. It was all too real, too fresh, too painful. And she was here. Standing right in front of him. The final piece in a puzzle he didn't understand but that he knew he needed to solve. Like the trial itself was telling him that her being here was *wrong*.

Something inside Cedric snapped. Fury rose in his chest, hot, searing, ready to burst free. The overwhelming mix of relief, confusion, and betrayal erupted.

Deep, deep inside, he might have known she wasn't responsible. She wasn't there. It wasn't her. But she knew *something*. She must. And he would get it out of her one way or another.

He lunged at her.

"What are you doing?" Elyria hissed as she dodged his attack. "I am not your enemy, you absolute plonker."

The line stirred something in Cedric's memory. He ignored it. Pivoting in the dirt, he charged at her again.

She countered with a sharp jab of her elbow to his side. "Stop this!"

The move didn't hurt Cedric, but it did cause him to stumble. He caught himself on the trunk of a nearby tree, then spun to face her, teeth bared. "Stop lying to me!"

"You've completely lost it," she said, eyes blazing. "I'm not—"

"Then tell me *why*!" Cedric's voice cracked as he threw a punch, his fist meeting the air when she ducked and rolled to the side. "Why is something inside me telling me that everything is tied to *you*? Did you orchestrate it? Did you lead them to us?"

Elyria's breath hitched. "You still think I'm behind your family's deaths." It wasn't a question. "Is that what this place showed you? Made you relive?" Her eyes flickered with something that looked like pity.

He hated it.

Cedric's hands trembled.

Her voice softened. "It wasn't real, Cedric. Not this time, at least. Whatever this place showed you, it's trying to break you. Don't let it."

Cedric touched the mana token hanging around his neck, and Elyria tensed as if bracing for another attack. But as suddenly as it came on, the fight drained out of him.

He ran a finger down the smooth front of the token, tracing the lightning-like streaks in the stone. "I'm not sure I know what's real anymore." His voice cracked. "How do I know *you* are real?"

"I don't know," she admitted, her voice quiet. "Sometimes *I* don't even know if I'm real. But even if I had an answer"—she breathed a laugh—"I somehow doubt there's anything I could say that would convince you. You just have to trust."

"Trust *you*?"

"Trust *yourself*. And yes, ideally, trust me while you're at it." She raised her hands, palms out in supplication. "I know how impossible that seems, believe me. But trust is a blade sharpened on both sides. It can cut, yes. But it also protects."

Cedric's shoulders slumped, her words slicing at the chaos in his head. It wasn't enough to clear it. "I don't know how," he said.

Elyria shifted her weight as if she meant to go to him, then thought better of it. "We start small, then. One simple truth. If you believe nothing else in this world, Sir Thorne, trust what I say next."

She inhaled deeply, like some grand confession was about to fall from her lips.

Cedric held his breath.

"I. Don't. Want. To. Be. Here. Anymore." She punctuated each word with a clap of her hands, her face the epitome of petulance.

A choked laugh broke from Cedric's throat.

The corner of Elyria's lip quivered. "So, we don't have to like it—we don't even have to like each other." She paused, daring him to respond to that obvious bait.

He held his tongue.

With a small sigh, she continued. "But I don't think I'm getting out of here without you. After all, this is your show, so to speak. I wouldn't even know where to begin finding a way out. What do you say?"

"Fine," Cedric muttered, pleased to find his hoarse voice hid the amusement he felt. "But if you—"

Elyria cut him off with a wave of her hand. "Yeah, yeah. 'If you betray me, I'll make you regret it.' Something like that, right?"

He wanted to smile at that, though he couldn't manage anything more than an exhausted exhale. Still, for the first time in what felt like hours—days, months, years—something light blossomed in Cedric's chest.

He and Elyria were bruised and battered both, each treading dangerous waters. But something had shifted.

It wasn't trust—not quite. But a truce, fragile and tentative.

It was a start.

"You're not alone in this, Cedric," she said, as if in answer to his very thoughts. Her voice rang like a bell, rinsing away the final traces of cloudiness in his mind.

"And if you still feel like throwing punches," she continued, "save it for whatever's waiting in the next trial. Or for Belien's smug face." She gave him a playful whack, her forearm connecting with his shoulder.

Then she winced, a breath hissing from between her clenched teeth.

"What? What is it?" Cedric asked, his words coming out in a frantic jumble that was far from how he'd intended.

"It's nothing," she said.

But Cedric didn't miss the way her hand twitched toward her forearm, the way her brow pinched in pain.

"You're hurt."

"I'm fine."

"Show me," he demanded.

With an overly dramatic roll of her eyes, she acquiesced, sticking her arm straight out in front of her like a child.

Cedric's eyes immediately went to the raw, pink skin on the underside of her forearm. Burned.

"How did this happen?" He turned her arm over in his hands, checking the rest of her for injury.

"Oh, I don't know. Couldn't possibly have been when I was trying to lug two hundred pounds of human deadweight out of a burning building, could it?"

Cedric wanted to retort, but guilt twisted at him. "I-I'm sorry."

She waved him off. "I've had worse." Her free hand flexed over her leg, like she was about to rub her thigh but stopped herself. She coughed. "Got it worse in my own trial, to be honest."

She pulled a corner of her blouse out from her waistband, lifting it to reveal a line of smooth pale skin over her stomach.

Cedric cursed himself for the way his pulse jumped at the sight.

"What are you doing?" he said quickly, dropping her forearm like it was suddenly poisonous.

"Calm yourself, Sir Prude. I just wanted to show you where I . . ." She trailed off. "Huh. That's odd."

"What's odd?"

"I got a nasty slice here when I was—" She paused. "I suppose it really was just all part of the illusion, wasn't it?"

An illusion. But if her trial had been nothing more than an illusion—a compelling, mind-bending one, he was sure, but an illusion nonetheless—then why had *his* trial left her nursing a burn wound?

If Elyria was wondering the same, he couldn't tell. No, she'd abandoned her own injury and was now running her eyes over Cedric's body. Scanning him, inspecting him.

"Where are you hurt? Where are your burns?" she asked, a fervency in her voice that only made the guilt burrow deeper in Cedric's gut.

He glanced at himself—checked his arms, his legs. His clothing was seared, scorched in places. He knew he'd felt the heat of the flames lapping at him. Yet, he couldn't find a single mark, any sign of where the fire had touched his skin.

It made no sense.

The lines between reality and whatever this was blurred further. Cedric didn't understand this trial, this test. What was the point of all this? Of any of it? How did this prove someone worthy of the crown?

"When I figure that out, I'll let you know," Elyria said.

Cedric ground his jaw. He hadn't realized he'd spoken aloud. Releasing an exasperated breath, he raked his hand through his hair, pushing a stray curl from his brow.

Elyria watched him closely, some emotion he couldn't identify on her porcelain face.

Cedric coughed. "How did you get here? How did you get out of . . . ?"

"Of my own personally curated nightmare?"

"Yes."

"I'm not exactly sure. Helpful, I know."

He snorted in affirmation.

"I just . . . I was there. I was surrounded by this—I don't know how to describe it. This nothingness, this—"

"—void." The word nearly got stuck in Cedric's throat.

A quizzical expression flitted over her face. "Yes, exactly. I had just . . ." She cast her eyes down, and Cedric thought—not for the first time—that she didn't seem to be doing that well with this whole trust thing either.

"You had just . . . ?" he prompted.

She looked up at him. When her jewel-toned eyes met his, Cedric had to actively work at *not* tearing his gaze away. They were so full of pain, so full of vulnerability. In them, he saw years of pent-up agony, of loneliness. But there was also the tiniest glimmer of hope. Some new kind of peace he would've sworn wasn't there before.

He didn't know what to make of it.

Apparently, neither did she. Because the next thing he knew, she was barreling on as if nothing had happened.

"I fell through the void, or it sucked me into it, or something happened. And then I was here. But I'm not sure I'm supposed to be? All I know is I heard—" She cut herself off again.

"You heard me," Cedric finished for her.

She nodded.

She'd heard him. She'd come for him.

He tried to sidestep how that revelation made him feel.

"Suppose you were able to get back to that void," Cedric said with forced lightness. "Suppose someone knew where one was around here. Do you think it would carry us out? Take us back?"

"I think it's as ridiculous and foolhardy a plan as anything else we might come up with." She grinned. "Let's give it a shot."

So, with a final look at the smoldering remnants of his childhood home—the illusion of it, the reality of it—Cedric and Elyria set off into the woods.

Reaching the wooden bridge didn't take long.

Working up the courage to jump off it did.

Every cell in Cedric's body screamed at him not to do it. Told him this was *the* absolute stupidest thing he could do, and four hells, was he *actually* contemplating this, and didn't he remember that this was still a competition? Shouldn't he be more suspicious that she was trying to get him to leap off a bridge?

Sweat beaded at his brow, his heart thundering as they stood on the edge of that void, staring into the endless nothing. But ultimately, when Elyria's hand wrapped around his, when her eyes met his with hope and, yes, *trust* beaming from them, Cedric leapt.

CHAPTER 25
A GILDED DAGGER

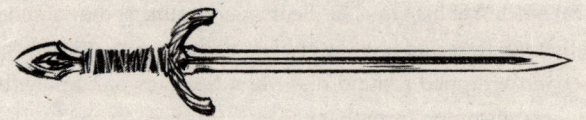

Cedric

Magic rippled around Cedric. The dark of the void exploded in a dazzling display of starlight and color as he and Elyria fell. It was like falling through worlds.

And then he was surrounded by stacked stone and closed walls. Torchlight glinted off his armor, neatly stacked in a corner. Their weapons were still propped against the wall.

They were back.

In front of them, the door to the main chamber, the one that had conveniently disappeared when they'd entered the room, sat open.

For a moment, Cedric and Elyria stood there, as if neither of them could quite believe that it was over. That they'd survived another trial. That they were one step closer to the crown.

Cedric opened his mouth. He closed it. He knew he should say something. He *wanted* to say something.

He just didn't have a single fucking clue what to say.

Not as his pulse was still a staccato beat in his veins, a stuttering reminder of everything he'd just been forced to witness—and all that happened after.

Should he be thanking her? The thought gnawed at him, bitter and relentless. He was supposed to be the strong one, the one blazing through these trials on his own merit. He'd trained for this. He was *meant* for this.

Yet here he was, all too aware that if it weren't for Elyria, he might still be trapped in that nightmare.

This didn't feel like a victory. It felt like he'd cheated, like he'd been carried to safety while the others faced their demons alone.

If Elyria shared his concerns, she certainly didn't show it. She was already in motion, her hand slipping from Cedric's as she scooped up her weapons and strode confidently toward the door.

He flexed his fingers against the absence of her.

Pushing what happened during the trial to the back of his mind, Cedric forced his feet to move. He couldn't name the emotions rolling through him as he strapped his gauntlets to his waist alongside his sword and dagger after donning his armor once more. Armor that felt somehow both heavier and lighter than it did before.

His eyes widened as he took in the scene in the Sanctum. The gilded table that spanned nearly the entire length of the room. The sumptuous display of roasted meats, ripe fruits, goblets brimming with wine and tankards full of ale. His fellow champions settled in large velvet dining chairs along both sides.

Flickering candles cast a golden glow over the tablescape, but the atmosphere was far from celebratory. Kit, Zephyr, and Thraigg had commandeered a corner at the near end of the table. Gael and Cyren sat across from them, exchanging stilted words. Tenebris Nox was by their lonesome, unsurprisingly, a few seats down.

Cedric found Belien and Leona at the other end of the table, scowls of disappointment evident on their faces as they muttered to each other under their breath.

The champions sat mostly in silence, poking at the food on their plates or taking long, deep pulls from their cups. All except for Thraigg, who seemed entirely delighted as he tore into a dripping drumstick with gusto.

Elyria stood at Kit's side. It had taken Cedric a few minutes to get his armor back on, so he hadn't witnessed their reunion. But from the soft expressions on both their faces and the way their little fingers remained affectionately hooked together, it wasn't hard to guess what they were both feeling. Relief, joy, perhaps the lingering hint of fear. It radiated from them both, like neither of them fully believed the other was there. That they'd both made it through.

Cedric's chest tightened as he watched Elyria murmur something to Kit, too low for him to hear. Kit nodded vigorously before wiping at the inner corner of her eye.

Cedric looked away, suddenly feeling like he was intruding.

"There he is!" boomed Thraigg, his words garbled in his full mouth as he waved Cedric over.

"Here I am," Cedric replied, exhaustion carrying him to an empty seat beside the dwarf.

"Took the two of ye damn well long enough. We've been waiting for *ages*." Balancing the drumstick between his teeth, Thraigg stretched across the table and grabbed a flagon of ale. Swaying slightly, he attempted to fill Cedric's empty tankard for him.

"Here, let me." Cedric reached for the flagon just as Thraigg jolted from a whole-body hiccup, sloshing ale over Cedric's outstretched hands.

"Whoopsie," slurred the dwarf, and Cedric couldn't help but grin at the juxtaposition of a word like that coming from someone who looked like him. He turned toward Elyria, curious to see if she'd heard the dwarf's unexpected exclamation. For some reason, he just knew she'd find it hilarious. But she was facing the other direction, having slipped into the chair next to Kit with a goblet of wine in one hand and an entire loaf of bread in the other.

A petite green face popped into Cedric's line of sight, cutting Elyria off from view. He couldn't tell if the reflexive emotion that flared in his chest was one born of gratitude or irritation.

Zephyr held out a cloth napkin.

"Ah, thank you," Cedric said. He took it and wiped the liquid from his hands. "I'm relieved to see you made it through."

She smiled, though it didn't quite meet her eyes. Cedric wondered what past horror she'd been forced to relive during the trial.

"I, too, am very glad to see you," she said quietly.

"Aye. We had a grand old time fighting our demons, didn't we, Zeph?" Thraigg said. "I must admit, though, she made for piss-poor company in there. All that pacing and wringing of her little hands. She seemed far more worried about ye than about the two of us getting through the trial."

Cedric swore the sylvan's cheeks turned a darker shade of green.

"I wasn't *worried*," she insisted. "I just wasn't sure where you'd gone, and it caught me off guard." Her eyes darted to the doors lining the back wall. "Thought we were heading to the same place. That's all."

"As did I," Cedric said, reaching for the now overfull tankard of ale in front of him. Its amber contents rippled as he took a careful sip. Then another, less careful one. And another, which was really more like a gulp.

He hadn't realized how desperately he needed a drink until this moment.

"But I suppose all's well that ends well," he continued after finally setting the tankard down, nearly drained. "Even if I ended up with a far less pleasant partner than I would have liked."

The good-natured jibe was barely more than a conspiratorial whisper in Zephyr's ear, inaudible to anyone else. But that didn't stop Elyria's head from whipping to the right, her eyes narrowing on Cedric as if she'd heard every word.

Already feeling emboldened from the ale, he tipped his chin at the fae with a lopsided grin. She responded by chugging the contents of the goblet in her hand.

He turned his attention back to Thraigg. "Are we the last to arrive?"

"Aye." The dwarf hiccupped. "Wait, no. Still waiting on that mousy li'l human bloke—the healer."

"Alden." Cedric scanned the remaining champions, confirming that the saint wasn't there.

Thraigg blinked slowly before nodding, like the action took some effort. "And that other fae fellow, too. With the blinding hair."

"His name is Paelin." Gael's voice cut across the table with no hint of the colorful humor Cedric had come to expect from her.

"I'm sure he will arrive any moment," said Cyren, tucking a lock of blue hair behind his ear. He patted Gael's shoulder, but Cedric caught the uncertainty flickering in his eyes.

Across the table, Elyria nodded in agreement as she refilled her goblet.

"That's what that ginger twit said 'bout the other one," Thraigg muttered.

Gael tensed.

Elyria shot Thraigg a warning glare.

"How long have you been waiting?" Cedric asked—an attempt to shift the dwarf's drunken focus.

Thraigg took a long drag of his drink before shrugging. "Dunno. A while."

Cedric was too exhausted to stop himself from rolling his eyes. "Very helpful."

"You two did seem to take quite a while. We thought . . ." Zephyr trailed off.

Cedric leaned back in his chair, understanding washing over him. The nervous way Kit clung to Elyria made a lot more sense now. They'd already thought them lost.

"Well, if we managed to squeak through," Elyria said, a sudden lightness in her voice that Cedric suspected was very much forced, "then I'm sure Paelin isn't far behind." Her green eyes met Cedric's for the briefest moment before flitting back to Gael.

For a long time, nobody spoke. Despite his efforts to dispel the tension in the room, it hung heavy in the air—a storm waiting to break. Cedric could see it in the way Gael's restless fingers tapped against the table, in the suspicious squint of Belien's eyes, in the perpetual sneer gracing Leona's lips. They may have survived the Trial of Spirit, may have all faced their truths, but bonds of camaraderie were thin, sparse, primed to snap.

Leona's sharp voice shattered the silence. "How long are we to be expected to continue waiting?"

"As long as it takes, Blackwood," said Gael.

"You had no problem moving right on when the one we were waiting for was my sister," Belien spat. "But now that it's your little fairy friend, I suppose we should wait forever. Is that right?"

Cedric's hand tightened around his tankard.

Lethal calm blazed in Gael's eyes. "The Crucible moved on. Is it my fault that the Arbiter declared the trial over? I would have waited as long as necessary. I expect whether Paelin will—"

"And Alden," Leona chimed in.

"I expect whether Paelin and Alden"—Gael's jaw ticked—"will best the trial still has yet to be determined."

Belien, evidently incapable of *not* stirring the pot, leaned forward with a smirk. "I think it's time you face the truth, Winters. After all, that's what the trial was all about, wasn't it? Your buddy is dead."

The air in the room shot up several degrees. The tangy scent of vinegar filled the air, along with the sound of . . . bubbling?

Cedric's chest tingled as he looked down. Gael Winters, flamecaller, had one hand flattened on top of the table. The other was wrapped around her metal goblet . . . which was full of *boiling* wine.

"Gael," Cyren murmured—a gentle warning.

"It's not personal," Leona added quickly, an attempt to soothe the escalating situation. Even she could not ignore the magic pulsing off Gael in angry waves. "Not all of us were cut out for the demands of the Trial of Spirit. Just look at how long it took Lightbreaker and Lord Church's golden boy."

Cedric ignored the cloud of shame hanging over his head.

He didn't know if it was ignorance or malice that drove Belien to say what he did next, but either way it was very, very stupid.

"Yes, exactly," Belien said haughtily. "Some of us are simply weak."

Gael looked ready to burst into flame.

Elyria spoke before she could. "You don't know what you're talking about. That trial forced us to confront our deepest fears, our darkest memories. It called on things that would fell even the toughest and strongest among us. If you think someone weak after they've stared down their worst nightmare, even if the nightmare won in the end, you're a greater fool than I thought."

Hard though that may be to imagine, Cedric quoted in his mind, remembering the way she'd hurled nearly those exact words at him before the trial.

"... hard though that may be to imagine," Elyria finished.

Cedric buried his grin in his tankard. It was rather nice when her vitriol was aimed at someone who actually deserved it.

Unfortunately, her words did not land with Belien the same way they had with Cedric. The sorcerer simply did not seem to care.

"Is that defensiveness I detect rankling the mighty Revenant?" Belien asked snidely.

"And is it for yourself . . . or on Sir Thorne's behalf, I wonder?" added Leona, her eyes narrowing on Cedric.

Her suspicious gaze was like a punch in the gut. Did she know? Did she know that he'd been unable to best the Trial of Spirit on his own? That the only reason he'd made it out of there, that he wasn't still trapped like Alden and Paelin, was because of Elyria?

He hadn't endured. He'd been dragged out of the darkness by someone stronger, someone who had faced down her own demons and still had the strength to save him. The others won their trials; Cedric had merely escaped his.

And somehow, Leona knew.

"Shut up, Blackwood," said Kit, interrupting Cedric's guilt-driven spiral.

"Was she talking to you, pixie?" Belien spat, his tone so vitriolic Cedric might have slapped him had he been closer.

Elyria stood, the movement so abrupt that it sent her chair scraping back several inches before toppling over. "By the fucking stars, how many times does the Arbiter have to say the word 'unity' before you two get it through your thick human skulls?"

Leona rolled her eyes. "You truly expect me to believe a death dealer like you is out here preaching harmony?"

"And what exactly is it that *you* hope to achieve by being an asshole? Other than making me want to crack said skull against this table."

"There! You see?" Leona slammed her goblet down, red wine splashing across the polished wood. "See how she threatens me? Unity, my *ass*."

"Can you blame her? We all have our limits," Nox muttered—an uncharacteristic contribution.

Thraigg snorted into his tankard.

"You're so blinded by your arrogance and bigotry, you can't even see how you are fighting against your own interests here," Elyria said, waving her arms animatedly. "Why would the Arbiter be constantly preaching the necessity of unity if it wasn't, oh, I don't know, *necessary*?"

Leona raised her goblet in a mock-toast. "Well, thank the celestials we have the Revenant here. Our ever-present reminder of the consequences of not sitting down and shutting up like good little humans. Will you slaughter us the way you slaughtered our people during the war?"

Elyria stilled, a sudden calmness overtaking her features that sent a chill down Cedric's spine. This was about to take a very bad turn.

"For fuck's sake, that's *enough*, Leona!" Cedric slammed his fist on the table. "Stop antagonizing every stars-damned champion that's left. We've all been through it today. We don't know what's ahead. Fighting among ourselves won't get any of us closer to the crown."

"Maybe not. But if it keeps it out of *their* hands, it'll still be worth it," Leona said. "You may have gone soft as shit on these magic-hoarding cretins, but not all of us are so quick to forget our roots, *Sir Thorne*."

With a huff, she turned to face Belien, content enough with having gotten the last word to end the conversation.

Belien, as it turned out, was not.

"Fairy fucker," he muttered, distinctly *not* under his breath. "All his morals tossed in the gutter for a soft piece of fae ass."

In a flash, Cedric was on his feet. He reached for his token before he could stop himself, heat flaring in his chest. He'd teach Belien to watch his words, to think twice before acting this way again. Even if it meant breaking whatever nebulous, unspoken truce the champions had been operating under thus far. He would pay the price, if it meant Belien paid one too.

Turns out, it didn't matter.

Because before Cedric could activate a single spark of his magic, a tendril of shadow had shot out from Elyria's outstretched hand and wrapped around Belien's neck.

Zephyr gasped. Leona screamed.

"What was that you said?" Elyria's voice was a gilded dagger— beautiful and deadly. "Not sure I heard you correctly."

Belien clawed at the shadow with both hands, straining for breath.

Cedric's stomach turned as he watched Elyria's magic coil around Belien's neck. He had heard tales of the power of the Revenant, of course. Spent night after night imagining it, dreaming of what it would be like to face it. To face her. To bleed her power from her, watch the light drain from her eyes, his parents' deaths avenged.

Seeing her wield it now was everything and nothing like he imagined.

It was so dark. So devastating. So breathtaking.

So similar to the power he had just watched tear his mother into pieces.

"Nightwielder." Nox's red-black eyes were locked on Elyria. Their voice was a reverent whisper, barely audible over Leona's screams and Belien's labored wheezing.

Kit stared at Elyria too, her mouth agape. Like this was the first time she was truly seeing her friend.

The shadow cinched tighter. Belien's face started turning purple.

That golden thread in Cedric's chest propelled him forward until he stood beside Elyria. Her body shook, though whether from the strain of using this dark magic or from *restraining* herself from using more of it, he didn't know.

"Elyria," he murmured into her ear, his voice low. "That's enough."

She didn't react.

He lifted his hand. Paused. Drew it back. Then, with as gentle a touch as he could manage, he placed two fingers on the side of her chin and turned her face toward him.

Magic sparked where their skin met, sending a shock zipping through Cedric. Elyria, too, from the sudden way her arm fell, her shadow dissipating into nothing.

Belien was on the ground, wheezing, gasping, crying as Leona fussed at his side. Cedric barely heard them. Not as emerald eyes bored into his, mere inches apart, his hand still on her face.

"Yes, that is enough," came the Arbiter's voice.

Cedric dropped his hand.

And everything stopped.

CHAPTER 26
RECOMPENSE

Elyria

"No." Gael's shoulders slumped the second the Arbiter's polyphonous voice rang through the room. Paelin would not be joining them. The Trial of Spirit was over.

"Champions who reign over spirit and truth," boomed the voice, "I offer my congratulations. And my sympathies."

Well, that was new. Elyria didn't think the mysterious being had expressed much of anything close to resembling sympathy after the first trial. Were they starting to get attached?

Elyria, unfortunately, knew the feeling.

Her chin still tingled where Cedric had touched her when he'd pulled her from her trance.

That fucking trial.

She hadn't meant to lash out at Belien like that.

He deserved it, sure. But what she'd gone through in the trial had changed something in her. And when she reached for her wild magic with the intention of intimidating the human with a *little, tiny, itty-bitty* earthquake, or maybe helping a few loose stones find their way to his smug face, her shadow had answered instead.

She didn't fully realize what she was doing to him until Cedric stopped her.

And she had absolutely no idea how to feel about that.

"Your journey is far from over." The Arbiter was still speaking. Oops. "Let the truths uncovered within yourselves guide you in the trials to come."

Elyria glanced at Kit. "Trials?" she mouthed. "Two down, two to go?" That was another tally for Kit's predictive prowess.

Kit simply stared back at Elyria, some inscrutable mix of emotions in her mismatched eyes.

At first, Elyria thought she simply didn't understand what she'd tried to communicate. Then the realization hit. Kit never knew about Elyria's dark magic. Elyria had never let her see it. Never told her.

Wonder, shock, and a little bit of hurt. That's what Elyria saw reflected back at her.

But not fear.

She could work with that. Could work with Kit's irritation. Her anger, even. As long as she wasn't *afraid* of her.

Elyria would check in with her as soon as she could. But it was all she could do at present to focus on the rest of the Arbiter's words, their next command. Especially with the hulking human knight still basically standing on top of her.

She considered elbowing him in the side, forcing him over. She needed space—to think, to breathe.

She could barely breathe with him right there.

"Emotional wounds cut deeper than physical ones," said the Arbiter. "Two nights you'll have to rest. Recover. Recuperate."

The doors at the back of the room swung open.

"And then the Trial of Magic shall commence. Your strength alone will not be enough to survive. Rely on the bonds you've forged, the trust you've built. Remember: Unity is the key."

And with that, the voice faded.

Elyria tried—she really tried—not to look at Cedric. She failed. And as she met his golden-brown eyes, something stirred in the hollow place where her inner shadow slept.

A recognition. An understanding.

They didn't say anything—there was no need for words. They were in this together now.

Whether they liked it or not.

The soothing stillness of night should have brought Elyria peace. The chance to just *be* after so much strife. Instead, she found herself restless.

Kit hadn't said much as they'd walked through one of the doors and their bedroom from the night before materialized before them. The agreement to hold off on any lengthy, emotional confessions until morning went unspoken as they'd poured themselves into their beds.

Elyria wanted more than anything to succumb to sleep. She couldn't. She lay on her side, staring at the wall beside her bed, the events of the day playing over and over in her mind.

The rush toward the doors. The golden mirror. The battle. The darkness. That burning house. The . . . aftermath. And interlaced with nearly every memory, permeating every image: *him*.

Why did Cedric loom so large in her mind? Was she just feeling the aftereffects of the Trial of Spirit? She thought about the scene she'd come upon after fading out of her own trial—his body curled up on the burning floor, flames dancing around him. She thought of the tightness around his eyes, the clench of his jaw as he fought against pain. It had been her first instinct to run to his side, to sing to him, to soothe his fear.

She thought about the way his eyes had widened when he'd realized it was her, how the pain and confusion on his face had shifted into something like awe. How he had lit up with relief . . . before crashing back into suspicion.

Elyria grinned against her pillow, recalling the way he'd come at her after that. He was a decent fighter; she would give him that. She wondered what it would be like to face off against the knight under less traumatic circumstances. She bet it would be fun.

And then she shook her head, burying her face in the cool cotton. What was *wrong* with her? Why did she feel his presence everywhere? Why was he always *there*? After each trial. Before she'd even entered the Gate. Even here, now, she felt him.

She didn't understand why. Didn't understand this flicker of familiarity that seemed to thread through her veins at the thought of him. Was it gratitude? It's not as if he'd done anything to help her. He had pulled her back from the edge with Belien, yes. But it wasn't the same as how she'd helped him—multiple times now. How she was here to help Kit.

And Elyria felt like something must be very, very wrong with her, because the more time she spent in this place, the harder it was to remember her reason for being here. Like her mind was pushing out thoughts of Kit and Evander and replacing them with this infuriating, self-righteous *human*.

And fine, she would admit that the man wasn't as absolutely loathsome as she'd initially thought. Especially now that he seemed to finally—maybe?—believe she'd had nothing to do with his parents' murder. And, yes, perhaps witnessing him in the wake of his lowest moments had softened her toward him.

A little.

But he was still insufferable. He still had a chip on his shoulder and a stick up his ass.

Elyria sighed. Her head hurt. She thought about how much had happened since that morning alone. It was as though an entirely different person had been the one hoarding bacon and trading barbs with the knight.

Every hour spent here felt like an eternity and like an instant. How much time was passing outside the Celestial Sanctum? Was it the same out there? Or was the ancient magic here warping their senses? Bending the very passage of time?

She rolled onto her back, clutching the blanket under her chin like an anchor, as if it might weld her to the present. She needed her spinning mind to stop, if just for a few moments.

It wasn't the darkness that kept her awake. She'd made peace with that—at least for now. It was something else. It *tugged* at her, not entirely dissimilar to the feeling of having forgotten something without any clue as to what it was.

Elyria sat up and swung her legs over the edge of the bed, her gauzy white sleeping dress dusting the tops of her knees. Her bare feet met the cool stone floor. With a glance at a peacefully sleeping Kit, Elyria crept from the room, not even bothering to slip on her boots. She just needed to clear her head. Needed space to think.

The moment she closed the bedroom door, unease washed over her. She didn't have to turn around to realize she was not in the Sanctum's main chamber, the room where they'd spent all their time outside the trials. She was in a long, empty corridor.

Flickering torchlight lit the hallway. Elyria hesitated for a moment, brushing her hand against the wall as if seeking reassurance from the cool stone.

The night was still. There was no sign of the other champions, not even their bedroom doors. No sign of life at all beyond the low hum of the Sanctum's ancient magic. It soothed something in Elyria's soul. A soft melody fell from her lips as she harmonized with the magic, the initial disquiet she'd felt melting away.

She stepped forward, allowing that *tug* in her chest to guide her down the winding corridor.

Rounding a soft curve in the hallway, Elyria stopped short.

Of course, she thought. *Of fucking course.*

It had guided her right to him.

Cedric sat on a stone bench in a small alcove at the end of the hall—head in his hands, shoulders hunched. Moonlight filtered in through a window above him. His armor was gone, leaving him in just a simple black tunic and pants.

Open.

Vulnerable.

Human.

He must have heard her because he lifted his head before she could take another step. His brown eyes were wide with an emotion that Elyria had trouble placing. It wasn't surprise, exactly. More like wonder. Incredulity.

Like he wasn't expecting to see her, but he wasn't *not* expecting it, either.

And Elyria understood that. Because, against all sense, it was how she felt too.

For whatever reason, the celestials or fate or the stars-damned Arcane Crucible itself seemed determined to push the two of them together.

To what end, she couldn't say. All she knew was that whatever dark and ancient thing she held within her seemed to recognize something in him—something that made her feel both drawn to and repelled by the knight in equal measure.

Elyria and Cedric watched each other for a moment, the air between them charged.

"Can't sleep?" Her voice was low as she cracked the silence.

Cedric let out a humorless laugh. "After all that? Not sure I'll ever sleep again."

She slid onto the bench beside him, her brow arched. "The great Sir Cedric Thorne, scared of a little shut-eye? What is the world coming to?"

One side of his lip curved up in a sad sort of smile. "Everything really has turned upside down in here, hasn't it?"

Elyria didn't know what to say to that. She cleared her throat. "What are you doing out here?"

He shrugged. "I don't know, really. Needed to get away from Thraigg's snoring. Zephyr's too."

Elyria snorted. "Now, I can see that from the dwarf. He has the look of someone who rivals a blacksmith's bellows when he sleeps. But are we talking about the same Zephyr? Sweet, petite sylvan gal?"

"She's worse than Thraigg," Cedric whispered conspiratorially, his smile finally reaching his eyes.

A giggle slipped from Elyria's mouth. Something flickered over Cedric's face at the sound, and she felt suddenly self-conscious.

"And how exactly did the three of you end up bunking together again?" she asked, eager to move past the moment. "You should have had your pick of rooms."

"Just lucky, I suppose. Neither of them would leave me alone after that display back there." He leaned back with a sigh, though she thought he already seemed lighter, less weary than he had been when she first approached. "Thraigg's thoroughly inebriated state didn't do much to help matters. And Zephyr, altruistic little thing that she is, didn't think it was very champion-like to leave an incredibly drunk, incredibly *handsy* dwarf to his own devices." He tilted his head and gave her a knowing look.

Another giggle escaped. Elyria clapped her hand over her mouth.

"It's not funny," he protested.

She dropped her hand. "Oh, come now. It's a little bit funny," she said, elongating the words so that they came out as a lilting melody.

Something clicked into place behind Cedric's eyes. "Ah," he said.

Elyria's brows drew together. "What?"

He chuckled. "I thought I heard singing before. And just now . . . It was you, wasn't it?"

"You heard that?" Elyria fought the urge to bury her face in her hands.

"Is that what you're doing out here? Kit got fed up with your singing keeping her up?" he teased.

"Firstly, Kit sleeps like the dead. She's always been able to sleep through *anything*. And secondly, I'll have you know that my singing is rather in demand. Folks often came to the Sweltering Pig just to hear little old me."

"The Sweltering Pig?"

"Best cider and third-best ale in all Coralith." She leaned back with a stretch of her arms, linking her hands behind her head. A smile twitched at her lips. "Artie says that—"

She cut herself off at the way Cedric suddenly stilled, as if every cell in his body froze in place. He was looking down.

She followed his line of sight.

Right to where her sleeping dress had ridden up, exposing the checkerboard of scars emblazoned on both her thighs.

The air grew thick, a heady sludge that Elyria struggled to pull into her lungs.

"What happened?" His voice was low, almost menacing.

Heat flooded Elyria's cheeks. The balm Zephyr had given her had taken the rawest edge off them, but the marks Raefe left on her were still unmistakable—an angry, twisted map on each leg. She scrambled to pull her nightdress down, but gentle fingers wrapped around her wrist, staying her hand.

She lifted her head to find two pools of golden brown staring at her—*into* her. Her heart forgot how to beat for several moments.

Cedric sucked in a slow breath, an eerie calm settling over him. "Who did this to you?"

She shot to her feet, breaking his grip on her wrist. "It's nothing," she said, cursing inwardly as her voice cracked.

"It's not nothing."

She didn't know what to say.

"Tell me."

Her nostrils flared as she inhaled deeply. "You're not the only one in this world who had grand plans for the day they finally met *the Revenant*." She fiddled with the fabric of the sleeping gown, glowing white in the moonlight. "But unlike you, this one wasn't inclined to listen to reason. More of an act first, talk never sort of guy."

Cedric had gone so still, Elyria thought for a moment he might have stopped breathing entirely.

She cleared her throat. "I wasn't thinking . . . I only partially healed the burns before I realized—"

"Burns?" He stood so quickly that Elyria found herself stepping back in surprise. "Those are burns? But they're so—"

"Precise? Yes, Raefe's mastery of his flametouch was actually quite impressive. Or it would have been, had he used it for anything other than making confetti of my breeches."

"Don't do that." His voice had a dark edge.

She swallowed. "Do what?"

"Make light of what happened. Of what this *Raefe* did to you." He spat the name like it was a curse.

No, not a curse.

A vow.

It sparked something in Elyria's core, even though she had no idea what to say in response. She shivered as Cedric's gaze ran up the length of her, slowing as it drifted over her legs before stopping at her forearm.

His jaw ticked. "I burned you too."

"What?"

"Your arm. In my trial. You got burned."

"That was hardly your doing." She extended her arm and gave it a wave. "And I appreciate the concern, Sir Worrywart, but fear not. It was an easy fix. See? Healed it right up. Nary a scar to be seen."

His weight shifted toward her, as if he meant to move closer. He didn't.

Elyria didn't understand why that disappointed her.

A few moments passed, thick silence hanging between them.

Finally, he said, "I hope you made him pay."

"Not enough," she muttered before she could stop herself.

"After we get out of here, we'll change that."

She snapped her head to him, the words washing over her like cold water. Awakening something in her. She never let herself think about *after*. She'd gone through the Gate knowing full well that there was almost no chance of coming back out, only caring about helping Kit make it as far as she could.

Yet here was this man, suddenly talking as if *after* was guaranteed.

The idea soothed her. Terrified her.

"After we get out?" Elyria said.

Cedric smirked. "After I win the crown."

That spark in her core fizzled out with the reminder of where they were, why he was here. Why she was. "Right. The crown. Because it's all about the crown."

"No, that's not what I—"

"I should leave."

"Why?"

She released a singular sharp laugh. "*Why?* We are on opposite sides here, Sir Thorne."

For a second, she thought he might have winced at her use of his formal name. She ignored it.

"You've trained for this your whole life, remember? Far be it from me to prevent you from fulfilling your duty." She hesitated. Bit her bottom lip. "Only . . . I *will* be preventing you. Because Kit is determined to win the crown to bring her brother peace, and I'll be damned to the fourth quarter if I let anyone get in her way."

She turned to go.

"Please." In a heartbeat, he closed the distance between them, his hand latching around her upper arm. His eyes searched hers. "Don't go yet."

Their proximity was suddenly overwhelming. Elyria's heart pounded in her chest, a wild, erratic rhythm. She should pull away. Should put distance between them.

But she didn't move.

Neither did he.

Instead, they both leaned toward each other, some invisible force drawing them closer. Her eyes lowered to his mouth, lingering on the scar cutting through the right side of his upper lip.

The *tug* in Elyria's chest throbbed.

Her breath hitched as her lips parted, the world narrowing to nothing but him and her and their unbearable closeness and the warmth of his body against hers.

"Don't run," he whispered. The skin on her arm felt hot under his touch.

"Don't run from yourself. You don't have to hide." Evander's words pealed in her head like a warning bell.

It broke the spell.

She yanked herself back, her skin prickling like she'd been doused in ice. "This was a mistake."

Without another word, she fled, leaving Cedric standing alone in a pool of moonlight.

CHAPTER 27
AN UNLIKELY PAIRING

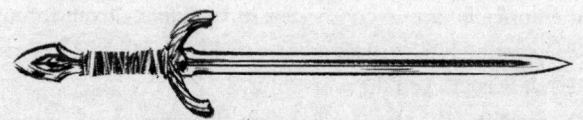

Cedric

All signs of the winding corridors Cedric found himself wandering last night disappeared with the rising sun.

As did Elyria.

She did not come out of her room the next morning. Not when the other champions slowly began emerging, looking more exhausted than they had when they'd gone to bed the night before. Not when Kit poked her silvery-hued head out of their room in search of breakfast. Not even when Thraigg stumbled out and immediately collided with one of the small tables now dotting the Sanctum's main chamber, sending platters of bacon and fruit flying with a deafening crash.

The Arbiter had given them two days to recover from the Trial of Spirit, and that, apparently, was what Elyria had decided to do. Alone.

"Good morning." A light voice filtered into Cedric's ears, and he tore his eyes from the row of doors at the back of the room. Zephyr held out a plate of yeast rolls.

"Thank you," he said, taking one and biting into it for show. Swallowing the hunk of bread was a chore. He didn't have much of an appetite, not after making such a fool of himself last night.

Satisfied, Zephyr walked away to offer the rolls around the room, gracefully sidestepping Belien when he reached for one.

Kit grinned at the sylvan healer as she grabbed two rolls, along with a pitcher from a nearby table, and retreated to her room.

Cedric watched her go.

Left alone with his fraying thoughts, he could no longer avoid the mental self-flagellation he'd been staving off since last night.

What had he been thinking?

He hadn't been. That was the only explanation. Or, at least, it wasn't his brain that had been doing the thinking.

He wanted to punch *himself*, the one-track-minded bastard.

Cedric had just been caught so off guard. His thoughts consumed by the memories he'd relived, the feel of the knife slicing through his lip, the fear rooting him in place as he stared at his father's lifeless body.

And that wasn't even the worst of it.

Those memories he was familiar with, the same ones that visited his dreams every so often. But the rest . . .

His nightmares hadn't included seeing the intruders searching for something. Hadn't involved that fourth figure, looming outside. Cedric hadn't remembered his mother's final words—ones that he still didn't understand. And he hadn't recalled seeing her torn apart by dark magic. He'd just known she died, as if his mind had been trying to protect him from the reality of what he'd witnessed.

Was this why he'd assumed the Revenant's involvement? As a child, Cedric heard tales of the Revenant's deadly exploits, of the dark powers that won the Arcanians a war. All children knew the stories.

Cedric's brow creased. Was it possible that the hatred that had fueled Cedric for the majority of his life, that had pushed him toward the Crucible, had been manufactured by himself?

Lord Church had never said anything to the contrary. Not that they often spoke about what happened before Cedric was taken in as a ward of the lord's estate. But if the lord had known anything more about who was responsible for Cedric's parents' murders, he'd never said. He had been perfectly content, in fact, to stoke Cedric's need for vengeance against the Arcanians—against *the Revenant*.

The infamous Revenant . . . who was, in reality, a woman like any other. A brash, reckless woman with a reputation so much bigger than her.

Impulsive. Petulant. Maddening.

Beautiful.

He groaned inwardly. He knew how foolish it made him, how disappointed Lord Church would be if he knew what Cedric was thinking. But there was no point denying it. She was a beautiful thing, more so last night than ever before. The way the moonlight caught on her periwinkle hair, making it glow silver . . . And the vulnerability in her eyes . . .

It had stirred something in him.

Cedric squeezed his eyes shut in an attempt to banish his thoughts—and those jewel-green eyes. This was not a helpful trail of thought to venture down. Dwelling on this wouldn't get him any closer to his goals. He was just exhausted. He was feeling too much. He was grateful to Elyria for seeing him through the Trial of Spirit, for getting him out. That's all this was—all it could be.

Because she was right. They were not on the same side. The Arbiter could espouse talk of unity until they were blue in the face, but the bottom line was that only one champion would walk out of the Crucible with the crown in hand.

And that person would be Cedric.

Cedric had thought the day would move slowly, knowing there was nothing to do other than sit around and "heal"—whatever the Arbiter meant by that. But time moved surprisingly quickly. Leona and Belien seemed to have learned yesterday to stay out of everyone else's way, so the remaining champions trained and talked and theorized about what the third trial would hold. Even Tenebris Nox seemed to be easing themself out of their self-imposed isolation and interacting with the rest of the group more.

The weight on Cedric's chest eased as he sat to the side of the room, watching Nox walk Thraigg and Zephyr through a few nocterrian sparring moves. The dwarf's eyes went wide when the sylvan spun on him, her dagger in hand. He slid backward, the ornaments in his braided beard jingling.

Cedric chuckled under his breath. Though they were nearly equal in height, the dwarf outweighed the sylvan by at least double. His stout, hardened demeanor and her delicate spryness made them an unlikely pairing, but it seemed as though the events of the Trial of Spirit had bonded them.

Cedric's eyes drifted toward the closed doors at the back of the room for the fiftieth time that day. He supposed he wasn't one to talk.

Something glinted in the periphery of his vision, and he turned his head to find Kit leaning against the wall to his right, an apple in her hand. Her wings glittered golden in the setting sunlight that filtered in through the high windows dotting the walls.

She bit into the apple, surveying Cedric with a playful gleam in her mismatched eyes. "She's fine, you know," she garbled.

His brows shot up. "What's that?"

"Elle—Elyria. She's all right."

He shifted in his seat. "I didn't ask."

She shrugged and took another large bite. Cedric suspected the fruit was hiding a rather smug grin.

"Can I ask you a question?" he asked after a moment.

Kit arched a brow. "I don't know, can you?"

He bit his bottom lip. "I'm not sure if it's considered impertinent."

"Spit it out, knightling."

"Your wings."

"What about them?"

"Well, you, Gael, Cyren . . . I've noticed you all keep yours, er, out quite a lot more than . . ."

"Than Elyria?"

He hesitated. "Yes."

Kit's tongue darted to the outside of her lip to snatch an errant speck of apple. She seemed to be debating with herself. "It's not my place to explain *her* exact reasons why, but generally speaking, a fae's wings are sensitive, easy to injure."

"A liability in a fight," Cedric said. That made sense. Elyria approached life as though a battle might erupt at any moment. He supposed that, for her, it often did.

His mind went to the scars on her legs, a bolt of anger tearing through him. She'd tried to play it off like it was nothing. But he saw the flash of panic, the pain simmering behind those jeweled eyes. He knew better. And the thought of what Raefe had done to her, the lingering scars he left on her—physically and otherwise—made Cedric's chest feel hot.

He had no real reason to be incensed. No right. But he was, nonetheless. And he knew whatever punishment Elyria had already meted out on the man who marked her could not possibly have been enough.

Kit nodded, though if she had any inclination of the dark path his thoughts had gone down, she didn't show it. "Some keep them hidden for that reason. But just as I imagine humans have varying tastes and preferences"—she looked Cedric up and down with amusement—"different fae feel differently. For most, it's not worth the drain on their magic to keep their wings concealed all the time. That's how I feel about it, anyway."

Gold shimmered as she flared her wings wide before folding them neatly against her back.

"I see," Cedric said.

"But for some . . ." Kit glanced around as if ensuring nobody was listening. "When fae are involved romantically, intimately . . . When it's a deep, *significant* sort of relationship, wings can take on a new meaning. And after one has felt their soulmate's wingtouch, it can be . . . challenging to stomach the idea of anyone else touching them." Her face fell. "Even after they are no longer together. Even if one of them . . ." She cleared her throat. "Elle is particularly protective of her wings."

Something tightened in Cedric's chest. A spark of pity, yes, but something else, too. "So, the two of you . . . ?"

"Four hells, no!" Kit made a gagging sound, and Cedric couldn't help but laugh. "She's like my sister. It was my brother who—" She cut herself off. "It's not important. I've already said too much."

Cedric tried to project cool confidence despite the wild churn of his emotions. They were flipping back and forth so rapidly, he thought the second trial might've stolen a bit of his sanity along with his innocence. Curiosity, fascination, sympathy, relief . . . and had that been *jealousy* pushing in on his chest before?

That couldn't be right.

"Rest assured, you've barely said anything at all," he told Kit, forcing a smile. "But thank you. This has been illuminating."

The corner of Kit's mouth quirked up. "Just don't tell her anything I barely said, all right?"

He placed a solitary finger against his mouth. "My lips are sealed."

"Well, fuck me right over the Chasm," Thraigg said with a low whistle from just beyond the open bedroom door.

Zephyr wrinkled her nose at the dwarf's words as she helped Cedric fasten his vambraces to his forearms.

Cedric sighed. "Honestly, Thraigg. It is first thing in the morning. Is that sort of language necessary?"

"Get out here and take a look for yerself, Ric. Then ye can tell me what's *necessary*."

Cinching his sword belt around his waist, Cedric dragged himself over to Thraigg, an admonishment on the tip of his tongue. One that he swallowed the instant he looked through the open doorway at the scene before him.

"Fuckin' told ye." Amusement danced in the dwarf's eyes as Cedric took in the sprawling, verdant landscape. Lush, feathery grass. A halo of oak trees encircling them, easily a hundred feet tall. And high above, a blue, blue sky—endless sky.

It was breathtaking.

"Impossible," Cedric whispered, though he didn't know why. He'd experienced firsthand that there were no rules when it came to the Sanctum. It switched antechambers for winding corridors at the twist of a doorknob and flipped night and day as easily as rolling dice. This new development should hardly have been shocking. And yet . . .

Cedric stepped through the doorway onto soft grass. He ran his fingers along the stone wall that stretched on either side of the doorway, as if verifying it was really there. It looked like the exterior wall of any building—perfectly normal, had he not known that this grassy clearing was a dining room twelve hours ago.

"Do you think this means the Trial of Magic has started?" Zephyr's voice came from behind him.

"What else could it be?" Tenebris Nox's voice filtered over the sound of footsteps—heavy boots crushing grass.

Cedric turned to see the nocterrian walking over with Gael Winters and Cyren Tenrider. The two fae hovered just over the ground, their glittering wings flapping behind them, flared as if they wanted to stretch as far into the sunlit scene as they could.

Farther down, Belien and Leona emerged from a door of their own, wonder plastered across their faces. One look at the other gathering champions, however, and their typical expressions of ire and disdain were back in place.

"Just like that?" Cyren asked. "No grand announcement this time? No *rules*?" He attempted a poor mimicry of the Arbiter's thoroughly inimitable voice. "Champions, the Trial of Magic awaits. Go forth! Only, make sure to hug and hold hands the entire time because *unity*!"

A melodious laugh rang through the air. Cedric's muscles seized.

"Not bad, Tenrider," said Elyria as she approached, Kit trailing behind her. She donned a cloak over a cream-colored top, smooth leather vest, and brown breeches, a lightness in her step that had been missing the last time Cedric saw her. She did not look at him.

Humming, Elyria bent low and skimmed splayed fingers across the grass. A delicate vine of white and purple flowers sprang from the ground. She plucked a few fresh blooms and tucked them into the periwinkle hair braided in an intricate coronet across her head.

Cedric clenched his teeth to keep his mouth from doing something stupid like falling open.

"Maybe the Arbiter thinks we should understand how it works by now," said Gael.

Kit frowned. "But then . . . *does* anybody know how it's going to work this time? What exactly are we supposed to be doing here?"

As if the Sanctum had been waiting for someone to ask that very question, the doors behind them suddenly slammed shut. The ground began to rumble and shake.

"What the f—" Thraigg's outcry was swallowed by a deep, rolling boom coming from the earth—like thunder.

"Elle?" Kit's voice jumped an octave.

"It's not me." Elyria's eyes moved frantically over the grass, as if trying to locate the source of the quake. "I'm not doing that."

As quickly as it began, the rumbling ceased.

Nobody was fool enough to think that was the end of it.

Gael and Cyren passed uneasy whispers back and forth. Hands on their tokens, Leona and Belien exchanged an urgent look. Thraigg spun the handle of his hammer in his palms, ready to start swinging. At his back, Cedric felt Zephyr step closer.

Green eyes met Cedric's for the briefest moment. Elyria's lips parted like she was about to speak.

And the ground erupted.

The earth split open, grass disappearing into fissures that cracked through the soil.

Champions scattered.

Belien and Leona howled at one another as they tucked themselves against the building.

Nox moved like a shadow, darting back several feet.

In an instant, and to Cedric's immediate relief, Elyria was in the air, wings materialized on her back, purple and green shimmering in the sunlight as if pulled from the aurora itself. She, Kit, Gael, and Cyren floated over the sundering ground, their wings rippling with an ethereal grace that nearly had Cedric forgetting about what was happening.

With a yelp, Zephyr pulled on the back of Cedric's armor, moving him back just as the dirt where he'd been standing crumbled into nothing.

"Move, Thraigg!" she cried.

Cedric's gaze shot to the dwarf, still braced in his battle stance, hammer aloft, as a crack ripped through the ground, racing toward him.

Cedric moved as if he could reach Thraigg before the fissure did. He wouldn't have been able to, but it didn't matter. A gust of wind rushed past him, hitting the dwarf squarely in the chest. Thraigg flew off his feet, soaring backward into one of the closed bedroom doors with a groan.

When Cedric looked up, he saw Cyren hovering in the air nearby, hands outstretched. He gave the stormbender an appreciative nod.

Thraigg grumbled a low thanks—first, to the fae who'd saved him, then to Cedric as he helped the dwarf to his feet. A cacophony of rustling and crunching overtook anything else Thraigg might have said.

Roots burst from the rifts in the earth, twisting as they snaked over the ground. They wound between the trees, locking the trunks together. Thorny vines crept down from the treetops, weaving together with the roots to create a nightmarish tapestry that seemed designed to showcase the dark side of nature.

Eventually, the roots and vines slowed. With a creak so loud it was as if the very earth was groaning in pain, they stopped, leaving behind an impossibly tall, impenetrable wall.

The champions were surrounded on all sides. Trapped.

"There's your answer, Kit," said Elyria as the two of them touched down in front of Cedric, her wings vanishing again with a burst of magic that left the scent of bitter almond grazing his nose.

"You asked what we're supposed to be doing here." She pointed to the trees. "We have to figure out how to get through that."

PART III
FLAME

CHAPTER 28
THE THIRD TRIAL

Elyria

Everyone froze for several heartbeats. There was nothing but the sound of settling earth and stunned breathing. The air felt thick, magic and tension clogging Elyria's nostrils.

To her mild surprise, it was Zephyr who broke the silence.

"What in the Earth Mother's name do we do now?" she asked.

Kit snorted. "Apt choice of words, given what we just witnessed. Fucking celestials. Aren't they supposed to stay out of mortal affairs?"

Thraigg guffawed as if that were the funniest thing he'd heard in ages.

Elyria rolled her eyes. "I doubt this was Gaia's intervention. More likely, it's the magic of the Crucible itself. And either way, it hardly matters. Not when there's a literal blockade preventing us from proceeding."

Stepping carefully over the fractured ground, she moved toward the wall of root and thorn. She reached out a tentative hand, feeling for the wild magic that pulsed within all of nature—some thread she could grab on to, could use to create an opening.

Her brow creased. She could sense it, could tell it was there. But it was faint. Blocked.

A spark of recognition flared in her chest as she heard footsteps behind her. "I'm not sure I'm going to be able to do much to break through here, Kitty Kat," she admitted.

"Why not?" asked a voice much lower and smoother than the one she expected.

She turned. "You're not Kit."

One side of Cedric's mouth curved up. "That sounds familiar."

Elyria scowled. "Yes, well, tit for tat, I suppose. Now you can call us even."

Cedric frowned. He opened his mouth as if to say something in response, then seemed to think better of it.

Elyria didn't like how much it bothered her not to know what he was going to say.

She cleared her throat and waved a hand at the wall. "The roots are too thick, too closely woven. Almost as if they've been welded together. There are a few weak spots I can sense, but I don't think I could open a passage big enough for even Zephyr to squeeze through."

Cedric drew his dagger from his belt, and for a fleeting moment, alarm zipped through Elyria. But the knight simply used it to poke at the roots and vines in the wall, as if testing their girth.

"Too thick to cut through, too," he said. "We can't force our way in. And you can't create an entry point for us. What about digging below it? From my understanding of wildshaper magic, you have some dominion over earth and rock as well, do you not? We could tunnel beneath it."

Elyria gave him a blank stare. "You want me to . . . dig . . . a tunnel? Underneath that?"

"While I'm sure she appreciates your confidence in her abilities, even the mighty Revenant has her limitations." Kit's voice was lit with amusement as she joined them by the wall.

Elyria shot her a grateful look. After a bit of time to process, Kit had taken the revelation of Elyria's hidden nightwielding magic in stride. While Elyria had hidden herself away in their room the previous day—well, not hiding, she wasn't *hiding* from anyone—Kit was a constant source of comfort. She brought her food, talked her through how to disentangle this new dark magic from her familiar, wild one. It felt almost like old times. Felt like something precious. As if twenty years hadn't passed and they weren't here at all. No, they were back at the Ravenswing Estate and Evander would walk through the door any moment, pat Kit on the shoulder, and sweep Elyria into his arms.

If she didn't know better, she would've sworn she'd felt his presence.

Cyren flitted over, his silver-white wings shimmering, and dragged Elyria's attention back.

"Can't go under it, can't go through it, why don't we just go over it? We could fly over this mess, get out of here like"—he snapped his fingers—"that."

"I think you're forgetting that not everyone here has wings, Cy," called Gael.

"He didn't forget," said Belien with a sneer.

Cyren flashed him an innocent smile.

"We could carry them," Kit said earnestly, as if actually considering this. "A couple of us will have to make two trips, but—"

"Now, wait just a moment." A look that could only be described as one of pure panic flashed over Cedric's face. "Let's not jump to any hasty conclusions here."

Elyria bit down on her bottom lip to halt the grin threatening to break out there. Was the great champion of Kingshelm frightened of flying?

"We don't even know whether bypassing this wall is what the Crucible demands," Cedric continued. "What if whatever we seek in this trial lies not beyond this"—he gestured to the wall—"but within it?"

"Finally, some sense," Belien said, though his tone made it clear he wasn't pleased to give Cedric credit. "It's idiotic to think the challenge here is as simple as getting over a wall."

Cyren raised an eyebrow. "If you're feeling inadequate about your ability to do so, know it truly would be my pleasure to carry you over, *friend*. As long as it's understood I can't be held responsible if you were to accidentally slip."

Belien flipped him an obscene gesture in response.

Cyren only laughed, before leaning toward Elyria and faux-whispering, "I'd be happy to carry you, too, gorgeous."

Elyria snorted. "This isn't helpful, you two." A weak attempt to broker peace. To be fair, she didn't particularly care about playing nice with the redheaded twat. But what she didn't want was the Arbiter's voice suddenly booming in her head, extolling more platitudes about the necessity of unity. And she didn't want any additional surprises.

So, of course, that was exactly what she got.

Faster than a lightning strike, the sky overhead erupted in a blaze of heat and light. The treetops burst into flame, fire racing across the canopy in a scorching wave. The heat of it grazed Elyria's skin, even from the ground, as the flames stretched up and out, reaching into nothing but air and blue sky.

It didn't stop the fire. The flames narrowed into lines that crisscrossed the sky. They danced across the open air—beautiful, smoldering threads that connected the treetops to the building with the doors they'd emerged from.

"Gael?" Cyren asked doubtfully.

She shook her head, her flame-red hair almost glowing. "It's not me but let me see what I can—" She was in the air before she finished her sentence, orange wings glimmering as she flew up to the tree line.

Cedric, standing to Elyria's right, tensed as Gael stretched tentative fingers toward the threads of fire. His hand moved to his chest. Elyria noted the movement from the corner of her eye and angled her head to get a better look at him without being too obvious. She'd been working so hard to ignore him, to not look, to not think about him. She wanted them both to forget that disastrous encounter in the moonlight.

But she couldn't ignore the look on his face, the rapture as he watched Gael attempting to—well, Elyria wasn't sure what she was attempting, but she was clearly using her magic to do *something*.

And Cedric was absolutely transfixed.

"Won't it burn her?" he asked nobody in particular.

"She's a flamecaller," Elyria answered, as if that alone would explain everything. It should. For someone who had supposedly trained his whole life for a deadly competition against his enemy, the knight seemed shockingly naive in his knowledge of Arcanian magic. He should already know that being impervious to burns was just one of the many benefits of wielding fire magic.

If only we were all so lucky, she thought, resisting the urge to palm her thighs.

Gael let out a yelp as the flames finally subsided. Wings flaring, she started spinning in the air, movements erratic. She'd lost control, Elyria realized, as Gael began careening toward the ground, fast.

Too fast.

Elyria felt Cedric move at her side, darting toward the falling fae to catch her. At the same time, Cyren shot a hand out, a gentle gust of wind soaring up to meet Gael's floundering body, slowing her descent. She landed softly in Cedric's arms.

"What was that?" Elyria asked, incredulity coloring her tone as she rushed forward to meet them.

"Neat bit of magic," Gael said, wonder warring with bitterness as Cedric set her on the ground, "but rather inconvenient. Flying is *definitely* not an option anymore."

"What do you mean?" asked Cedric, and Elyria resisted the temptation to laugh at his obvious relief.

"The fire burned some sort of ward into place." She pointed at the sky. "The magic hooked into me as soon as the flame winked out. All of a sudden, I couldn't fly anymore."

Elyria unsheathed her wings with a frown, taking in the somewhat slack-jawed expression on Cedric's face with pride. Sure enough, as soon as she attempted to lift off the ground, some unseen force pushed on her, keeping her down.

"Great." Elyria turned to Cyren. "I don't think the Crucible much cared for your plan, Cy."

Kit chuckled. "Exactly. Not very 'unity' focused."

Cyren's wings flared irritably before he folded them against his back. "Don't talk about the Crucible as if it's some living, breathing thing."

"Isn't it though?" Elyria said under her breath, squinting at the sky.

She didn't think anyone heard her, but when she pulled her gaze back, Cedric was looking at her with bemusement.

Gael stepped forward, inspecting the wall of trees as if she might be able to see what lay beyond. "What now, then?"

Elyria took another step toward the wall, sweeping her eyes over the tangled mass of roots and thorns once more. "What else can we do?" She sighed, pulling her staff over her head and discarding it in the grass, then folding her wings flat against her back. "Let me try again."

"Are you sure you—" Cedric cut himself off at the dangerous look Elyria shot him.

Holding both hands in front of her face, Elyria splayed her fingers. She closed her eyes. Let her awareness sink past the grass, past the soil, into the heart of the earth. And she reached for the magic she could feel thrumming deep within each twisted vine, each gnarled root. It was faint, a veil placed over it. But it was there. The melody of *life* woven into the fabric of all wild things—a hymn of growth and potential.

With painstaking focus, she grabbed hold of the whispers humming within each root, the magic in each vine, beckoning them forth until she could feel them, grasp them.

And Elyria *pulled*.

It was like dragging an anchor through tar. Sweat beaded on her furrowed brow as she attempted to coax the roots apart. They did not want to budge, did not want to move. But eventually she managed to unwind enough of the thorny tendrils to create an opening—barely two handspans wide.

"Kit." Elyria's whisper was a plea.

Kit sprang into action, three fingers pointed at the opening. Water shot from her hand, crystallizing as it met the roots, frost creeping along the vines. In seconds, the opening was encased in a thick sheet of ice.

Elyria let out a shuddering breath as she let go, stumbling back several paces. She met a column of stone, sturdy at her back as she slumped against it. Then the column placed two steadying hands on her shoulders, and she realized that it was not, in fact, a column at all.

It was a knight.

"Are you all right?" Cedric asked.

Elyria straightened as she whirled on him, color rushing to her cheeks. She didn't have a chance to answer him, however, before Leona's nasally voice snared her attention.

"That's it? All that, for what? A window?"

"A window's better than nothing," Zephyr said, nimbly skipping over a crack in the ground as she joined the group in front of the wall. "At least now we can get an idea of what to expect whenever we do get through."

Leona snorted. "Pray, tell us then, little greenfoot"—she gave Zephyr a poison-laced smile—"what lies ahead for us in this great trial?"

Beside Elyria, Cedric tensed.

Zephyr cleared her throat. "Um, I see . . ." She strained on the tips of her toes to peer through the pane of ice. "Hallways? That can't be right."

"Let me see." Leona shouldered Zephyr out of the way, the sylvan releasing a pained gasp as the sorcerer trampled her foot.

Elyria fisted her hands at her sides to keep herself from strangling the bitch.

"Not hallways," Leona said, her voice suddenly serious. Studious. "Passages, perhaps. Narrow. Winding. Sh—" She jumped back, startled.

"What? What is it?" Belien asked, elbowing Cyren aside as he stepped next to Leona.

Her eyes met his with some unspoken understanding. "Shifting," she said, her voice low.

"Shifting?" Nox was suddenly there, movement silent as the wind. They peered through the makeshift window and released a long breath. "It's a labyrinth."

CHAPTER 29
UNITY

Elyria

"A labyrinth?" Zephyr was back on her tiptoes, trying to look through the icy window once more.

"Will ye all stop repeating one another?" Thraigg said with a grunt. "Yer echoes are bound to drive me insane."

Sunlight glinted off Nox's horns. "The real challenge is in there, then. We're merely at the starting line."

"And who knows what is held within," added Cedric.

"Well, we know one thing," said Leona, drawing her shoulders back.

Elyria caught Kit's eye and tried not to groan. "And that would be . . . ?"

"There's always a prize at the center of a labyrinth."

"Oh, there *always* is, is there?" Kit said. "Says who?"

Leona's eyes narrowed. "I—" She cleared her throat. "It is simply known."

"Do you have any idea how daft that sounds?"

Belien stepped in front of Leona as if to shield her from Kit's sarcasm. "Do you have any idea how stupid *you* sound? What if it's the crown in there?"

"Precisely." Leona dipped her chin at him in thanks. "Which is why we need to get in."

"I tried," Elyria said. "You *saw me* try."

"Clearly, you didn't try hard enough."

"How about you give it a go then, Blackwood?" Kit spat.

"Gladly." Leona stepped forward, her hand clutched around the token hanging from a chain around her neck. Her lips moving with some silent spell, she raised a hand and pointed at the wall of roots as if she might scold it into movement.

Nothing happened.

"Belien!" Leona hissed. The sorcerer scrambled into position next to her, mimicking her movements, the two of them working together to try to break through the wall.

Still, nothing happened.

Kit snorted.

Cyren released a loud laugh. "Very impressive."

Leona huffed, the cold expression typically adorning her face still in place as she turned back to Belien. But Elyria saw the way the tips of her ears turned pink.

Cedric went next, hacking at the wall with his sword as if he hadn't already determined the roots were too thick to cut through.

Panting, he scratched the back of his head. "This might take a while."

And so, they tried.

Time and time again, they tried. Thraigg joined Cedric in attempting to hack their way through with blunt force, but every time they made it through a layer, more vines would instantly replace the ones they cut. Gael set the entire wall ablaze, only to have it snuff out as if the roots absorbed the flames. There wasn't even a single scorch mark left behind.

Zephyr attempted to climb over at one point, her nimble feet scaling the wall with impressive speed. But like snakes, the roots shifted and slid over themselves, making it impossible for her to grab hold, and she found herself on the tail end of Cyren's stormbending magic more than once as he kept her from plummeting to the ground.

No matter which champion tried what method, nothing worked. It was as if the labyrinth was fighting them.

No, refusing them.

Arguments rose as patience wore thin. The sun began to dip low in the sky.

Nox's voice cut through the din of complaints as the nocterrian sidled up to Elyria where she now sat in the grass. "Why don't you use your shadows?"

"Excuse me?"

"We all saw what you can do. You're a nightwielder. A powerful one. I myself have just enough control to shadowstep, to hide myself among them when the need arises. But to manipulate them the way you did when you . . ." Their gaze flitted to Belien and back. "Your shadows are strong. You can create constructs. Why don't you try them on the wall?"

Elyria didn't know how to answer. Didn't feel like going into how she'd spent the entirety of yesterday trying to figure out how she managed to do what she did to Belien. Didn't feel like admitting she'd failed.

She had been able to separate her wild magic from her shadow. But all her attempts to re-create that solid dark tendril had gone up in smoke.

It didn't matter how much she pulled or begged or cajoled. It was as if her darkness simply went back to sleep. She had barely been able to coax out more than a wisp of shadow. And while she didn't love the idea of the nocterrian knowing this, what she really wanted to avoid was Belien and Leona overhearing. Nothing good would come from the humans learning about this weakness of hers.

Elyria might have accepted her inner darkness. But here, outside of the Trial of Spirit and the illusion she had lived through, she still had no fucking clue how to control it.

Thankfully, she didn't have to come up with an excuse for Nox, because Kit approached at that same moment.

"Will you try again, Elle?" Kit tried to keep her voice bright, but Elyria could hear the undercurrent of dejection. Kit had tried several times to carve into the wall with her magic, freezing the vines, trying to embrittle them so Thraigg could smash them. Each time, his hammer had bounced back as if the wall were made of rubber.

Nox surveyed Elyria with interest in the wake of Kit's question.

"I can try." Elyria hated the uncertainty in her voice as she got to her feet. "But I don't think I'm strong enough on my own," she said—a deflection, but not necessarily a lie. Even if she could reliably call on her shadows, she didn't think she could do this by herself. There was ancient magic preventing her from wielding the roots, locking her out.

As if it needed a key.

Elyria stopped midstep. A kind of calmness washed over her. Clarity.

"Remember: Unity is the key."

The Arbiter's voice rang through Elyria's head, their words echoing like a chorus. The realization came to her so clearly, she felt like an idiot for not understanding sooner.

"That's it," she said, awe filling her voice as she neared the wall.

"What's it?" Kit asked.

"Unity."

Belien groaned. "Not this shit again."

Elyria shot him a silencing look. "I don't think I'm *meant* to be able to get through on my own. None of us are. The Arbiter's been shoving the idea that we all need to work together down our throats this entire time. What for, if not to ensure we thought to actually, you know, do so when the need arose?"

"What are you saying, exactly?" Gael asked.

"'Unity is the key.' That's what the Arbiter said. If we want to unlock this trial, I think we need to work together—truly together."

"And how exactly do you propose we do that?" Cedric's baritone unexpectedly soared into Elyria's ear as he came up next to her. She suppressed a shiver.

Swallowing hard, Elyria took in the looks on her fellow champions' faces—hopeful, eager, wary . . . except for the two wearing matching expressions of irritation. "It's the Trial of Magic," she said evenly. "I need you all to lend me your power."

Silence stretched between the nine of them, so taut Elyria could have snapped it in half.

Then Leona laughed—a mirthless sound.

"You're dreaming, pixie," said Belien. "Over my dead body."

"Your reaction shocks me," Gael deadpanned.

"Ignore them," said Kit. "You have my magic, Ellie."

"And mine," said Cyren and Gael together.

Thraigg grunted. "Aye."

"Whatever I can give," added Zephyr meekly.

"Yes," said Nox.

Then, as if they'd purposefully synchronized it, each champion turned toward Cedric in one fluid movement.

Elyria noted the tick in his jaw, as if even contemplating this—loaning her his magic—was causing him physical pain. She tried to see it from his perspective. Even after his informal alliances with Zephyr and Thraigg, and his begrudging truce with Elyria, the idea of merging magic was something else entirely. It opened him up to a new kind of vulnerability.

Golden-brown eyes met Elyria's. *Please,* she thought. *Trust me.*

Several tense seconds passed, and then he nodded.

Something throbbed in her chest.

Leona sucked in a breath through clenched teeth, as if horrified that her fellow human would agree to this.

"Do you know what to do?" Cedric asked.

Elyria nodded, a memory of Evander overtaking her for a split second—his golden eyes crinkling as a wry smile appeared on his handsome face. The way he confidently sliced open his palm, soothing her worries, assuring her that this is what soulmates did. How sharing their magic would prove that they belonged to each other.

She blinked the image away. "We have to"—she drew her dagger from her hip—"merge our blood."

Cedric's eyes widened as she took the pointed tip and dug it into her left palm. "Blood magic?"

Blood pooled in Elyria's hand as she held it out. "Not the kind you're thinking of. It's not *sanguinagi* magic. There's absolutely nothing nefarious about this, I assure you."

"You're sure?"

Elyria nodded. "I've done it before." She flicked her eyes to Kit, then back to the knight. "Trust me."

The seven champions fanned out in a crescent before her, the wall of root and thorn at her back.

Kit took the dagger and sliced the tip of her finger. She let a few drops fall into Elyria's palm.

Nox went next, their maroon blood tinting the mixture a darker shade. Then Zephyr and Thraigg, her droplets of green blood swallowed up by a rivulet of his, red and bright.

Cyren and Gael added a few drops each.

Finally, it was Cedric's turn. He eyed Elyria's bleeding palm dubiously.

"I only need a drop or two," she said. "It won't take much."

"You don't—" His throat bobbed, his gaze darting between the other champions with nervous energy. "You don't actually need me, right? We wield magic through our tokens. It's not in our blood. There's nothing to merge."

"There is magic in everything," Nox said.

"And what kind of *unity* would this be without you, knightling?" Kit added with a grin. She looked at Leona, who sniffed and took a few steps back. The grin fell. "Last chance," Kit offered.

"No fucking way," Leona spat.

Cedric sighed as he sliced the tip of his finger, blood trailing down his knuckle until it dropped into Elyria's open palm.

As if Elyria's own blood understood that this was the final contribution, it started to swirl in her palm, shimmery and glistening. Then, so quickly she would have missed it if she blinked, it was gone—sucked back into her, merging with her bloodstream, not even the puncture wound on her hand left behind.

Elyria beheld her hand, the magic thrumming in her veins. The swell of untapped power that swept through her was unlike anything she'd felt before. It sang in her blood, lighting her nerves.

Something tugged at Elyria, right in the center of her chest. She raised her eyes to look at the champions surrounding her. They stared at her in awe, a luminous web weaving around them, binding them together. To her.

And amidst those shimmering threads of light, one glowed golden.

"Is it working?" Cedric asked, something like astonishment in his voice.

"Yes," she breathed, stunned by the power washing over them.

"There's just one more step, right?" Kit said, prompting the words that were stuck in the back of Elyria's throat.

"Right. Yes. You all need to wield your magic—together." Elyria took a deep breath and raised her other hand. "Call it. Cast it. Now."

They didn't hesitate.

Kit raised a hand, water swirling, darting between her knuckles.

Periwinkle hair whipped around Elyria's face as Cyren's wind freed several strands from her braid.

Shadows bloomed at Nox's feet.

Healing light poured from Zephyr's fingers.

Heat warmed Elyria's skin as Gael kindled a flame in her hand.

Thraigg grunted as he plucked a rock from the ground and gripped it tightly in his gloved hand. Elyria found herself momentarily captivated as the rock crumbled into dust, leaving a brilliant gemstone in the center of the dwarf's palm.

And then Cedric wrapped his hand around his mana token, and Elyria lit up.

Like a birthing star, fiery and bright, she felt it all. Each thread of their magic, flame and wild and water and wind mixing in her veins, in her breath, in her very being. Her inner shadow woke and joined the tapestry of magic swimming within her. She had never felt so powerful, never felt so alive.

So complete.

Elyria spun to face the wall, and this time she didn't even need to reach out and pull on those threads of wild magic within. With little more than the flex of her hand, the ice melted from the window that had taken so much effort to create. The frozen barrier dissolved, revealing the tangled vines beneath. Vines that no longer resisted, no longer fought her.

The opening widened, thorny tendrils moving with ease. As if sighing with relief, the roots unwound, untangled. They bent to Elyria's will with barely more than a thought.

Within moments, a wide, arched doorway stood in front of the group.

And as quickly as the glorious mélange of magic had come on, that thrumming power in Elyria's veins decreased, dampened, softened . . . until it was gone.

She stepped back, dabbing at her cheek with the back of her hand. "See? What did I tell you?" she said between panting breaths. "Unity."

All seven champions stared at her, disbelief etched on their faces.

"What?" she asked, suddenly self-conscious.

"That was . . ." Gael trailed off.

"You were . . ." Zephyr seemed at a loss for words.

Nox just watched Elyria with that keen crimson gaze.

Several more moments passed before Kit finally spoke. "You were glowing, Ellie," she said. "The second Cedric's blood dropped into your hand it was like . . . I can't describe it. You were like a living aurora." She paused, wringing her hands, then lowered her voice. "Was it . . . ? Was it like that before? With Ev?"

Elyria bit her bottom lip. It wasn't. That had been nothing like this. Not even close. Not just because of the number of people or the amount of power involved, either. It *felt* different. And Elyria thought Kit might have understood that because without waiting for an answer she strode toward the newly created doorway.

"Shall we?" Kit said, peering into the passage beyond.

The labyrinth loomed before them, dark and twisting pathways stretching ahead, cutting off to the left and right. The walls seemed crafted from the same roots and thorns as the outer perimeter, reaching all the way to the tops of the trees—to the barrier. There would still be no flying ahead, no peeking overtop.

No cheating.

Elyria thought she saw something move deep inside the maze, something flickering in the shadows. But before she could be sure, the walls shifted, root and thorn unwinding and rewinding to change the path before their eyes.

"Of course," Cyren muttered, his wings flicking in irritation as he joined her. "Couldn't just be a straight path, could it?"

Suddenly, Kit spun, her eyes narrowed on a spot behind Elyria's head. "No. Not you."

Elyria turned to see Leona and Belien standing unnervingly close. The back of her neck prickled in warning.

"We've seen enough," said Leona, taking another step toward the doorway. "We're off to get our crown now."

Gael stepped into their path, between the pair and Elyria. "You shouldn't even be allowed in! You didn't help. You didn't do *anything*."

"Now, that's not fair," sneered Leona. "We had to sit here and wait for your pathetic asses to figure it out. That took a great deal more effort than you'd think."

"You're a disgrace," Kit said. "You give all humans an even worse name than you've already got."

Belien tensed. "Watch your tongue, pixie witch."

"It's thanks to one of us 'pixie witches' that you even have the option of moving ahead. Elyria still has yet to hear your thanks."

Leona laughed—a shrill, piercing sound. "Of course, how rude of me. *Thank you*." She sketched a mocking curtsy. "All hail the mighty Revenant—champion of Nyrundelle, slayer of humans, living nightlight."

Elyria's hand twitched. The light from the champions' combined magic might have faded, but some remnant still thrummed in her veins. She could feel it sparking at her fingertips, right alongside her now very awake shadow.

She fought the urge to lash out at the two humans. To fight now would go against everything they just accomplished, everything they now knew about how the Crucible worked and what it wanted.

Leona didn't seem to care. With a glance at Belien, she took a step toward Elyria, full of menacing promise. "In truth, there is something we should thank you for, I suppose," she said.

Elyria's brow creased. "Oh?"

"You demonstrated so beautifully how we might even the magical playing field once we've won the crown. If all it takes is a little bit of your blood to wield Arcanian power, maybe things really can start to change after all."

Elyria rolled her eyes. "That's not even how it works, you insane bit—"

She didn't get a chance to finish before Leona's hand darted to her token. Elyria barely had time to yell a word of warning before she was thrown aside.

Kit and Gael darted out of the way as Leona and Belien barrelled toward the labyrinth entrance, narrowly avoiding the magical strikes Leona continued dealing left and right.

The blow that hit Elyria was like a punch to the gut. She gasped for breath as she scrambled back to her feet. She ran after the sorcerers, tossing a disbelieving glance at Cedric as she passed him. He was frozen, indecision stamped into every line of his face. Thraigg and Zephyr cast nervous looks at him, as if waiting for him to tell them what to do. Nox was nowhere to be seen—had they already taken off into the labyrinth without anyone noticing?

Fucking nocterrian.

A stream of fire flew over Elyria's head, catching the tail of Leona's cloak just as she crossed the threshold. Gael whooped victoriously, standing a few paces behind Elyria as Leona shrieked, stopping mid-run to stomp out the flames licking her feet.

Without a thought, Elyria shot out a hand, dark tendrils forming a ribbon of shadow, the edges sharp as a blade as they raced for Leona. Whatever flicker of surprise she might've felt from her shadows finally emerging was quickly smothered by the need to thwart the sorcerer. She would stop her. She would bind her. And then they would deal with her.

But Elyria had momentarily forgotten about Belien. He jumped into the path of Elyria's shadow. With a burst of mana, he deflected the sharp ribbon, sending it in a wide arc over Elyria's head.

No. No, no, no, no.

Elyria knew what had happened before she heard Gael's shocked, pained gasp. Before she felt the earth shudder with the impact of Gael's body hitting the ground. Before she saw the blood splattered across the grass or the severed wing laying at a grotesque angle nearby.

Bile rose in Elyria's throat.

"Monsters!" Cyren's roar was a battle cry as he raced into the labyrinth after Belien and Leona. There wasn't even time to try to stop him. With a flash of silver-white wings, he was gone. As were the humans, having disappeared into the curving maze.

Elyria rushed to Gael's side, her heart pounding. The flamecaller's breaths were shallow as Elyria brushed a lock of wine-red hair back from her forehead. She was already so pale.

"I'm sorry, I'm so sorry," Elyria muttered, frantic.

Zephyr and Kit were a blur as they worked in tandem to stop the bleeding.

"Stay with me, Winters," Kit commanded as she wrapped tendrils of healing magic around what remained of Gael's right wing.

"You're going to be okay, I promise," said Zephyr, her hands glowing as she ran them across Gael's body and whatever unseen injuries lay within.

Guilt burned under Elyria's skin. Ice slithered through her gut. Heavy footsteps and scraping metal sounded behind her head, and she knew without looking who was standing behind her.

"This is your fault!" she yelled, whirling on Cedric.

He backed up several paces. "Me? That's—"

She didn't let him speak. Advancing another step with every accusation, she screamed, "You just stood there!" *Advance.* "You let them get away!" *Advance.* "What were you thinking?" *Advance.*

"I—"

"That's right, *nothing*. You stood there like a fucking coward while your *human brethren*"—she hurled the words at him like a poisoned dagger—"tried to cheat their way to the crown."

Cedric's face fell. "And do you think they deserve to die for cheating?" His voice was low.

It stopped Elyria's rage in its tracks for a fleeting moment. He wasn't just talking about Leona and Belien. "No," she said with conviction. "But they do deserve it for what they just did to Gael. What they could be doing to Cyren now, for all we know."

Gael coughed weakly. "Some . . . someone . . ."

Elyria was back at her side in an instant. "Shh," she said. "Save your strength. Focus on healing."

"Someone has to go help him," Gael pleaded. "Help Cy, *please*."

Elyria met Zephyr's forest-green eyes. "Can she move?"

Pulling vial after vial from her belt, Zephyr shook her head. "Not yet."

"Then we need to split up," Elyria said, getting back to her feet. She scooped up her staff from where she had discarded it earlier and thrust one end into the ground, leaning into it as though she might collapse without the support. "I'm going after them."

Kit stood. "We'll go." Her instantaneous assent had Elyria's heart clenching. She made it only two steps before stopping again, however. Casting a nervous look between Zephyr and Gael, Kit said, "What if they need—"

"I'll stay." Thraigg's deep voice was uncharacteristically solemn.

Elyria gave the dwarf a nod of thanks. "Don't proceed until she has recovered enough to move—not a moment before. We will find Cyren . . . and deal with Leona and Belien. And we'll meet you on the other side."

"I'll go too." Cedric's voice was heavy with some emotion that made Elyria's chest tighten. She couldn't deal with that right now—didn't *want* to. She knew she wasn't being fair to him. She knew she was projecting, her own guilt over the role she'd played in Gael's mutilation tearing at her heart.

She didn't care.

"No," she told him, and she thought he might have shuddered at the chill in her voice. *Good.* "You stay here with Gael. It's the least you can do."

And with a final look at the butchered wing lying on the grass, Elyria ran into the labyrinth.

CHAPTER 30
IN THE LABYRINTH

Elyria

The narrow, suffocating corridors of the labyrinth were formed from more of the same tightly wound roots and vines as the outer wall. They were just as tall, too, the tangled walls reaching the tips of the surrounding trees, towering over Elyria and Kit—an imposing maze.

Heavy, humid air covered them like a blanket, the light filtering in through the treetops overhead muted and overcast. There was no sign of the crisp air or fresh sunshine they'd experienced before crossing the threshold into the labyrinth. It was as if they had traveled to an entirely different place.

Kit at her heels, Elyria turned corner after corner, searching for a flash of blue hair or the glint of silver-white wings—any sign of Cyren. The farther they ran, the deeper they went, the more things started to change.

Walls shifted, roots unraveling and re-forming in a slow, deliberate dance that altered their route midstep. More than once, they had to stop and change course as the path they'd been heading down came to an abrupt end.

The ground beneath them grew uneven, dirt giving way to jagged stone. Elyria kept her staff in hand, her eyes continually scanning their disorienting surroundings. She was alert, focused . . . but she also couldn't help the sinking feeling of hopelessness that was starting to press on her shoulders. They were already so, so lost.

"I don't like this," Kit said, her voice low as she followed close behind Elyria.

"Neither do I. Stay close and be ready for anything."

They slowed their pace as the ground began to slope downward. The thick walls of root and thorn started to morph as well, soon replaced by long stretches of smooth, solid stone.

Elyria knew they were still technically outside, that the sky was still somewhere overhead. But there was something about the construct of the labyrinth that felt familiar too. It reminded her of the winding hallways she found herself traversing the night before last, when she'd met Cedric in the moonlight.

The narrow pathways widened. The air grew cooler. The ambient light filtering from above dimmed. The walls and pathways continued shifting. If the maze already had them this turned around, they would have no chance of locating Cyren once they were wandering around in the dark.

Thankfully, they wouldn't have to find out.

Elyria's breath caught in her throat. Like something out of a dream, the cool stone on either side of the passage began to shimmer, reflecting a kaleidoscope of color.

Whatever stone was used to build this part of the labyrinth, whatever magic it held within, was absolutely breathtaking. Even in the dimming light, a rainbow of hues danced across its iridescent surface.

Luminous.

Otherworldly.

Like the aurora itself had been snatched from the sky and held within.

It was incredibly beautiful. And, for some reason, deeply unsettling.

Kit extended a hand toward the stone, brushing her fingers against its surface, equally transfixed.

The distant sound of rattling rock drew Elyria's gaze away from the mesmerizing walls. "We have to keep moving."

Melancholy flashed across Kit's face, but she nodded all the same.

The maze's path continued to slope down—gradually at first, then in a steep decline. It made the iridescent stone walls on either side seem like they were growing taller, the treetops and outside world disappearing as the walls curved over their heads, creating a tall, arched ceiling.

A tunnel.

They could very well have been deep underground, the opalescent walls emitting an ambient glow strong enough to light the passage before them. It guided them—whenever they came across a split in the tunnel, whenever a wall shifted or they got turned around, the light would glow, would shimmer, beckon.

The faint noise of clashing steel and shouting drew their attention.

Faster, Elyria thought, exchanging a look with Kit as clangs reverberated off the tunnel walls and the heady scent of magic stung her nose. They chased the sound, rounding a corner and—

Elyria's eyes widened at the scene before her. The *battle* taking place. Not just between Cyren and Belien, who were weaving around each other like dueling serpents, hurling attack after venomous attack, but between the champions and the labyrinth itself, which seemed to have come alive around them.

The walls pulsed with energy. The smooth panels of stone shook and rumbled, vibrating as if irritated with the fight that had unfolded. With this blatant display of disunity—of *enmity*.

As if the labyrinth—the trial itself—was itching to join the fight.

They were in a dead-ended section of the tunnel, wide and empty. A cavernous room that stretched overhead, moonlight flowing through a perfect circle cut from the stone ceiling.

Had they really been traversing the labyrinth that long? Or was this the Sanctum's uncanny magic at work again? Elyria couldn't dwell long on the thought as a blur of blue and silver darted in front of her.

Cyren moved almost too quickly to see, a dagger in his right hand, his left conjuring gusts of wind that boosted him forward, sideways, back, allowing him to dodge Belien's attacks. An ornate, needle-pointed rapier flew through the air as Belien used his magic to wield it from afar, keeping himself out of the stormbender's reach.

Kit ran forward, her hands already weaving patterns in the air, calling upon her magic. But before she could reach Cyren, could aid him, the shimmering walls pulsed, a shock wave ripping through the room. Kit stumbled, her magic faltering as she fought to keep her balance—as if the labyrinth was blocking her attempt to interfere.

And where was Leona? Elyria's eyes darted around the room until they landed on the sorcerer leaning against the wall on one side, clutching her arm. Blood stained her sleeve, Elyria noted with grim satisfaction.

It wasn't enough to keep her from rejoining the fight though. Leona's eyes narrowed on Kit, and Elyria found herself moving forward at the same time as the sorcerer. Gripping her staff tightly, Elyria thrust it into Leona's path, tripping her.

Leona stumbled forward, then whirled on Elyria. "You!"

Elyria wiggled her fingers in greeting. "Me."

With a furious sneer on her face and a dagger Elyria hadn't noticed suddenly in her hand, Leona lunged.

Slamming the end of her staff into the ground, Elyria spun herself on the shaft, pivoting her body out of harm's way and rounding on Leona from behind. With a swift kick, she planted her boot on Leona's ass and shoved. Leona plummeted toward the nearest wall, crying out as she caught herself with her injured arm.

The air around them crackled with magic, the ground beneath their feet gently rumbling. Leona flipped her dagger to the other hand, releasing her token for a moment. Elyria noted the way the gem at its center looked dull, its light waning. Leona was almost out of mana. Which meant this fight was all but over.

"Enough, Leona." Magic crackled at Elyria's fingertips. "This is insane. You have no reason to fight us."

"You would say that," Leona snarled. "You truly have no idea, do you? You selfish, *spoiled* Arcanians. We aren't the ones fighting! You have all that magic, have centuries upon centuries to learn and grow, to live and *let us live*, yet you make it your priority to fight, to keep us from that which you don't even need.

"The crown is our chance to change things, to take back what should be ours. To ensure we no longer live under the shadow of your kind, at the mercy of those like you." Her voice shook, a crazed look in her eyes. "So, no, Revenant. You do not say when it's enough. I do." She lunged forward and levied a vicious swipe at Elyria with the dagger.

Elyria stepped back and swung her staff wide. Leona cried out as the wood connected with her injured arm, the sound reverberating off the labyrinth's shuddering walls.

"You're running out of time," Elyria said, her tone even. "You're injured; your mana is almost gone. You won't walk away from this if you keep this up. Stop fighting and work with us. We might still be able to get out of the Crucible alive."

Leona panted, her ruined arm clutched against her chest, bloody fingers wrapped around her token. The dagger she had been holding moments before hovered threateningly in the air between them.

"What point is there in leaving the Crucible alive without the crown in hand?" Leona's voice was raw, her eyes wild. With a furious shout and a burst of mana, the dagger went flying.

Elyria sidestepped the attack. The dagger flew into the wall at her back, embedding deep in the stone. Tossing her staff aside, she curled both her hands into fists, grabbing on to the tendrils of shadow she could feel simmering under her skin.

She shot them at Leona.

But these were not the razor-sharp ribbons that had sliced Gael's wing. They were soft wisps of dark smoke that wrapped around Leona's ankles and good arm, pinning her in place.

Leona let out a scream of frustration and bellowed Belien's name, calling for help. But a cursory look to the other side of the cavern showed Elyria that he had more than his hands full.

Belien's rapier danced through the air as Cyren dodged and parried, his movements a windy blur. From the side, Kit was throwing blockades of ice up between them, attempting to slow Belien down, to keep Cyren obscured from sight.

Face me and fight fair, you winged bitch!

Elyria froze, her eyes shooting to Leona, still pinned in place, lips pressed tightly together. But Elyria could have sworn she heard her speak.

Realization nearly knocked her over. She *had* heard Leona. She'd heard her the same way she'd heard Brandon Cormac in his final moments back in Castle Lumin.

With sudden clarity, Elyria recalled the moments of seemingly silent communication she'd observed between Leona and Belien. The insufferable *knowingness* she exuded.

Leona was a mindwielder. She was a fucking *sage*.

And with what must have been the last dregs of her mana, she unleashed herself on Elyria.

Static filled Elyria's mind. It blurred her vision, crept into her ears. She couldn't think, couldn't hear anything but white, hot noise. The cries of a hundred dying soldiers, the squelching sound of weapons tearing through flesh, the coppery tang of blood, the stench of death. Every life she'd taken as the Revenant, every wound she'd inflicted, every cry of pain and scream of fear.

It overwhelmed her. Warmth trickled from her nose. She stumbled. Nearly lost her grip on the shadows shackling Leona.

But she didn't.

Elyria held firm, pushing back and focusing her thoughts on cinching those wisps of shadow tighter. A pained whimper slipped from Leona, and the static in Elyria's mind cleared.

With a surge of wild magic, Elyria sent a fracture through the wall behind her, cracking the slab of stone into a hundred pieces, calling each one to her.

Leona pulled on her shadowy restraints, crouching, cowering before the looming barrage—a hail of fractured stone that could easily have crushed her to a pulp.

Elyria held fast, allowing the stone fragments to encircle Leona, twisting around her threateningly. "Stop. Fighting. Us," Elyria repeated through gritted teeth.

Leona's breath grew ragged and desperate, and for the first time, Elyria saw something other than fury flicker in her hazel eyes.

She saw fear.

The kind of fear that makes people do crazy things.

Leona screamed—a loud, defiant roar. Hot static filled Elyria's mind again. Ringing filled her ears. Louder, sharper, more painful than before. It shattered the grasp she had on the shadows that shackled Leona, made the hail of splintered stone fall to the ground.

And it wasn't just her.

Elyria's head whipped to the side as she heard Kit's cry, Belien's shout, Cyren's pained bellow. Her bleary eyes sought out the other champions—all three were on the ground, heads clutched in their hands.

Leona was no longer targeting just Elyria. Her psychic magic flooded the entire cavern, bombarding them all.

Elyria fell to her knees, hands pressed against her ears. Leona's magic pulsed inside her skull, filling the cracks and crevices in her mind, as if it sought to rip her consciousness apart from the inside.

I'll see you all dead before I let you take it.

Kit let out another high-pitched cry, pain radiating from the sound, and Elyria's blood began to boil. Leona was going to kill them all.

Elyria couldn't let that happen. She *wouldn't* let that happen.

Blood dripping from her nose, she dug deep inside herself. She curled her mind's eye around a thread of her darkness, coiling it like a spring.

But before she could release it, a massive quake rattled the cavern.

It wasn't her.

She didn't *think* it was her.

And it was all Elyria could do to roll to the side as the floor beneath her feet split open. Just like outside the labyrinth, a rift tore through the ground. Only instead of roots and vines erupting from within, the cleft continued to widen, a deep, endless chasm unraveling beneath them.

A despairing noise fell from Elyria's lips as she watched her staff tumble into the void. She couldn't dwell on the loss. As if the labyrinth was hunting those who had disturbed its peace, the rift chased Elyria. Still flattened to the ground, she rolled away, over and over, until her back hit a wall and she could roll no farther.

The rift didn't stop.

Elyria gasped as the floor beneath her crumbled away, as she felt that split second of weightlessness.

And then she fell.

CHAPTER 31
NOTHING TO LOSE

Elyria

Elyria clawed at the dirt, her feet kicking wildly as she plummeted. Her boot caught in the soft earth making up the sides of the fissure, and she managed to stop herself before she fell in completely.

With effort, she grappled with the steep side until she was able to boost herself back up over the edge, hauling her torso onto solid ground. For a moment, she hung there, bent at the waist, hips and legs dangling into the open chasm below. The tendons in her back strained painfully as she tried to pull more of herself out, but the ground was slick beneath her sweating palms.

Turning her head, she locked eyes with Kit, crouched on the other side of the rift. There was terror in her blue and green eyes as she rose, her head twisting as she looked for a place where she could get across. Could get to Elyria.

It didn't matter. She was too far away.

And Elyria was slipping.

She flared her wings uselessly, that pressure still weighing down on her, preventing her from flying to safety. She called on her wild magic, willed the soil below her to move, to solidify, to boost her back onto solid ground.

But she couldn't grasp it, not as she continued to slide, her fingers bleeding as she dug her nails into the ground.

This was how she would die, then. The Revenant, swallowed by darkness in the most literal sense. Elyria wanted to laugh at the poetry of it.

She threw her head back, a curse at the celestials for this trial and the existence of the entire infernal Crucible on the tip of her tongue. Something shiny glinted at the edge of her vision, and her eyes shot to the source—the golden hilt of Leona's dagger, embedded in the wall six inches to the right and a foot above her.

Hope sparked in her chest as Elyria reached for it.

Then, with one final rumble of the cavern, that hope sputtered out. A woman's earsplitting scream filled the space just as Elyria's bloodied fingers scraped the hilt. She lost the tentative bit of balance she had garnered and slipped farther. She relatched her hands to the ledge, her heart plummeting into her stomach.

"Kit!" she shouted, fear coating every inch of her insides. She couldn't even turn her head to check for her friend.

"I'm okay!" Kit called back, and relief flooded Elyria's veins so rapidly she nearly burst into tears. But if it wasn't Kit she heard, then . . .

Leona screamed again; the sound was sharp at first—a panicked shriek that softened as it faded. It was followed by Belien's agonized howl, and Elyria knew Leona had fallen.

She wished she could bring herself to care.

Bootsteps pummeled the ground, the vibrations shaking Elyria's grip on the ledge. Kit's moonlight hair flew into Elyria's line of sight a few seconds later, that look of terror still sketched on her young face as she wrapped her hands around Elyria's wrists.

"Just hang on, Ellie," Kit said, her voice cracking. "On the count of three, grab hold of me. I'll pull you up."

Elyria nodded, pressing her sweaty fingers into the ground with as much force as she could muster.

"One . . . two . . . three!"

Another moment of weightlessness as Elyria let go and grabbed hold of Kit. Grunting, Kit pulled. Elyria pushed against the rift's side walls, gritting her teeth against the bite of the jagged ledge scraping against her stomach. And then Cyren was there too, wrapping an arm around Elyria's waist, the three of them working together to haul her out of the pit.

"Thank you," Elyria managed to gasp, looking between Kit and Cyren after they'd scrambled to a stretch of unbroken ground. "That was a bit close for comfort."

"No thanks necessary. Though I'm sure I can come up with some creative ways you can show your gratitude if you insist." Cyren grinned, the humor in his eyes only slightly dimmed by the wince that followed.

"Are you hurt?" Elyria asked, examining the fae with alarm.

He waved away her concern. "Fear not, beautiful," he said, the flirtatious lilt of his tone dragging Elyria's inspecting gaze back to his face so she could give him a pointed look. "I'll survive."

He shifted his focus across the cavern to where Belien sat on his knees, staring over the edge of the chasm. There was something vacant about the look on his face, something sharper than despondence, darker than disbelief over Leona's fall. It sent a shiver up Elyria's spine.

The ground was still, the cavern hauntingly quiet. As if Leona's death had satisfied the labyrinth. With a groan, Elyria sat up, testing her limbs and prodding gently at her abdomen. Pain radiated through her body, her muscles tender and strained, but nothing was torn, nothing broken. She raked a hand down her face, grateful to note that her nose had stopped bleeding too.

Her shoulders sagged, relief and exhaustion chasing the adrenaline from her blood, and for a few moments, all four champions sat in silence. Elyria didn't think she could move even if she wanted to.

The sound of shifting metal and that *tug* from within her forced Elyria's eyes to the cavern entrance just as Cedric came into view, his chest heaving. Surprise and an annoyingly disproportionate amount of relief lit her from the inside when she saw him.

Zephyr emerged at the knight's side, her large green eyes taking in the scene before them—the piles of shattered stone, the champions on the floor, the split in the ground.

Kit's head whipped to the newly arrived champions. "Gael?" she asked.

Zephyr nodded and cast a look behind her, where a pale-faced Gael stepped out from a shadow. Elyria's eyebrows shot up as she realized the fae was propped up by the formerly missing Tenebris Nox.

"Well, fuck me," Thraigg whispered as he skidded to a stop next to them, his blue eyes scanning the broken cavern before falling on Elyria, Kit, and Cyren. He cleared his throat with a low cough. "Glad to see ye're still alive."

"Most of us," Kit said, a sadness in her tone that had Elyria's throat tightening with pride. She had such a good heart. As awful as Leona was, Kit didn't relish her death.

Unfortunately, her empathy didn't seem to make much of a difference to Belien, who was suddenly whipping his head between the two groups of champions—Elyria, Kit, and Cyren still sitting on the other side of the rift, Cedric, Zephyr, Thraigg, Gael, and Nox at the cavern's entrance—as if he just remembered he wasn't alone.

He staggered to his feet, his face a twisted mask of anguish. Eyes bloodshot, his breaths came in shallow gasps—speeding up and slowing down in an erratic pattern, like he was fighting a growing panic.

A pang of pity ran through Elyria. Belien was an absolute asshole, but he had now lost his sister and Leona both. He was without allies. How alone he must have felt. Elyria's eyes flicked to his token, which glimmered weakly with his residual mana. How alone and how powerless.

"You." His voice was a rasping snarl, filled with venom and despair. Elyria returned her gaze to his face, expecting to find his malice directed at Cyren, Kit, or herself.

It wasn't.

Belien's hand trembled as he raised it at Cedric, his expression shifting—turning darker, more hateful—with each infinitesimal degree he lifted his arm. "You were supposed to be the one to save us. We came to try, came to do right by our people, but it was always supposed to be you, wasn't it? Champion of Kingshelm. Savior of Havensreach." Sneering, he took several steps toward Cedric. "Look at you now."

Cedric mirrored his movements, moving away from Zephyr, Gael, Thraigg, and Nox, all of whom had fanned into the cavern behind him. "I never claimed to be anyone's savior."

Belien's laugh was bitter. Hollow. "Now you stand with *them*. From the instant you arrived at Castle Lumin, you've been clamoring to join forces with them. Jumping at every opportunity to work with our enemy. Betraying your own kind. Becoming a *traitor*. And for what? So they can steal the crown right out of your hands when you make it to the end? So they can continue to hoard the land and power of Arcanis while more of us die each day?"

Cedric's jaw hardened. "That's not true. The Arbiter said—"

"Fuck the Arbiter." Belien took another step toward Cedric, the two of them now standing on parallel sides of the rift in the ground. "All this talk of unity, of *harmony*. It's bullshit. They'll only continue doing what they always do. Stepping on our necks to raise themselves higher."

Elyria's breath hitched. The tension in the air was so thick she could have sliced right through it. But the labyrinth had already shown them what became of fighting in here. "It's over, Belien," she said. "Let it go. You don't have to end up like them."

It was the wrong thing to say.

Belien whirled toward her, his hand clamped around his token. "I won't let this be what Belis gave her life for. I won't let Leona have died for nothing."

Belien raised his hand, and time seemed to slow. Using his magic to draw a jagged piece of stone from the floor, he carved its razor-sharp edge into the underside of his forearm. Crimson spilled down both sides of his wrist, dripping onto the floor like raindrops summoned straight from the fourth quarter of hell.

That's when Elyria felt it.

Felt the power emanating off the sorcerer in palpable waves. Heard the magic crackling through the air. Saw the dark scarlet veins blooming under Belien's eyes.

"Blood magic." Kit's voice was barely a whisper as the group watched the heinous transformation unfold.

Magic rolled off Belien, ricocheting off the stone walls of the cavern in random bursts as if he couldn't contain it. The other champions were in disarray, trying to avoid the crimson bolts of power. Zephyr yelped as one struck alarmingly close, Nox pulling her into the shadows just before it bounced back.

But Elyria's gaze was still on Belien. Gray-blue eyes transformed into a deep, burning red as he met Elyria's wide-eyed stare. The side of his mouth tipped up in a dark smile, and she knew. He was going to kill her.

Pain blossomed in Elyria's muscles as she moved, angling herself in front of Kit. There was no time to do anything else, and Elyria could only pray that her body might protect Kit from the magical blow—the final act of defiance from a man with nothing left to lose.

Then, just before he released the wave of dark magic roiling around him, Belien shifted. He twisted his body, guiding his bloodied arm until it was pointing at someone else.

And Elyria's heart plummeted into her gut.

"Cedric!" His name ripped from her throat. It was too late. She could do nothing but watch as Belien's magic arced through the air, a twisted bolt of blood-red lightning that hit Cedric in the center of his chest.

The knight soared backward, the deafening clang of his armor echoing through the cavern as he slammed into the wall and slid limply to the floor.

The entire world narrowed as Elyria leapt to her feet, pain and exhaustion a distant memory. She sprinted to Cedric's side, her stomach twisting as she spotted the smear of red on the wall behind him. His eyes were closed, his face drained of color, but his brow was furrowed, his lips moving. Relief and terror tugged at her chest in equal measure. He was hurt—very, very badly—but he was alive.

An inhuman growl sounded from behind her. She turned her head. Belien was still alive too. Hunched over, panting, veins of scarlet continuing to creep over his skin, even as he bled out onto the cavern floor. His crimson gaze locked on Cedric's pained face, on the slight movement there.

"No." Elyria's voice was made of stone and steel as she stood, positioning herself between Belien and Cedric. Her eyes flared with a promise as the ground trembled beneath her feet.

This time, it wasn't the labyrinth.

It was the Revenant.

There was no second guessing. No pulling or begging or cajoling her power. With a single thought, ribbons of shadow shot from her hands, cinching around Belien's arms, waist, neck.

With another, Elyria tore open the fissure in the ground.

And Belien didn't even have time to shout his final words before she released him into the chasm and the earth swallowed him whole.

CHAPTER 32
SURVIVOR'S GUILT

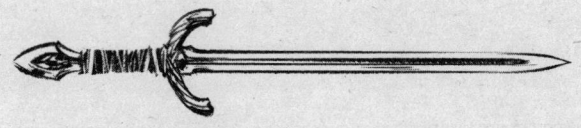

Cedric

Fog clung to Cedric's consciousness. He felt heavy. He tried to move, but his limbs were distant, detached. He was drifting, unsure of where he was, *when* he was, exactly what happened during those last moments in the cavern. Glimpses cut in and out of his mind—the cold sneer on Belien's face, sparks of red lightning, Elyria's panicked voice calling Cedric's name, and then . . . pain.

Pain and this tepid, foggy nothingness.

There was no pain now. It was peaceful, in fact. He thought he might like to drift like this forever.

The sensation of someone hovering nearby tugged at the edges of his awareness. It pressed against his consciousness, a familiar warmth, the feeling of being right on the cusp of waking from a pleasant dream.

The fog parted. His eyelids fluttered.

And Cedric knew he must be dead.

Because there, leaning over him, was the most beautiful being he'd ever beheld. And surely nothing like *her* existed in a place as harsh as the one he'd left behind.

Otherworldly beauty seeped from every plane of her face, radiating from the soft curve of her jaw, beaming from her jewel-toned eyes. Her loose periwinkle hair was luminous in the faint light as it spilled over her shoulders.

She was a goddess, watching over him as his soul slipped into the Hereafter.

He opened his eyes farther, and the world began to sharpen around him. Pain lanced his chest, surging through his veins like molten iron, and Cedric suddenly longed to return to that fog of nothingness.

If he was dead, why did everything hurt so damn much?

The sharp intake of breath drew his attention back to the ethereal figure floating over him, and reality struck him like a hammer.

Not a goddess.

A fae.

Elyria's face was impossibly close, her bottom lip between her teeth, green eyes filled with worry as they ran down his face, his neck, his chest. Searching. Pleading.

Maybe he really was dead. Because that was the only possible explanation for why she would be looking at him like that.

"Cedric?" Her voice turned his name into a song, a melody that washed the vestiges of that mental fog from his mind. Her hand rested on his upper arm, a gentle touch that sent a spark across his skin. It was then that he realized he was bare from the waist up, save for the long bandages wrapped around his chest, shoulder, and head.

With a low groan, Cedric shifted and tried to prop himself up on his elbows, each breath sending a sharp pain through his ribs.

"Don't move." Elyria leaned back, the lilt of her voice shifting into something commanding. Protective. "He's awake," she called over her shoulder, and Cedric heard the soft patter of footsteps before Zephyr's frowning face entered his field of vision.

"Thank Gaia," said the sylvan, immediately ducking down and fussing with Cedric's bandages.

"How"—he coughed, his words trapped in his dry throat—"how long?" he rasped.

"A few hours," Elyria replied, some emotion flicking across her face that belied the casualness in her voice.

"What happened? Where is Bel—"

"Dead." The word was calm but laced with tension, the kind that made Cedric feel like he was missing something important.

He blinked, his mind sluggish as it struggled to piece together what had transpired in those last moments. Belien was dead. So was Leona, he remembered. He hadn't witnessed her fall, but he'd certainly had the honor of bearing the brunt of Belien's grief.

Elyria stood abruptly, leaving a sudden chill in the place where her hand had lain upon his arm.

Stiffly, Cedric pushed himself into a sitting position, ignoring the protestations of Zephyr and his body alike—the spike of pain that pulled across his ribs and the throbbing at the back of his head. He tracked Elyria's movements as she ventured toward the small campfire burning nearby, the rest of the champions lounging around it.

Thraigg's burly frame was curled over his hammer, the metal glinting in the firelight as he cleaned it. Cedric met his eye, and the dwarf offered him a stout nod. Next to him, Nox sat with their legs crossed and eyes closed, absentmindedly stroking one of the dark curved horns on their head, deep in thought. Cyren and Kit had their heads bowed together, speaking in low tones. They took turns tossing surreptitious glances at Gael, who sat in front of the fire, hands wrapped around her knees, staring blankly into the flames.

They were still in the cavern. Cedric's eyes widened as he realized the ground he sat upon was once again whole and even. Evidence of the battle remained—piles of broken stone strewn across the floor, sections painted with the dark stain of blood. But there was no sign of the wide rift that had cut the cavern in half. Had Elyria sealed the sundered ground?

He looked at her retreating form, her head turned to the side as she braided her hair down one shoulder, offering the slimmest glimpse of her face as she walked away. He would've sworn her eyes kept darting back to him, though he couldn't read the emotion there. Was it . . . guilt? Or something else? She was acting as though the sight of him pained her.

He didn't understand. If anyone should be feeling guilty, it was him.

Traitor. Betrayer.

Belien's accusations ran on a loop in Cedric's mind. He should have felt something like relief or satisfaction—justice?—knowing the sorcerer was gone. He'd been a poison on the entire Crucible, spreading nothing but bitterness and animosity since before they'd even gone through the Gate. Leona, too. In direct conflict with what the Crucible clearly expected of its champions. Time and time again, their behavior had proven them a stain on humanity's reputation. The idea that one of them might be the one to claim the crown had been humiliating at best, terrifying at worst.

And that was *before* a blood-mad Belien had tried to incinerate Cedric on the spot.

But all Cedric felt was a sort of sinking feeling around his heart. He couldn't get the accusations out of his head. Was he a traitor to his kind? Was that what his legacy would be? He was the last remaining human champion. And he'd only gotten here because time and time again, an Arcanian had been willing to put their pride and personal gain aside to help him.

Cedric had never felt smaller. Even now, he was sure he was only alive thanks to their machinations.

He rubbed his hand over the bandage on his torso, at the spot where Belien's blood magic had struck him. How *was* he still alive? He'd felt the bolt cut straight through his armor, felt that sharp, piercing pain in his chest. He was certain that the only place he should have woken after a blow like that was in the Hereafter.

Zephyr was still fussing behind him, and Cedric winced as she lifted the bandage wrapped around his head to apply a foul-smelling balm. Between her and the quartet of fae present, all blessed with a modicum of healing magic, Cedric knew that his injuries must have been very grave indeed for him to still be in this much pain.

He sighed, inwardly chastising himself. He'd become soft, already entirely too used to the convenience and comfort of magical healing. His nose scrunched and his lips pursed as Zephyr rubbed the pungent balm on his chest wound, his head swimming from the stench.

A melodic laugh floated into Cedric's ear. Drawn like magnets, his eyes shot to the source.

He'd thought Elyria would have joined the other champions at the fire by now. Instead, she reapproached Cedric, a small bundle in her hands.

"Here," she said, holding it out to him. Then, wrinkling her nose and looking assessingly at Zephyr, she added, "Although, perhaps you won't have much of an appetite until that . . . aroma . . . fades."

Cedric's brows drew together as he took the bundle from Elyria and unwrapped it to reveal five strips of bacon folded in a cloth napkin.

He looked at her.

Her eyes still wouldn't quite focus on him, and she chewed her lip as if self-conscious, though Cedric couldn't possibly imagine why she'd be feeling that way. Was this about what just happened with Belien? Or was it about what *almost* happened between the two of them?

"I recall you being rather stingy with sharing," he said, his lips tilting up on one side. He shoveled a piece of bacon into his mouth, savoring the rich, salty flavor as it washed over his tongue.

She shrugged. "I took extra from breakfast, and you caught me in a generous mood. Don't get used to it."

"Right. Of course." His grin widened.

"I mean, if you don't want it—"

"No, no," he said hastily. "I want it."

The silence that hung in the air felt incredibly heavy.

Zephyr stood, a grunt of self-approval piercing the tension as she looked over Cedric's bandages one final time. "I'm not sure *bacon* would have been my first choice in recovery foods, but I suppose it's a good sign that you have an appetite."

Elyria sprang into motion. "Oops. Well, you heard her, Sir Knight. Healer's orders, so sorry." She bent down and snatched the remaining bacon from Cedric's hand, ripping off a piece and popping it between her lips with a laugh before sauntering away.

"How about some water and crackers instead?" Zephyr had a knowing look in her forest-green eyes that Cedric promptly ignored.

"You have crackers?" he asked.

She pointed at a pouch on her belt and grinned. "Oh, I am always well stocked when it comes to snacks."

Cedric felt his lips curving up in a smile, though a new thought quickly wiped it from his face. What about the rest of them? They all had to be hungry, especially if they'd been waiting for Cedric to wake up all these hours. A wet trickle of guilt spread down his spine, worming its way into his stomach.

His concern must have shown on his face, because Zephyr went on to say, "Everyone else has already eaten."

"Gotten full off your crackers, have they?" he asked skeptically.

Zephyr chuckled and jutted her chin toward Elyria and Kit, who were now speaking by the fire. "When you've a wildshaper and a tideweaver in your midst, one doesn't need to worry too much about finding sustenance."

As if she felt Cedric's gaze fall on her, Elyria glanced over her shoulder. She wore a wry grin as she offered him a mock salute with two fingers, then crammed another piece of bacon into her mouth.

"You just focus on healing up," Zephyr continued, "and we can be on our way. I think we are all quite eager to get to the end of this trial."

Unease settled further in the pit of Cedric's stomach as he nibbled on a cracker. The trial wasn't even over. They were still in the thick of it—in the midst of this literal maze. So why were they all still here? Why had they lingered, delayed?

He knew the answer, yet he didn't understand. They'd been waiting for him to wake up—*he* was the reason.

Everyone was always waiting on him.

"You were supposed to be the one to save us."

Belien's words were a dark curse settling in Cedric's mind. He clenched his fist, a flicker of something other than guilt—something hotter, wilder—stirring in his chest. He dared another glance at Elyria. If he was the one supposed to be doing the saving, why was he continually being saved? Why did she continue to bother?

Traitor. Betrayer.

He didn't deserve it.

She should have left him to be burned into ash by the dragon in the first trial. Should have left him to be consumed by the flames of his memory in the second.

Cedric shook his head, anger and confusion and self-pity rattling around in his mind like dice in a cup. This line of thinking was pointless. Pathetic. This wasn't over yet. He couldn't lose sight of the reason he was here. And despite the Crucible being so damn insistent on them all working together, a sense of knowing sank deep into the marrow of his bones that only one person would emerge as victor in the end. Only one of them would walk away with the crown—only one side would obtain its power.

And he was the only chance his people had left.

To the credit of whatever disgusting ingredients were in Zephyr's balms and poultices, they did their job credibly. The ache at the back of Cedric's head and the sting in his chest were already considerably lessened by the time the sylvan finished catching him up on everything that had happened after Belien's near-death blow.

Zephyr detailed the interest on Elyria's and Cyren's faces when the enigmatic Tenebris Nox had demonstrated their shadowstepping ability, explaining how Gael, Thraigg, and Cedric were able to catch up. She recounted Kit's demand for an explanation from Nox as to why they abandoned the group outside the labyrinth. Then her begrudging acceptance of the answer—that they'd hidden in the shadows, followed Leona and Belien through the labyrinth, and returned when the fight in the cavern broke out.

"So, you're a spy," Kit had said.

"I'm an observant person," Nox had replied.

Zephyr grinned when she recounted their exchange. It faltered when Cedric asked her for more details on exactly what had happened to Belien.

"Perhaps that's a question better served for . . ." She turned her head, her gaze landing across the cavern, where Elyria leaned against the far wall, one foot propped up behind her and a distant look in her eyes.

"Right, then." Cedric stood, marveling at how much better his body already felt as he plucked his arming doublet from where it had been folded and set aside. He pulled it on, making a mental note to beg Zephyr for the ingredients of her magical mystery cure once they were through this.

Stretching his neck—first to one side, then the other—he buttoned his doublet and strode over to Elyria.

She didn't look at him as he approached.

Didn't look at him as he took up a spot beside her, touching his back to the wall.

Didn't look at him as the voices around the campfire quieted, then surged, as if the other champions realized how obvious they were being.

Finally, Cedric couldn't take it anymore. "Thank you," he said, his eyes searching Elyria's face for some kind of reaction. Any reaction. "For helping me. For saving me. Again."

She drew her eyes from the spot of empty air they'd been fixed on and met his gaze, just for a second.

"Zephyr is the one who healed you," she said, waving her hand as if trying to dissipate his gratitude.

"But she isn't the one who avenged me."

Elyria's hand stilled in midair. Several silent seconds passed between them before she dropped it back to her side. "It wasn't for you," she said. "You saw him. Belien had gone mad. The blood magic . . . He was corrupted. What was I supposed to do?"

"What did you do, exactly?"

"Ask them." She tipped her head at the campfire and the conspicuous champions who were definitely *not* eavesdropping.

"They told me to ask you."

She pinched the bridge of her nose between her thumb and pointer finger. "I see."

"So . . . ?"

"So, I stopped him."

"You killed him," he said. A statement, not a judgment.

"I did."

A beat of silence passed between them.

"And how do you feel about that?" he asked.

Her head whipped toward him, so quick that it nearly threw Cedric off-balance. "How do you think I feel?" she hissed.

"If I knew, why would I ask?" he said, keeping his voice level. This was not how he envisioned this conversation going.

She released a shaky breath. "I've killed many people. So many. Why should this be any different?"

Cedric's chest tightened at the vulnerability in her voice. Like it wasn't a rhetorical question. Like this *was* different, only she didn't understand why.

Because everything in here is different, he wanted to say. *Because I feel like I am a different person from the one I was when I walked through the Gate. And I think you are too.*

But he didn't say that.

What he said was "And the rift in the ground?"

Elyria's shoulders sagged, visible relief flooding her face at the subject change. "I sealed it up. The labyrinth didn't complain. And we've been dithering about here since, waiting for you to wake from your beauty rest."

Emotion flickered in her eyes even as she made light of his injuries. He knew it had been bad. He just didn't know why she cared. And Cedric couldn't resist. "Beauty rest, huh? So . . . you think I'm beautiful?" he said, smoothing down the arm of his doublet, then fiddling with the end of the sleeve at his wrist.

She huffed, and Cedric couldn't quite tell if it was with irritation or humor. "I think *you* think you're beautiful."

His chest swelled.

"And I also think you're not nearly as funny as you think you are."

"I never claimed to be funny," he said, grinning.

"Ah, but how did you put it? You're considered by many to be 'positively delightful,' yes?"

His grin widened. "That is, in fact, precisely how I put it. And consider me *positively delighted* to know I made so great an impression that you memorized my words verbatim."

He would've sworn he saw her cheeks turn a shade pinker.

"Well, don't," she said simply.

"Don't what?"

"Don't think you've made that much of an impression." But the edge of her lips quivered, and satisfaction spread through Cedric's insides like warm honey. "And *don't* look so satisfied with yourself," she added.

Cedric stared at her.

"What?"

"Nothing. Just, sometimes it feels like you can read my thoughts. You can't, can you?" He narrowed his eyes in mock suspicion.

She snorted. "I hardly need to be a mindwielder in order to be able to tell what you're thinking."

"Is that so?"

"Everyone else may only see the stoic knight in your visage, but I'm afraid I find you incredibly easy to read. I don't even need to be like Leona to discern your thoughts."

The air was pushed from his lungs. "What? Leona?"

"Right. You were still getting that *much-needed* beauty sleep when I told everyone else." She smirked at him. "Turns out she was keeping quite a secret from the rest of us. The mindwielding bitch nearly managed to melt our brains before the ground split. Not fun."

She gave him a moment for that to sink in. Cedric thought about the times when he felt like Leona looked at him a little too long, the knowing way she'd taunted him about the Trial of Spirit, the silent communications he'd witnessed between her and Belien. Of course. Not just an advanced sorcerer, but a sage. No wonder she had gained such notoriety. He almost had to respect the fact that she'd successfully kept her telepathic abilities a secret for so long. Couldn't have been easy.

Cedric frowned. Now he was feeling posthumous pity for Leona? Of course he was. Abhorrent as she'd been, she was still human. In the grand scheme of things, they were here for the same reasons. They had been cut from the same cloth, had the same goal.

And now Cedric was all who remained.

"You aren't the same as them," Elyria said quietly, and for the second time in as many minutes, Cedric found himself staring at her in disbelief.

"Stop doing that," he said.

She arched a brow. "Doing what?"

Cedric bit the inside of his cheek. "Seeing right through me."

At first she didn't say anything back, just returned to staring at that spot of empty air in front of her, brow furrowed in thought.

Cedric leaned his head back against the wall, his eyes roaming to the tall, curved cavern of the ceiling.

"I don't see through you," she said, her melodic voice so soft that he thought he might have imagined it. "I just see you."

Still braced against the wall, Cedric turned his head toward her, thoughts swimming. Two silver-flecked pools of emerald green beamed at him. He opened his mouth, no idea what in all four hells he was going to say in response to that but feeling strongly like he needed to say *something*.

He was rescued from the task when Thraigg let out a grunt, stood, and lumbered over. "Glad to see ye back on yer feet, lad. Feeling all right?"

"Better." Cedric rotated his shoulders, testing the feel of his body. "Might even venture to say I'm feeling good."

A sort of bereftness sank into him as Elyria pushed off the wall, offered the dwarf a friendly nod, and proceeded to take the spot he'd just vacated by the fire.

"Glad to hear it," Thraigg said, oblivious to and unaffected by Elyria's sudden departure. "Think it'll be much longer before you're back in fighting shape? Can't imagine this damned maze will stay idle forever."

Cedric hated the confirmation that they really were only still here because they'd been waiting on him. He made a mental vow. *No longer.*

"Right," he said, jaw tight. "I'm ready when you all are."

CHAPTER 33
MAKING FRIENDS

Elyria

Get it the fuck together, Lightbreaker.

Elyria was half a heartbeat from slapping her palm clear across her own cheek in the desperate hope that it might mean smacking some sense into herself. What was *wrong* with her?

She could still feel the ghost of her power throbbing in her chest, as if ribbons of shadow were wrapped around her heart. They'd been in place ever since she'd used them to drop Belien Larkin to his death. She didn't know how to get them to loosen.

Elyria was a killer. Many times over. That was a fact. And despite her best efforts over the decades, killing with the shadow was certainly nothing new.

Killing with *her* shadow felt different.

It's not as if the crazed sorcerer didn't deserve it. He'd careened over the edge of sanity so fast it was a miracle that he didn't take more of them down with him. She didn't doubt that the others would have made the same call, the same choice, had they been able to act just a little faster.

But there was still something momentous about the seconds after Belien struck Cedric.

Because when Elyria saw him fall, her power didn't overtake her. It wasn't a knee-jerk reaction, the result of shock or self-defense. She wasn't being ruled by desperation or guided by the whims of her inner darkness.

She was in total control.

It was a purposeful, conscious choice she'd made. To hurt. To kill. To protect.

Her heart had beat an uneven rhythm as she'd wielded her shadow like a deadly rope against Belien with one hand and held on to something else with the other. That golden thread that started somewhere in her chest and led straight to that infuriating, confounding, reckless fool of a knight. A thread that had pulled taut when that crimson lightning bolt struck his heart—strained almost to the point of snapping.

A thread that she refused to let go of.

She would not let *him* go. And after she released Belien into the depths of the labyrinth's chasm and sealed the ground overtop, she turned all her focus inward and *tugged* on that thread.

He would not die today. She would make sure of it.

And so, she did.

Zephyr said she didn't understand how he had survived the hit, how he hadn't passed instantly into the Hereafter.

But Elyria knew. Knew that there was something *other* about this thing between the two of them. A bond that could have been forged with whatever they went through in the Trial of Spirit or could have simply been placed there by whichever celestial seemed to love fucking with Elyria most. And she couldn't deny its existence anymore.

Even if she could barely look Cedric in the eye now.

What the fuck is wrong with me? her inner voice reiterated, a haunting, judgmental refrain that accompanied her as she wandered toward the campfire.

She fisted her hands at her sides. *"I don't see through you. I just see you."* Elyria groaned inwardly as she recalled what she said. She didn't even know where that had come from. Thraigg's interruption could not possibly have been more timely. On the infinitesimal chance they did end up getting out of the Crucible alive, she owed the dwarf the largest mug of cider the Sweltering Pig offered.

Elyria caught Kit's eye as she approached the other champions around the fire, immediately scowling at the haughty look on her friend's face. Kit saw too much. Saw everything. And that knowledge only caused that bud of guilt in Elyria's chest to grow.

A bud that might very well bloom into a fully grown plant of misery any second if she didn't stop looking at Gael. The flamecaller was still hugging her knees to her chest, eyes pinned on the dancing flames in front of her. Her undamaged wing fluttered listlessly behind her while what remained of the other was bandaged against her back.

The sight of her twisted Elyria's insides. She knew she wasn't exactly responsible for her losing her wing, but it was partly her fault that Gael was like this. There was barely any sign of that fiery fae she'd met in Castle Lumin. Between losing Paelin in the second trial and now her wing, Elyria feared for whatever thoughts were brimming under that head of wine-red hair.

"Can't imagine this damned maze will stay idle forever." Thraigg's gruff voice carried from where he and Cedric stood, and something in Elyria's gut clenched. Had the knight recovered enough to move on yet?

With a quizzical look, she sought out Zephyr on the other side of the fire. The sylvan responded as if reading the question in Elyria's eyes, nodding gently. "Once he woke up, the rest of his injuries began healing remarkably well. More quickly than I would have thought. He should be more than ready to move on. And I think we all should—soon."

"Couldn't agree more," said Cyren, his voice lacking its usual teasing lilt as his wary eyes went to Gael.

As did Kit's. "Is she going to be able to . . . ?" she started to ask, putting voice to the question Elyria was sure they were all wondering. Cedric's injuries healing was one thing, but whatever was plaguing Gael seemed to be another entirely. Was she going to be able to pull herself together? To go on?

Cyren's brow furrowed. "I'll keep an eye on her," he said quietly. "But we all know we can't stay here."

Kit nodded. Zephyr made an eager squeak of agreement. Nox didn't say anything at all, only continued surveying the group with the faintest hint of a smile on their lips, as if enjoying watching the way things were unfolding.

Elyria couldn't figure the nocterrian out. Didn't understand what they were doing here in the first place, let alone why they had decided to work with the rest of them so seamlessly. Just as Kit had warned, Elyria had felt their crimson eyes boring into her back on more than one occasion. And she still hadn't had a chance to ask them what they were doing in that Coralithian jail cell to begin with.

Four hells, had that really been only a week ago? It felt like *years* had passed since then.

"Come on, let's get going," Elyria said, more to herself than anyone else. The command wasn't met with any resistance. The others began gathering their scant belongings—weapons, bits of food, the various vials and tins Zephyr had used on Cedric.

The sylvan also helped Cedric back into his armor, though one look at the mangled remnants of his cuirass—the metal of his chestplate scorched and blackened around the hole where Belien's blood magic had struck—and the knight deemed it unsalvageable. Elyria hated the way her chest tightened seeing the physical reminder—proof of just how deadly the blow had been.

Gael remained motionless by the fire until Cyren knelt beside her and placed his palm on her shoulder. Only then did she turn and acknowledge him, getting to her feet and extinguishing the fire with the wave of a hand. All while not saying a single word.

As a group, they filed out of the cavern, following the singular tunnel in the only direction it went, its luminescent walls lighting their way. Logically, Elyria recognized that they must have been going back the way they'd come—it was the only path—but nothing about the tunnel felt familiar. She grimaced thinking about how much the labyrinth must have shifted and changed while they warred and rested in the cavern.

Elyria felt strangely bereft without the familiar weight of her staff on her back and found herself brushing the hilts of the twin daggers strapped to her legs on more than one occasion. As if she needed the reassurance that she wasn't unarmed.

A silly thought, she recognized, as perhaps the most powerful magic wielder present. Wildshaper and nightwielder, both. She wondered how many others like her there were in all of Arcanis. It wasn't a pompous, ego-driven question. Just one born of curiosity. She'd spent so long burying half of herself. Now that she had finally given that half the freedom of acknowledgment—started to embrace it, even—she suddenly wanted to know more about it. Wanted to know everything.

They'd only been walking for a few minutes when Elyria felt that unfortunately familiar rumble. The grinding sound of shifting stone followed, and then the walls began to shake. Before their eyes, solid stone shifted until the path ahead was no longer a path at all, but a fork in the road. Two twin tunnels unrolled before them, equally dark, equally bare. There was nothing to differentiate them, aside from the fact that one lay to the left and the other to the right.

"Great. Now what?" Kit rolled her shoulders back as she glanced down each tunnel.

"Anyone have a particularly gifted sense of direction?" Elyria asked.

"Zephyr had a keen nose for where to go when we were in the arena," Cedric offered.

"We figured that out together." Zephyr ducked her head, as if unsure of what to do with the compliment. "Besides, I can think of at least one person with the skills required here."

She looked at Thraigg, who stepped forward with a grunt. He stroked his chin thoughtfully, the decorative beads in his beard jingling as he placed a hand on the wall. After a few moments, he said, "This way," and pointed down the right-hand tunnel.

"How do you know?" Cyren asked, tucking Gael behind him as if he expected some fire-breathing monster to come charging out of the tunnel Thraigg chose.

"The dwarven people are blessed with stone sense," Zephyr said, her light, high voice steady and matter-of-fact.

At the looks of puzzlement the sylvan received from multiple members of their party, she went on to add, "Really? Nobody knows?"

"We don't much bother spreading it around," Thraigg said with a shrug.

Zephyr sighed. "Well, would you like to educate the group, or shall I?"

Thraigg chortled heartily and gestured for her to continue.

"They can . . . Well, it's sort of self-explanatory, isn't it? They can sense the stone. Feel it. Hear it. It's not unlike wildshaping magic." She looked at Elyria with an odd expression. "The stone speaks to him, in a way, and so he can sense where it might change, end, lead."

"Stone sense, nightwielding, telepathy . . ." Cyren's shoulders heaved with a dramatic sigh as the group ventured into the right-hand tunnel. "Anyone else feel like revealing their secret power to the rest of the class?"

"If only," Kit said with a snort.

"Wasn't a secret." Thraigg let out a grunt of amusement. "Not my fault ye're all so uncultured ye don't know boots from beard when it comes to my people."

"Yer people," Cyren said in a disastrous impression of Thraigg's accent that had Elyria choking back a laugh, "absolutely keep secrets. It's why your smithing skills have remained unmatched throughout the millennia. Why do you think the rest of the realm is always clamoring for dwarven-made steel?"

Thraigg grinned as he reached up to clap the fae on the shoulder. "That's just good business."

The group ambled along, the walls continuing to shift every so often, Thraigg stopping each time in response—*sensing* where to go next. Elyria couldn't help watching Gael out of the corner of her eye as they went. The flamecaller was little more than a specter, face blank, steps slow and measured as she shuffled along behind Cyren. Elyria's chest ached at the sight, and she found herself purposefully falling to the back of the group. As if she needed to put physical distance between herself and Gael—the embodiment of her guilt.

She hadn't meant to hurt Gael.

She *had* meant to hurt Belien.

She felt guilty about both for different reasons.

And she didn't quite know where that left her.

Dawdling several yards behind the rest of the champions, Elyria trailed one hand along the luminescent walls.

"You feel it, don't you?" Tenebris Nox stepped out of a shadow and took up pace next to Elyria, startling her.

"Don't do that," she said with a scowl.

Nox lifted their hands in supplication. "Sorry, old habits."

"And feel what?" she asked.

"The magic trapped in the labyrinth walls," they said.

"Trapped?"

"Trapped, placed there. Pick your phrasing. But I am relatively confident that it wasn't always like this."

"What makes you so certain?"

"Shadows talk," they said. "You'll see."

"Stop doing that, too."

"What?"

"Fixating on my . . ." She gestured to herself, waving her arm up and down her front. "All this."

"I'm fixating?"

She levied a pointed look at them. "'Why don't you use your shadows, Elyria?' 'You're a nightwielder, Elyria.' 'Your shadows are strong; why don't you try them on the wall, Elyria?'"

Nox chuckled. "Fair point. But I'd still hardly call that fixation. It is simply . . . interesting to me."

"What is?"

"You have all this power at your literal fingertips yet are so reluctant to use it."

"Who says I don't use it? Hells, you saw what happened back there."

"Yes. But was it not reluctant?"

Elyria's fingers twitched, her jaw clenching. "So?"

"So, nothing. I'm merely an interested observer. One who knew you were something special from the second they hauled you into that cell back in Coralith."

"What were you doing in that jail anyway?" Elyria asked, eager to derail the track that this conversation was currently on.

The nocterrian ignored her question. "I couldn't put my finger on exactly what it was then, but there *was* something. And now I know. It was that shadow of yours, talking to mine."

Elyria didn't know what to say to that.

Nox released a long breath. "I can't think of the last time I met a non-nocterrian nightwielder." Elyria caught a flash of white fangs, evidence of some amusing thought flitting through their mind, before they went on to say, "Finding you out here almost feels like it was designed by Noctis himself."

"Out here?"

"So far from Nocterrum."

Elyria made a noncommittal noise. "Many of us shadow-wielding fae running around your homeland, are there?"

"No," they said. "There are not."

Whatever amusement might have been there before had been entirely chased away by a look so suddenly serious that it made Elyria want to immediately avert her gaze.

"Yes, well"—she cleared her throat—"speaking of Noctis, I'm guessing you're about to tell me that I should be calling on the Warden of Shadows now, given my new magical affinity?"

They huffed. "I couldn't possibly care less who you pray to. Though, your powers are hardly new, are they?"

"Did your shadows tell you that?"

They shrugged.

"Show me," she said. It wasn't a command, not exactly, but it wasn't a question either. If Tenebris Nox was going to continue giving her shit about her own shadows, it was more than fair to ask for another demonstration of the nocterrian's power.

Nox's mouth tipped up on one side as they raised a hand, pulling a shadow from the wall. Unlike the misty tendrils or sharp ribbons that Elyria's shadows seemed to prefer corporealizing as, Nox's was more like . . . a mist. It wasn't a wholly separate thing from the actual shadow where it began—simply a space the light failed to reach. But that space expanded, grew, and widened. It felt half like an invitation to see what lay within and half a warning to stay as far away as possible.

"Fascinating," Elyria said, lifting her hand as if to touch the shadowy mist as it crept closer. Then, just as quickly as it had come, it slunk back, folding into itself. She barely had time to blink before Nox's shadow was gone—or at least, returned to its original state—once again nothing more than a pocket full of absence.

"I find *you* fascinating," Tenebris replied.

Elyria's neck prickled with irritation, the thin thread of her patience fraying. She recognized that it wasn't a wholly rational reaction. She probably should have been excited by the nocterrian's attention. Hadn't she just been thinking how she wished to know more about her power? Well, here was a bona fide expert, a nightwielder who'd already expressed an understanding of the very magic she needed to learn about.

But she was not some specimen for them to be fascinated by. She'd spent enough of her life under the watchful eyes of others. And she just needed the space and time to start untangling her feelings from her magic.

Time she didn't have and space she wouldn't get. Not in here.

"What is it that you want, Nox?" she asked, coming to a stop and turning to face them.

"What do *you* want, Revenant?" they asked in return. "Why do you keep holding back?"

"Leave it alone," Elyria warned. "Whatever you may claim to know—"

"I know more than you think," Nox interrupted, their voice dropping to a whisper. The shadows around them seemed to flicker and grow darker as they spoke. "I could help you. We're not so different, you and I. I know—"

Elyria took a step forward, her own darkness rippling at the edges of her vision. "You *think* you know. Everyone *thinks* they know so much about the mighty Revenant. You don't."

"Don't I?" Their magic surged again, swirling around them like a cloak. It *pulsed*, as if the shadow had a heartbeat of its own, as if it meant to cross the space between Nox and Elyria and weave itself over her.

Expecting exactly that, Elyria braced herself. Her heart racing, she waited for the cold grip of Nox's power to blanket her, to tighten around her, to squeeze the breath from her lungs.

But that didn't happen.

Because just as it seemed like this strange confrontation might spiral into something worse, Cedric's voice cut through the air, calm but firm. "Everything okay back here?"

Both Elyria and Nox turned to face him. The knight stood a few feet away, his hand resting lightly on his sword hilt, his expression unreadable.

Nox took a step back, their shadowy aura receding. "But of course, Sir Thorne," they said, sketching a bow that Elyria felt was undoubtedly mocking, but either Cedric didn't notice or he didn't care. Not as Nox stepped back and let their shadow swallow them, reemerging farther down the tunnel where the rest of the group had continued walking, seemingly oblivious to what just occurred.

Elyria shook her head, her annoyance with the nocterrian warring with her fascination of seeing their nightwielding magic in action. She'd heard of the practice of shadowstepping, of course. Knew about it in theory. But prior to today, even in her two centuries of life, had never seen it herself. She wondered if that was something her own shadows could do.

"Making new friends all over the place, aren't we?" Cedric said before she had a chance to follow that thought further.

The tension in Elyria's shoulders eased—just slightly—as the two of them started walking again. "I don't know what their problem with me is."

"I'm sure I could come up with a few ideas."

"Har, har, very funny."

"I thought so."

Elyria had a jibe on the tip of her tongue, but a cry of surprise slipped out instead. Cedric had stopped short, and she'd had to quickly brace her hands in front of her to prevent her entire torso from colliding with his back.

What this meant, however, was that Elyria was now standing with her two hands attached to Cedric's unarmored back . . . and the hard muscles that lay there.

She quickly retrieved her hands, face reddening, but Cedric barely seemed to register the touch. He stared into the distance, his fist rubbing idle circles on his chest.

"What in the four hells are you looking at?"

He didn't answer. Didn't need to. Not as Elyria realized that mild embarrassment wasn't the only thing causing her face to turn red.

The heat hit her in a slow wave—putrid and blistering. The scent of sulfur and smoke settled on her skin. Sweat immediately began beading on her brow as she and Cedric shuffled forward, squinting their eyes against the increasing brightness coming from ahead.

Elyria thought she might have heard Kit calling for her, not in a panicked, worrisome manner, but in a "hurry the fuck up, would you?" way. It was hard to know for sure though, when for a searing moment, all Elyria could see was the labyrinth's latest obstacle.

And what an obstacle it was.

Kit, Cyren, Gael, Zephyr, Thraigg, and Nox were lined up at the end of the tunnel they'd been traversing, open air stretching overhead as if the group had finally emerged from the underground maze. Only, it wasn't grass and blue skies and green trees that greeted them like at the beginning of the trial.

It was a lake, at least three hundred feet across and of a seemingly infinite width.

And it was on fire.

Elyria twisted her neck from side to side, trying to discern what they were supposed to do, how they were supposed to cross. There was no pathway. No bridge. Just an ocean of roiling flame.

And on the opposite side?

"Noctis take me," Elyria said with a groan. "Another fucking gate."

CHAPTER 34
OBSIDIAN

Elyria

"Well, at least we can feel relatively confident we've made it to the end of the trial." Kit flourished her hands at the gate lying across the fiery lake. Heat rose in tangible ripples, melding into the darkening sky overhead. The ground beneath their feet sloped down, a rocky shore that met the molten fire. Flames leapt and danced over the lake's surface, swirling around what looked like a small island of glossy black stone roughly halfway across.

"Figures we go through all of that"—Cyren waved an arm back toward the labyrinth tunnel—"only to find yet another stars-damned gate instead of an actual prize." He dabbed at the beads of sweat running down the sides of his face, then swept long strands of cobalt hair off his neck and fixed it in a bun high atop his head.

"Maybe the crown is just beyond?" Kit suggested.

"Ever the optimist," Elyria said, squinting against the orange glow coming off the lake. Beside her, Gael's head was tilted down as she stared at the flames licking the shoreline.

The heat was oppressive—a feverish wall. But it was also the one thing standing between them and the exit. And Elyria was more than ready to leave everything that had happened during this trial behind.

"Gael?" Elyria asked. She had little more than a foolish hope that Gael—now a ghost of the fiery fae she'd once been—might be able to help. Elyria asked anyway.

Gael didn't respond.

Cyren bent low, whispering in Gael's ear, urging her to help, to react, to say or do anything.

She just kept staring into the fire.

"All right, so our resident flamecaller is not an option at the moment," Elyria said, wishing the brightness she forced into her voice would cover the sour taste at the back of her throat. "Anyone have an idea for how we get from here"—she gestured at the ground, then pointed to the gate across the fiery lake—"to there without her?"

"Can't you shadowstep us over there?" Cedric asked Nox.

"Sadly, I cannot," replied the nocterrian, not really sounding all that sad about it. "It's too far to make it in one step. I'm not powerful enough."

Their crimson eyes landed on Elyria at the last part of their sentence. She avoided their gaze.

Cedric stepped closer to the edge of the shore. "So, we aim for the island in the middle first, then."

"If it's made of what I think it is, that would be even worse," Nox said.

Cedric's brows drew together. "Why's that?"

Zephyr drew in a fast breath. "Ob-obsidian."

"And that matters because . . . ?"

"Gaia's tits, boyo," Thraigg muttered. "Yer mystical tutelage is a bit lacking, innit?"

Elyria bit back a laugh at the truth in those words. Hadn't she thought as much before they'd entered the labyrinth? Whoever was responsible for Cedric's magical training seemed like they'd been awfully selective.

"Arcanian obsidian has powerful properties," she told him. "Essentially heatproof. Spectacularly malleable, if you know how to work it."

Thraigg released a grunt of affirmation. "My people have crafted many fine blades and even finer pieces of armor from obsidian."

"But it's also known to have rather . . . temperamental . . . reactions to magic. Though its impact is, blessedly, limited," Elyria continued.

"To shadow magic, specifically," Nox added.

Cedric's brown eyes widened. "So, shadowstepping to the island might mean . . ."

A gravelly noise emerged from the back of Thraigg's throat, and he spread his fingers wide, throwing both hands outward in an exaggerated burst—an imaginary explosion. He wiggled his fingers in the air as he lowered his palms, mimicking scattering debris. "Exactly."

Cedric's throat bobbed. "We find another way to get across, then."

"Brilliant," Elyria said. "Why didn't anyone else think of that?"

Cedric's face scrunched with irritation, and she hid the grin that threatened to emerge.

"It's just, how exactly do you propose we do that? We still can't fly." Elyria flared her wings to make her point before she cursed inwardly at her insensitivity. Luckily—or perhaps concerningly—Gael didn't seem like she was even listening. Elyria quickly cloaked her wings anyway, then turned to face Kit. "An ice bridge, maybe?"

"Sounds like the knightling here isn't the only one who needs a magical refresher," said Kit.

"Not even in magic," grumbled Nox. "Just physics."

Elyria resisted the urge to toss obscenities at the nocterrian.

"Opposing elements, Ellie," Kit continued. "Even if I could conjure enough ice to cover the expanse—already an impossible task, mind you—it would melt before we made it halfway."

"And even if we were to make it there, how do you suggest we do so without melting ourselves?" Nox added, wiping their hand across their sweat-drenched brow as if to make their point.

"What about a mist?" Cedric asked. "A fog—just enough water in the air to cool it slightly and just enough of it to cover us while we cross."

Elyria sucked her bottom lip between her teeth. "To what end? Wouldn't it also evaporate in seconds?"

"Not if Cyren disperses some of the heat at the same time," he said. "You can do that, right?"

Cyren glanced up from where he was still whispering pleadingly in Gael's ear. "What?"

"Can you use your wind magic to keep the air moving? Help disperse the heat while we cross?"

"I . . . Yes, I think so. I'll have to be careful not to fan the flames instead." He rocked his head from side to side, weighing his options. "But if I balance depriving the fire of oxygen while circulating the air around us . . . it might work. I might be able to lower the temperature by a few degrees if we work together."

Zephyr cleared her throat. "This still doesn't solve the issue of how we're supposed to walk across a sea of flames though."

"True, not all of us are fireproof." Elyria dared a small glance at Gael while the other champions continued discussing possible strategies. The flamecaller's gaze had roamed to the island in the midst of the lake, the shiny black stone reflecting the flickering flames.

A thought struck Elyria. She let her consciousness drift down, sinking into the ground searching through thick layers of sand and rock and sediment until she hit something cold, sharp. Dangerous.

Her eyes snapped open. "Thraigg," she said, interrupting Cedric midsentence and relishing the pinprick of satisfaction that brought her. "Can you *sense* whatever is below the fire? The material that lies at the bottom of this lake?"

The dwarf knelt, placing his hands on either side of his bent leg. "Mmm," he started, eyes closed, head tilting from side to side as if trying to obtain some kind of magical equilibrium. "Yep. Obsidian," he said, standing back up after a few moments. "Sheets of it, from what I can tell. Same stuff making up that bit in the middle."

Elyria nodded at the confirmation, her lip finding its way between her teeth once more. It wasn't ideal, but it wasn't as though they had many options at this point. "Okay. I can work with that."

Kit's eyes widened as the realization of what Elyria was about to attempt sank in. "Ellie, are you sure you can—"

"Yes," Elyria said, cutting Kit off.

"Can what?" Cedric asked, eyes darting between them.

"But won't it—"

"Maybe," Elyria replied, again not giving Kit time to voice her concern. "But I don't see many other options."

"What were you going to say?" Cedric asked, his voice growing louder, sterner. "Won't it what?"

"Won't it be dangerous for her," Nox answered on Elyria's behalf, stepping forward. The indigo skin on their forehead was creased, and for a second Elyria thought they might genuinely be concerned.

Every cell in Cedric's body seemed to go still. "Why would it be any more dangerous for her than the rest of us?"

"It won't be," Elyria said, eyes narrowing at Kit and Nox alike—a silent command to shut their mouths. "I'll be fine."

"You don't know that," Kit said, brushing off Elyria's glare like it was a pesky bug. She turned to Cedric. "As we said earlier, obsidian has the potential to interact with magic. There's no way to know what kind of reaction it'll have to being manipulated."

"Manipulated how? Stars above, is it truly so difficult to tell me plainly what it is you're planning?"

"Don't trouble yourself with the details, Sir Worrywart," Elyria said, twisting her head until her neck bones cracked in a simultaneously satisfying and revolting way. "Let us do the heavy lifting, and you just worry about scurrying your handsome self across."

Cedric's stern expression seemed to falter for a moment at Elyria's deliberately chosen words, but it didn't last. "Tell me," he pleaded.

Kit blew out a sigh. "She means to tear some of the rock from the bottom of the lake and bring it to the surface, so that we can get across. And she means to do it with her magic."

"Yes, but with my *wildshaper* magic, not my shadows," Elyria said. "Thus, your concern, while appreciated, is wholly unnecessary."

Kit's mismatched eyes met Elyria's. "You know better than anyone that it's never that simple."

Nox stepped forward and said what Kit didn't. "What if your

shadows leak out? What if the obsidian senses it within you, regardless of whether you're actively wielding it or not? There are too many variables, too many unknowns."

"And we don't have many other choices!" Elyria threw her hands in the air.

"Why can't we just merge power again?" The ground rumbled the instant the words left Cedric's mouth. The flames lapping at the shore jumped at the mention, and Elyria swore it was as if the Sanctum was issuing its disapproval.

Cyren barked a wary laugh. "If we're worried about her shadows and the obsidian, what exactly do you think will happen should she be primed with the rest of our magic? Or, worse, should any of us be offered the temptation of wielding hers?"

Kit frowned as she looked Gael over, taking in the blank expression on the flamecaller's face. "I doubt we'd be able to get this one to willingly contribute, anyway. Let alone cast as necessary to activate the merge."

"Well then. If everyone has said their piece, mind if I get on with it?" Elyria didn't bother hiding her annoyance as she pivoted to face the fiery lake. They'd already wasted so much time arguing about this.

"I can help."

She felt Cedric's presence before she heard him. Turning her head to where he now stood beside her, her eyes darted to the token hanging from his neck. The green emerald embedded within it pulsed dully. "I think it's better if you sit this one out. Save whatever human magic you have left for when you really need it."

Squaring her shoulders, Elyria tried to block out the heat pressing in on her from the outside, as well as the doubts crawling through her insides. It was fine. This was fine. She was fine. She could do this.

"Thraigg, tell me the best places for me to pull from," she said.

He nodded, his thick brow creasing as he knelt once more. "Aye. Right about"—he slapped his calloused palm against the ground—"here." The dwarf stood, brushing rocky sand from his hands. "Best start pullin', lass."

CHAPTER 35
HOT GIRL THINGS

Elyria

Elyria closed her eyes and raised her hands, letting her focus slip back into the ground at their feet. Farther, deeper, cutting through fire and flame until she felt it—the obsidian that lay beneath.

She paused, sucking in a sharp breath.

"What? What is it?" Cedric's voice sounded far away, but she could hear the concern in it.

She didn't answer him. It didn't feel like the rock and stone she was used to reaching for. It felt like a wall. A wall made up of thousands of steel bands. Keeping her out.

Making sure to keep her shadow tucked away, Elyria reached out with her wild magic. She searched. She prodded. She tried to pull the bands apart, to get through to the thread of magic that she knew must lie within. Each band felt like a shard of ice against her own power—sharp and jagged, so cold it burned.

She dropped her hands.

Cracking her eyes open, she said, "I—I don't know if I can reach it. It's fighting me." She took a single step closer to the edge of the lake, the heat licking at her like a taunt.

"Like outside the labyrinth?" Kit asked.

"No, not exactly. It's more like . . . I don't know how to describe it. Not so much tangled as . . . inaccessible? I can't find a way in. I just need . . ." Elyria closed her eyes again. Tried again.

She let out a frustrated huff. And then a hand was resting on her shoulder, a warmth seeping into her that felt so different from the boiling air around them. That familiar feeling in her chest throbbed, as if her body recognized his touch.

"Let me help," Cedric murmured, his breath caressing the shell of her ear. "Just tell me what to do."

A shudder trailed up her spine. Her fingers twitched. And her voice was barely more than a whisper when she said, "Okay."

Elyria and Cedric drew a deep, synchronized breath. The warmth trailing through her intensified as he stepped squarely behind her, and that *tug* inside of her pulled her backward until she was leaning against his chest. He rested his other hand around her waist as she settled, and Elyria had to push aside the warring, conflicting thoughts that entered her mind.

Later, she thought. *I'll deal with that later.*

"Follow the trail of my magic." She didn't know how much he would really be able to do, but she understood enough about human magic to know that the mana he wielded should be able to recognize her own, at the very least.

Cedric adjusted his hand on her shoulder to touch his token. His mouth moved against her hair, a silent spell on his lips. Elyria extended her senses once more, letting the wild beat of her magic hum in her veins. She followed it down, down, through the dancing flames. And this time, when she reached that steel-banded wall of obsidian, he was there too.

She felt him tense at her back as he parted the bands with ease, as if they *wanted* to comply with his magic. She didn't understand why, but she couldn't dwell on it. Not as tendrils of her own power were finally able to reach inside.

Her eyes shot open as she grabbed it—that cool, slick thread of magic beating within the heart of the obsidian at the bottom of the fiery lake.

It was slow at first. Elyria focused on pulling—not too fast, not too hard—until she felt the earth shift. With a grunt of effort, she dislodged a long slab and drew it to the surface, the black stone shining like rippling glass as it broke through the flames.

"Ye're doing it." Approval radiated from Thraigg's voice.

Elyria's hands began to shake as she locked the first slab into place.

"Just four more, I think," said Nox, their keen crimson eyes pinned to the first part of the makeshift bridge Elyria had just created.

"Oh, is that all?" Elyria gritted out.

Sweat dripped from her temple as she pulled up another slab. Then another. And another.

Cedric's hand tightened around her waist, and she could've sworn she felt a boost of strength flow directly into her.

Which didn't make any sense. Because as far as she knew, that was not how human magic worked.

Later.

With Thraigg guiding her and Cedric maintaining an opening in the obsidian's shield, she drew a final slab up, overlapping its edge with the previous one until a shiny floating pathway cut across the fire.

"Well done, Ellie," Kit said, voice soft, as Elyria placed the final piece.

Through sheer mental grit, Elyria resisted collapsing into Cedric's arms. Wiping a hand across her exhausted, sweat-laden brow, she straightened and pulled herself out of his embrace. She then ignored the distinctly bereft feeling that came after as she faced Kit. "Your turn."

Kit and Cyren exchanged a glance, the smallest of smiles playing on their lips.

"Thought you'd never ask," Cyren said, his signature wink making an appearance before his gaze fell back on Gael and his expression grew serious again. With the slightest flicker of hesitation, the pair moved forward, wings folded tight, hands raised.

"Oof," Kit said, stepping onto the bridge with a wince. Elyria was sure the temperature must have jumped ten degrees in those few paces alone.

"On three?" Cyren asked.

Kit rolled her eyes, already swirling droplets of water in the air. "Just do it, Cy."

Long strands of hair pulled free from the bun on his head as Cyren began to cast in parallel with her. A gust blew over Elyria's shoulders, whipping a few pieces of her own hair around her face. While she wished the air were cooler, even just feeling it moving across her skin was a balm in this oven.

Cyren's wind swept through the tiny droplets of moisture Kit hung in the air, stirring them into a cooling haze that spread over the bridge—a misty tunnel.

"Time to go, everyone," Kit said, her voice strained but measured as she and Cyren started to move, their steps matching each other's as they strode forward.

"Don't have to tell me twice," Thraigg said, darting to his feet in a surprisingly nimble motion and striding onto the bridge.

"Gael?" Zephyr's small voice asked. Unshockingly, the flamecaller didn't respond, only continued staring blankly into the flames. Zephyr looked past Gael to where Nox stood and exchanged a look with the nocterrian. Each of them took one of Gael's arms and placed it in their own, guiding her forward.

"Ready?" Cedric asked, his hand outstretched. He stood on the edge of the bridge, looking back at her with an expectant expression on his chiseled face. Elyria hadn't noticed when he'd stepped around her, but she was now the only one remaining on the shore.

She bypassed his proffered hand, striding past him with one brow raised. "Of course. I was born ready," she quipped, then clamped her lips together when she heard him chuckle in response.

The heat was still stifling, each step like walking through a sauna, but it was bearable. Elyria glanced at her feet, surprised at how steady the bridge was below them. She'd thought it would feel more precarious, that the bridge would be more akin to a raft floating on this sea of molten fire. But it was as if the surface lay right below the flames, like they trod a path on solid ground. Flames lapped at both edges of the obsidian slab, but that's all they did, never creeping closer.

"Not bad," she muttered to herself, a flicker of pride surging in her chest even as a wave of heat broke through Kit and Cyren's vaporous tunnel.

"Not bad at all."

She glanced up and to the right, where Cedric was looking at her with a confounding expression she didn't know how to categorize. It wasn't discomfort or pain, despite the still-smoldering air. In fact, the knight seemed mostly unaffected by the surging heat. If she didn't know better, she might think that the blush of pink creeping into his cheeks had nothing to do with their surroundings at all.

"Hurry up!" Kit called back, her pace faltering as she strained to keep her magic aloft. "Keep it up, Cy. Almost there."

"I'm trying, woman," Cyren muttered through clenched teeth, the words soaring back to Elyria on a weak gust.

Elyria caught the way Zephyr winced as she and Nox hurried Gael along. The sylvan's face was pale, her normally vibrant eyes dulled, as if exhaustion was about to overtake her. Still, it didn't stop her from tossing her gaze behind her every few seconds, making sure Cedric and Elyria were keeping up.

The black glass of the island glimmered ahead. "We're almost there. Keep going," Elyria shouted, though again, she wasn't sure who she was really talking to. Even as she said the words, her own steps slowed. They were almost to the island, but that only meant they were nearly halfway. Fatigue pulsed in her bones. Her magic was spent from putting the bridge into place. The heat was too much. And she would have to do it all over again.

A wave of hot air swelled at Elyria's back, as if on cue. She glanced at the faltering mist around her. Kit and Cyren couldn't keep this up. The tip of Elyria's boot caught on a small divot in the stone slab, and she stumbled, drenched with the realization that she couldn't keep going much longer either.

She couldn't help the despondent thought that bubbled up in her mind. Could this have been where Evander's journey through the Crucible ended, too? So close, yet so far? Because she felt like she had to be. Close, that was. She was so close.

The gate on the other shore pulsed with a soft light, beckoning her.

An awareness settled deep inside that something important lay within, and the Crucible itself was inviting her to see it.

A hand brushed the small of her back, and Elyria grimaced at the feel of the fabric of her shirt, soaked through with sweat, clinging to her skin as Cedric steadied her.

"Just keep moving. We'll make it." There was no question in his voice, and once again, Elyria felt that boost of energy, that small thrum of power, flow into her.

She nodded, forcing her tired limbs to pick up the pace. Together, they crossed from the makeshift bridge to the island, trading one form of obsidian for another. Elyria braced her hands on her knees and bent at the waist, doubling over as she sucked in breath after breath. Nearby, Kit and Cyren were in much the same state, the latter having fallen to his knees on the dark, glassy surface, though they kept their hands loosely raised, magic continuing to swirl weakly around the group.

"We can't"—Elyria panted—"can't stop . . . We have to—" She blinked, looking from the champions surrounding her to the beckoning gate on the other shore and back again.

It was difficult to tell previously, but they did not actually appear to be in the dead center of the lake. As if getting to the island had shrunk the distance behind it, they were far closer to the shore—and the gate—than Elyria thought. Moreover, it turned out the island was tied to the shore by a strip of obsidian rock. It was thinner than the bridge she'd constructed, but similar. And, most importantly, looked just as traversable.

A kernel of hope took root inside Elyria's chest. One that only swelled in size as she realized something else about the place they now occupied.

She straightened. "Is it . . . ?" Elyria started, her voice trailing off as she grappled with the very real possibility that she could be hallucinating. "Cooler?"

The air around them was still thick, still heavy, but there was a distinct, distinguishable difference in the temperature. Elyria glanced at Kit and Cyren, the two of them exchanging a wary look.

Biting her lip thoughtfully, Kit let her hands drop, the swirls of misted water dropping with them.

The heat didn't return.

"Another ward?" Cedric mused, walking over to the rocky edge where Elyria's makeshift bridge met the island. Peering into the flames, he raised a palm before him, facing out, like he was greeting the air. "There's definitely something here. Some kind of magic."

"Whatever it is, I'll take it." Cyren dropped his hands to the ground and sat back on his ankles, chest heaving.

Zephyr guided Gael toward a raised section of rectangular rock and helped her sit on it—a makeshift bench. "I suppose it wouldn't be fair if the Crucible let us all burn to death."

"Right, because fairness seems to be of the utmost importance in here," Cedric said flatly.

Elyria stared at him.

"What?"

Her lips tipped to one side. "I believe that's the closest you've ever come to criticizing the celestials' grand design here. One might think you positively sacrilegious."

She laughed at his answering scowl, though there wasn't much force behind it. Not with her strength and power sapped as it was. Elyria was so tired she could have curled up into a ball on the glossy ground and slept right there. If it weren't for . . .

As if it called her name, Elyria drew her eyes back to the glowing gate. All that stood between them was another stony bridge. They were so, so close. So close to that *important thing* that she knew—she just *knew*—lay beyond it.

"We're almost there," she repeated, unexpected hope surging in her chest. "Surely crossing was the last part of the trial. Now we just need to—"

A deep, guttural rumble reverberated through the obsidian beneath their feet. Elyria cut herself off, her body tensing. The other champions froze in place, their eyes flicking between the still-churning lake of fire, the ground, and one another.

"What in all four hells was that?" Cyren said, his voice a harsh whisper, his hand already reaching for the hilt of the blade at his hip.

Elyria's heartbeat thundered in her ears as the rumbling beneath them grew louder. The ground shook, the flames around them flaring in response. A crack sounded from the obsidian near Elyria's feet, steam hissing from a sudden fracture in the surface. Out of the corner of her eye, she saw Kit, Thraigg, Nox, and Cyren close ranks around Gael and Zephyr by the bench.

"Get ready." Cedric's voice floated into Elyria's ears as he moved behind her, turning so his back was to hers. His sword was already in his hands.

Her own hands trembling, she pulled one of her daggers from its sheath at her thigh. She scanned the horizon, searching for movement, for any sign of whatever cruelty the Crucible was serving them now.

Nothing happened.

The champions exchanged cautious glances. "Was that supposed to be some kind of warning?" Kit asked, clearly dubious.

"Yes, perhaps the trial has gone on too long and the Crucible is simply urging us along," Zephyr agreed, though she didn't sound too convinced.

Cyren exhaled. "How anticlimactic." Sheathing his sword with a theatrical flourish, he grinned at Elyria. "Here I was thinking we were in store for some kind of dramatic finale after all this."

Elyria rolled her eyes. "Crossing a flaming lake by the very skin of our teeth wasn't dramatic enough for you?"

He winked, grin widening. "I suppose I'll have to find another way to drum up some excitement. You wouldn't happen to—"

A deafening roar split the air.

The flames around them surged upward, creating a fence of fire that licked at the obsidian surface of the island and the invisible barrier that seemed tied to the edge.

And then the lake came alive.

Liquid fire churned and roiled as a massive form burst from its depths. A towering serpentine creature with scales that gleamed bright orange, like iron newly pulled from the forge.

Glowing red eyes narrowed on the group from below horned brows.

Elyria's breath caught in her throat.

"Fyre wyrm."

CHAPTER 36
HEADS WILL ROLL

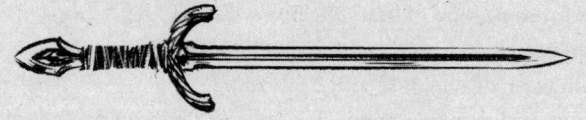

Cedric

The lake of fire surged as the wyrm's roar sent a tremor down Cedric's spine. It wasn't just the sound—deep, guttural, primal—but the sheer power of it. It rattled through his bones, echoing off the glassy obsidian ground like a physical force.

Stupid. He'd been so stupid. He thought that after the bullshit of the labyrinth itself, the trial's final challenge had ended when they found a way to get across that stars-forsaken lake. The cooling relief he'd felt as they crossed through the ward, the nearness of the gate . . . he'd thought it all a sign that they'd made it to the end.

He should have known better. Now, as the huge, snakelike body of the fyre wyrm slithered out of the flames, he realized the Crucible never gave freely. Not the respite from the heat, not that brief moment of hope.

"Solaris save us," Cyren muttered under his breath, all traces of humor wiped from his face as he stared at the beast.

It was massive, its sinuous body easily spanning the length of the island they stood upon. Glowing orange scales darkened into a deep purple, turning matte as more of the wyrm's body rose from the lake, almost as if they were cooling—molten metal forging into blackened armor.

A head crowned with jagged horns topped the creature's monstrous form, eyes like coal burning within its sharp, reptilian face. Cedric swallowed hard, his hand tightening around his sword hilt. He could feel the heat coming off the wyrm in waves, the nearness of it sending a ripple of fear and wonder through him. The great beast was as horrendous as it was mesmerizing, and he found himself unwittingly taking a step closer as the wyrm's massive head tilted, regarding the group.

"Get ready," Elyria muttered behind him, her voice tense but steady.

They all moved at once.

"Go!"

With a hiss, the wyrm lunged forward, the speed of its movement startling given its size.

The others were already scrambling, scattering like leaves in a gale, as the lower half of the beast's body swept across the island. Cedric dove to the side just as its tail whipped past where he'd been standing, shattering the glassy surface, shards of obsidian pelting his skin.

"Hit it with all ye've got!" Thraigg yelled, brandishing his hammer. He was the first to charge, smashing the blunt end of his weapon into one of the wyrm's coiled segments, the ground beneath it cracking under the impact.

The beast reared back, writhing in pain, but it didn't stop. Its molten breath sizzled in the air, filling Cedric's nostrils with the acrid stench of sulfur and burning rock. He rolled to his feet, his heartbeat pounding in his ears.

"Eyes up!" Elyria's voice carried above the din of the wyrm's hisses and the sound of flames crackling around them. She was a purple blur as she spun away from another swipe of the creature's tail, then whirled right back around, brandishing her dagger.

Cedric tracked her instinctually, watching the way her body twisted as she fought. Still, she was slower than he thought she should be, the toll of what she'd done to construct and cross the bridge evident. An involuntary gasp left his lips as the side of the wyrm's head came so close to Elyria that its jagged horns drew blood from her arm.

Then, as if a line had been drawn straight from the fierce fae warrior to Cedric, the wyrm's head snapped toward him. He barely managed to lift his sword in time to angle his blade and leap out of the path of the beast's open maw.

Teeth the size of small blades gleamed in the fiery light as Cedric slashed his weapon. A pain-drenched roar shook the air, the creature's molten scales glowing bright. Dark blood leaked from the gash Cedric had scored into its snout.

"Aim for the face!" Cyren's voice cut through the chaos, his hair whipping behind him as he leapt into the fray, daggers flashing. He darted in and out of the wyrm's reach with impressive ease, relentlessly targeting weak spots in the creature's hide. Each wound was minor, but it was enough to keep the wyrm off-balance and allow the other champions to come forward.

"Now!" Any traces of the exhaustion that had overtaken Kit from crossing the lake dissipated as she raised her hands, ice crystals forming in the air above her. A frozen spear shot forward, striking the wyrm in the side. It melted before piercing deep enough to do significant damage, but it managed to force the wyrm back another few feet, the length of its body now lined up at the island's edge.

Nox charged forward, twin batons raised in front of them as they battered the wyrm. Zephyr dug a dagger into the tip of its thrashing tail before darting back. Thraigg continued slamming his hammer down, landing the occasional hit but meeting the obsidian ground more often than connecting with the wyrm itself. It was moving too fast. Still, Cedric was awestruck by the way their ragtag group worked together to beat the creature back. Even Gael, dazed and struggling as she was, raised a hand and sent a weak burst of flame at the beast, though it seemed to do little more than annoy it.

The wyrm twisted in the air, crashing back toward Elyria, snapping its jaw at her. Cedric shouted in warning, but the realization hit her too slowly, her movements too sluggish. She leapt to the side, but there wasn't enough power behind the move to clear the wyrm's path.

The panic in her eyes had Cedric's heart lurching in his chest, and his hand was on his token before he knew what he was doing. He focused his remaining magic into stopping the creature's charge, feeling the mana drain as he halted the wyrm mid-lunge—just long enough to break its momentum.

He was almost too late.

Elyria scuttled out from between the wyrm's dripping maw, her eyes wide with shock as they met Cedric's, her chest heaving. Another second and she would've been gone. Another second and she would've—

The wyrm let out a mind-bleeding screech, whirling on Cedric as his magical hold on the creature faltered. But before it could exact its monstrous revenge, Zephyr was at his side, resolve burning in place of her typically quiet demeanor. She hurled a vial at the wyrm, glass shattering on its scales as a burst of silvery mist drifted up toward its head.

The wyrm recoiled, hissing as the mist clung to it. It retreated until it was nearly next to Cedric, its movements erratic and confused, like it had been blinded.

This was their chance.

He didn't waste it.

Cedric darted forward, slashing deep cuts into the creature. Elyria ran up beside him, her breathing still labored as her wild magic wove shattered shards of obsidian like a wave of tiny daggers, slicing at the wyrm, digging into the soft spots next to and under each scale.

The wyrm struggled, but it couldn't focus, couldn't fight back—if only for a moment. Its massive tail thrashed as it slipped off the edge of the island and sank partway into the fiery lake, its head bouncing off the ground.

"Now, Cedric!"

His sword was already raised when Elyria's cry rang in his ears. He poured every ounce of strength into the swing as he brought the blade down. The metal connected with the wyrm's thick neck—once, twice, three times. Dark blood splattered Cedric's face as he finally sliced clean through.

The wyrm's head fell from its body with a revolting *thud*.

For a moment, there was nothing but stunned silence. The wyrm's body slumped to the ground, steam rising from the severed stump of its neck. Then, as if the flames were reclaiming it, its coiled, twitching body sank farther into the lake until it disappeared beneath the surface. Cedric placed his boot on the dismembered snout of the beast and sent its head rolling in after it.

The champions stood there, gasping for breath, the magnitude of what they had just done settling over them. They had bested a *fyre wyrm*. They had won. They had actually won.

"By Gaia," Thraigg breathed, leaning heavily on his hammer.

Cedric wiped sweat and blood from his brow. He looked over at Elyria, bent at the waist, a hand on her ribs. She was panting, gasping for air, but she was alive.

Something deep in his chest tightened painfully at the knowledge that she very nearly hadn't been.

"We did it," Zephyr whispered, eyes wide. "It's dead."

"Didn't even break a sweat," Cyren quipped. "Could've done that all day." He exchanged a relieved glance with Kit, though the exhaustion that had already plagued the pair of them seemed to return with a fervor, their faces rapidly paling as the adrenaline left their systems.

Elyria gave him a weary smile. "Let's not test that theory."

It took several minutes before their hearts stopped racing and their breathing returned to normal, but eventually the group began to move toward the thin strip of obsidian connecting the island to the shore—and the gate. One by one, they crossed the rest of the fiery lake, stepping carefully as the obsidian walkway seemed to sway under them.

Nox was the first to reach the opposite shore, followed by Thraigg and a massively relieved-looking Zephyr, tugging Gael along behind her.

The moment her boots touched the rocky sand, Kit's body visibly relaxed. Her hands dropped to her sides as she turned to cast a weary glance at Cyren, Elyria, and Cedric, still on the walkway. "Well, that was exciting."

Cyren laughed, the sound both tired and triumphant. "I take back everything I said before. That was absolutely climactic enough to last me the rest of my life." He flashed a grin, pushing his sweat-drenched hair back from his face. Pointing to the gate, he added, "Looks like we might actually make it out of here in one piece."

Before either Cedric or Elyria could respond, the ground rumbled beneath their feet again, so violently they stumbled. Cedric grabbed hold of Elyria's arm as she pitched toward the flames lining the side of the walkway, steadying her as that same deep, bone-rattling sound split the air.

The same, but different. Louder this time. Too loud. Almost like—

"It can't be." Kit spun toward the lake, eyes wide with fear.

Cedric whipped around just in time to see the wyrm burst from the fiery surface—the same, again, but different. Because this time, three ferocious heads snapped and roared with fury, where only one had been before.

"Everyone, run!" Elyria shouted. "Nox, get them out! Get them to the gate!"

Back on rocky sand and no longer restricted by the surrounding obsidian, Nox didn't balk at the command. With the briefest of nods, the nocterrian grabbed the two nearest champions—Thraigg and Zephyr—and stepped into a shadow. They emerged beside the gate, and with an unceremonious push and against much protestation, they shoved the sylvan and the dwarf through the glowing archway.

And that was all anyone had time to do before the wyrm's three heads were careening toward Cedric, Elyria, and Cyren.

"Quickly now, get—" Cedric's words died in his throat as one of the wyrm's heads lunged forward with blinding speed, its jaws closing around Cyren in one swift motion.

And the fae's scream was cut off in an instant as, with a sickening crunch, the monster took him from this world.

CHAPTER 37
ASHES TO ASHES

Elyria

Gael's cry cut through the chaos, a raw, animalistic sound emanating from where she stood, sending chills down Elyria's spine. The wyrm's three-toned roar split the air and shook the walkway beneath her feet as its heads twisted and snapped.

Cyren was gone. The reality of it barely registered as Elyria stumbled backward, body numb, mind spinning. But there was no time to grieve. The wyrm's three heads hung over them, their glowing eyes flashing with seeming indecision about just which champion it wanted to consume next.

The others were in motion—Nox stepped back into a shadow. Gael fell to her knees on the shore. Kit started running back toward the walkway—to Elyria.

Cedric, chest heaving, still had his bloody sword gripped in one hand as he pulled Elyria back with his other. He moved forward to stand between her and the wyrm, knees bent in a defensive stance as he braced for the next attack.

The wyrm obliged, all three heads aimed right at him.

"No!" The word left her lips before she could even think about what she was doing. Elyria's shadows lashed out, dark whips shooting forward, wrapping around one of the wyrm's heads and pulling it backward, yanking the entire beast back with it.

Her shadows tightened, a riotous wave of power surging through her. She could do this. She could stop it. They just needed a few seconds. Enough time for Nox to get to them, for them to get to the gate.

For a moment, it worked.

The wyrm recoiled, its heads jerking back as her shadows bit into its scales. Elyria felt a glimmer of hope.

But then the wyrm dove, dragging Elyria's shadowy leash down, down . . . until it touched the obsidian at her feet.

The reaction was immediate. The ground surged with dark energy, the obsidian amplifying her shadows into something wild, uncontrolled. She barely had time to gasp before an explosion of power tore through the air.

The wyrm screeched in pain, rearing back and convulsing like it had been struck by lightning. Hot blood sprayed Elyria's arm, but she couldn't tell where or how badly the creature had been hurt. Not as that same shock wave slammed into her, knocking her off her feet, her ears ringing.

And she wasn't the only one.

Horror lanced her every thought, every nerve, every heartbeat as the wave of her dark power struck Cedric. His body flew across the obsidian walkway, disappearing into the lake of fire with a burst of flame and a shocking splash.

Her insides iced over.

Elyria's vision went hazy.

And everything else faded into the background as her heart plummeted into the molten fire with him.

Elyria's mind blanked as she stared at the spot where Cedric had sunk beneath the flames. It wasn't real. It couldn't be real. Not after everything they'd been through, not after what he'd just done to help them—help *her*—survive.

Not after she'd just gotten him back.

Darkness bloomed from that spot inside her chest, shadows misting over her skin, swirling in her hands. They threatened to spill over, to cover the obsidian ground, to cause another burst of power that would obliterate everything—the writhing wyrm, the bridge. Herself.

Time slowed, froze.

"Ellie!" Kit's cry snapped Elyria back to the present. Her shadows dissipated. On the shore, Nox had their arms wrapped around Kit as she thrashed and kicked against their hold. "Let me go! I won't leave her!"

Grief washed over Elyria as she nodded at the nocterrian, a silent command. Kit was always the priority. Nox would see her through the gate. Hopefully, along with Thraigg and Zephyr, they would see her through to the end.

Just as Elyria thought it, the nocterrian stepped into a shadow, reemerging by the gate and walking through with Kit, even as she continued flailing against their hold.

Elyria was alone.

No, not alone.

A flash of red drew Elyria's eyes to where Gael still knelt on the edge of the shore. Nox hadn't gotten her out yet.

Elyria swallowed hard, her limbs heavy with exhaustion, her heart pounding a desperate drumbeat in her ears. Or was that the sound of it breaking?

Gael's body was unnaturally still as she stared into the fiery lake, eyes tracking between the wyrm—still jerking in pain—and the spot where it had taken Cyren. Her single wing fluttered weakly behind her, and the expression on her face . . .

Elyria's heart clenched.

She knew that look.

"Gael, you need to move!" Elyria called, careening down the rest of the obsidian walkway to get to the fae. Panic gripped her as the wyrm finally regained its faculties, pulling back, preparing once more to strike.

Elyria's eyes widened as she took in the steaming blood dripping from a deep, grotesque gash that had opened up on its neck, a souvenir from the explosion of her power.

Gael showed no sign of acknowledgment. She didn't respond to Elyria's shouts. She was lost in her grief.

Her madness.

A defiant roar rent the air, swallowing Elyria's warnings.

Three heads hissed, three heads bowed, and three sets of wide-open jaws lunged for Gael.

But she was faster.

It was so sudden, so unexpected, that it took several moments for Elyria to understand what was happening. One second, Gael was standing still, lost in her own mind. The next, she was charging into the fiery lake, barreling toward the wyrm, her face twisted in a mask of rage.

"Gael, no!" Elyria screamed, but it did nothing.

Gael's power ignited with terrifying force, flames licking up her arms as she threw herself at the beast with feral rage. Her movements were frantic, erratic, as if she were nothing more than a conduit for the raw, uncontrolled power burning inside her.

The wyrm snarled, its heads snapping at Gael, but she didn't stop. She didn't flinch, only dodged the heads with blinding speed, flames erupting from her hands. She hurled balls of fire at the creature. They bounced harmlessly off its scales, and Elyria's heart fell. Of course they did. It was a fyre wyrm, and Gael was a flamecaller.

She wasn't letting that stop her, though. Gael was nothing but a frenzied hail of fire and fury as she continued hurling wave after wave of power at the wyrm. A one-winged angel come straight from the fourth quarter of hell.

Miraculously, it started to work.

The wyrm recoiled from the flames, hissing in pain as Gael's fire worked its way past its scales to strike the exposed, bleeding flesh Elyria had unearthed. It wasn't enough. The creature's torso rose from the lake, towering above Gael as if ready to crush her with its massive body.

And still, she didn't stop.

She leapt, flames surging around her, and threw herself onto the wyrm. Elyria watched in horrified awe as the flamecaller latched on to its neck and thrust her hands into the gaping wound at its throat.

Gael's eyes locked with Elyria's for a fleeting moment.

And then she was nothing but a living flame—every inch of her, from her long, cascading hair to the tip of her remaining wing, was on fire. And she channeled that fire directly *into* the wyrm, letting it coat the great beast's organs, setting its blood alight. The scent of burning flesh singed Elyria's nostrils as Gael charred its insides.

Elyria had never before heard a sound like the one the wyrm released in triplicate as its massive body convulsed, each head thrashing, then buckling, as it was consumed from within.

Gael was quiet. She made no sound as her face contorted with rage, with pain, with grief. She was utterly silent as her remaining wing withered, as her skin turned black, cracking and splitting. Still, she pushed deeper, her fire growing brighter, burning hotter.

With one final roar, the wyrm fell.

And Elyria's heart shattered as Gael collapsed atop it, flames still sputtering from her body, while both she and the great beast were reduced to ash.

Elyria stood frozen, her breath coming in shallow gasps, her mind struggling to process what she'd just witnessed. She thought maybe she should be screaming, crying, lashing out at the unfairness of it all—but she didn't. Couldn't. She was numb. Hollow. Alone.

It was over.

Gael was gone.

Cyren was gone.

Cedric was . . .

She dropped to her knees, her body collapsing under the weight of that loss.

She couldn't say it.

Couldn't even think it.

It was too much.

And that was when she saw it—movement, out of the corner of her eye. A figure crawling out from the flames.

Her heart stopped.

It couldn't be.

Her breath caught in her throat as Cedric emerged from the fire, body smoking, armor blackened.

Illogical. Impossible. Inconceivable.

But it was him.

He was alive.

Cedric dragged himself onto the shore, the smoldering remnants of his clothing still glowing with heat as he rose—first to his knees, then to his feet. His face was pinned in a silent expression of shock.

Staggering forward, his eyes blazing with something other than fire, he lifted his head and locked eyes with Elyria.

She moved toward him, finally crossing onto the shore, her feet surprisingly steady.

He opened his mouth, drew in a shaky breath as if he was going to speak.

She reached for him.

And he collapsed in her arms.

CHAPTER 38
MONSTROUS THOUGHTS

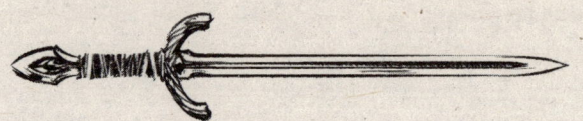

Cedric

Cedric's eyes fluttered open, and for a moment, all he saw was darkness.

Thick, suffocating blackness that clung to his mind, sticky as syrup. He moved, stretching his fingers, his toes, searching for that full-body ache, waiting for the pain to hit him, to feel as if he'd been trampled by a herd of warhorses.

But there was nothing.

Nothing except a strange, unfamiliar coldness in his chest.

I'm still alive.

He let out a shaky breath, the weight of that realization pressing down on him from all sides. Memories flooded his mind in fragmented bursts—the triple-toned roar of the resurrected fyre wyrm, flames dancing on the lake, the blast of power lighting him up, the feeling of soaring backward through the air . . . and then the heat. Surrounding him, consuming him, corroding him. Yet here he was. Whole. Intact. Present.

When he shouldn't be.

Cedric tried to sit up, his body protesting. A hand pressed firmly against his shoulder, easing him back onto the bed. No, not a bed.

He blinked, the shadows in his vision slowly giving way to dim, familiar light. A stone ceiling loomed overhead, intricate etchings spiraling into the corners. It felt as if it was watching over him where he lay, splayed on a loose pile of pillows in the middle of the room.

In the middle of the Sanctum.

He was back in the Celestial Sanctum.

Glancing over, Cedric found Zephyr kneeling beside him, relief pouring from her, so thick it was nearly tangible.

"Welcome back," she said softly. "You've been out for quite a while."

"What's a while?" Cedric's voice came out rough and strained, his throat burning as if he'd inhaled smoke.

She bit her green-tinged lip. "Almost a whole day," she admitted.

Surprise zipped through Cedric as he rose to his elbows, then glanced down at himself. He took in the black tunic draped over his torso, the loose pants curving around his waist. The melancholy that had overtaken him at the creeping memory of what happened on that lake of fire momentarily dissipated as he said, "Did you dress me?"

Zephyr's cheeks turned a darker shade of green. "W-we couldn't very well leave you as you were," she stammered.

Cedric heard a low chuckle and turned to see Thraigg ambling over. "Aye, even dead to the world as ye were, I doubt ye would've found charred armor makes for comfortable bedclothes, boyo. What's left of yer armor can be found o'er there." The dwarf thrust his thumb in the direction of the bedroom doors that lined the back of the antechamber before adding, "Which is where we found these for ye too."

"You seem rather untroubled to see me like this," Cedric said.

Thraigg let out a single laugh. "Would you rather I be wringing my hands at your side like this one?" He jerked his thumb at Zephyr.

"Don't let his dwarven bravado fool you," she said with a shy grin.

"He was just as worried as the rest of us." She gestured at Kit and Nox, sitting a few paces away and wearing matching expressions of concern.

Cedric barely noticed. There was only one person his vision sought.

Elyria sat on a long bench, wings hidden, her back pressed against the stone wall opposite him. She circled her finger around the rim of a goblet, her expression flat. She wasn't looking at Cedric. Her eyes were drawn halfway shut, like it was a labor to hold them open. She seemed tired—something more than exhaustion sitting heavy on her shoulders—and the sight of it made Cedric's stomach squeeze.

He tore his eyes from Elyria to survey the other champions. Kit offered a small smile that didn't quite reach her eyes, Nox sitting beside her with a thoughtful expression on their face. Thraigg, meanwhile, had wandered over to a small table nearby, immediately digging into the bowl of fruit that lay upon it. Whatever the Crucible still had in store for the remaining champions, Cedric was relieved to see that starving them out didn't seem like part of the plan. The usual display of pitchers and platters dotted the antechamber, put there by whatever ancient magic still ran through the Sanctum.

And with Zephyr at his side, now offering him a flagon of water and a small yeast roll, that accounted for everyone.

There was nobody else there.

He didn't really need to ask, but he found the word slipping from his lips anyway. "Gael?"

Zephyr shook her head.

Something prickled behind Cedric's eyes. Their group had become so small. He knew it was absurd to get emotional about it. He could practically hear Lord Church hissing in his ear, telling him to *control his emotions*. And regardless of the fact that doing so had been nearly impossible from the moment he stepped foot inside Castle Lumin, it was true that there was little point in dwelling on this. It was what was supposed to happen, after all. Only one person was ever supposed to walk away a victor at the end of this.

Contrition settled uncomfortably on Cedric's skin. It was more than shame though. More than guilt. Something more like grief. Not just for Cyren and Gael and the others they had lost, but for the person *he* was supposed to be—the man who had died somewhere in the Crucible.

The person who cared more for his mission than the people around him. Who wanted nothing more than to win the crown for Havensreach, to do his duty to the king, to prove Lord Church had been right to place his faith in him.

He hardly knew that person now. He could barely remember the resolve he'd felt when walking through the Gate in Castle Lumin.

Perhaps that was the point of all this. In the second trial, he'd been forced to shed parts of himself in order to reveal his truth. Was that the only time that had happened? Perhaps each of these trials—all of his near-misses with death—had been slowly chipping away at the person he was when he entered.

"Tell me what happened," he said, pulling himself up to a sitting position.

Zephyr stilled. "After Cyren was"—she cleared her throat—"taken, Tenebris pushed Thraigg and me through the gate, so I didn't see any of it for myself. But my understanding is that Gael burned herself out taking down the wyrm. That was right after you . . ."

"Right," Cedric said, his voice low. Flashes of obsidian-laced power and orange-red flames danced in his mind. "After me."

"You have no idea how relieved we all were to see Elyria come through the gate with you," she continued, her voice high, like she might banish the sorrow in the air with forced cheer.

"She brought me through?" His gaze immediately drifted back to where Elyria sat. This time, as if she sensed his returning attention, her heavy-lidded eyes shot open, brilliant green meeting his warm brown before she tore them away.

Why was she avoiding his gaze again? Unlike the bewilderment that had washed over Cedric when she'd done this after he woke from Belien's attack, anger sparked in him instead. Was this to be their new dynamic, then? He would nearly die, and she would save him, only to act as though he didn't exist when he awoke? Why bother saving him at all?

A gnawing sort of fear twisted inside him—a coiled serpent. That icy feeling in the center of his chest grew colder.

Cedric forced himself to sit up fully this time, ignoring Zephyr's quiet protest. His head spun, but he gritted his teeth, the need for answers far stronger than the pain that tugged at his limbs.

"I should be dead," he said.

No one responded at first, the silence hanging in the room like a shroud.

"I shouldn't have made it out of the trial."

"Why would you say such a thing?" Zephyr's voice was calm, but Cedric thought he caught the flicker of something else behind the words. "Of course you should have."

He clenched one of the pillows by his legs in his hand, the plush fabric at odds with the rough, grating feeling scraping under his skin. He couldn't explain where this was coming from, why he was suddenly so *angry*, other than that he was so tired of feeling worthless. So tired of being the weakest link among them.

"You know it's true. *She* knows it's true!" He pointed a finger at Elyria, who put her goblet down, stood, and started pacing toward him. "How many times should I have died in here? The wyrm should have killed me. The dragon should have killed me. My own memory should have killed me!" His voice cracked. "And that stars-forsaken lake of fucking fire should *absolutely* have killed me."

He slammed his fist into the pillow, his breathing growing erratic as the memories of the end of the trial swirled around him—sinking into the firestorm, unbearable heat crawling up his limbs, the way his body had felt for a moment like it was turning to ash. And then . . . nothing. No pain. No death.

He looked at his hands, his palms up, as if searching for answers in the unscarred skin.

"What is this?" he breathed.

It was Elyria who finally spoke, her melodic voice shockingly gentle. "Cedric, it's nothing to—"

"Don't," he snapped, cutting her off. "Don't tell me it's nothing. Don't tell me I'm fine. Don't tell me there's nothing shameful about the fact that despite being the supposed 'great champion of Kingshelm,' I wouldn't have even made it past the first fucking trial without your help."

He tipped his head back and released a hollow laugh. "Maybe that's the point though. Look how easily my fellow humans were all taken by the Crucible. Did we even have a chance? Or were the Arbiter's claims for unity just sweet lies? Something to whet our appetites for victory, encourage us to help you all go further."

"Humans aren't the only ones who have been lost to the Crucible," Elyria said, her tone sharpening.

The others exchanged glances, the air in the room thick. Several long moments passed before anyone spoke again.

"No matter how it happened, what matters is that you survived, Cedric," Kit finally said. "We can all try to reason the whys and hows and—"

"There's no reason to be had here, clearly," Cedric said. He could feel the tenuous grasp on his sanity slipping the more he argued this. How could they not see? There was something *wrong* here, for him to have survived when he shouldn't have. "I should be dead. I felt it."

"Well, you're not," Elyria snapped. "And you're right, you did almost die. Again. But for once, I'm not the one who saved you—by some miracle, you seem to have done that yourself this time. Lunara knows how you managed to do it, but don't try to weasel your way out of the accomplishment of actively preventing your own fiery death."

Cedric bolted to his feet, opening his mouth to protest. She wasn't finished.

"But if the situation arises again, if you get into danger again—and you're right, you do seem to attract death like moths to a fucking flame, so I'd say there's a pretty big stars-damned chance it'll happen—you should know that I wouldn't hesitate to save you. I'd do it again and again and again, because I don't want you to fucking die!"

Her eyes blazed as she came to stand in front of him, her nose only a few inches from his own.

"You're the one who put the idea in my head that we might just have a chance to finish this thing and get out of here alive. I don't even care who ends up with the fucking crown at this point, I just want *that*. I want the *after* that you promised. And I'm not willing to lose anyone else to the celestials' mad games."

Cedric shook his head, his breathing growing shallow, his pulse pounding in his ears. That icy cold in his chest was spreading, a squirming feeling creeping through his veins. It felt a little bit like mana, though he didn't even have to look at the drained token still hanging from his neck to know that was impossible.

"I—" He pressed his trembling hands over his heart, trying to tamp down the feeling spreading there. "There's something wrong with me."

"Breathe, boyo. Just breathe." Thraigg's voice was low, restrained, the kind tone one might use to calm an animal thrashing about its cage. He shuffled close enough to reach out a thick hand and pull Zephyr back.

"Cedric..." The silver fire in Elyria's eyes was immediately replaced with concern as she lifted a hand to reach for him.

He recoiled instinctively. "No," he said, voice tight. "There's something . . . wrong." His mind was spinning. He didn't belong here; he wasn't meant for this. Lord Church had gotten it wrong. All of Havensreach had gotten it wrong. He wasn't capable of winning. He wasn't made for this.

The air in the room felt suddenly charged—too hot, too cold, too thin, too thick. His erratically tracking eyes met Elyria's for a split second, some unreadable emotion flicking across her face.

"Cedric, you need to calm down," she said. "You're going to—"

And that's when Cedric realized that it wasn't ice that had been slowly spreading from his chest and into his veins.

It was fire.

A heat simmering just under his skin, so piercing, so bright, it had felt freezing.

Light exploded from Cedric's chest, filling the room from floor to ceiling.

And he combusted.

CHAPTER 39
MAN ON FIRE

Cedric

I can't breathe.

The fire is suffocating.

It's everywhere, crawling up my limbs, roaring in my ears, scorching my throat, my lungs. My vision is warping, the walls of the Sanctum bending and twisting like they're dissolving under the heat.

I look down, see the white-gold flames licking at my body, searing my clothes. Are they melding into me? Fusing with me, replacing my flesh with charred fabric? Or is it melting off me along with my skin?

But no. There's no blistering flesh, no skin dripping from my bones.

Scalding, oppressive heat is everywhere, and yet I still feel . . .

Cold.

And that's when I realize the fire isn't just around me.

It's in me.

I can feel it radiating from my chest, pulsing out through my limbs with every erratic beat of my heart. It's expanding, surging. It's trying to burst free.

It's succeeding.

I press my palms against my chest, where the flames are hottest. And like sparks igniting a pile of kindling, mental images start to unfurl, one after the other.

Charred fingerprints on a wooden training post.

The mesmerizing call of Gael's magic.

Wild, swirling flames blazing through the attackers who murdered my parents, melting their *clothing, searing* their *flesh as my family's cottage burned.*

Every time I felt that burning spark in my chest, every time my hands heated or my neck prickled with warmth.

I'd always thought it was just my emotions, the burn of anger, the way rage was supposed to feel.

I see it now.

I didn't just feel like I was burning.

I was *burning.*

Just like I am now.

"What's gotten into you, my little phoenix?"

The memory of my mother's voice is a soothing balm against the fire weaving around me, through me. Her little phoenix.

She knew.

Did she know?

I stumble back, my breath hitching. The heat flares, the flames dancing on my skin growing erratic, leaping off my body in wide arcs.

This is wrong. Everything about this is wrong.

I am wrong.

I squeeze my eyes shut, clench my fists, trying to stop the fire from spreading.

I don't know how.

Panic squeezes me from all sides.

I'm a monster.

I've always been a monster.

I should have known. I should have—

Something presses in on my consciousness, a shadow shifting over me. I feel it settle on me like a blanket, the calming wisp of something else.

Of someone *else.*

A hand wraps around my arm, gentle but firm.

Stop.

Don't.

I'll hurt you. You'll—

I shake, thrash, shudder. Trying to dislodge it.

The grip only tightens, holding fast. Even as the hand starts to tremble. Even as the hiss of pain reaches my ears—first a whisper, then a scream. It still doesn't let go.

And so I cling to that shadow, that cooling calm. An anchor in this firestorm.

I cling to her.

And slowly—ever so slowly, the inferno inside me starts to fade.

CHAPTER 40
SMOKE

Elyria

Cedric was fire incarnate.

It wasn't the same orange-red blaze that had covered Gael from wing to toe, though. White-gold flames danced across Cedric's skin, rippling in waves over his chest, his arms, his face. The heated air around him shimmered, distorted, the pillows by his feet crumbling into black ash as flames consumed them. The thin golden ring in his warm brown eyes expanded, his irises glowing like liquid fire as they were pinned open, unseeing.

Elyria couldn't move. Could hardly breathe. Could only stare, her mind desperately trying to piece together what she was witnessing with what she knew.

There had always been something *other* about him, hadn't there?

Some reason she felt drawn to him, called to him. Something that only grew more apparent as the trials went on. She *saw* him fall. She could still feel the way her heart cracked as he sank into that fiery lake.

Yet here he was.

And it was like he brought all the fire with him.

Movement suddenly returned to Elyria's body, that trilling *tug* in her chest propelling her forward. She let it, not sparing a single thought to the idea of resisting.

As if in response to her approach, Cedric stumbled back, his breath catching. He tensed, his molten eyes squeezing shut. He clenched his fists. The fire licking at his limbs grew higher, suddenly leaping off his body like it was trying to ward off an attack.

He was a blazing beacon in the void, an empyreal effigy.

Awe and terror swelled in Elyria's chest as she took another step closer. "Cedric," she whispered. He didn't respond. Didn't react. Perhaps he couldn't even hear her over the roaring heat.

Still, Elyria kept saying his name, her eyes never leaving him, barely noticing the shouts and movements of the others. Kit darted forward, her hands aloft, water flowing through the air, weaving around him, only to evaporate in a wave of steam. Zephyr was still, rooted to the spot, green lips parted in shock. Thraigg's mouth hung open.

"He's going to burn out," Nox said evenly, as if they didn't particularly care but thought perhaps someone ought to know.

"Cedric," Elyria repeated. "Cedric. Cedric!"

Still no response. His fists were still clenched, his body shaking. This fire, this flame—*his* flame—whatever it was, wherever it came from, it would consume him. The image of Gael's blackened fingers, her skin crumbling into ash, tore through Elyria's mind, and she swallowed back bile.

Not him.

He was not allowed to go like this.

The Crucible could not have him, too.

Like a marionette being pulled by that golden thread, she reached for him. The agony was immediate. White-gold flames bit at her flesh.

For a fleeting moment, she wasn't here. She was pinned to a table in a ransacked tavern, Raefe's disgusting flametouch searing her legs.

No.

This wasn't then.

He wasn't him.

Cedric was *good*.

And he needed help.

He needed her.

Screaming through the pain, Elyria fully thrust her right hand into the blaze and wrapped it around Cedric's forearm. It hurt. Badly. The flames gnawed at her skin. She bit down hard on the inside of her lip, tasting blood, in an attempt to distract from the pain.

But still, she held on, her fingers digging into him as he tried to pull away, thrashing to dislodge her. With a gasping breath, she summoned her shadows, letting them flow from her hand, wisps of smoke that coiled around him.

Shadows twisted with his fire, wrapping him in a blanket of cooling darkness. One heartbeat or a hundred could have passed as Elyria and Cedric stood there, entwined.

Flame and wild, shadow and sun.

Inch by inch, the raging inferno subsided until only smoldering embers remained, flickering weakly beneath his skin.

Little by little, the shadows—*her* shadows—smothered the flames.

Elyria's legs buckled, her power dissipating into the ether. Cedric fell with her, their arms still intertwined, their bodies crumpling together, limp and empty.

For a minute they lay there in the middle of the room, chests heaving, eyes wide with shock. Cedric was pale as a ghost, his clothing in tatters, all color drained from his face. His entire body trembled.

Still shaking herself, Elyria ignored the pain blazing up her right arm and reached for his hand with her uninjured one. "You're all right. I've got you," she said, déjà vu washing through her.

Painstakingly, as if it required every iota of focus and concentration he possessed, Cedric nodded. Together, they got to their feet, each leaning on the other as they staggered to a bench along one side of the chamber. Zephyr and Kit tittered around them, unsure as to how they might best help.

Elyria wished they would all step back, step away. He needed a minute. They just needed a minute.

Cedric's voice was raw, his head hung low as he rasped, "What am I?"

Elyria didn't know how to answer that. She was wondering the very same thing herself.

CHAPTER 41
SCARS

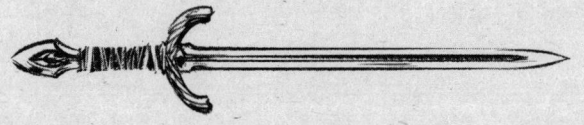

Cedric

Cedric sat on the stone bench, his elbows on his knees, his hands scrubbing his face. He could feel Elyria at his side, silence stretching between them, a strain in her typically irreverent presence that he knew was only there because of him. She was stretched tighter than a drawn bowstring.

He knew the feeling.

His chest still ached—not from the flames. They were long gone at this point, fizzled out in the time he'd spent sitting here, silent, still, after his . . . combustion. It ached from the memory, though, of the heat that had consumed him from the inside out, that had burst from him so uncontrollably that he knew he might have very well burned the entire Sanctum down had Elyria not been able to stop him.

He rubbed at his chest, his fingers bunching the black fabric of his tunic, as though he could sense the fire smoldering just underneath. Absently, he thought about what a shame it would be to ruin yet another set of clothing.

A clang echoed across the chamber, drawing Cedric's focus to the other four champions. Kit and Zephyr had made a hasty retreat to the other side of the room when Elyria, fed up with their hovering after they'd tended to her wounds, issued a reprimand sharp enough to have taken their heads clean off. Now they sat with Thraigg, who appeared to be in the middle of telling some tale—quite animatedly, from the way he was gesticulating with his hammer.

Half-covered in shadows, Nox sat a few paces away, sipping from a bronze goblet. Brow furrowed, their eyes flitted between Cedric and Elyria, as if the two of them were a puzzle they were trying to piece together.

Thraigg's story must have ended, because suddenly all Cedric could hear was the soft hum of magic layered with Zephyr's and Kit's hushed voices. His ears pricked at the sound of his name, barely loud enough for him to hear.

"Is Cedric all right?" Kit asked.

He felt like he should be the one to answer the question, to tell her that of course he was. And of course he wasn't. But both responses stayed stuck in his throat, tangled and muddy.

"There are different kinds of injuries," Zephyr said after a moment, her voice layered with an emotion Cedric couldn't place. "Not all of them are so easily healed. Some leave scars long after all signs of the wounds themselves have faded."

They lapsed back into silence.

Pulling his hands from his face, Cedric stared into his open palms. They looked so . . . ordinary. He flexed his fingers, half expecting fire to burst from his hands, but nothing happened. There was just that tingle under his skin, the smoldering embers of magic somehow *in* him, a furnace he had no idea how to extinguish.

What was that?

What was he?

He clenched and unclenched his fists, willing the answers to appear in the lines of his palms. But there was nothing. No seared flesh, no scars—none that were visible, at least.

He reclined against the wall, tipping his chin up until the back of his head came to rest on the cool stone behind him. His upper arm brushed Elyria's shoulder as he did, but still, she said nothing. Turning his head, he flicked his eyes to the long bandage that started at her hand and wrapped its way up her arm. Guilt spiked in his gut. He hated that she'd gotten hurt—that *he'd* hurt her, again.

"I'm sorry," he suddenly blurted, his voice piercing the tense silence between them.

"It's fine." The words were clipped, her body tense, as if she was angry. She wouldn't look at him. But she also hadn't moved from her spot beside him.

He didn't understand why. It wasn't as if she didn't have the entire open Sanctum to retreat to. Hells, she could take her pick of bedrooms. There were more of them than the remaining six of them could occupy at this point, a fact that had Cedric's shoulders sagging with heavy sadness.

Fourteen champions had entered the Arcane Crucible—fifteen, if you wanted to get technical. Six remained.

His attention turned back to Elyria and the simmering tension he felt radiating from her at his side. Her uninjured hand was fisted in her lap, her exhalations coming fast and indignant through her nose. Yes, she was definitely angry. Outraged. Livid, even. And she had every right to be.

Once again, she'd had to come to his rescue. Once again, he'd proven himself the weak link among them. Once again, they were forced to wait on *him*.

Although . . . that wasn't *entirely* true this time, he supposed.

In the hours that had passed since Cedric awoke back in the Sanctum, there had been nary a sign as to what was to come next. No accolades or congratulations from the Arbiter rang through his mind. No doorways glowed. And Cedric suspected part of Elyria's obvious frustration was due to the fact that not a single one of the champions knew what they were supposed to do next.

"I understand that you're angry with me," he said, coughing to clear the scratchiness in his voice. It still felt like there was smoke in his lungs. "And I know—"

Her head whipped to him. "Of course I'm fucking angry," she hissed, not quite meeting his eyes. "I'm *pissed*."

"You could have let me burn." His voice was hoarse, and though he hadn't intended to sound so pathetic, the words came out as barely more than a whisper.

Elyria stiffened but didn't answer immediately. She was silent for so long, in fact, that Cedric wondered if she'd even heard him.

Finally, she released a long, shaky breath, tilting her head so that she met his gaze straight on. "And that, right there, is *why* I'm so pissed."

He blinked, surprise flickering through him.

"All that shit that you said before you lit up like a fucking bonfire," she continued.

Flashes of all the fears Cedric had put into words ran through his head.

"I shouldn't have made it out of the trial."

"How many times should I have died in here?"

"I wouldn't have even made it past the first fucking trial without your help."

"Look how easily my fellow humans were all taken by the Crucible. Did we even have a chance?"

"I should be dead."

Elyria's silver-flecked emerald eyes burned into him with a fervor, a rawness, that locked his gaze in with her own. He couldn't have looked away even if he wanted to.

He didn't want to.

"You think you're so expendable, that you're not worth saving? I disa-fucking-gree. And I really wish you would stop with this self-pitying, self-sacrificing bullshit." Her words were like acid, but her voice was thick. "Did you ever think that maybe I didn't *want* to let you go?"

Cedric swallowed hard. What was he supposed to say to that? "I'm . . . I'm sorry—"

"Fucking stars above!" She threw her hands in the air, her bandage slipping slightly as she stood. "Stop apologizing for being alive, Cedric."

Her words struck him like a slap. Not malicious though. A plea. A demand. Like she was still waiting for him to wake up.

And hadn't he sworn he would no longer keep anyone else waiting?

With a sigh, Elyria turned away from him and attempted to walk off. Cedric reached out, wrapping his fingers around her unbandaged wrist with a featherlight touch. The instant his skin made contact with hers, he felt that weight in his chest settle, the ache dispersing like steam evaporating into temperate air.

With the gentlest pressure, he pulled her back. She complied, turning to sit on the bench once more, apprehension painted all over her perfect features.

She looked as lost as he felt.

He opened his mouth to say something, but once again, the words were stuck just behind his tongue.

"I need to check your bandage." Zephyr's soft voice fell over the pair, and Cedric tore his eyes from Elyria's face to where the sylvan now stood in front of them, shifting awkwardly on her feet.

"Sure," Elyria said impassively, holding her injured arm aloft as if it were barely a bother, as if nothing strange and unexpected had occurred in this chamber at all.

Zephyr went to pull something from her belt.

In one swift motion, Elyria yanked her arm back, her eyes narrowing on the small tin Zephyr now held. "How's the smell of that one?"

The sylvan huffed a quiet laugh. "I'm afraid you already know," she said. "Same stuff I gave you for your legs."

Cedric couldn't stop himself from glancing at Elyria's legs, from thinking about the checkerboard of burns he knew lay under her leathers.

Elyria groaned melodramatically. "Fine. But only because I also know how well it works." With her uninjured arm, she pinched her nostrils closed and squeezed her eyes shut, her visage suddenly far closer to that of a spoiled child than a centuries-old fae warrior, and it made that formerly aching spot in Cedric's chest start to throb.

"Here, allow me," he said, taking the tin from Zephyr with one hand and tenderly lifting Elyria's bandaged arm with the other.

Elyria's eyes flew open, and she seemed to instinctively pull her arm closer to her body. "No, you don't have to—"

"Please," he said, his eyes meeting hers. "Let me."

She hesitated, her face inscrutable. She leaned toward him. The movement was subtle, small. And were it not for the thick fog of tension suddenly pressing on the two of them, Cedric might have wondered if he'd imagined it entirely. But tense, it was. The kind of tension that made him feel like the two of them were seconds away from clashing . . . in some manner or another.

Whatever she saw in Cedric's expression must have softened her resolve, however, because a long sigh slipped from between her lips moments later, and she allowed him to gently retrieve her arm.

Cedric's breath caught in his throat as he unwrapped the bandage to reveal the angry red burn beneath. It was worse than he'd imagined—her pristine skin was cracked, raw, and blistered from her palm to her elbow. And this was *after* Zephyr had already tended to it. He could see a few patches of new skin poking through, shiny and pink, but more of it was still charred, dark, and peeling.

Swallowing hard, he tried to quell the twisting in his stomach as he dipped two fingers into the balm—which did, in fact, smell *absolutely foul*—and gingerly applied it to the burn. Elyria released the faintest whimper as he touched a particularly heinous-looking spot, and it was all Cedric could do not to crumple at the sound.

He froze, tempted to pull back entirely, but he thought that delaying would only make it worse. "I'm sorry," he said. "You know I never meant to—"

"I know," she interrupted, something that sounded a lot like pity in her voice. "It wasn't your fault."

His jaw clenched. "It was."

"I told you to stop apologizing," she gritted out. "It's not the first time, won't be the last."

"I know. But it should be," he said, his voice tight. "And I swear, I will never be the cause of your pain again."

There was a sad smile on her lips when he looked up. "You can't promise that," she said.

"I can. I do."

He owed her that much. Owed her more than that. He'd done this to her. The hot sting of shame crawled up Cedric's spine as he thought of the animosity he'd held for the Revenant—for her. There was much he wanted to make up for.

A clean bandage was suddenly dangling in front of his face, held there by a small green hand. Cedric blinked, having nearly forgotten Zephyr entirely.

"Thank you," he said, taking the bandage and wrapping it back around Elyria's arm. Zephyr patted him on the shoulder, and for a second she looked hesitant, torn. Like she might have wanted to say something. It was gone as quickly as it came though, and Zephyr was heading back to her previous position on the other side of the chamber before he could ask her about it. He had enough going on in his head at the moment anyway.

As if she could sense his thoughts, Elyria placed her hand on top of his, warmth radiating from the spot. A different kind of warmth than he was used to feeling. Less like heat. More like . . . light. And that throbbing in his chest only intensified.

If she felt anything similar, she didn't let on. She only continued holding Cedric's hand as she said with a steady voice, "I know something of having a power inside you that you don't know how to control."

"I have barely the comprehension to understand that this 'power' came from inside me at all, let alone that it's something that can even *be* controlled. You should stay away from me," Cedric replied, though despite being the one to say the words, something in his chest roiled at the suggestion. He couldn't find the strength of will to enact it, to put any actual distance between them. Everything in him seemed to be screaming to do the opposite, in fact. So instead of pulling away, he flipped their hands so hers was face up, his fingertips dancing across her palm.

She scoffed. "I'm not afraid of you."

He looked up from where he'd begun tracing the lines on her hand and met her glowing green stare. "Maybe you should be."

"Maybe you need to stop being afraid of yourself." Her gaze was unwavering as she wove her fingers between his. Her voice dropped. "You're not alone in this. We're so close, I can feel it. So close to the end. Whatever happens next, we can face it . . . together."

Together.

The word was a chorus swelling in his ears, loosening the lingering remnants of whatever had constricted around his heart. For the first time since he woke, he felt like he could take a real breath.

"I'm sor—"

"I swear to Solaris, Lunara, Gaia, and Noctis alike, Cedric, if you say 'I'm sorry' *one more time* . . ."

He pressed his lips together. "I shall try to apologize less," he said after a moment, his mouth tipping up sheepishly as he called upon the words they'd exchanged at the beginning of the second trial, "if you promise to try to loosen up a little when the occasion calls for it."

Elyria's lips pursed, her cheeks flexing, and Cedric knew she was fighting a laugh. He was very pleased when she lost that fight, a beaming smile overtaking her face. It was like the first rays of sun breaking through an overcast sky.

"That sounds like a losing proposition for us both," she said, and the lopsided grin playing at the corners of Cedric's lips bloomed until he found himself laughing.

A true, full-bodied laugh.

Elyria stared at him, the silver flecks in her eyes winking like stars on a windy night. "He laughs! Consider me utterly aghast." She flexed her bandaged arm as if testing his handiwork, her voice teasing. "Did the fire burn away your broodiness?"

The question was said in jest, an attempt to stretch the lightness that had just finally broken through between them. Cedric knew this. It hit him like a hammer to the chest, nonetheless. A reminder that he had been changing—that he had changed—since being here. Making him question just how much of that change was due to the Crucible, or simply because whatever was in him had been slowly awakening this whole time.

It had haunted him since the moment the fire surged from his body. No, earlier. Since he crawled out of that lake of flame and smoke like he'd been born from it. Maybe since the first time he'd felt that heat coiled in his chest, waiting all along to break free.

His next words came out as a broken whisper. "What is wrong with me?"

Elyria cracked a grin. "Oh, come now, that's far too easy." When

Cedric didn't respond, her expression softened. She shifted, straightening her back even as she left their fingers intertwined, their hands lying on the bench between them. "There's nothing wrong with you, Cedric."

"It feels like everything that's happened is my fault," he said, voice shaking. "It's my fault you got hurt. It's my fault Gael died. It's my fault that—"

She lifted her other hand, her first finger raised to halt him. A contemplative look crossed her face, as if she was carefully weighing her next words. "I know what it's like . . . to carry that ever-present weight of guilt. Of blame. To feel like something inside you is wrong, to let it eat away at you until nothing of you remains but wisps of smoke and a collection of scars.

"I ran from my power for years. Ran from myself. After Evander died, I blamed myself for not being strong enough. For not controlling it. I thought maybe if I'd been stronger, if I hadn't been so scared of what I could do, he'd still be here."

She looked across the chamber and met Kit's eye, a bemused expression on the other fae's face. "He only did it to help me, you know. Only entered the last Crucible because he thought that with the power of the crown, he might be able to free me from this." She opened her free hand, and a wisp of shadow danced over the bandage crossing her palm. "That he might finally be able to give me peace."

Her voice cracked on the last word. Cedric didn't have a response to share. He also didn't think she needed one. That this confession was as much for her as it was for him. So, he simply listened, rubbing his thumb in slow circles on the back of her hand as she spoke.

"For twenty-five years, everywhere I looked, all I saw were the places he wasn't. Every time I walked into a room, every time I turned the corner, my eyes would go to the places I thought I would find him. The places he should have been. Sitting in his favorite chair. Reading a book on his side of the bed. Filling a water basin for the housekeeper with the snap of his fingers. Even things I used to complain about him wasting his time on . . ."

With a sigh, Elyria closed her hand, snuffing out that wisp of magic. "Things that, now, I would give anything to be ignored for again. If it meant he was still here."

"He never would have wanted you to stop living, Ellie." Kit's voice was low as she crossed the space between them, coming to kneel at Elyria's side. "And I wish I'd known this was the burden you carried all these years."

A single tear rolled down Elyria's pale cheek. Cedric resisted the urge to wipe it away.

"If only you'd endangered your life sooner, we might have had more time to enjoy this," Elyria said with a choked laugh.

Kit reached out and lightly smacked Elyria's shoulder. "We'll have plenty of opportunities to make up for lost time after we get out of here," she said.

Elyria pulled her hand from Cedric's to take her friend's instead. "After," she said, and his heart clenched all over again.

He wanted to speak, to say something, to acknowledge this strange thread between them. To ask if she felt it too.

She must feel it too.

But before Cedric could say anything, Kit stood, pulling Elyria to her feet before they dropped their hands and drew apart.

"First things first, though," said Kit.

"The whole 'getting out of here' thing?" Elyria asked.

Kit nodded, then turned to address Thraigg and Nox in addition to Cedric and Elyria. "Anyone have a clue what we're supposed to do now?"

Nox hummed as they got up and approached the rest of the group. "It is rather curious that we have not received any additional communication from the Arbiter, is it not?"

"Curious? It's damned baffling," said Thraigg.

"Precisely," said Kit. "Where's our congratulations for surviving another trial? Our ominous instructions on what is to come in the final one?"

"What makes you think only one remains?" asked Cedric.

"Oh, she hasn't shared her theory with you yet?" Elyria asked.

Cedric shook his head.

"Kit's convinced that the Arbiter's proclamation back in Castle Lumin painted a map through the trials for us."

"Was I wrong?" Kit looked affronted. "The Arbiter told us that the trials would demand strength and power and test our resolve and spirit. Trial of Strength, check. Trial of Spirit, check."

"Trial of Magic?"

"Power, magic." Kit glared at her friend. "As I've said before, *semantics*."

Elyria clucked her tongue. "Which would mean that we have, what, a Trial of Resolve remaining? That doesn't make any sense to me."

"Is the trial seeing how long we resolve to wait here like bumbling idiots?" Thraigg grumbled.

"Perhaps the Arbiter's words are not an exact match for what we've come to experience, then," Cedric said. "But the prophecy still is."

"The prophecy?" repeated Elyria.

Cedric cleared his throat. *"From shadow and fire, champions rise, forged in the Crucible of fate. Strength, spirit, magic, and concord test the trials beyond the Gate."*

Elyria was smirking at him when he finished his recitation, and embarrassment kept him from repeating the final two lines. Nobody else seemed to notice, though.

"So, not the Trial of Resolve, then, but the Trial of Concord?" Kit asked, her brow furrowing over her mismatched eyes.

A chill fell over the chamber, blanketing the group of champions like a shroud. Cedric didn't understand why. Didn't understand why Elyria went suddenly stiff, her breath catching, her gaze pinned on a spot somewhere behind Kit's moonlight-silver head. Didn't understand the expression of pure, unbridled disbelief on her face.

Not even as a voice—low and male and gentle and one that Cedric had certainly never heard before—cut through the silence like a knife.

"I always knew you were the smart one."

PART IV
FORGED

CHAPTER 42
IMPOSSIBLE REUNION

Elyria

It was impossible.

More than impossible.

Every cell in Elyria's body was immovable, frozen. She could barely breathe. But there he was, almost exactly as she remembered him.

Dark hair. Bronze skin. Shimmering wings of black and gold.

Next to her, Kit gasped as Evander walked out of the shadows.

Gasped, and then collapsed, right there onto the stone floor of the Sanctum, her blue and green eyes pinned to her brother as thick tears carved tracks down her brown cheeks. "H-how?"

"I was starting to worry you had given up on me, Kitty Kat," he said, and his voice had that same smooth lilt, that same mirthful intonation Elyria had known. Had loved.

Her heart pounded, each beat slamming against her ears like the tone of a bell. She felt like she was being held underwater, suspended in time, in space. The desire to rush forward, to touch him, warred with the instinct whispering warnings in the back of her mind.

She didn't understand, *couldn't* understand.

And she wasn't the only one.

"Who are you?" Nox's voice wasn't exactly accusatory, more curious, though it was still laden with something that felt like apprehension.

"What is this?" Cedric asked at nearly the same time, his voice spiking across the haze in her head like a crystal whip—clear and cutting.

"You've already met my sister," Evander said, kneeling next to Kit and wrapping an arm around her shoulder. She sobbed harder.

Elyria still hadn't moved an inch, though she felt heat emanating off Cedric's body as he stood and took a step closer to her. He was tense, suspicion radiating from him, his fingers twitching at his sides as if itching to go to the hilt of his sword.

Evander's golden eyes flicked to Elyria, and her heart might have stopped beating. "And you've also met my love," he said. "My name is Evander Ravenswing, and I've been waiting for you all for a very long time."

"Tell me again." Elyria's voice trembled as she gazed at Evander, sitting just to her left, legs splayed wide, sucking the juice of the strawberry he'd just eaten from his thumb.

"I've already told you everything I remember," he said.

"Which is why I said *again*, obviously."

Evander smiled at her, and her stomach clenched. His eyes crinkled in exactly the same way. His dimple—just on the left side, not the right—emerged in exactly the same spot. And Elyria wanted—wanted so, so badly—to believe it was real.

She couldn't. Couldn't trust his measured expression, his controlled reactions—so perfect, it was as if they'd been crafted for just this occasion. Couldn't trust the overwhelming feeling of relief that wanted to crest inside her. She refused to let it. Refused to think that this wasn't some new cruel trick, some illusion of the Crucible.

Kit had no such qualms. That much was evident in the way she gazed at her brother as though he was every present she'd ever wished for and the realization of every dream she'd ever had.

Evander sighed good-naturedly, his smile unfaltering, like he was slightly exasperated but would humor her, nonetheless. It was a sigh Elyria remembered well, though she felt a kind of sharpness just under the surface. As though his reaction, this replica of the past, was a little *too* perfect.

"My fellow champions were felled, one by one, by the trials," Evander said. "Ultimately, by the time we got through the Trial of Magic, only I remained. Me . . . and him."

"Varyth Malchior," Nox said, shaking their head as if it might erase the ludicrous notion. Elyria didn't blame them. She herself had nearly laughed out loud when Evander first mentioned his name. But it was only because the infamous leader of the dreaded Cult of Malakar felt more like the villain in a children's story than an actual person by now.

Evander's next sigh was far less good-humored. "Yes. As I've said."

"You'll have to forgive our skepticism, Lord Ravenswing," Cedric said dutifully, and Elyria choked on her wine upon hearing the honorific spill from the knight's lips.

Evander turned to face Elyria. "Your human is very polite," he said, a smirk playing on his full lips. She took a measured sip from her goblet to keep herself from scowling.

Cedric ignored the barb. "You must understand, we simply find it difficult to wrap our heads around the knowledge that Varyth Malchior not only entered the Crucible last time, but allegedly made it out? Despite the fact that none have ever managed to do the same?"

"Yes, well, what else would you expect of a descendent of the dark sorcerer himself?" Evander's golden gaze ran down Cedric before flicking back to his face, like he was sizing him up.

A defensive prickle surged in Elyria's chest.

"I realize how it sounds," continued Evander. "How I might hear it, even, were our current roles reversed. But believe me, the man is real, and he certainly has not been trapped here with me all this time."

"He is out there," Zephyr said quietly.

"Yet the crown remains unclaimed, does it?" Thraigg added, voice gruff.

Evander nodded. "Not for his lack of trying, believe me. But it would appear the celestials understood at least one thing about the influence of Malakar's dark magic when they crafted the Crucible."

Cedric arched his brow. "Meaning?"

"*Meaning*, it wouldn't let him claim it. Not even after we made it to the final trial."

"The Trial of Concord?" Kit asked eagerly.

"Yes. The final barrier standing between champion and crown." He bounced his finger on Kit's nose, and she beamed at him. "Malchior couldn't best it, and I refused to help him. But with his wicked magic came wicked ways to manipulate some parts of the Crucible, enough so to break his tie to the Sanctum and escape, abandoning me here."

"And you've been here this entire time?" Cedric asked, at the same time Elyria said, "And you've been alone all these years?"

"Yes."

Shame spread through her like poison. Twenty-five years. He spent twenty-five years trapped in this prison, while she drowned herself in drink and between the legs of anyone who caught her eye. "Wouldn't . . . ?" Elyria started, then bit back the words on her tongue.

"Say what you are thinking, love," Evander encouraged, leaning toward her. "I would hope we wouldn't start keeping secrets now."

Cedric tangibly stiffened at Elyria's other side. "Wouldn't it have driven you mad?" she asked.

"I suppose I just knew that if I waited long enough, someone would come for me. I prayed to the celestials for it every day and every night. I prayed it would be you."

Elyria's heart cracked.

"Why have we not seen you until now?" Nox asked, again their tone filled with curiosity . . . and laced with something sharper.

"Dare I presume to understand the designs of the celestials?" Evander said with a chuckle. "I simply could not be seen until now."

Well, that's convenient. The thought crossed Elyria's mind before she could stop it. Couldn't stop the questions burning there, either. She didn't get a chance to ask them, though.

"I saw you, however. I've been watching, waiting," Evander continued.

Elyria's cheeks heated. She didn't want to know if he'd witnessed the *almost* with Cedric in the moonlight, or the many moments shared between them since. The words felt sticky on her tongue as she said, "I had no idea. I thought you were lost."

Evander placed his large hand over hers on the table and she froze. "That's a shame. I was hoping you would know there's nothing in this world or the next that could have kept me from you forever."

Several heartbeats of thick silence passed. Elyria's heart was suddenly beating too fast. She stared at their hands, Evander's heavy atop her own. His eyes flicked to her shoulders, almost as if he was looking for the wings she hadn't even considered uncloaking. She couldn't. Not with the familiarity and foreignness of him at war in her heart.

She wanted to grab hold of his hand and keep it tucked in hers forever. She wanted to fling it off her. Her body split the difference by tensing so tightly, she was sure she was the one who would combust this time. She didn't know how to process his presence—his return—on top of everything else.

Cedric's arm brushed against Elyria's, the reminder of him calming her, grounding her. Her shadows buzzed, the *tug* in her chest pulling the slightest bit, even as she noted the way Cedric's gaze flicked from her to Evander to their hands on the table.

"So, now what?" Thraigg finally asked, a welcome interruption to her spinning thoughts. "Where do we go from here?"

Evander cocked his head. "Whatever do you mean?"

"He means, we don't know what we're supposed to do now," Kit said, shaking her head. "The Arbiter has not issued any instruction since before the last trial. We don't have any idea what the Trial of Concord entails."

Evander paused. "I see," he said simply, though there was something in his voice as he spoke the words that set Elyria on edge.

"But don't worry, brother." Kit jumped to her feet. "We're here now.

We're together, and we will not stop until we are all free of this place. Fuck the crown. If Varyth Malchior was able to escape this place without winning it, we can too. It was never my reason for coming here anyway."

Evander hummed thoughtfully before releasing Elyria's hand. He pushed his chair back and stood, clasping his hands casually behind his neck.

Elyria's faculties returned the instant he broke contact. She flexed her hand as she drew it back to her chest, an instinctive kind of retreat. Well, perhaps that wasn't the whole truth. If she'd been following her instincts, if she'd listened to the call of her shadows, she would have grabbed Cedric's hand instead.

Evander pressed his lips together into a tight line as he watched her. Like he knew.

Eager for distraction, she was quick to say, "You've been here before." *Been here all along,* added her guilt. "Do you know what to do?"

Evander's dark brow furrowed. "I fear I do." He paced back and forth behind Kit and Elyria, as if in deliberation. But beyond the thoughtful crease on his forehead, the purse of his lips, there was a predatory grace to his movements that sent a chill up Elyria's spine.

"You fear? What does that mean? What needs to happen next?"

His golden eyes locked on hers, and in that heartbeat, her world spun on its axis. Because there was nothing warm or jovial or kind in those eyes. Nothing familiar, only cool calculation and icy resolve.

It paralyzed her. So much so that her legs remained rooted to the floor, her voice trapped in her chest when Evander came to a stop right behind Kit and said, "Someone needs to die."

And then it happened—too fast, too sudden.

A flash of darksteel.

A soft gasp.

Time froze.

Then, all at once, it resumed in a clangor of screams and shouts and cries, none of which were louder than Elyria's as she stared at the deep crimson stain blooming across Kit's chest.

And the bloody blade Evander had just thrust into his sister's back.

CHAPTER 43
ANGER & AGONY

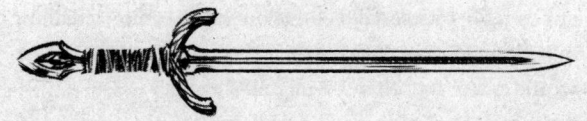

Cedric

There was blood on the table. Cedric watched a heavy droplet bead at the edge and drip, unhurried and languid, onto the stone floor.

He could hear no other sound, see no other movement. Logically, he knew there was plenty of both. The moment Evander's sword burst through Kit's chest the world erupted. Cedric was sure Elyria's scream still rang in the air.

Nox and Thraigg leapt over the table, the former grabbing hold of Evander and shadowstepping him to the far side of the room, the latter there to catch Kit just before she crumpled to the ground.

And yet, to Cedric, it was like the entire universe had condensed into a single heartbeat of sickening stillness. All he could see was the small "oh" that Kit's lips had formed, the betrayal and hurt—not just physical pain, but deep, soul-killing *hurt*—in her mismatched eyes.

In the silence, he thought he could hear that sole droplet of blood as it splashed onto the floor. His thoughts churned, rapid waves crashing into one another. *I should have known. I should have done something. I could have prevented this.*

He'd known something was off. Evander's sudden appearance had struck Cedric all wrong. After twenty-five years of separation, how was the fae full of nothing but confident smiles and charming swagger?

From that first moment, he was too perfect. Too smooth. Cedric's fingers had itched for his sword the instant he laid eyes on the man. But . . . *Elyria*. He saw it—the way the disbelief in her eyes had morphed into something else. More than relief, more than joy. Something like *hope*. He heard the way her breath hitched at the sound of Evander's voice. And all of Cedric's unease and wariness was suddenly blanketed with a thick cloud of something he had absolutely no right to feel.

He was *jealous*.

And so, he'd forced himself to dismiss his better judgment, worried he was imposing his personal feelings on their reunion, chalking up the suspicion lurking in his gut to his own traitorous emotions.

He would never ignore those instincts again.

Kit's ragged gasp pierced through his stupor, and Cedric came crashing back to the present. Back to the maelstrom of panic and shouting and screaming.

I could have prevented this.

Elyria fell to her knees, cradling Kit's head in her lap. Zephyr seemed frozen by the shock of it all, hesitating before swarming the fallen fae, green light glowing in her hands. Pain radiated from Kit in waves so large and looming Cedric swore he could see it—misty clouds pulsing into the ether, as if her own magic was trying to escape the agony.

The metallic tang of blood coated the air.

Not just Kit's, either, Cedric realized, as a shout drew his attention to where Nox and Evander were engaged in battle. Evander held another darksteel blade, having seemingly snatched it from thin air, while Nox twirled twin batons in their hands. The nocterrian already had a long gash running up their forearm, their shadows gathering around Evander's legs, struggling to restrain him. With the wave of his free hand, the shadows dissipated, and Evander walked through them as if they had never been there at all.

A cry rent the air, followed by a squelching sound that turned Cedric's stomach. Metal clanged against stone as Zephyr pulled the darksteel blade from Kit's torso and discarded it on the ground. Thraigg wasted no time in grabbing it, charging toward Evander with a curse. He hurled the weapon at the dark fae. Droplets of blood spun off the blade in a splattering arc as it cut through the air, aimed at a spot in the dead-center of Evander's back, right between his wings.

Cedric held his breath. But Evander pivoted at the last second, twisting on his feet so fast, Cedric would have missed it if he'd blinked. The blackened edge of the dark blade sliced across Evander's ribs, eliciting a hiss of pain and forcing him to stagger back.

Now, Cedric thought, his hands reaching for his sword, his body finally leaping into motion. They would have to subdue Evander now, before he could draw any more blood, cause any more pain. They would get to the bottom of why he'd done this after. Later. Once they made sure Kit was all right.

He refused to think she would be anything but.

With one final look at Elyria, head bowed over her friend, her body covering Kit's as she whispered soothing shushes in her ear, Cedric moved. Together, he and Thraigg dashed across the chamber to close ranks with Nox . . . only to stop short as a deep, menacing laugh began emanating from Evander.

Shivers ran down Cedric's spine, the laugh echoing around the chamber, cold and *wrong*. Evander's jerking backward stagger came to a halt. Cedric's eyes narrowed on the fae's side where the darksteel blade had cut him, dark blood pooling on his skin.

Not blood.

Black liquid, thick as tar, seeped from the gash. Cedric stared, lips parting in shock as the strange, viscous substance spread. It beaded and dripped onto the floor, but also curled up Evander's ribs, moving like it had a life force all its own. His bronze skin darkened and faded, the color draining as the substance skittered over his body, black veins bulging in its wake. His shimmering gold wings flickered—the wavering wick of a candle about to be blown out.

Elyria's choked cry cut through the air as those once-magnificent wings tore, their delicate membranes shredding like aged parchment. Pieces flitted to the floor like ashes while the ragged, tattered remains fluttered loosely.

No longer the wings of a princely fae in his prime, but those of a creature long since corrupted. Veins crept from Evander's eyes, the whites of which had turned an unholy, unnatural black.

"No . . ." Elyria's voice was almost lost amidst the maniacal chuckle still coming from the creature before them. She was standing now, Cedric noticed, having taken just a few steps toward them, fear and indecision slowing her movements. Behind her, Kit lay on her side, eyes closed, ribs lifting with shallow breaths, while Zephyr continued working hurriedly to contain the fallout of her wound.

"Evander, please, no," Elyria continued, taking another step. Her voice was weak. Cedric had never seen her like this. She seemed so . . . frail.

Evander's head whipped toward her, a grim smile plastered on his vein-streaked face. "My love," he said, as if in greeting.

Shock fixed her soft features in place. Her eyes were pinned open in horror, her lips parted with dawning realization.

Cedric tightened his hand around his drawn sword, stepping into Evander's line of sight, cutting off Elyria from view. "Why do this?"

Evander's cruel smile widened, twisting his formerly handsome features, now more monster than man. "Wouldn't you like to know, *my lord*?"

Cedric balked at the way Evander's lip curled around the words, throwing them back at him, mocking him. And was there something else hidden in those two little words? Cedric couldn't begin to understand the dark fae's meaning.

Nox drew their batons together, crossing them in an X in front of their face, crimson eyes burning a hole into the dark creature before them. "What are you?"

"I'm not sure you're ready to know," Evander replied. Then he lunged.

In the blink of an eye, his darksteel blade collided with Nox's batons, showering the nocterrian in sparks. Cedric leapt forward, drawing his sword up in a long slash poised to knock Evander's weapon from his hands.

But the fae was too strong, too fast. With a grunt of effort, he broke through Nox's defense and slashed across their torso, sending them stumbling back. A wet streak bloomed across their dark clothes. At the same time, Evander's free hand twisted in the air, an icy shield forming right as Cedric's sword swung up.

The clash of steel and ice rang in Cedric's skull. He cursed under his breath. Spinning on the spot, he brought his sword down toward Evander's shoulder. The fae parried with a swift upward motion, darksteel meeting Cedric's sword with such force that the impact reverberated up his arm.

He ducked to dodge Evander's returning strike. Behind him, Thraigg let out a shout, charging with his hammer raised high. He swung. Evander *laughed*. Then, as if dancing to the sound of the alarmed shouts coming from Nox, Cedric, and Elyria alike, he gracefully stepped into a shadow.

Thraigg's hammer connected with nothing, throwing him off-center.

Everyone in the room held their collective breath as one heartbeat ticked by, then another. The shock of learning Evander could shadow-step was incredibly heavy as it settled on Cedric's shoulders. The tideweaving magic, Cedric knew to expect based on what Elyria had told him earlier, but this?

A glance at her told him she was just as stunned. He backed up another step, moving that much closer to where Elyria stood frozen in the center of the room. Having regained his balance, Thraigg exchanged a wary glance with Cedric.

Another few seconds passed. Confusion settled deeper into the lines of Cedric's frown. Where did Evander go? Had he . . . run away? No. The champions may have technically outnumbered him, but all one had to do was take one look at Nox, clutching their abdomen, and Kit and Zephyr still on the floor on the opposite side of the room, to see that the champions were at a serious disadvantage.

Cedric's focus flew back to Kit, unconscious but breathing steadily.

Zephyr wiped at her forehead and got up from the ground, nodding at Cedric as he caught her eye. Kit would live. For now, at least.

The briefest flash of relief ran through Cedric as he tracked his gaze to Elyria, hoping to convey some kind of reassurance, even as every hair on his neck still stood on end.

And then Thraigg was roaring, Evander having materialized in the same spot he'd disappeared from. As if rather than stepping through the shadows, he'd simply been . . . hiding in them.

Disgust and alarm mixed in Cedric's stomach as a dark, veiny hand grabbed Thraigg, black nails curling around his wrist. A hideous crack sounded as he wrenched the dwarf's arm in the wholly wrong direction, the hammer falling to the ground with a heavy *thud*. Thraigg's howl of pain echoed in the chamber as he dropped to one knee, clutching his shattered arm.

Zephyr screamed, darting forward with a furious grace. Cedric wanted to warn her to stay back, all too aware that though she might have stabilized Kit, the threat was far from over. They couldn't risk their best healer jumping into the fray. But he barely had time to take a single step before Evander raised his hand and sent a wave of rushing water at the sylvan. It slammed into her, sending her flying into the stone wall behind her with a wet crunch.

"Zephyr!" Cedric ran forward once more, meeting Evander's darksteel sword with his own in a flurry of chaotic blows. Strike. Dodge. Lunge. Parry. Tables and chairs fell over in their path as they battled their way across the chamber. Sparks flew from the places where their blades met. Around them was only chaos. Blood. Screams. Pain.

And through it all, Evander laughed. A deep, hollow sound that seemed like it was coming from the very walls of the Sanctum, as if he were enjoying every second of the carnage.

Cedric's breath grew ragged. He was slowing, his body screaming in protest as he drew his blade up once more to meet Evander's most recent blow. Somewhere deep inside, he tried to stir that spark of warmth, to kindle that heat. If ever there was a time for him to erupt in flame, let it be to take down this dark creature before he destroyed them all.

As if he sensed his resolve, Evander's black eyes locked onto

Cedric's. For a moment, the two men just stared, their swords grating against each other, the air thick with magic and the tang of blood.

"You truly think you can stop me, little knight?" Evander sneered. "You have no idea what I am trying to do here."

"I do not care," Cedric said. "Whatever it is you aim to accomplish, you mean to do so with death and blood. No more."

That cold, calculated laugh emerged once more. "Oh, the irony. I told him many times how fruitless this would be." He reared back, blade crashing down on Cedric's with a clang.

Cedric drew back, holding his sword in front of him with both hands, the sharp tip leveled at Evander's chest. "Who is *him*?"

"I told him there was little point in binding me here without a fleshed-out plan to conquer the next Crucible. Without a true champion to take the crown. It won't let just anybody take it, you understand. You have to be *worthy*."

"Isn't that the whole point of the entire stars-damned Crucible?" Cedric asked, his sword starting to waver in the air. "To prove only the worthiest will emerge as victor?"

Ignoring him, Evander continued. "Still, he insisted. He told me it would be worth it, in the end. That he'd already heard whispers of where to go next, of what he needed." His eyes narrowed, never leaving Cedric's face. "Who he needed. And so, I agreed. I let him use me to free himself from the bindings of the Crucible, let him plant a bead of his power in me before he left."

"W-what are you saying?" Elyria snapped free of her paralysis, her voice cutting through the air. "You . . . you *chose* to stay here? You chose to become *this*?"

Evander finally broke his gaze from Cedric, turning to face his former love. He curled his fingers in toward his palm, conjuring a tiny stream of water and letting it dance between his blackened fingertips. "When one is caught in a riptide, is it truly a choice to allow yourself to be swept up in it?"

"Yes," she said. "It is."

"Even when the alternative is to swim against the stronger tide? To paddle until exhaustion takes you, until you sink, until you drown?"

"There is always a choice."

"Hmm. Rather a lofty position for you to take, my love. I would think you of all people should understand where I am coming from."

She shook her head. "This isn't you." Her voice was thick, her hands trembling. "I know you're still in there. The real you. Let me help you."

For a moment, Evander hesitated. Cedric thought he saw his dark eyes soften, saw the veins around them recede ever so slightly. "Help me?" His voice was softer. "You cannot help me, love. Not anymore. Varyth saw to that."

Elyria took another step closer, and like he was tied to her, Cedric stepped with her, closing the distance between them. Tears streamed from her eyes, and Cedric yearned to drop his sword long enough to wipe them from her cheeks. But he didn't, keeping the blade trained on Evander, even as it appeared he'd all but forgotten about Cedric entirely.

"Tell me what happened," she pleaded.

Evander's expression shuttered, all traces of whatever emotion had broken through gone. "A life for a life," he said, matter-of-factly. "That was the price. Varyth escaped the Crucible by using my life-debt to sever his own. Only instead of killing me outright, his dark magic kept me alive. Tied to this place"—he gestured widely, repulsion on his face—"but alive. I was his little secret. His watchdog, waiting in the shadows. I was to stay out of the Arbiter's line of sight. Stay hidden. Until the next Crucible came and brought with it someone worthy enough to free us all."

He began pacing then, twirling his darksteel blade at his side like it was a toy rather than a deadly weapon. He barely spared a glance as he passed the other champions, still collapsed or crumpled in their various corners of the room. Thraigg hissed as Evander came close but showed no sign of otherwise moving.

"But, alas, waiting is an exhausting game," Evander continued. "And he may need someone worthy to win him the crown, but his promises have grown rather thin over the years. I was no longer content to sit back and wait. I was tired of watching. The Arbiter is so slow about things, you see. I thought it better if I offered a helping hand instead."

Elyria sucked in a breath through her teeth. "Did you . . . ? What have you done with the Arbiter?"

"Nothing," he said with a scoff. "Were I but capable of 'doing' anything to her . . . Sadly, power does not exist on this plane strong enough to do a stars-damned thing to a celestial. But I was able to keep her from contacting you. Is it such a terrible crime to have wanted to see how my darlings fared in the third trial without her guidance?"

Her? A celestial? What does that—

Nox's guttural groan sliced through Cedric's whirring thoughts.

"The magic in the labyrinth's walls," they said softly.

Evander grinned as he strode past them.

A soft gasp slipped from Elyria's lips. "The walls . . . and the chasm that opened in the cavern. That was you?"

Evander tutted. "I couldn't very well have allowed that human witch to kill you all, could I?"

"You nearly killed *her*, too," Cedric said through gritted teeth, tipping his head toward Elyria. He recalled the panic that had flashed through him when Zephyr relayed all that had occurred in the cavern prior to his arrival. How Elyria had been perhaps seconds from meeting the same fate as Leona.

As if she was chasing the same thought, Elyria went on to say, "And our inability to fly?"

"Alas, no," Evander said. "That was simply the Crucible at work. A futile attempt at providing an even slate, even odds. All that sort of rot." He slowed as he returned to where Elyria stood, stopping little more than an arm's width away. "You did so, so well during the trials, by the way. You faced your inner darkness, like I always knew you could, and look at you now. I am so proud of you, my love. Did I tell you that already? If not, you will have to forgive me."

She scoffed, her eyes going to Kit's prostrate form, disbelief distorting her features. As if she couldn't fathom the fact that he would ask forgiveness for some perceived slight of manners when he just tried to kill his own sister.

He followed her gaze and clucked his tongue. "Ah, yes. Sadly, Katerina's performance has been less admirable."

Elyria stiffened. "She came here for *you*," she hissed, emerald daggers shooting from her eyes.

Her reaction eased some of the tension in Cedric's gut. He was worried Evander's serpentine words might have wormed their way under her skin. But this dark thing was clearly not the man Elyria knew. No matter how many pretty words he spun.

Evander's head dipped. "I know," he said, and if Cedric didn't already know better, he might have thought a flicker of genuine sadness shone through the dark fae's gravelly voice. "And her sacrifice will not be in vain. Her death paves the way for my freedom. You and I can leave together. Just pick one of them"—he waved a lazy hand at the injured champions strewn around the room—"to do the same for you. The stronger the emotional connection you have, the greater the magic will be, but any of them will do. And we can walk out of here."

A horrified expression dawned on Elyria's face, and Cedric watched the last shreds of hope that the true Evander—*her* Evander—was still somewhere inside crumble into dust.

"You're mad," she said, moving her head from side to side as if she might shake the terrible words from her ears.

Evander stepped toward Elyria. She balked, mirroring his movement and moving back at the same clip so as to maintain the distance between them. Cedric rushed to her side, his arm brushing her back, his hip grazing hers.

"I'd never do that," she continued, her back straightening. A bolt of pride zipped through Cedric. "And Kit isn't dead. You failed. *We* will tackle whatever final challenge the Crucible may hold, one of *us* will win that crown, and then *we* will leave. I can only hope that when the Crucible is won, your soul will be able to find peace."

Cedric tensed at the renewed malice in Evander's gaze.

"You force my hand, Elle," he said, that fake sadness coating his words again.

She spat at his feet. "Don't call me that."

"You are the only one among them who is worthy." Evander's black eyes flicked to the places where Cedric and Elyria were touching before landing on his face. "No matter what *he* may think. And if you will not choose, I will choose for you."

"No!" Elyria screamed, but before Cedric could even lift his sword again, water was spinning from Evander's fingertips. It encircled Cedric, a massive orb of churning water that lifted him from the ground, his sword falling away uselessly as he was swept inside.

Water was everywhere. There was no up; there was no down. He spun and spun as icy liquid filled his nostrils, ran down his throat.

It tasted shockingly bright.

Cedric punched his arms out, kicked his legs, trying to swim, trying to move forward or backward or up or down in a desperate search for the surface. For the life-giving air on the outside.

But he had no purchase. No sense of up or down or left or right. He couldn't gain an inch in any direction as the roiling water kept him spinning.

Darkness crept into the edges of his vision. He clawed at his throat and beat at his chest, as if he might physically pull the water from his lungs. He begged that spark inside him to ignite, to burn it all away, but it had extinguished right alongside his will.

He was drowning.

He was dying.

And as a blur of purple flashed past the opaque walls of his aquatic prison, he was sorry about that.

CHAPTER 44
DARKNESS FORGED

Elyria

Time shattered around Elyria, each fractured second dragging out longer than the last.

She could see it—could feel it. The water swirling around Cedric, his body thrashing inside the orb. His mouth was pinned open in a silent scream, his hands scrambling at his throat, searching for breath that wouldn't come.

Elyria's pulse raced, a scream building in her chest, thoughts spiraling, panic gripping her mind.

This can't be happening again.

Not him.

Not like this.

"Evander, stop!" She beat against his shoulder, his chest, his back.

He paid her no notice, like he didn't feel the strike of her fists or hear the screams tearing from her throat. Even as the decayed strips of his tattered wings sheared off and floated to the floor, he simply stared at the knight he was drowning, a placid smile on his vein-stricken face.

Movement stirred in both corners of Elyria's vision. Thraigg was getting to his feet, his face still twisted in pain as he lumbered toward the floating sphere, broken arm clutched close to his chest. Dark blood stained the floor where Nox tried to rise as well. Zephyr let out a small whimper, pulling her limbs in toward herself.

All three of them were moving—against pain, against exhaustion, against defeat—drawn by Cedric's suffering.

Suffering that, injured as they all were, Elyria knew only she could end.

Do something.

Her hands trembled. Or was that the ground—the very Sanctum—shaking? A familiar darkness whispered in her gut, her shadows leaking out and trailing over her skin with the softest caress. Heart pounding, she shifted her gaze back to Evander. His black eyes glittered with amusement, like he was savoring watching the life drain from Cedric.

He is gone. The thought pierced Elyria's panic, a truth that cut deeper than any blade. She didn't mean Cedric, who still clung to life within his watery prison. *Evander* was gone. This creature, this corrupted shell of a man, was not him.

Or at least, this was not what he would have wanted to become.

The thought was as clarifying as it was painful—the sharp sting of a slap rousing one from slumber. She would try to remember him as the man she knew before all this. Before the Crucible and Varyth Malchior robbed the world of Evander's true light.

Do it now.

Her body moved almost on instinct, hands rising, shadows curling from her fingertips like smoke.

Like he could sense the magic, Evander whirled on her, his eyes as thin as slits. "Put those away, Elyria," he hissed. "What good are your shadows when I have my own now?"

Just as he'd done with his tideweaving magic before, he conjured a ribbon of shadow and let it dance between his fingers, weaving between each knuckle.

"Varyth granted me a seed of his magic—magic born of Malakar himself." His mouth tipped up in a smug grin. "And I've had twenty-five long years to tend it, nurture it, let it grow. How long have you been controlling your shadows? A handful of days? We are not the same."

His fingers jerked, barely a flex, and the ribbon of shadow lashed out, binding Elyria's hands together, her palms touching as if in prayer. She released a frustrated, feral sound, and inside, her darkness reared back and roared.

"Now stay there and wait like a good girl," Evander said, lips pursing. "This will all be over soon."

Rage sparked up her spine. It was hard to see him through the churning water of the orb, but she knew Cedric was running out of time. She felt for that golden thread in her chest, alarm seizing her when she found it limp and listless.

"You're right," she said, grabbing hold of that thread with whatever mental power she could spare. She let a pulse of magic rise to the surface.

Evander peered at her, dark brow furrowing.

"We are not the same."

Much like she'd done to Cedric when he was burning, her shadows wrapped around her, a dense blanket of mist.

And much like he'd done to Nox earlier, she dissolved Evander's shadow ribbon with a thought.

His eyes widened as he took in Elyria prowling toward him like a wraith sent by Noctis himself. She wasn't just wielding her shadows. She *was* shadow.

And she was pissed.

"Varyth Malchior may be of Malakar's line," she said, her darkness swirling over her like a second skin. "And the dark sorcerer's magic may have trickled down over the generations, eventually saddling him with the powers he so magnanimously shared with you. But me?"

Her fingers curled into a fist, her shadows gathering, layering, solidifying in the empty space beyond it. Creating something sharp. Something new. Forged from her grief. Forged from her love. Forged by the darkness that had once nearly consumed her. "I got it straight from the source."

She lunged, thrusting the shadow-forged blade forward and plunging it directly into Evander's heart.

For a moment, everything was still. Evander's eyes were pinned open in shock, his mouth parting as if some word sat on the tip of his tongue.

No words came out.

Hot black blood sprayed Elyria's face as she withdrew her fist—and the shadow-forged blade attached to it—from Evander's chest.

Her shadows dissipated.

Evander fell to his knees, shock etched into every corrupted plane of the face she used to touch and kiss. The face she'd once thought she would love forever.

The water orb burst in a wave, and Cedric fell to the floor, unmoving. There was a moment of terrible, heartbreaking silence, and then he retched, water spilling from his mouth. Next came the gasps, his breath ragged and spluttering.

It was the most beautiful sound Elyria had ever heard, followed by the worst.

Evander groaned, a long, harsh, soul-weeping sound. His wings crumbled into ash, his body sagging as blood poured from his wound, surrounding him in a viscous pool of black.

Elyria knelt beside him, hands shaking, body heaving. His blood painted her legs. Fat tears carved tracks down her cheeks. She placed one bloodstained hand on his chest, over his heart, right where she'd stabbed him.

It was not an attempt to stifle the wound—not that it would have made much difference had she tried. It was a reminder for herself of what once lay there.

"This isn't what I wanted." Evander's breaths were uneven as he lifted a hand to her face. She didn't stop him, didn't turn away. "He told me so many things. Made me so many promises. And I didn't . . . I thought we . . ." Recognition sparked in his eyes, understanding of what he'd done crashing into him, overtaking him. Regret and sorrow broke across his face—the final remnant of the real Evander.

Elyria never knew it was possible for a heart to break so many times.

"Kit." With a whimper, he shifted, attempting to turn his head toward his sister. "I'm sorry." His words were garbled, spoken through a mouthful of blood. "I'm so sorry."

"I know," Elyria said.

Evander's eyes met hers once more as he drew a shaky breath, and Elyria knew it was one of his last. "Tell her I'm—"

"I will."

"And, Elle . . ." Her name was barely more than a wet whisper now, the dark veins receding from his skin, his eyes shifting back to brilliant gold.

Her throat tightened. "Yes, Ev?"

"Thank you."

And then he was gone.

CHAPTER 45
LONG OVERDUE

Elyria

Elyria once told evander that he felt like good luck. When he laughed and asked her what she could possibly have meant by that, she grinned.

"Your eyes," she said, heat burning in her cheeks from the admission. "They look to me like twin pools of liquid luck. I feel like I could dive straight into their golden depths and never surface. Never want to. And I only have to stare into them to feel like the most fortunate fae in all Nyrundelle."

Now those eyes stared at nothing. Their golden glow was extinguished. Elyria drew a trembling finger over Evander's eyelids, shuttering them for the final time.

Evander's own black blood traced lines down his face as she let her touch linger. The weight of what she'd done clutched her in a vise, suffocating her, squeezing her insides. She took a strangled breath, and it was like the very air had turned to bitter ash.

He was the whole reason Elyria was here—why Kit had dared to take on the Crucible, committed herself to the Sanctum. They'd had no idea of knowing that the heinous visions they received of him in this corrupted form were sliced straight from the truth.

Elyria had thought it a nightmare. Kit had thought it a calling. She'd thought that coming here and conquering the Crucible might bring her brother peace.

Was that what Elyria had given him?

With his final breath, when the Evander she'd known and trusted and loved had returned—if just for a moment—he'd thanked her. Perhaps he had long wished to free himself from Varyth Malchior's corruption and the dark magic tying him to this place.

She hoped beyond hope that was true.

Nearby, Cedric coughed, still recovering. Elyria breathed infinitesimally more easily when she saw that he appeared to be doing so quickly. There was a blue tint to his lips and a tremble in his limbs, not to mention the fact that he was sopping wet, but he seemed mostly unharmed. He was conscious and aware, shivering but straight-backed as he continued hacking into his hands.

Thraigg slumped down next to him, clapping the knight on the back with his unbroken hand as if doing so might help expel any remaining water from his lungs.

Zephyr, her skin paled to a sickly shade of green, helped Nox into a chair before waving her hands over the nocterrian's wounded midsection. Elyria couldn't help but notice how weak the glow of her magic seemed.

Across the room, Kit was still unconscious on the floor, her chest rising and falling in a steady but shallow rhythm that had Elyria's heart constricting with every breath. Elyria had just taken a step toward her friend when a sudden flash of light stopped her in her tracks.

She watched with wide eyes as Evander's slain body lit up from the inside and a celestial mark—the same one she'd watched the Arbiter place on each and every champion's forehead before they'd entered the

Sanctum—appeared between his brows. Ribbons of shadow snaked out from the hole in his chest, scattering in the air as his body erupted in blue flames, just like those that had consumed Brandon Cormac's body before Elyria went through the Gate.

The chamber shook, the walls reverberating as if the Sanctum itself was erupting too. Or perhaps the magic that Evander had trapped within its walls, whatever sick machination he'd employed to interfere with the third trial, was simply being released.

And then Evander's body was gone, the fire consuming even the pool of corrupted blood that had gathered beneath him. Nothing remained but the gaping hole in Elyria's heart and the lingering stain of him on her clothes and skin.

Long overdue, the Crucible finally claimed him.

"Any change?"

Zephyr shook her head as she checked the blood-soaked bandage wound tight around Kit's chest. The sylvan mumbled a few words in a language Elyria did not know and waved her hand. The red that had wept through the bandage evaporated, leaving only a fresh, clean, flesh-colored wrap in its wake.

Elyria might have been impressed by the way Zephyr wielded her healing power had this not been the fourth or fifth time she'd seen this particular trick over the past several hours. Despite both Zephyr's and Elyria's attempts at repairing the hole in Kit's chest, all they'd been able to do was stem the very worst of the bleeding. Her wound was not healing as it should. It had slowed, thank the stars, but she was still losing blood.

Worse still, she had not yet regained consciousness, and in the hours that had passed since the stabbing, she'd developed a fever as well.

Elyria thought she knew what helplessness felt like, but as she watched sweat bead on Kit's forehead, it was all too clear she didn't know a thing.

This would not do.

Standing so abruptly that Zephyr let out a noise of surprise, Elyria strode over to the table where Cedric, Thraigg, and Nox were eating. She tried to hide her look of disgust over the fact that they could do so at all. She was certain the wafers, cheese, and grapes would all taste sour and ashen on her tongue. But she supposed she couldn't begrudge them the replenishment of their energy. Surely they would all need it.

Whatever magical manipulation Evander had enacted, it clearly hadn't affected the Crucible's more hospitable interferences. Food and drink appeared in the Sanctum, as it always had. Still, there was no sign of what came next, no word regarding the next—the final?—trial.

"What do you think he meant when he said those things about the Arbiter?" she asked, bracing her hands on the tabletop and looking pointedly at the three champions.

Cedric blinked at her. "Hello to you too."

Elyria rolled her eyes. "Hi. Hello. Good morning, good afternoon, good night." The right side of Cedric's mouth quivered, scar and all. "Now, what do you think he meant?"

"Ye might want to be a little more specific, lass." Thraigg squirmed, his fingers toying with the makeshift splint Zephyr had fashioned him.

"Stop touching it," Nox scolded, smacking the dwarf's good hand.

"It itches."

"And it will continue to do so as it heals. Zephyr said as much," Nox said flatly. "So, you might as well get used to it."

"Ye're one to talk. I see ye pawing at yer stomach every few minutes. Leave the bandage be or it'll start bleeding again, ye stubborn bastard."

"Do as I say, not as I do." Nox shrugged, though Elyria caught the hint of a wince as they did, as if the motion pulled at their wound.

Thraigg let out a noise that might have been somewhere between a whine and a growl, but he did as the nocterrian commanded and placed his hand on the table. "As I was saying, ye may need to repeat it for those of us who were nursing our wounds—"

"Wounded egos, more like."

"—while that maniac was monologuing." Thraigg drummed his fingers on the table and shot Nox an annoyed look.

Their exchange was so sibling-like that Elyria momentarily found herself at a loss for words. She didn't think Nox and Thraigg had spoken more than a handful of times the entire while they'd been in here. Though she supposed if any experience was going to bond people, it would be this one.

Or perhaps she hadn't noticed because she'd been preoccupied with . . . other things. Her eyes flicked to Cedric before quickly returning to Thraigg's rugged, scarred face.

"He revealed that he was the reason we did not hear from the Arbiter before the Trial of Magic," she said. "And when I asked what he'd done with them, he said—"

"Something about not being able 'to do a stars-damned thing to a celestial,'" Cedric finished for her.

Elyria nodded. "What do you think he meant by that?"

"Maybe the bastard misspoke," Thraigg said. "The Arbiter's s'posed to be the mouthpiece of the celestials. In his twisted mind, maybe he lumped 'em together."

"He also referred to the Arbiter quite specifically as *her*," Elyria said.

"I caught that too," said Cedric.

Elyria felt his warm brown eyes settle on her face, but she didn't feel like he was really looking at her.

"But I don't understand it either," he added.

"And either way, if whatever he did is what sealed the Arbiter away from us, shouldn't we have heard from her—them—whoever, again by now?" Elyria asked.

Nox stroked a long indigo finger along one of their horns. "Curious."

"Why is it curious?" Cedric asked.

Several seconds passed before Nox responded. "How much do you know of the Crucible's history?"

"I know it all," Cedric said, pride buffeting the words.

Nox raised a brow. "Do you, now?"

Elyria couldn't tell whether their tone was mocking or sincere, but she supposed it didn't really matter.

Cedric's jaw flexed. "It was—is—my duty as a champion representing the realm of Havensreach to learn as much as possible about the Arcane Crucible, of course."

"Of course," Nox repeated, and again, Elyria found the sentiment behind their words difficult to discern.

"Why do you ask?" she prompted, eager to learn where this line of conversation was going and what it had to do with what Evander said about the Arbiter.

"Tell me what you know of the origins of the Crucible," Nox said to Cedric, ignoring Elyria. Both she and the knight frowned at the nocterrian.

"I—surely you don't need me to give you a history lesson," Cedric protested, clearing his throat as if he was suddenly nervous.

"I'm simply curious as to whether the human version of events matches what I've come to understand after being in here myself."

"And what is it you've come to understand?" Elyria asked.

Yet again, Nox ignored her. Her face heated. If Nox was after a history lesson, she would gladly give it to them. If only to refocus this conversation on what she wanted to know. "After Queen Daephinia sundered the realm in three and the Shattering took both her and the dark sorcerer Malakar from this world, the celestials—"

"Not you," Nox interrupted, their crimson eyes flashing between her and Cedric. "Him."

"Why?" Elyria asked sharply.

Finally, Nox deigned to reply to her. "Because I have a hunch, and I like to see if my hunches play out. Take a seat and listen, Revenant. You just might learn something too."

Elyria groaned but fell into a chair next to Thraigg, pulling one knee up in front of her and wrapping her arms around it. She looked expectantly at Cedric and Nox, her chin tilted up, head cocked to one side—the picture of impatience.

Cedric sighed and scrubbed his hands down his face. "Fine. How far back do you want me to start, exactly?"

Nox smiled, their teeth glinting in the light flickering from sconces dotted about the chamber. "Start where all stories should," they said. "At the beginning."

CHAPTER 46
ORIGINS

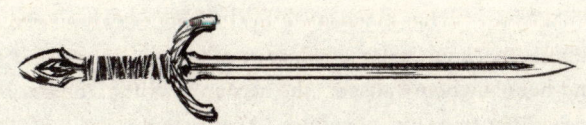

Cedric

With a nod and another clearing of his throat he'd hoped would nudge some of the nervousness from his body—even though he didn't quite know what he was nervous about—Cedric began.

"As Elyria said, after the Shattering—"

"Ah-ah, I said to start at the *beginning*," Nox interrupted.

"This is the beginning—what led to the creation of the Arcane Crucible."

"Not just the beginning of the Crucible."

"You want an, 'In the beginning . . .' type of tale here? Don't you think there are better things to be doing with our time?"

"I don't see anyone coming to rush us out of here, do you? We have nowhere to go, no one to see. Not until the Crucible shows us what comes next, or we all go mad—whichever comes first."

Cedric sucked in a breath, tempted to roll his eyes at the nocterrian. But alas, they weren't wrong. In the hours that had passed since the confrontation with Evander, the Sanctum had been eerily quiet. Until the next chime blared or glowing doorway appeared, they were stuck.

"In the beginning"—Cedric affected a deep, booming baritone, eliciting a chuckle from Elyria that pulled a smile from him—"there were the Five. Solaris, the Sun Goddess; Lunara, the Time Keeper; Noctis, Warden of Shadows; Earth Mother Gaia; and Aurelia, Guardian of Balance."

At the mention of Aurelia, both Thraigg and Elyria huffed in unison. Cedric ignored them.

"Through the celestials, Arcanis flourished. Though they had taken oaths never to interfere directly with the affairs of the mortals that populated their world, their benevolence"—another huff from Elyria—"led the peoples of Arcanis, human and Arcanian alike, to prosper. There were periods of unrest, disputes that arose between races, to be sure. But for the most part, we all lived our separate lives on our separate sides of the continent. Until, eventually, came the rise of the fae queen, Daephinia. And with her marriage to the human king, Juno, the disparate realms were connected, made into one."

"And here is where I suspect the accounts written in your history books may differ from Arcanian ones," Nox mused.

"Why is that?" Cedric arched a brow. "Do the Arcanian texts paint prettily over the misery that humankind went on to suffer under Queen Daephinia's ironfisted rule?"

"Ain't a damn thing wrong with being an Ironfist," muttered Thraigg, at the same time Elyria said, "What suffering?"

Cedric answered Thraigg first with a sidelong look. "You know very well I meant nothing to do with your surname." He then turned to a bemused Elyria, equal confusion on his own face. "Surely you are not serious."

"Queen Daephinia and King Juno's rule was star-blessed," she said, brow furrowing. "Arcanis prospered, cities sprouted, and the birth of the princess heralded the arrival of many other babes born."

"Mixedborn babes," Thraigg corrected sullenly, "and look how well that all turned out."

All four of them fell silent for several moments, and Cedric couldn't keep his mind from conjuring a memory of that human woman, pregnant with a mixedborn child, wailing as if her life was ending while Cedric and his fellow knights hauled away the fae father. Perhaps her life did end that day. Perhaps she refused to allow her baby to be taken from her after it was born, as all mixedborn babies were upon discovery.

Perhaps she shared her child's fate.

"Yes, well." Cedric cleared his throat again. "I wouldn't expect any of you—any Arcanian—to think otherwise. But even with a human king ruling at Daephinia's side, it was hardly rainbows and roses for us. Humans may outnumber Arcanians, but with your magic, your physical advantages, and a fae queen ruling over all, we were never going to come out on top."

"But there was peace—" Elyria protested.

"Peace was an illusion," Cedric said, and it was as if a chill fell over the entire Sanctum as the words escaped his mouth. "There was much unrest. There was misery and pain."

"There will always be misery and pain," Nox said thoughtfully, and while Cedric didn't disagree, that was hardly the point.

"I cannot say I'm surprised by the inaccuracy of Arcanian accounts of what life was like before the Shattering," Cedric said, unable to keep the bitterness from his voice. "After all, it isn't as though it affected you."

Elyria pressed her lips into a flat line. The group lapsed into a tense silence. "Regardless," she finally said, "what does any of this have to do with the Crucible or the Arbiter or Ev—or any stars-damned thing relevant to our present situation?"

Cedric did not miss the way she stopped herself from saying Evander's name aloud. How she hadn't said it at all in the time since the Crucible claimed his body.

"I believe we were just about to get to that, weren't we, Sir Thorne?" said Nox. "You did just bring up the Shattering, after all."

Cedric grimaced. "Right. So, the humans were unhappy. The realm was technically united. But in reality it was nearly as divided then as it is now. And the celestials, for all their original intentions for a happy, whole, and prosperous Arcanis, turned a blind eye to the suffering of more than half its people. All but one of them."

"Aurelia," Elyria whispered.

"Yes. The Guardian of Balance was not blind to the injustices happening in the world, to how distinctly *un*balanced its people had become. And so she broke her oath. She interfered."

Elyria's eyes narrowed. "She sided with you."

"She wanted to give humanity a leg to stand on," Cedric shot back, his voice insistent. "She granted us knowledge of how to wield the land's mana."

"How to leach it, you mean," Elyria grumbled.

Cedric rolled his eyes and opened his mouth to respond, but Nox beat him to it. "Thus, she earned humanity's devotion. Now if nature would not bless humans with magic, they would bless themselves."

"Yes," said Cedric, nodding. "And it worked. Things became . . . better, for a time." He bit the inside of his lip, something akin to shame bubbling up from his gut. "But though Aurelia sought balance, eventually some would—*one* would—take advantage of her gift. Would twist it for his own gain. For it was not balance that he sought, but power."

"Malakar."

There was something about the way Elyria said the name that made a shiver run down the back of Cedric's neck. Not reverence. Not fear. A quiet rage—something that felt a little bit like vengeance.

But before he could call it out, her cool mask slipped into place. It was the first time she'd donned it since before the third trial, and something about it made a sudden, bone-chilling cold take Cedric over. Like even the kernel of heat kindling in his own chest was sucked away by her veil of indifference.

Cedric took a breath before continuing. "Yes. A trusted advisor to the king, Malakar could wield mana like no other human. More than a sorcerer, more than a sage, it was like mana filled his very veins. And eventually, he came to wield what did flow through those veins as if it *were* mana."

"Ye speak of blood magic," Thraigg said, and though he didn't mean to, Cedric found himself rubbing idly at the spot in the center of his chest where Belien had struck him.

Nox ran an indigo finger along one of their horns, nodding thoughtfully.

"It corrupted him," Cedric continued. "And soon, even as powerful as he became, as his *followers* became, it wasn't enough. Most humans resented Arcanians and their innate magic, but none more than Malakar. He considered King Juno a traitor for having married Daephinia. Thought their mixedborn daughter's existence made a mockery of our suffering. And so he plotted their fall."

"And started a war." Elyria said it matter-of-factly. Emotionless. Her detachment only made shame burn hotter in Cedric's cheeks. She'd fought in the war. Had killed many in the war. Had become "the Revenant" because of the war.

It was the Revenant who spoke now, Cedric was sure.

He swallowed hard, determined to finish despite the knot forming in his stomach. "Technically, the war came after. Malakar plotted against the crown. He assassinated the king and the young princess. And in her grief, Queen Daephinia's rage split the realm in three. *That* marked the beginning of the War of Two Realms."

"Which you lost." Again, spoken in that detached, emotionless voice. Nothing haughty or proud about it—it was not a boast.

Cedric almost wished it were.

He forced a laugh in a desperate attempt to pull some of that quick-fire wit he felt he knew so well from her. "Well, not *me*, of course. *I* didn't lose anything. Not even my grandparents would have been alive at this point."

She blinked at him.

He blinked back.

The tension in the air pulled so taut, Cedric half wished he would combust again, just for the distraction.

It was Thraigg who finally snapped it, his voice gravelly and rough when he said, "I still don't get what the bleeding fuck this has to do with anything."

Nox smiled—a sharp, catlike grin. "We're almost there, but if it would help, I can speed the rest along?"

"Gaia's tits, yes. *Please*."

"Fine. As Malakar's power rose, Aurelia realized her mistake. Saw what had become of her generosity and sought to fix it. So, for the second time, she defied her fellow celestials and interceded—this time, for the other side."

Cedric's ears perked up. This was one aspect of the story he was not as well versed with.

"As the ultimate symbol of balance, she crafted an artifact, fusing it with her own power, as well as that taken from Arcanian and human alike."

Nox paused, as if for dramatic effect, and it took all of Cedric's willpower not to roll his eyes. He glanced at Elyria, hoping to see a similar expression on her face. But she simply watched the nocterrian, expectant but patient. Cedric frowned.

"The Crown of Concord," Nox finally said, "designed for just one person. A gift for the living proof that harmony between the peoples of Arcanis could exist." Another pause. "The mixedborn princess, Selenae. Prophesied to bring everlasting balance—true peace—to the land."

"The crown is a celestial-forged artifact?" Cedric clenched his teeth to keep his jaw from going slack.

"Indeed. Something that was only discovered at the culmination of the final battle between Daephinia and Malakar, when the queen's sacrifice revealed its true nature." Nox's crimson gaze narrowed on Elyria, appraising her. "You were there, were you not? You should know better than anyone that the kind of power that burst from the crown upon its Shattering could only have been celestial in origin."

Elyria was as still as a statue.

Scratching idly at their horn, Nox continued. "What do you think made the other celestials so angry they would banish Aurelia from their ranks?"

Cedric drummed his fingers on the tabletop. "I thought she was exiled for siding with humans in the first place." He didn't give voice to any of the other dozen thoughts running through his head, starting and ending with what either the humans or the Arcanians could do—would do—after winning the crown. What might happen if either side wielded celestial power. What might happen if that power fell into the wrong hands.

Nox shrugged.

"How do you know all this?" Elyria asked, a bit of that familiar color returning to her voice, to Cedric's relief.

"How does anyone learn anything?" Nox said.

"That's not an answer," Cedric grumbled.

Elyria stood. "Well, thanks for the history lesson, Tenebris, but I still don't see how this has anything to do, nor how it will help, with our current predicament."

"Do you not?" Nox looked amused.

"Spit it out."

"Where exactly do you think Aurelia was banished *to*?"

"I don't—"

"I believe it was a rhetorical question" came a chorus of voices, speaking as one.

Cedric nearly jumped out of his seat at the sound. The voice was not ringing in his mind. It was in his ears. It was in the room.

He turned toward the source of the noise. To the white-robed figure standing directly in front of the doors at the far side of the chamber, hood no longer drawn, face no longer hidden.

"Hello, champions," she said, something forlorn folded into the layers of her voice.

Zephyr gasped. Thraigg's mouth dropped open. Elyria had frozen midstep.

Tenebris Nox smiled. "Hello, Aurelia."

CHAPTER 47
FOR ALL OF US

Elyria

Her skin was like the sky.

She couldn't possibly have been a physical, tangible being. Not with the way the expanse of endless night swirled where her skin should be, constellations twinkling across the bridge of her nose, nebulas swirling in her eyes. But Elyria remembered the firm grasp from below those billowing robes when the Arbiter—when *Aurelia*—grabbed her in Castle Lumin.

She was real.

And she was here.

Her hair—if you could call it that—rippled as the celestial inclined her head at the champions. A greeting, an acknowledgment. Waves of color—violet, green, pink, cerulean—flowed from the crown of her head in an ethereal mass, each strand shimmering as though spun from light itself.

Aurelia's eyes glinted, the white glow of dying stars bursting at the center of each iris as they drifted from champion to champion. They lingered on each of them for just a moment before finally settling on Elyria, whose breath caught in her throat under that heavy, nebulous gaze.

"I sense surprise," she said, her layered voice dulcet, more harmonious than it sounded before. It was a jarring experience, Elyria decided, to see those lips move in sync with the kaleidoscopic voice she had come to expect to hear only in her head. "I sense apprehension. Fear. Guilt. Grief."

"Are you surprised about that? After everything you've put us through?" Elyria blurted out.

Thraigg, Zephyr, and Cedric released a collective gasp. It was then that Elyria realized the three of them had planted one knee on the ground, their heads bowed in veneration before the banished star god.

Nox, on the other hand, had their feet propped up on the table in front of them, thoroughly unbothered by the primordial being in their midst. Rather, they surveyed the scene with that same air of amusement they typically bore, like they had a ringside seat at a rather entertaining show.

Figuring she was already knee-deep in smiting territory, Elyria continued. "And you 'sense' it? Shouldn't you, you know, *know*? You are a celestial." She couldn't help the note of betrayal that played in between her words. She felt as though she'd been duped. Used. Like her choice to enter the Crucible was never a choice at all, not with this all-powerful being pulling the strings.

Aurelia smiled wanly, something like sadness sitting at the corners of her starlit lips. "I am. Or . . . I was. I am diminished. So long as my powers and presence remain tied to this place."

The darkened tone at the end of her sentence made it clear that was as much of an answer as Elyria was going to get, and she couldn't blame her for it. She supposed her questions were rather rude. Bordering on blasphemous. But after three trials and a week that felt nearly as long as the twenty-five years that preceded it, she had met her quota for caring.

"What are we to do now, then?" she asked.

The celestial smiled at Cedric, Zephyr, and Thraigg, still genuflected before her. "Please rise."

Thraigg's hammer clinked against the floor as he stood, his good arm wrapped around the handle, leaning into it, letting it take his weight like a crutch. Elyria found herself wishing she still had her staff so she could do the same.

She looked at Aurelia with an expectancy that a more devout person might have considered downright sinful. "Well? Don't keep us in suspense."

"Now you take on the Trial of Concord." Aurelia swiveled on the spot, her robes billowing in a wide arc. She gestured toward the row of doors behind her. The center one began glowing with an all-too-familiar silvery light. "You finish this."

Thraigg and Zephyr exchanged a nervous glance, the latter's eyes darting to Kit's fevered form, still unconscious. The reminder caused Elyria's insides to ice over.

"Now? What about her?" She pointed at Kit, then to the three other injured champions. "What about all of them?"

Zephyr's face paled. Thraigg shifted, as if trying to hide the sling holstering his injured arm from view. And despite an attitude that might have suggested otherwise, Nox's bandage was weeping, and a sheen of sweat clung to their indigo skin.

"They are in no shape to tackle another trial yet. Our magic is spent, and they need to *heal*. What happened to all that grace given during the earlier trials to rest, to recover, to recuperate?" Elyria glanced in Cedric's direction, halfway expecting to see he'd succumbed to some unseen injury himself. But despite the literal hell his body had gone through over the past few days, he was the only one other than Elyria who seemed unimpaired.

"I am sorry for the losses you have suffered and the wounds you have sustained, but I fear there is little time left. What happened . . ." A stricken look overtook her cosmic features. "It is evident there are forces at work here we did not anticipate."

Cedric cleared his throat. "With all due respect, are we to understand that you did not know Varyth Malchior escaped the last Crucible?

That he left someone behind"—his eyes flitted to Elyria—"to manipulate events, to enact his own designs? How can that be?"

The celestial was silent for several long moments. When she spoke again, her multifaceted voice was low. "Even before my banishment, in the height of my prime, I was never omniscient. Neither I nor my sisters and brother can know precisely what mortals feel, what you think, what you've done or what you'll do, at any given time. We might watch the occasional person more closely, track figures of particular interest, plant seeds of foresight or prophecy. But our role has always been simply to provide the means for—"

"Then what's the point of you?" Elyria said, and Zephyr gasped again. Elyria ignored her. "How can you have the power to do all this"—she gestured broadly in the air—"yet be caught unaware when dark magic infiltrates the very game you created?"

Aurelia had the decency to look chagrined. "Make no mistake, this is no game. When the crown was shattered, I knew the mistake I made was very grave indeed. Not that I regret my desire to restore balance, but I do regret the manner in which I chose to do so. The power I granted."

"Because of Malakar?" Cedric asked.

Aurelia nodded, her starry face solemn. "Yes. If only I did possess the power of foresight. Maybe then I could have known what would happen. What my attempts at balance would cost Arcanis."

"If balance is what you sought, why create the peoples of Arcanis with such an imbalance of power in the first place?"

Nox leaned forward in their chair. "Who says she is the one who created them at all?"

Aurelia's eyes flashed at the nocterrian's words. "The Crucible was designed to repair the flaws in an already flawed system, the cracks of which were only widened by my interference. My siblings agreed to help me restore the glory of Arcanis in a way that could draw out only the truly worthy, someone strong enough not only to wield power, to reign with truth and justice, but one who would be able to resist its darkest temptations upon their success. One to herald in the dawn, one to bring a new day."

Cedric inhaled sharply, his eyes going glassy. "The prophecy."

Aurelia nodded. "Granted to Arcanian oracle and human seer alike, in the hopes that one day, the worthy would be called, their path forged through strife and unity, to lead them to the crown."

Elyria bit the inside of her lip, trying to remember the lines of the prophecy. And despite the celestial's protestations of not being able to read minds, it seemed like Aurelia knew exactly what Elyria was thinking when she began her recitation, her many voices sliding together like silk.

> "In the twilight of Arcanis's strife, long past a luminous fall,
> Visions pierce the veil of time, foretelling the stars' plan for all.
> A shattered crown shall be united, a sundered land restored.
> A severed people shall be made whole or fall to darkness once more.
> From shadow and fire, champions rise, forged in the Crucible of fate.
> Strength, spirit, magic, and concord test the trials beyond the Gate.
> From bitterest rivals to heartbreaking ends, two bloods shall
>   find their way.
> Through sacrifice, darkness, and friendship betrayed, as dawn
>   brings a new day.
> So will they reclaim the One True Crown, wielding its
>   terrible might.
> A choice will be offered, an offer then made: Heal the realm or cast
>   it into night."

The celestial exhaled, a sigh of the ages, and it was as if a great weight lifted from her shoulders when she finished speaking the words. Elyria's chest deflated, as if the prophecy pulled the air from her lungs. She glanced around, taking in the reverent bow of Thraigg's head, the wetness glistening between the lashes of Zephyr's closed eyes. Even Tenebris Nox had wiped the mirth from their expression, solemnity carved into the planes of their striking face.

Cedric's brow was furrowed, the top of his upper lip curling under his nose like he smelled something noxious.

Elyria smothered her desire to grin. "What's wrong?"

Aurelia tipped her head to the side, like she, too, was curious about his reaction.

"It's just a bit different from the version I was taught," he said, his eyes not meeting the celestial's.

Elyria snorted. "I didn't even remember half those verses existed, so I think you're in good company, Sir Fretful."

"It is understandable that some parts might have been altered or lost in translation," Aurelia said.

Elyria's amusement at the knight's reaction was swept away as she considered the prophecy, the difference between his version and the one she'd just heard. Words she'd been fretting about for days now.

Through sacrifice, darkness, and friendship betrayed . . .

"Well, I suppose if there were any doubts as to the veracity of *this* version, they can be laid to rest. I don't believe the lines you recited for me, Sir Scholar, included that part about 'friendship betrayed,' and yet . . ." Elyria cast a long look at a still-unconscious Kit, then thought about the line that preceded it.

From bitterest rivals to heartbreaking ends, two bloods shall find their way.

Evander had broken Kit's heart—and her own—with his betrayal. Hopefully that meant they were well on their way to seeing the end of this damn prophecy come to fruition. Granted, Elyria cared little for the "One True Crown" and its "terrible might." All she wanted was to leave this stars-damned Sanctum with Kit and move on. Let the rest of the kingdom worry about healing the realm. All she cared about was healing her friend—her sister.

That was what she told herself, at any rate.

Elyria faced the celestial. "Will they be safe here?" She looked pointedly from Kit to Zephyr to Thraigg to Nox. In the light of all they'd endured in the Crucible, one part of the prophecy was patently clear: two bloods, two people, were needed to earn the crown. This must have been why the Arbiter—why *Aurelia*—had urged them toward unity from the beginning. Two had to be deemed worthy.

You are the only one among them who is worthy.

Despite Evander's words, or perhaps because of them, Elyria wasn't entirely convinced that she was. But she couldn't let that stop her from trying.

"No further harm will befall them," said Aurelia, her many voices aligned in solemnity. "I swear it."

Elyria worried her bottom lip between her teeth, still hesitant.

"It has to be you two, Elle," Zephyr said, voice quiet. She slipped a green hand into Elyria's unbandaged one, then did the same to Cedric. "Take this to the end. For all of us."

"Aye," said Thraigg, exhaustion evident in the way he leaned heavily on his hammer. "We'll keep an eye on Kit. Ye just focus on workin' yer magic like ye have all along, eh?"

"Claim the crown, Revenant," added Nox, another flash of fang appearing as they grinned at Elyria. "After all, you've already been through the first three quarters of hell at this point. What's one more?"

The corners of Elyria's eyes burned as Zephyr drew their hands together, placing Elyria's in Cedric's before stepping back. Bolstering warmth flowed into Elyria from the contact, hot resolve surging from the place their skin met.

That *tug* in her chest pulsed.

She squeezed his hand.

He squeezed back, looking at their linked hands with an expression that danced on the line between surprise and affection. And maybe she imagined it, but something greater than that too.

Elyria cleared her throat, slipping on her proudest, most imperious mask. "Well, *this* bitter rival"—she waved a hand down her front—"is quite done with wading through 'heartbreaking ends' and would very much like to get on with the 'bring the dawn' portion of the show." She met Cedric's eye—that ring of gold in his bold brown eyes burning into her own. "Think our two bloods will do, Ric?"

She thought his eyes might've widened at her use of his nickname, but he did little more than grunt his assent, reaching for his sword before Aurelia cut him off with a gentle click of her tongue.

"You won't be needing that," she said, before gesturing toward the shimmering door.

Elyria gave the celestial a quizzical look but did not protest, putting down the dagger sheaths she had begun to strap to her thighs.

Aurelia's voice carried through the chamber like a dozen whispers on a soft wind as she went on to say, "Come, champions. The crown awaits."

CHAPTER 48
A LONG WALK

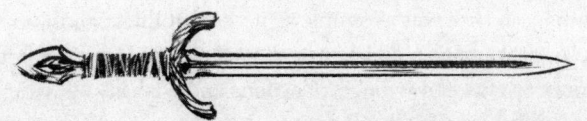

Cedric

By the time Cedric and Elyria emerged on the other side of the door, Aurelia was nowhere to be seen. Cedric kept his hand wrapped tightly around Elyria's, feeling exposed without the sword normally slung at his hip. He would never admit it, but he was also afraid of what might happen if he let her go. Like she might very well disappear if he did.

She held on just as tight, and for the life of him, he could not discern what she was thinking as the two of them strode forward down a long corridor. Night had fallen, and as moonlight filtered in through high windows, mixing with the flickering torches lining the walls, Cedric was hit with a powerful wave of déjà vu.

The feeling deepened as Elyria began humming, a delicate melody that seemed to match the tone of the ancient magic vibrating around them. For a moment Cedric was in another corridor, under another beam of moonlight. He was perched on a bench of stone, the most mesmerizing song drifting into his ears. He was looking up and seeing *her*.

In the present, he glanced at their hands, still laced together, hanging between them as they walked, their footsteps echoing off the stone walls on either side of them.

"I owe you an apology."

Cedric's gaze flew back to Elyria's face—her furrowed brow, the tick of her jaw. "Why? For what?"

"For many things," she said. "For berating your indecision outside the labyrinth. For doing the same thing, for freezing, when Ev-Evander . . ." She closed her eyes for a heartbeat. "It took me entirely too long to act, to do what needed to be done. Even after he hurt Kit like that, even while he was fighting you all, I just—"

"I know," Cedric said. He wasn't sure what else to say. Because he did know. He knew the paralysis that came with the knowledge that the lines one had drawn in their head might have been wrong all along. That nothing in here was as simple as it was out there. Humans versus Arcanians, past versus present. In here, it all blended together, a muddy whirlpool of rights and wrongs, of actions and wishes.

It was why he'd hesitated to act when Belien and Leona charged into the labyrinth, even after Gael was hurt.

"Betraying your own kind. Becoming a traitor. *And for what? So they can steal the crown right out of your hands when you make it to the end?"*

Belien's voice rang in Cedric's head, his final words more haunting than ever now that he was so close to said end. And to said crown—a prize he wasn't sure he even wanted to win anymore.

"I need to thank you too."

Cedric had been so momentarily lost in thought he hadn't noticed that Elyria had slowed her steps, gently pulling him to stop in the middle of the corridor.

Cedric gaped at her. "Forgive me for sounding repetitive, but again I must ask, for what?"

She faced him, chewing on her lip. "For the same thing. You did not hesitate to defend us, to defend Kit. You did not falter as I did."

He shook his head. "Do not do yourself such a disservice as to think you did nothing. You moved in the end. You made it count." He sighed. "In all honesty, I should have done more. I knew from the moment he appeared that something was wrong but I . . ."

"You what?"

He opened his mouth to say more, but at the sight of the pain swimming in her eyes, his explanation died on his tongue. She'd just been forced to kill the love of her life. For him. How could he explain he'd ignored his suspicions because he was *jealous*? Everything he might have felt seemed petty and inconsequential in comparison.

If Cedric could go back in time and kill Evander before he attacked Kit, he would. He should have struck him down the moment he appeared in the chamber. Elyria would have hated him for it. Might have murdered him right where he stood in retaliation. But to prevent her from seeing what had become of the man she loved, it would have been worth it.

She stepped closer, their hands still linked, and that thread tied somewhere deep inside Cedric's chest pulsed, a beam of light amidst the simmering fire inside.

"I should have done more," he repeated. He tried to turn away, to face forward, to launch back into motion, but she held him back, wrapping her bandaged hand around his wrist as if she meant to pin him down.

"Don't run," she said, her mouth curving wryly.

That light in his chest pulsed again, the memory of their near-miss in that moonlit hallway surging forth. She remembered. She still thought about it too.

"You saved me again," he said. "I don't even know what to say about that at this point. I suppose I should be used to it by now."

He didn't let himself think too hard about what he was doing when he lifted his arm and pressed his lips to the back of her hand.

"Thank you," he whispered against her knuckles.

Her lips parted, her brow jumping up her forehead in surprise. He half-expected her to protest, to pull away—hells, to slap him. Instead, she simply swallowed hard, and Cedric couldn't keep his gaze from following the gentle bob of her throat.

"I don't need your thanks," she said, the slightest tremble in her voice. "I just . . . I couldn't let it happen again."

He let their hands drop back between them, fingers still intertwined. "I know," he said. "But you have it anyway."

"I do believe this officially qualifies as the longest hallway in Arcanis." Elyria huffed, blowing a lock of periwinkle hair out of her eyes. "It feels like we've been walking for an hour."

"Two," Cedric said, though if he was being honest, it hadn't felt that long at all to him. Silence hung in the air, as it often did between them. But unlike the tension-filled droughts of sound that plagued them before, this one was comfortable, casual.

"Doesn't it seem strange that the Trial of Concord has thus far consisted of nothing more than what equates to a nice stroll?" she asked.

"I don't know, I'd say I'm feeling rather *concordant* right now." He grinned. "And a nice stroll, eh? Is this your way of telling me you've been having a good time?"

"You'd like to think that, wouldn't you?" She flashed her teeth in a teasing grimace, simultaneously squeezing his hand. "What I meant was, surely there has to be more to the Trial of Concord than this."

"I suppose we are about to find out," Cedric said, pointing ahead to where the winding hallway had finally straightened, revealing a large wooden door at the end.

Elyria stopped walking. "What do you think is beyond there?"

He shrugged. "Is there any point in speculating? We tackled the trials that preceded this. Surely this one will be a piece of cake too."

Elyria's mouth popped open in protest, closing when she saw the widening of Cedric's grin.

"Noctis take me," she said, dropping his hand in a dramatic show of mock surprise. "Once more, the knight makes a joke. Who *are* you, Sir Cedric Thorne? And whatever shall I tell that lord of yours when he asks what happened to you?"

At the mention of Lord Church, Cedric's face fell. He thought of how far he'd come—how far he'd fallen—from the "great champion" that had walked through the Gate. Cedric looked down at the black tunic draped over his armorless chest, his unguarded forearms. He didn't know what reuniting with Lord Church once this was all over would look like. He wondered if the lord would even recognize him like this. Bare. Unarmored. Unmasked. The quiet, thrumming power of the simmering embers deep in him pulsed in his chest. Was he even capable of donning those old pieces of himself again? He didn't think he could go back to being that same obedient, subservient knight.

Elyria must have noticed the change in Cedric's mood, because she was quick to add, "Only joking, Your Broodiness."

He nodded absently.

She frowned. "What will you do with the crown once we've claimed it?"

Cedric recognized the blatant attempt to change the subject, yet the question still caught him so off guard, he stumbled over his own feet. "What will *I* do with it?"

"I mean, I certainly don't want it. All I want is for all this to be over so I can get Kit to the first healer I fly across." She paused, as if weighing whether to say the next part aloud. "And I cannot deny that this 'imbalance' between our peoples would surely only grow more vast were I to present the crown to King Lachlandris. He may be a fair enough ruler, but he is still a royal. With celestial power in his hands, I cannot imagine he would do anything but make the situation in Havensreach worse."

Cedric stared at her, the light in his chest thudding in parallel with his heart. "A few days stuck in the Crucible with me, and I've turned you into a human sympathizer, have I?"

She chuckled darkly. "I could say the same about you, could I not? Don't think I missed the murderous glint in your eye when first we met in Castle Lumin, Sir Knight."

Her tone was teasing, but the reminder of the visceral rage he'd felt upon learning of her identity as the Revenant had shame swelling in him. He wished he understood more about why he'd thought—why he'd been led to believe—for so long that she was the one responsible for the blood and fire of his past.

Cedric took a steadying breath. "Knowing what we know now, I'm not sure anyone should wield power such as this."

"Not even your lord? Your king?"

Traitor. Betrayer.

He swallowed. If she was being honest, he could be too. "Perhaps especially not them. Just look at what power like that does to a man—what even the desire for power like that does. I am sure Varyth Malchior painted many beautiful lies for Evander in order to sway him to his plan."

The mention of Evander's name had Elyria tensing, but it was a less severe reaction than Cedric expected. As if the long walk down this simple hall had helped heal some of the hurt already.

"I dread to think of what would happen should the crown fall into Malchior's hands," Cedric added.

Elyria bit her lip. "What of the Chasms?"

"I—I don't know. Without access to the Midlands, the situation in Havensreach will surely grow more dire. There are too many of us for the land we possess. There is too little mana. But the risk . . . If only there was a way to use the crown to restore the land while also ensuring it never falls into the wrong hands."

Elyria looked at him thoughtfully, her lips scrunching to one side like an off-kilter kiss, and his insides warmed. "What if there was a way to do just that?"

"Is there?"

"When we merged power outside the labyrinth, there was a moment there when I thought I could have accomplished *anything*."

Something stirred in Cedric's core at the reminder of how Elyria had looked in that moment—the sheer waves of power rolling off her, the way she'd unwoven the trial's thorny barrier with the twitch of her fingers. Her otherworldly glow, her light pulsing in his own chest like she was made of starfyre.

He cleared his throat, the back of his neck growing hot. "I recall."

Blessedly, she didn't appear to notice his reaction. "Now, imagine that magic expanded tenfold—a hundredfold. With the crown, bolstered with that kind of power . . . I think I could fill the Chasms and bridge the realms." She sucked in a breath. "After which, we would get rid of it—hide it, bury it, destroy it. Anything. Everything."

"So that nobody ever has the opportunity to abuse its power again." Awe and respect and something else wove through Cedric's words.

"Yes. Is that crazy?"

"No," he said, eyes wide. "I don't find that crazy at all. After all, it was with the crown that Queen Daephinia was able to sunder the land in the first place, was it not?"

Elyria grew quiet for several long moments. So long, that Cedric felt that thread of light in his chest pulling him toward her, pushing him to reach for her. To ensure she was all right, that she was safe, that she was real. But he knew if he did, if he touched her again now, the fragile control he was holding on to would snap.

By the stars, how he wanted it to snap.

"Would you trust me to do it?" she asked. Her voice was quiet, unsure. Like she was afraid of his answer. It squeezed at his heart, and for a second, he was back in the second trial, in that dark place Elyria had found him.

"How do I know you are real?"

"I don't know. Sometimes I don't even know if I'm real. But even if I had an answer, I somehow doubt there's anything I could say that would convince you. You just have to trust."

"Trust you?"

"Trust yourself. But yes, ideally, trust me while you're at it."

"I don't know how."

"We'll start small, then. One simple truth."

In the present, Cedric blinked.

His truth was that for the first time in what felt like a lifetime, he had real hope. Hope that they would leave this place, that they could make a difference. Hope that his being here wasn't a mistake or a miscalculation.

He wasn't a knight sent to fight a war he didn't understand. He wasn't Lord Church's champion, trained to win a challenge he'd never truly been prepared for. He wasn't a frightened boy witnessing his entire world burn around him. Right now, in this moment, he was a man who knew without a doubt that the woman at his side was meant to do this. That he was meant to do it with her.

She knew what it was to conquer darkness. To resist its temptation. To use power for *good*. To save and to help and to love without limit.

You are the only one among them who is worthy, Evander had said.

Of that, he had been right.

"One simple truth," said Cedric, his voice thick. "If you believe nothing else in this world, Elyria Lightbreaker, trust what I say next."

Elyria's eyes widened in recognition of the words.

"You are the only one I would trust to do it."

She smiled then, bright and beaming, color blooming in the ivory planes of her cheeks, and Cedric could have sworn his heart skipped several beats. The golden thread shimmered, sealing up the cracks that had formed in Cedric's soul, and he knew without knowing that something had shifted—cemented—between them.

"All right then," she said, striding toward the door at the end of the hall. "Let us finish this."

CHAPTER 49
THE FINAL TRIAL

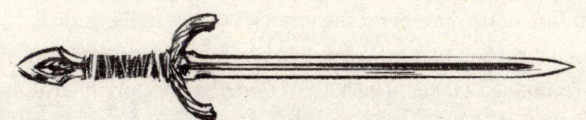

Cedric

The air was crisp and cool. Cedric looked up and soaked in the endless night. There was no aurora to light their way. Just a thousand diamonds spilled across an ocean of inky black.

The ground below their feet lit up, as if the starlight above had been gathered and infused into the dirt, creating a luminous path. It did not wind, did not meander or wander. It cut straight ahead, leading them to the end of a steep amphitheater. A pit carved from stone, surrounded on all sides by steep stairs and rows upon rows of empty benches, as if an audience of ghosts waited to watch the final trial.

The Trial of Concord.

At the center of the pit stood a familiar silhouette, shrouded in white. Cedric put his hand on the small of Elyria's back as they descended the stairs, a kind of finality settling on his shoulders with each step.

More than once, Cedric's hand tightened on Elyria, wrapping his fingers around her waist like he meant to steady her. She huffed, clearly annoyed that he thought she might actually lose her balance walking down some stairs. She even went so far as to uncloak her wings, flaring them out as if to prove a point. She could fly. She did not need his help *walking*.

Her reaction drew a low chuckle from Cedric, but he didn't pull back. Balance was the least of his reasons for doing it.

He'd gotten far too used to the feel of her hand in his, to the way her touch grounded him, kept him pinned in reality. She calmed the furnace in his chest, let the light there bloom instead. He *needed* to touch her. Needed to feel the pulse of her blood and the magic beneath her skin, each beat a reminder.

She is real.

This is real.

We are at the end, and we are going to get out of here.

The pit itself was clean, stark, barren. Empty, save for a lone pedestal standing at its center and the white-clad celestial beside it.

Aurelia's robes were drawn, her hood shielding her hair, though her face remained visible. The back of Cedric's neck prickled at the sight of the pillow that lay atop the pedestal. It was tufted, crafted from a velvet of deepest red, a sparkling gem in the center of each divot. It was the kind of pillow meant to hold something precious. Something regal. Something royal.

But no crown sat atop it.

There was only a silver dagger, ornate carvings etched into its double-edged blade. They curved up its hilt, where a sparkling ruby was set in the center of the pommel.

Aurelia focused her starlit eyes on Cedric as he and Elyria approached, and that prickle turned into a shiver that crawled down Cedric's back. Beside him, Elyria stiffened, her hand searching for his, her fingers tightening when she found him. She folded her wings flat against her back as the two of them came to a stop before the celestial.

They held their collective breath as Aurelia began to speak, the multitudes of her voice stretching into the open air.

"You have done well, my champions. So well, to have made it this far. Truly, it is beyond my wildest hopes that you stand here before me today."

Elyria shifted her weight, an unease poking through her typically resilient demeanor that only made Cedric more nervous in turn.

"You have fought, you have learned, you have shown power and mercy, both. And most of all, you have done it *together*. Through darkness and doubt, fire and shadow, life and death, you have forged a true bond—the kind that is difficult to craft, yes, but also difficult to break. Tested in the fires of trust, bound by something deeper than ambition. And you have emerged, both of you champions, both of you victors."

Aurelia's voice echoed off the empty stone benches of the amphitheater, and Cedric bit back the sensation that this all felt far more like a show than a trial.

"And the crown?" he asked, a knot twisting in his stomach.

"The crown is waiting," she said, her star-filled eyes glassy. "And while this bond of trust has carried you here, while you have brought each other to this point . . ."

There was no mistaking the sudden sadness in her voice, and Cedric's blood went cold as her nebulous gaze fell on the dagger atop the pedestal.

". . . only one will walk away with the prize you seek. A piece of a power greater than any mortal mind can comprehend."

Elyria went still, all notions of her nervous shifting eradicated by the celestial's words. "What does that mean?"

Several moments passed before Aurelia answered. "To wear the crown is to carry the weight of its past. Every broken oath, every good intention turned wrong, every fallen comrade . . . every regret buried with them. Rulers are not made by crowns and titles alone—they are forged in the crucible of sacrifice. Those unwilling to burn do not deserve the throne."

Cedric stared blankly at the celestial. "Sacrifice," he repeated.

"Who said anything about ruling?" Elyria's voice was sharp, cutting. "Fuck the throne. Fuck wearing your crown. We only want it because it is the key to getting out of here."

Aurelia did not deign to acknowledge her protestations. The celestial did not pause, did not falter or stutter as she continued. "The crown cannot be won through strength or will or magic alone. This, here, is the final test of the Arcane Crucible and of the bond you have forged. For the claim of one must be laid down, their life willingly given, for the sake of the other." She paused. "This is where all others have failed."

"A life for a life." Cedric's mind spun in frantic circles, Evander's earlier words whipping through his head like shards of glass. No wonder Varyth Malchior had been unsuccessful. He and Evander might have made it to this place, might have heard these same words, but to think that whatever existed between them could pass for a true bond seemed ludicrous. Cedric wondered if they'd already come to their nefarious truce by the time they stood here, or if Malchior's dark promises only came after he realized he could not claim the crown. He supposed it didn't really matter, in the end.

"A life for *all* life," Aurelia corrected. "One must trust enough to give, and one must trust enough to receive. For balance."

"For *balance*?" hissed Elyria. "Where is the balance in demanding death for no reason?"

"Power demands sacrifice. You came through the Gate with doubt in your heart and enemies at your back. You overcame them, repaired bonds where they existed, and forged new ones where there were none. It is with great pride and triumph that I can see you have shown yourselves truly worthy of this prize. Now the time has come to claim it."

"You're mad," Elyria seethed, her body trembling. Shadows began leaking from her skin, wisps of black smoke wafting over her. "This . . . this was the end goal all along? Force us to ally, make us work together, make us *care*? Knowing all along that one of us would be served up like a lamb for the slaughter?"

Aurelia said nothing.

"This is all your fault! Because of your interference! Your best-laid plans that failed!" She was breathing fast now—too fast, shadows spinning off her in waves. "*You* are the reason Malakar came to power, the reason the world was split in three. Where is *your* sacrifice? *Your* loss?"

The stars above seemed to burn brighter as the celestial's divine composure finally cracked. "Do you think I enjoy this? Do you think I have rejoiced in all the lives lost in the Sanctum? Do you think this is what I wanted? This is *never* what I wanted! I am bound to this forsaken place, the same as you. I want this to be done just as much as you do."

"Then give us the crown!"

"I cannot."

Elyria let out a yell of frustration, and Cedric wanted nothing more than to wrap his arms around her, to help her find her breath, to assure her that they'd figure something out, that they would find another way. But one look at the tortured expression on the celestial's face and he knew it was impossible.

Aurelia sighed, her multi-tonal voice solemn, the sound heavy. One by one, the stars dotting her skin blinked out, until more and more she blended in with the sky above. "You are both worthy champions. This final choice belongs to you."

Then she was gone in a burst of dazzling starlight. Moments later, the night sky filled with glorious color—green and violet and scarlet and gold—as the aurora unfurled above them.

Elyria barely noticed. "Coming here was a mistake. This whole entire stars damned fucking Crucible was a mistake." She wrung her hands, pacing as shadows twirled between her fingers. The ground rumbled beneath her feet. She was spinning out. He knew what she must have been thinking. To *not* claim the crown would ensure not only their deaths, but those of Kit, Zephyr, Thraigg, Nox. They would all be trapped in the Sanctum, until death or madness—likely both—came for them. But in order to claim it . . .

His eyes went to the dagger, moonlight glinting off it like some twisted beacon of fate. His heart hammered against his ribs as icy resolve washed over him.

"It's all right, Elyria," he said, grabbing her hands and forcing her to still. He studied her face, the points of her ears, taking in the freckle on her left cheek, the wave of periwinkle hair above her right eyebrow that always seemed to be slightly out of place. Lifting one hand to her chin, he traced the curve of her jaw, the line of her bottom lip.

She released a shaky breath, her eyes shuttering as she leaned into his touch.

"Don't," he whispered, and her eyelids fluttered back open. "I want to see you." He stared into her jewel-green eyes, tried to memorize their exact shade, the sheen of the silver flecks within. When he blinked, his lashes were wet.

"Cedric, what—"

"I just wish we had more time," he said, steeling himself as he drew in one last, slow breath.

"Wait, what are you—"

Cedric ran to the pedestal.

He reached for the dagger. A zing of power ran up his hand as his fingers grazed the ruby in its hilt. But it was gone in the next blink as a pale hand knocked it from his grasp.

"No." Elyria whirled on him, eyes blazing. Metal and stone rang through the amphitheater as the dagger clattered to the ground between them.

Cedric lunged for it.

Once more, Elyria was faster. With a kick, she sent it skittering across the stone floor until it collided with the stairs on the other side. He moved to go after it, but she was already in front of him, blocking him, throwing her shoulder against his chest, pushing him back.

Fuck, he'd forgotten how strong she was.

Planting his feet, he braced against the force of her, grabbing her arms in an attempt to steady them both. For a moment, she complied, something in her visage softening. He had no time to analyze what it meant, ducking low and sweeping his foot against her boot to throw her off-balance. With a yelp, she stumbled, then righted herself by grabbing hold of the pedestal.

It only gained him a single second, maybe two, but he wouldn't waste them. He launched himself across the pit, rushing toward the dagger with a burst of speed he hadn't known himself capable of. He snatched it up, angling the pointed tip at his chest.

A blur of periwinkle flashed past his vision before a blow to his temple had stars bursting behind his eyes. He felt the dagger being pulled from his grip. With a wince, he forced his sight to clear long enough to take in the ethereal figure floating before him. Elyria hovered in the air, wings flared, a vision of shimmering purple and green. He leapt for her, catching her around the waist and yanking her downward before she could fly away.

"I have to do this," Cedric grunted as she tried to free herself from his grip, spinning in his arms, the dagger still in her hand. "You know it has to be me."

She growled, elbowing him hard in the ribs. The air rushed from his lungs, but he did not let go. Instead, he hauled her backward, using his greater weight to keep her grounded, even as her wings flapped against his pull.

They crashed to the floor in a tangled heap, Cedric twisting midfall so his back hit the stone first, pulling her on top of him. The dagger went flying, once more clattering against the stone.

"Let go!" Elyria hissed, voice ragged, desperate. They were both panting now, breaths coming in too short and too long, too shallow and too deep.

Pain flared across his jaw as she landed another hit.

"Stop it!" With one arm still wrapped around her waist, he managed to pin both her wrists in one hand, gripping them tight in an attempt to hold her still. "You have to let me do this."

Her chest heaved as she glared down at him. "I'm not letting you die for me."

Shadows danced along the edge of Cedric's vision, curling around his arms and legs, binding him in place until she could extricate herself from his hold.

"Elyria!" he yelled, struggling against her shadows as she leapt to her feet and ran for the dagger again.

Two could play at this game, he decided, and this time, when he called upon that spark in his chest, it ignited. Her binding shadows burned away in a flash of white-gold flame.

Elyria stopped in her tracks, the briefest flicker of wonder and something a little bit like pride overtaking the fury on her face. It was just enough of a distraction for Cedric to scramble to his feet and quickly catch up to her, yanking her back by her leathers before she reached the dagger.

Her back hit his chest, his hand accidentally skimming the edge of one of her silken wings as he pivoted from behind her. She gasped, chest heaving as they stood there, face-to-face, something unnamed hanging in the inches between them.

For one breathless moment they were still, their hearts hammering against the silence of night. And then he was racing past her, lunging for the weapon once more, only for a ribbon of black smoke to surge forward and snatch it from him.

Cedric spun, helpless to do anything but watch as the dagger soared into Elyria's outstretched hand, her chest rising and falling with labored breath. She gripped the hilt tightly, her hand trembling, eyes bright with tears. "You can't," she said. "I won't let you."

"It has to be me," Cedric said again, this time softer, his voice imploring. He took a step closer to the dagger—to her. "I have to be the one to die for the crown, because you have to be the one to wield it. We agreed. You'll use the power of the crown to seal the Chasms, and then you'll destroy it."

"I don't care! I don't care about the Chasms! Let someone else fix it; let someone else find a way. It's not worth your life, Cedric. You deserve"—her voice cracked—"to live. You've already given everything to this place!"

"But it's worth yours?" A surge of anger fed the flame in his chest. How dare she think she wasn't the important one here, the worthy one. He closed the distance between them, and she drew the dagger behind her back, but he didn't reach for it. Instead, he took her free hand in his—gently, tenderly, that burning rage calming the instant he closed his fingers around hers.

He laid her palm against his heart. "Do you think I'd let *you* die for this? For me? Do you think I could live with that?"

"You will learn to—you will *have* to." Her voice shook, but she didn't pull away. "I couldn't save him, but I can still save you."

"Don't you understand?" His voice was desperate, pleading. "There's only one reason I survived this long already. I should have died five times over in here, and I know, deep in my bones—in my soul—that this, right here, is why. I am only alive because of you. Let me be the reason you get out, save Kit, save everyone."

"No fucking way."

"Elyria—"

"I said, no, dammit! I didn't save your life over and over again just for you to end it now." Now she did try to pull away, to yank her hands back, to put space between them. He only drew her closer. "You don't get to make this choice."

"There is no other choice to be made," he said. "What's the alternative? We waste away in here forever? Kit dies, Thraigg dies, Nox dies, Zephyr dies? Or worse yet, what happened to Evander happens to you? I'd rather die than see that happen anyway."

He steeled himself. "I think I've always known that my story was meant to end like this." Sorrow leaked out with every word, with each limited beat of his heart. "And if it means saving you, if it means ensuring the crown doesn't fall into the wrong hands, then it's all worth it. *You* are worth it."

She shook her head, her hair loose and wild after their struggle. Her hand tightened around his. "I've lived enough for two lifetimes already. I accepted my fate the second I decided to follow Kit through the Gate. But you—you deserve an *after*."

"*After* was always just a dream for me. It doesn't have to be for you."

They stood there, frozen, the weight of this impossible choice pushing on their shoulders.

"This is what I'm meant for," Cedric said. "It's the only thing that makes sense."

Elyria let out a small, broken sound, and Cedric knew he had won. He wondered if she could hear the way it made his heart crack.

"You're wrong," she whispered. "None of this makes sense without you."

The words echoed through his blood like the worst kind of prayer. If they kept this up, he would lose his resolve. He would falter. They would fail.

Just one more look, he thought as he stared into her blazing green eyes, at the fire burning there, wholly different from the one kindling in his chest. He took in the way the aurora lit up her hair, the swaying colors illuminating each strand, making them shine—purple and silver and green and gold.

He looked at her and he saw her. *Her*. Not the warrior, not the Revenant. Not the friend or the ally or the sister or the grieving ex-lover. Just her. And he knew that everything he'd thought, everything he'd been taught, the weight he'd carried since he was a child wasn't real, wasn't true.

This. This was real.

Lord Church had been so wrong about her. About all of them. And if he was wrong about this, what else was he wrong about?

Cedric's fingers trailed along the end of Elyria's disheveled braid, pinching strands of periwinkle between his knuckle and the pad of his thumb. Her almond scent filled his nose, and it felt like a punch straight to the gut. He knew from the first moment he saw her, from the instant that sugar-and-poison scent filtered through his senses, that she would be the death of him.

It just wasn't anything close to the way he imagined.

Just one look, he'd told himself. It wasn't enough. It would never be enough. But if not now, when?

So, without letting himself second-guess or lose his nerve or think about it for even one second longer, Cedric leaned forward and crushed his lips to hers.

CHAPTER 50
FALLING

Elyria

He is kissing me.

His mouth is on my mouth, capturing me, pinning me here. It's soft at first—testing, tender.

And then our lips are moving with urgency—need. A clash of anger and sadness and regret and want.

So much want.

I've been running from wanting—true wanting—for twenty-five years. And for years longer than that, I lived behind walls, built high and impenetrable. I carved doors for Evander, Kit. Windows for my family. But they were small and controlled, and I was always in charge of whether they stayed open or if they got locked up tight.

I should have known he would bring it all crashing down.

My lips part and his charred sandalwood scent is surrounding me and my hands are tangling in his hair, pulling him closer. He tastes like fire and power and light. He is warm and he feels safe.

His arm is wrapping around my waist and he—

A full-body shiver runs through me from my toes through the tips of my wings, because his fingers are there too, running loosely along the edge. His wingtouch is the first I've felt since before Evander went into the Arcane Crucible. I always thought it would horrify me, that the familiar feeling at the hands of another would throw me into a panic.

It's nothing like that.

And even before, it was never like this.

It's as if heat is flowing from his very fingertips, his fire lighting up my wings. Not scorching, not searing.

Illuminating.

He's not a pyre. He's a hearth.

He is home.

And he is mine.

"Elle," he whispers, and I shiver again. Hearing my name on his tongue does something to me. I hate it. I love it. I crave it.

Gently—so gently—he pins my wing between his fingers, languidly stroking the edge with the pad of his thumb as his lips move to my ear, my throat. And that heat moves elsewhere.

Warmth pools in the center of my core, right below my belly button, and if I wasn't so sure that Aurelia was watching our every movement, waiting on us to make this impossible choice, if I thought we were alone . . . I would take him to the floor right here and now. I would strip us both of this clothing that feels too tight, too constricting. I would pin him between my thighs, and I would make sure he understands what it truly means to live.

I would show him everything.

I press another tender kiss to his lips before peeling back to stare into the heat of his gaze. My eyes trace the ring of gold in his irises, the strong line of his jaw, the scar cutting through his upper lip—that memento of his heartbreaking past.

He smiles at me, the aurora painting a sunset on his beautiful golden skin.

I smile back.

And then he's so still, I might've thought time had frozen.

Except for the way his eyes go wide.

Except for the smallest gasp escaping his mouth.

And he's not still anymore.

He's falling out of my line of sight, his arm slipping from my waist.

And I don't understand.

Until I look down, where he's collapsed to his knees.

And see his other hand fisted at his chest.

Wrapped around the jewel-hilted dagger I didn't even notice him slip from my back.

The dagger he's just used to pierce his own heart.

He might as well have thrust it right into mine.

I wish time had *frozen.*

I wish we'd had more of it too.

I sink to his level, pull him against my chest. He's leaking a different kind of heat now, and it's too warm, too wet, too thick.

I want to cry and scream and yell and thrash and hit.

No tears come. Do they?

The line where his lips meet is dark with blood. A bead of it swells at the corner of his mouth and dribbles down the side, a single weeping tear.

His hand cups my face, his thumb wiping wetness from my cheek.

"Make it count, Elle," he whispers.

His eyes close.

And Cedric Thorne dies with a smile on his lips.

CHAPTER 51
FLICKER

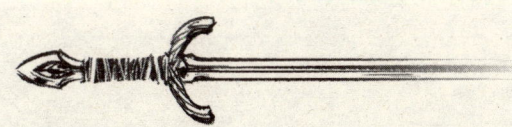

Cedric

The pain is sharp—a flash of white-hot fire.

It starts at the point in my chest where the blade pierced my skin, and it spreads outward in waves. Searing. Scorching. Searching. And then, just as quickly as it came on, it dulls. It fades.

A different kind of pain follows. Softer. Familiar. A flickering light, the last embers of a dying flame.

The breaking of a heart.

I expected it to hurt more. I expected it to hurt less.

There's a coldness now at the edges of my mind. A creeping numbness, biting, like the chill of winter frost. I feel it—feel me—slipping away.

I look at her.

Her face.

Her eyes.

Two glimmering pools of emerald, liquid silver lining the edges. They're full of life. She's full of life.

She's going to live.

She's going to change the stars-damned world.

It eases some of the chill that's taking me over, if just for a moment.

She's looking at me and her face is wet.

She's crying.

For me.

I wish she wouldn't.

But she's so fucking beautiful, even when she cries.

CHAPTER 52
FADE

Cedric

It's getting dark.

Not her.

She's still here, a glowing light in the endless shadow, burning brighter than the stars scattered in the sky above us.

The pain's all but gone now. Faded into nothingness.

I am very nearly nothing too. All of me, ebbing, waning.

Passing.

There's still something left—something small, infinitesimal. It pulses in my chest, throbs.

A tiny tug, a golden light.

I feel it flickering there, that thread tied just behind my ribs, tethering me to this world. To her.

It's weak, thin, stretched too far. But it's still there.

She's still there.

It's flickering, but it doesn't die. Not yet.

My hand reaches to cup her cheek, and I relish the softness of her skin, even as it's slick with tears.

I try to hold on.

I can't.

CHAPTER 53
SNAP

Cedric

The thread pulls tight.

Too tight.

"Make it count, Elle," I tell her.

My eyes close, a heavy tiredness soaking into every cell of my being.

Her hands are on me. I can feel the heat of her, clutching me close. Holding me together even as I fall away.

A spark of regret flares in the hole in my chest, that flickering light pulsing one final time, an echo of all the things I wish could have been different.

But I'm already slipping, too far gone to stop it now. I've gone too far.

And this is a place she cannot follow.

The tether behind my ribs strains, stretches—please—I want to hold on, I want to reach for her—no—I don't want to go yet, I—

The thread snaps.

CHAPTER 54
A GOLDEN CROWN

Elyria

He looked like he was sleeping.

If it weren't for the blood growing cold against Elyria's skin, she might have thought he was.

She was soaked in it, a thick layer of red coating her hands, pooling in her lap, creeping up the bandage still wrapped around her arm. There was so much of it. Too much.

Bile rose in the back of her throat.

This wasn't real.

It couldn't be.

This couldn't be how it all ended.

He promised. He swore that he wouldn't be the cause of her pain again.

He lied.

Elyria's vision blurred, her racing mind going still and silent as she searched for that golden thread, that warm, familiar *tug* in her chest, that thing that had led her to him time and time again. She'd used it to pull him back from the brink before, and she would do so again.

It wasn't there.

She could barely breathe. She knelt, frozen fingers slackening where they clutched the black fabric of Cedric's tunic. She should've been sobbing, screaming, something.

She did nothing, felt nothing.

Only the void of him.

She looked at the dagger lodged in Cedric's lifeless chest, saw the river of red pouring from the crimson jewel in its pommel. It was as if it were painting his body with the lifeblood of all who had come before him—died before him. The lives lost to the Crucible.

She barely noticed the aurora starting to undulate in the sky above, ribbons of swirling color weaving, dancing, condensing, until they formed a single beam of rainbow light that descended on the pedestal in the center of the amphitheater.

Elyria lifted her head as the light faded, her eyes falling on what was left behind. The thing that Cedric gave his life for. That all who had taken on the Crucible gave their lives for.

The crown.

Only it wasn't a crown.

Not quite.

The cracked remains of Elyria's heart plummeted into her stomach as she stood and approached the pedestal, dripping hands fisted at her sides. What sat on the bloodred velvet was something *like* a crown. A golden crescent, sharp spires topped with radiant gems . . . that abruptly came to a stop just as it started to curve around.

Incomplete.

A fragment.

"What is this?" Elyria whispered, lifting a red-stained finger as if to take it. She didn't. She let her hand drop limply back to her side. The very thought of touching the half-crown made this all too real.

She was still hoping that it wasn't.

"Is this what all this was for?" Her voice was hoarse, hollow. Aurelia had to be listening. "You push us through your trials, watch us fall, break, bleed . . . and for what? To wield a broken crown? To win half of what was promised?"

"I'm sorry." The celestial's voice came from behind, a chorus of whispers on a phantom wind.

Elyria's head snapped toward the source of the sound, a bitter laugh searing her throat. "You're *sorry*?"

Aurelia's hood was down, her aurora-streaked hair shimmering in the starlight. The galaxies in her eyes swirled with something that might have been sorrow as she passed Cedric's body, and rage lit up Elyria's chest.

"Don't tell me you're sorry," she spat. "Don't even look at him."

"I take no pleasure in what occurred here tonight, Elyria Lightbreaker," said the celestial, though even as she spoke the words, Elyria could sense a kind of lightness to her voice. A relief that hadn't been there before.

"Your Crucible has been completed," Elyria said, eyes narrowing. "Your useless prize won. Are you not free? Your sentence commuted? Your spirit unbound? Let's get on with it, then. Tell me how to get out of here, how to get back to Kit and the others, and how all of us can leave this place. You can even keep your shattered crown. I don't want it."

Aurelia's answering sigh was a symphony of emotion—longing and resolution and, unfathomably, irritation. But she did not speak, and her refusal to respond had Elyria's inner shadow rearing back. She was done with this. Done with the Crucible and the celestials' games. Done with cryptic non-answers and half-truths.

"On with it," she pressed. "Give me your final instruction, and you can go. I *want* you to go."

"Until the One True Crown is claimed, I remain bound to this plane," said Aurelia.

"Fine, I claim it. Happy?" Elyria flung her hand out to pick up the half-crown. The instant her fingers wrapped around one of its pointed spires, her blood began to sing, her nerves lit on fire.

She gasped, dropping it back on the pillow.

"How?" she hissed. "What is—"

Elyria cradled her hand to her chest, fingers tingling. When she looked down, she saw they were not covered in red anymore. Neither was she. Her pants, her blouse, her vest, previously dark and slick with blood, were pristine. As if the mere act of touching the crown had burned away all evidence of Cedric's sacrifice.

She blinked, unwrapping the bandage from her arm to see her skin completely healed, all remnants of the burns from when she'd calmed Cedric's flaming form gone. It made her feel empty. Like the last trace of him had been erased.

The sheer power in that single touch made her dizzy.

"Now you see why only one truly worthy could be allowed this privilege," Aurelia said.

Black smoke coiled around Elyria's feet, tendrils of living night snaking up her body. "*Privilege?* What privilege? To walk alongside death as it comes for the people I care for? You say I must be *worthy* if I am standing here, but *he* was worth more." She jerked her head toward Cedric's body, still laid out on the cold amphitheater floor.

"He paid the ultimate price, and it didn't mean anything in the end. I might be able to leave this place, but it won't be with the prize we sought." Her voice cracked, sorrow coming in relentless waves that crested over her broken heart. Cedric, Evander, Gael, Cyren . . . even Leona and Belien, Paelin and Alden and Brandon and every champion who'd ever been lost to this cruel place, unknowingly in pursuit of a prize that didn't exist.

That flash of celestial power that Elyria felt was just that—a flash. A taste. A fragment. It wasn't whole, wasn't complete. Her shadows closed in around her, wrapping her in a dark cocoon as if trying to shield her from this reality. Elyria couldn't seal the Chasms with half a crown.

Blinking back tears, she asked, "What was the point of any of it? Why did you tell us the crown awaited when you knew this was all there was?"

"The crown does await," Aurelia said, starry eyes glazing over. "*A shattered crown shall be united, a sundered land restored.*"

Elyria's jaw tensed, her nails carving crescents into her palm from how tightly she clenched her fist. "Stop," she said. "If I go years without hearing another word of that stars-damned prophecy, it'll still be too soon."

Aurelia didn't seem to hear her. Didn't seem to care. "*A severed people shall be made whole.*"

"I said, stop. I don't want to hear it."

"Or fall to darkness once more," the celestial continued. *"So will they reclaim the One True Crown, wielding its terrible—"*

"Fuck you! Fuck your prophecy!" Elyria exploded, cutting off Aurelia's recitation with a scream. Shadows shot in all directions, knocking the pedestal over, the crown bouncing on the floor with a riotous clang before rolling to a stop near Cedric's body. The sight of it, with its shattered edges and its mocking glint, so close to him—the physical, visceral reminder that his sacrifice had been in vain—drove her into motion. In a heartbeat, she was next to him, one hand pressed gently to his chest as she knelt to snatch the crown up and fling it away.

But again, when she touched the gilded surface, a surge of power shot through her like a bolt of lightning. Raw, pure, overwhelming. Her hand shook as her fingers clenched around the crown. A strangled cry poured from her lips when she realized she couldn't release it. It was as if the golden spires were fused to her.

Neither could she pull her other hand from Cedric's body. It was pinned flat against his chest, power surging through her like a conduit.

Magic rippled in her blood, pulsed beneath her skin. She let out a whimper when the dagger lifted from Cedric's chest, pulled free by the otherworldly power coming from the half-crown.

Life thrummed in her veins. She had never felt anything like this. Nothing could compare. Nothing came close, not even those seconds outside the labyrinth, with the blood of the other champions roaring in her veins, with Cedric directing his magic through her. Then, she'd felt powerful, alive. Like she had every thread of magic at her fingertips, like she could bring it under her command.

This was different. Elyria couldn't control this magic.

She *was* this magic.

She was the birth and death of every star, the darkness born in shadow. She was life and she was light.

She knew this light.

A memory pricked at the furthest reaches of Elyria's mind— blinding white light bursting across a battlefield, a tidal wave of energy rolling through bodies and buildings.

And that's when she felt it.

Deep behind her ribs, wrapped in her shadows, buried in her grief. A tiny, fragile flicker.

A *tug*.

Elyria's breath caught. Her fingers tightened around the metal of the crown, somehow searing and numbing, hot and cold at once. Her shadows stretched out, covering Cedric's body, dark tendrils weaving around him. Searching. Reaching. Not for a golden thread—that bond was gone; it had snapped when he died—but a tether, spun from the darkest part of her, seeking that whisper of light.

It was here. It had to be.

Her heart pounded in her chest as she leaned closer to him, her whole body shaking under the weight of the celestial force roaring in her veins. "Please," she begged. "Please."

And there it was—that flicker, the final ember, the last echo of Cedric's light, buried deep within him. Elyria grasped it with all that she had, all that she was, and she *tugged*.

Vaguely, she thought Aurelia might have been speaking—yelling, cursing, screaming—at her. Elyria didn't hear it. She could feel the magic start to wane, that cold exhaustion spreading in her veins, like the star-blessed power of the crown was making her burn out twice as fast.

She didn't care. Not as her shadows surged, twining around the pair of them, wrapping the piece of the Crown of Concord in ribbons of black. They encircled that small, fragile flicker inside Cedric, coaxed it, nurtured it, pulled it to the surface.

And just as that coldness spread to her chest, burnout having almost fully consumed her . . . she felt it.

Not a flicker, but a spark.

A pulse of warmth.

A golden *tug*.

A gasp of life.

And a beating heart.

CHAPTER 55
ABSOLUTION

Cedric

At first, there was nothing.

Not the biting cold, not the dull numbness of death, not the weight of the blade in his chest.

Just a quiet emptiness.

Oblivion.

And then, there was light.

A flicker, distant at first, a firefly dancing in a faraway field. It flew closer, grew stronger, brighter, until it was everywhere. Searing warmth poured through him, heating his blood, setting his veins alight. And he felt himself being pulled back into his body, a tether fastening him to this world.

Cedric gasped, a ragged breath filling his lungs.

He wasn't sure if he was alive. It wasn't like before, floating in that murky in-between. This time, Cedric was certain beyond a doubt that he had died.

His eyes flew open. He blinked against the blinding brightness of the world, ribbons of gold and silver flashing in his vision. His heart beat a slow, steady rhythm beneath his ribs. And there she was, trembling hands pressed to his chest, her face hovering above him, eyes wide and wet with tears and disbelief.

"Elyria." Her name broke from his lips like a prayer.

She didn't move. For a second, Cedric wondered if this was a dream—a single moment, frozen, for him to remember. His final gift before passing into the Hereafter. Then, without a word, Elyria pulled him into an embrace, her arms snaking around his waist, locking behind him.

Real.

She was real.

And he was back.

He coughed, clearing the lingering stain of death from his voice. "We must stop meeting like this. Eventually, you'll have to stop saving me," he murmured.

Elyria's laugh was broken, choked with relief as she lifted her head just enough to look him in the eye. "No," she said, a trembling smile pulling at the corners of her mouth. "No, I don't think I will."

Cedric wrapped his arms around her, drawing her back into place, her face cradled where his neck and shoulder met. He pressed a soft kiss to her forehead, holding her as tightly as his recovering strength allowed, the feel of her grounding him, knotting that tether in his chest, binding him to the here, the now.

The last time he'd touched her like this, it had been a goodbye.

For several long moments, neither of them said a word. They simply sat there, tangled in each other, taking in breath after breath. And finally, not because he wanted to, but because he had to, he looked down.

Cedric's brow furrowed as he peered at the place where he'd pierced his own heart. There was a hole in his tunic where the jewel-hilted dagger should still be embedded in his chest, but that was all. No scar. No blood. No pain. All he felt now was that smolder of his inner flame, its embers crackling back to life.

"How?" he asked. "I died. I should be dead. I *was* dead."

"I know," Elyria whispered. "I felt you go." She unhooked her hands from his waist, and it was only then that Cedric noticed she had something clutched in one of them. Static sparked in the spot where the pointed spires of the crown grazed against his tunic as she drew it up to show him. "I guess even half of a celestial-forged crown was enough to pull you back from the brink."

Well past the brink, Cedric thought with a shudder, before her words registered. "Half?"

Elyria sat back on her ankles, holding the half-crown in her lap, and Cedric saw the places on either side where the crescent of gold was broken, its edges jagged and sharp.

"Yes, half." A chorus of voices rang out behind them, and Cedric turned to look over his shoulder at the white-robed celestial standing there. Aurelia's gaze was fixed on the two of them, the galaxies on her skin swirling, churning—agitated. "And though I delight in seeing you breathing once more, Cedric Thorne, this should not have been possible."

"What do you mean?" Elyria asked, her tone guarded, hackles raised. Like she was afraid Aurelia would take him from her. The thought made the corners of Cedric's eyes prick.

Aurelia looked truly baffled, her brows drawn together tightly over her star-filled eyes. Cedric had a difficult time reconciling the thoroughly *human* expression with the celestial's otherwise otherworldliness.

"I do not know," Aurelia said, her layered voice strained, like it pained her to admit as much. "I cannot explain how you are alive."

Elyria stood, helping Cedric to his feet before turning to face the celestial. "The crown has done this before."

Cedric's gaze flicked between Elyria's face and the half-crown, the faintest buzz of power pulling him toward both in equal measure. It took a moment for her words to sink in. Who else had the crown brought back to life?

"A miracle never before seen and never since replicated," stated Aurelia. "As well as a moot point. None of my siblings nor I predicted what would happen when Daephinia's power split the crown, but the Shattering is long since past. And with only half of it here, half its power held, I am at a loss for how this"—she gestured to Cedric—"is possible."

Not particularly caring for being spoken about as if he were not present, Cedric cleared his throat. "It's been nearly two centuries since you and your siblings created the Arcane Crucible, since you locked this piece of the crown away in your Sanctum. You have admitted twice now that there are things beyond the knowledge of even your celestial family. Is it truly so impossible to think that the crown—even just half of it, as you say—might have been changed by this place?"

"He has a point," said Elyria.

"High praise," responded Cedric, and humor sparked in those green eyes.

"It makes a certain sort of sense, don't you think? The blood of many lost lives poured from the dagger after the"—Elyria glanced at Cedric, her jaw tight, her eyes no longer sparkling—"sacrifice was made. Is there a chance that the magic of all those lost within these walls went to the crown?"

Aurelia pursed her star-kissed lips, seeming to contemplate this. "It is . . . possible," she conceded after a few moments. "And I would confer with my siblings to determine as much but, alas, I remain unable to do so."

"Answers would be nice," Elyria said, inspecting the piece of the crown in her hands like it was the first time she was really looking at it. "But either way, it seems as though whatever magic this thing may or may not have been holding on to has been spent. Feels empty. Sorry about that."

She tossed the crown up in the air, let it spin, and then caught it between her nimble fingers. Cedric could've sworn he saw Aurelia flinch. He also knew that Elyria wasn't sorry at all, and the thought had the fire in his chest flaring with an absolutely inappropriate sense of pride.

"Wait, why are you unable to confer with your siblings?" Cedric asked, eyes darting back to the celestial.

"Oh, right. You were dead during that part," Elyria said, the solemnity in her eyes belying the flippancy of her tone. "Evidently, despite our conquering of the Crucible, our fair Arbiter here is not yet free. She needs the crown to be united in order to escape from this place."

Aurelia nodded. *"A shattered crown shall be united, a sundered land re—"*

"Yes, yes, we get it," Elyria interrupted. She was acting more and more like her old self with each passing moment, and Cedric couldn't have been more thrilled to see it. "Until the One True Crown is claimed, blah, blah, blah. No freedom for you, no filling the Chasms for us. We understand."

"All right then," said Cedric, suppressing the laugh that threatened to bubble up from his gut. "If this is but one half of the crown, dare I ask what happened to the other?"

With a sigh, Aurelia made a sweeping gesture with both arms. "If only I knew. It was given to the mixedborn princess."

Cedric frowned. "Princess Selenae? But Daephinia's daughter was killed in the same assassination attempt that took the king's life. You must be mistaken."

"I am not." The chorus of Aurelia's voice took on a dark quality. "Do not take my admission of lacking total omniscience to mean I do not know the truths of this world, boy."

Shame burned in Cedric's cheeks. Perhaps he was letting Elyria rub off on him. He'd forgotten that, for all her faults and mistakes, even if her power was diminished, he was still in the presence of a celestial. The Guardian of Balance. One of the Five. A goddess of starlight and ruin.

"But surely if Selenae had survived, the queen would not have sundered the realm as she did," Elyria said, voice sharp. She clearly had no such qualms about continuing to disrespect the star god before them. "I do not understand."

Aurelia's eyes narrowed. "The queen believed her daughter had been killed, yes."

Elyria and Cedric waited for her to continue.

The celestial's cosmic gaze softened, a brief flash of something like regret passing across her starlit face. "Malakar's purpose in enacting the Great Betrayal was to wipe out the royal family so he could take control of the crown. His strike against his king was as swift as it was brutal. And in the chaos that followed, the princess could not be found. The destruction had been so great, you see. It was easy to think that Selenae, no more than eighteen winters old—"

"Meaning she was just a child," Elyria said to Cedric. He nodded, suppressing the shiver that ran across his skin as she whispered her explanation in his ear. His knowledge of mixedborns was limited, to be sure, but he was aware that they fell somewhere between their two heritages when it came to their growth. Meaning Selenae could have been the equivalent human age of anywhere from six to sixteen, depending on how much she took after her mother.

A child either way.

"—had perished alongside her father," Aurelia finished. "And yes, she would have been but a child. A mix of her mother's fae blood and her father's humanity, Selenae was to be the embodiment of the peoples of Arcanis coming together as one. Born to rule over a united Arcanis." She paused. "A balanced Arcanis. But that dream died when her father did, buried like so many things, under the weight of Queen Daephinia's grief."

A heavy ball of guilt settled in his stomach, and he tried not to think of what he knew happened to mixedborn children in Havensreach.

Elyria sucked in a breath. "So, if Selenae didn't die alongside the king, then . . ."

"She was taken from the castle. Spirited away by one charged with her protection, a well-meaning soul who thought to save her from the fate that befell her father. Who knew how far Malakar would go to wipe out the one for whom the crown had been forged? Better to let him—let everyone—think she was dead. Only . . ."

"Only the queen's grief was too great," Elyria said. "Her actions too severe. And by the time it might have been revealed that her daughter was still alive, Daephinia had already ripped Arcanis apart."

"Why would whoever took Selenae not reveal the truth to the queen?" Cedric asked, aghast. To think that this all might have been avoided had Daephinia only known the truth.

"The one who took her likely believed it necessary to keep her safe." Aurelia drew a slow breath. "Surely, they feared what would happen if Malakar got his hands on her. Perhaps they meant to return the princess to her mother after Malakar's defeat. But they could not have foreseen how deep the queen's grief would run. Could not have imagined the madness of her actions."

Elyria's jaw flexed. "So, all of this—the war, the breaking of the world, the Chasms—was because of a single random person's choice? Because someone thought hiding the princess would protect her?"

"Nothing is so simple as to come down to one singular choice, least of all an event so monumental it echoes through the annals of time. The princess's caretaker chose to hide her away, just as Malakar chose to enact his villainous plan, just as Daephinia chose to wield her terrible grief."

Elyria snorted, her hand tightening around the fragmented crown she still held. "Grief. As if that is an excuse to rage upon an entire realm. We *all* grieve."

Cedric thought he saw her eyes flick to him once more, but it was too fast to be sure.

"Then you should know better than most how grief can make monsters of us all," Aurelia said, another flash of that almost-human sadness touching her features.

Silence fell over the three of them for several moments before Cedric asked, "So the other half of the crown was given to Selenae?"

Aurelia nodded once more.

"And where is she now? Why has she not come forward? Why have we not heard a single thing about her in all these years?"

"You ask the right questions, but I'm afraid I do not have the answers."

Elyria shifted on her feet, her shoulders raised, eyes darting to the amphitheater stairs as if reminding herself where the exit was. "If there's another piece of the crown out there, how do we know Varyth Malchior hasn't already gotten his hands on it? How many people know about this?"

"None that I know of," said Aurelia.

"Wonderful. Very reassuring." Elyria scoffed. "How *would* you know? You've been trapped in here this whole time."

Cedric inwardly braced for some sort of cosmic retribution to befall Elyria for her blasphemous attitude, but Aurelia just sighed. The celestial seemed . . . tired.

"The princess was well hidden," Aurelia said. "I do not think anyone could have—"

"Yet somehow you expect us to find her? Find the other half of the crown, reunite it, heal the land, *bring the dawn*?" Elyria hissed the last words.

Another multi-tonal sigh rent the air, and Cedric put a hand on Elyria's back in a feeble attempt to calm her. He'd half expected her to whirl on him and smack his hand away, but she just leaned into it with a deep sigh of her own. Like she was exhaling a breath she'd been holding for a long while.

"One piece will lead you to the other," Aurelia said, her voice placid and peaceful once more as she cast a pointed look at the crown piece clutched in Elyria's hand. The swirling stars on her skin stilled, as though Elyria's faltering anger had reset the celestial's mood as well. "I suggest you take it one step at a time, starting with leaving this place."

Her white robes billowed behind her as she turned and began walking. "Come, victors," she beckoned. "I may not yet leave this place, but you have earned your freedom from the Sanctum. The others await. It is time for you to go home."

CHAPTER 56
THE PRICE OF VICTORY

Elyria

Like before, Aurelia ushered Elyria and Cedric into that winding stone corridor, then disappeared, leaving them to make the return trip alone. Unlike before, the journey back to the Sanctum's antechamber seemed to take no time at all, possibly due to the fact that Elyria had all but sprinted the entire length of it.

She couldn't stomach the idea of another leisurely stroll back to the Sanctum—not with their escape from this place finally so close, not without knowing how Kit had been faring since the final trial began. Elyria needed to keep her focus on what was right in front of her.

She dared a quick look over her shoulder. Cedric jogged behind her, his face the epitome of inscrutability. She hated that she couldn't tell what he was thinking.

She was such a hypocrite. Here she was, doing everything she could to keep herself from ruminating on all that had happened during the final trial—the choice they'd been forced into, his heartbreaking decision, the dizzying relief that came with bringing him back, and, of course, that kiss. Yet she couldn't stop thinking about how *he* felt.

Did he regret it? she wondered. He'd known he was about to die. She couldn't blame him for wanting to grasp on to one last piece of life with his final moments. Even though the idea of that being all it was made Elyria's stomach clench painfully.

Right. Forward thinking. Kit. Getting out of here. Those were the things that mattered, the things that were important. Not to mention, they still had to figure out whatever in all four hells they were going to do about the other half of the crown being somewhere out there.

Elyria's knees nearly buckled the second she stepped foot back in the chamber. Kit was upright, conscious, and appeared to be in the middle of a rather animated conversation with Thraigg. Elyria could see the edges of the red-stained bandage under Kit's billowing blouse, noted the ashen look on her face, the lingering sweat still dampening her forehead. But she was awake, and she was *alive*. The sight of it lifted almost all the remaining weight that had been pressing on Elyria's shoulders these past twenty-five years.

"You're back!" Zephyr stood abruptly from a different table, shock written across her green face. As she approached, Elyria noticed the pallor of her skin, the anxious furrow of her brow. It was as though the sylvan was sick with stress. Guilt zipped through Elyria—she could only imagine the toll that all the healing Zephyr had provided the other champions had taken.

Elyria glanced at the crown in her hand. They were nearly done. At last, Zephyr could get the rest she very much deserved—that they all deserved.

Wringing her hands as she approached them, Zephyr's forest-green gaze flicked from Elyria to Cedric to the door behind them, which closed with an audible finality as soon as the knight stepped through it. Her eyes widened as they landed on the crown. "Is that—"

"Yes," Elyria said, vanishing her wings with a small sweep of magic. "The Crown of Concord, at your service. Well, half of it, anyway."

"Half?" Zephyr asked, her voice shaky. "It's only half?"

Elyria frowned. "Unfortunately, yes. The other half is out there somewhere and must be retrieved before the crown's power will be complete. But the good news is that this"—she shook the crown in the air—"is supposedly enough to get us out of here."

"Is it really?" Kit's typically boisterous voice was somewhat subdued as she stretched in her seat to get a better look, but to hear it at all was a song in Elyria's ears.

"So said the Arbiter. Said *Aurelia*." Elyria strode over and placed a gentle hand on Kit's shoulder. Her eyes burned as she breathed, "Welcome back."

"Never left," Kit said, running her eyes over her friend. Relief flashed across her face as she took in Elyria's lack of visible injuries. Then her expression settled into one of melancholy. She knew.

Of course she knew. What had Elyria expected, that they wouldn't tell Kit what happened to her? What had happened to her brother? What Elyria had done?

Like she could read Elyria's mind, Kit's voice was soft when she said, "Thank you, Ellie."

Elyria let her hand drop. "Don't thank me."

"You saved my life. Saved us all."

"I killed him." The truth of that was a sharp blade, cutting the breath from Elyria's lungs. Evander may have become a monster, but he was still Kit's brother. If Kit had been awake to witness it, would she truly be so willing to forgive?

Kit sucked in a deep breath. "He was already lost. You told me as much, back in the camp. I didn't want to hear you." She looked up, a tear glistening at the edge of her green eye. "I didn't want to see it. Didn't want to see the truth of him."

"None of us saw what he did coming," Thraigg said, leaning over the table to pat Kit's other hand. "There's no blame to be dealt here, lass."

Elyria shook her head. *Oh, there was someone to blame*, she thought. *Just not anybody here.* Rage scalded her throat as she held back the curses she wanted to hurl at Varyth Malchior. He was behind so much of what had gone wrong. Because of him, Evander had cost Leona and, indirectly, Belien, their lives. He'd nearly killed Kit, nearly killed them all.

In fact, without his dark magic twisting Evander in the first place, Elyria and Kit would surely never have received those visions of him. Would not have attempted the Crucible at all. Would still be—

Would still be drowning her sorrows under Artie's judgmental eye. Would still be filling her days with songs and her nights with strangers. Would still be estranged from Kit, would never have this closure, would never have met . . .

Her gaze found Cedric lingering by the closed door they'd come through. Zephyr shifted anxiously on her feet, looking him over, checking him for injuries, her eyes lingering on the hole in his tunic where the dagger had gone in. A strange mix of guilt and relief kept flickering across Zephyr's face, and Elyria couldn't quite figure out why. Perhaps despite her distinct encouragement to do so, the sylvan felt bad that Cedric and Elyria had been forced to take on the final trial alone. Perhaps this was just her strange way of showing she cared.

To his credit, Cedric hardly seemed to notice Zephyr's fussing. Over her head, his gold-ringed eyes met Elyria's, and the intensity of his stare had her breath catching in her throat. It was like he could see the emotions battling in her mind—relief and rage and rapture and restlessness all overlapping, all fighting for dominance.

Kit took Elyria's hand, drawing her attention back. A pang of guilt rang through her as she realized Kit had started speaking again and Elyria hadn't been listening.

"But I hear you now"—Kit hooked their little fingers together, just like they often used to—"and I'm so grateful. You gave him the peace I sought for him, in the end." She took a deep breath. "I never thanked you properly for coming in here with me in the first place, and I almost didn't get the chance to. So, let me say it now. *Thank you*. You are the reason we all survived this long." She inclined her head at the crown. "And you're the reason we're going to get out of here."

Elyria swallowed hard, resisting the urge to look at Cedric again. He was the one who'd made the necessary choice, had paid the price to grant them their freedom from this place. But she didn't know how to begin explaining that. So, she said nothing, simply nodded and gave Kit a tight-lipped smile.

"So . . . the Trial of Concord," Kit said after a few moments of awkward silence, disentangling their little fingers. "What happened? How did you end up with half a crown? What did the final trial entail?" She extended a long brown finger to poke one of the crown's sharp golden spires.

Elyria watched with rapt curiosity, wondering if she would feel a spark of that tremendous power that had seized Elyria when she first touched it. But Kit had barely any reaction. The corners of her lips turned down slightly, perhaps, but that was all. Elyria noted that the crown still held that feeling of being, well, not powerless, not exactly. But dormant. Whatever awe-inspiring celestial power had flooded into Cedric to bring him back had indeed been expended. It was just a pretty piece of royal jewelry for now.

"That is a rather long story, best left for another time, I think," Cedric said, giving Zephyr an affectionate squeeze on the shoulder before stepping around her. "I think we are all more than ready to leave this place. I pray you will not take this the wrong way, but you still look like you could use a trip to the healer, posthaste."

Kit snorted—a half-indignant, half-amused sound—but didn't protest. She did still look pale, weak. Like just having this conversation required a great deal of effort. The thought made Elyria antsy. What were they waiting for? They needed to *leave*.

"Speaking of which . . ." Nox's voice came from a shadow to Elyria's left, dulcet and calm, though the unexpectedness of it still made her jump. In her rush to get back, the relief of seeing Kit, she hadn't even realized the nocterrian wasn't present. "Did Aurelia happen to say anything about *how* we would be able to leave this place?"

"Oh, yes." Elyria placed a hand on her hip. "She wrote down instructions, in fact. Numbered them. She was absolutely, one-hundred-percent crystal clear and not cryptic or ambiguous at all."

Nox did not appear amused. "How do you know we are truly done here, then?" they asked. "I might have expected a bit more fanfare to accompany the Arcane Crucible finally being conquered. Part of a crown and your reports that 'we won' hardly inspire much confidence."

Elyria held up the crown in her hand. "What she *did* say was clear enough. She told us we earned our freedom from the Sanctum, and it was time to return home."

She felt a sudden warmth seep into her side as Cedric came up beside her, his hand brushing hers for the briefest of moments.

"Indeed, she did. So, any ideas, Elle?" he asked.

She inwardly scowled at the fluttering in her stomach caused by his casual use of her nickname, though her annoyance at her body's traitorous reaction was quickly replaced by a sinking feeling.

"Make it count, Elle." That was the last thing he'd said to her before he died. Had she? If they didn't reunite this slumbering piece of the crown with its other half, if they couldn't seal the Chasms and help bridge the literal divide between the peoples of Arcanis, would any of it count? With Malchior out there, scheming, plotting, would any of this matter?

She thought of Gael, of Cyren, of Paelin and all the rest. She thought of Evander. She thought of the terrible *what-if* that was Cedric. How easily he could still be counted among those who gave their lives and ambitions to this dreaded place.

Elyria bit her lip a little too hard, hoping the pain would help her focus. If she did want to make their lives count, they had to get out of here. And, of course, it couldn't be as simple as Aurelia having actually told them what to do.

She scanned the antechamber, took in the scattered tables and benches, the pillows and pitchers. Crown still in hand, she walked over to the wall of doors and tried a few handles. None of them glowed. None of them led anywhere special at all. They opened up into bedchambers and bathing rooms, as they always had between trials. Finally, her gaze landed on the empty wall opposite the doors, where the archway from which they'd entered the antechamber after the first trial had been.

There was something about the blank expanse, the layers of stacked gray stone. There was nothing to indicate there was, or had ever been, an archway or gate there. But as Elyria wandered closer, crown still in hand, it suddenly felt like she was being pulled toward it. When she was only a few feet away, the stone started to shimmer with an all-too-familiar silvery light. Before long, a glowing archway stood before them.

A Gate.

A way out.

Through it, Elyria could see the vague outline of the grand hall of

Castle Lumin stretching before her. More importantly, she could *hear* it—the cacophony of cheers and raucous chants coming from the cavernous room. The voices were muted somewhat by distance and whatever magic lay within the Gate, keeping the Sanctum separate from the real world, but they were there.

"You wanted fanfare," she called over her shoulder to Nox. "I think we're about to get it."

The nocterrian made a noise that sounded somewhat like a *harrumph* but said nothing else. Elyria heard stirrings behind her, the sounds of chairs scraping and hushed encouragement as Thraigg helped Kit to her feet.

"They're all still here," Cedric murmured, stepping next to Elyria.

They were. Blurred and indistinct as her vision through the Gate was, Elyria could see dozens of spectators lining the walls of the hall. Whether thanks to some ancient magic woven into the rules of this tedious contest, or by Aurelia's hand, the people already knew the Crucible had been conquered. They thought the crown had finally been won.

Elyria wasn't sure what that meant for what was to come next.

"Well, Sir Victor, your adoring legions await." She took his hand and placed the crown in it.

"*Our* adoring legions," he corrected with a grin, closing his fingers over hers just as she tried to pull back—keeping her hand, along with the crown, firmly clasped in his.

Elyria tensed, a spark running up her arm, the shadows in her chest stirring. She wanted to lace her fingers with his, to exit this cruel and fantastical place hand in hand.

"Tested in the fires of trust, bound by something deeper than ambition. You have emerged, both of you champions, both of you victors."

It was a strange thing, standing here on the threshold of freedom, this new precipice. In some ways, it felt like this was the true test of that bond. Because while they had fought beasts of tooth and claw, they had burned and bled and *lost* in here . . . they had done so together.

"Are you ready?" Cedric asked.

She wasn't. The moment they stepped through that Gate and back into the real world, this—whatever *this* was—would be over. There was so much still unknown. So many questions. Elyria wasn't ready for them to go back to their separate sides of the continent, for their peoples to once again be at odds.

What *did* this mean for their peoples? *Both of you champions, both of you victors*, Aurelia said. Did that mean something? Would the king—the kings, both of them—honor that fact? Would they even believe them?

The promised power of the crown was no longer on the table. Neither side would claim that celestial might, would be able to wield it against the other—Elyria would make sure of it. Was there a chance that could possibly mean the start of something like . . . peace?

She shook her head. For all their talk of working together to seal the Chasms, of healing the land, and of *after*, Elyria and Cedric had not discussed what that might actually look like. It had seemed simple at the time. Now it seemed to grow more impossible the longer she stared at the Gate.

They needed to hunt down the other half of the crown. They needed to ensure Varyth Malchior stayed as far away as possible. They needed to plan and strategize, and they needed time together to do all of that.

Together.

The word stuttered in Elyria's mind, reality starting to fray the edges of the hope that had been building against her will. There was no *together* once they left the Sanctum. She and Cedric had two wholly separate, wholly disparate *afters* waiting for them.

Her cheeks heated at the foolishness of longing for anything different. She started to gather the mess of emotions churning in her chest, tying them in knots, digging a hole deep inside herself where she could bury them.

At the gentle squeeze of her hand, Elyria turned to find Cedric looking right at her. Something like determination and maybe even a hint of longing was sketched into the strong set of his brow, the clench of his jaw.

"Find the other half," he said, finally releasing her hand and leaving the crown piece in her open palm.

She immediately felt the absence of him, the heat of his touch fading. It felt . . . final.

"Unite the crown, seal the Chasms. Finish what we started."

"And you?" Elyria banished the tremble she could feel in her chest from showing in her voice. "What will you do?"

"I will make sure Varyth Malchior never gets his hands on it. I will ensure he pays for everything he did here." Conviction. Confidence.

Elyria's heart simultaneously swelled and deflated. A bittersweet taste coated her tongue. She didn't know how he hoped to accomplish that, but she supposed if anyone was in a position to hunt a mad sorcerer through the human realm, it might just be him.

Cedric smiled—small, sad, but capped with the barest hint of hope. Like maybe, just maybe, this didn't have to be goodbye forever.

She hoped it wasn't.

She wanted to believe it wasn't.

Needed to believe it wasn't.

Even if she knew it was. Knew they'd always been playing this game from different sides of the board. And nothing that occurred between the two of them really mattered outside the confines of the Sanctum.

Even if it mattered to her.

She dug deeper.

Leaning on Thraigg, Kit finally came up beside Elyria. Zephyr shuffled up next to Cedric on his other side, Nox lingering a few paces behind the line of champions. Former champions. Survivors and victors, all—in Elyria's eyes, at least.

Her fingers closed around the half of the crown.

And she stepped through the Gate.

CHAPTER 57
A FINAL BLOW

Cedric

The roar of the crowd was deafening. Cheers and cries echoed through the grand hall, surrounding Cedric, coating him in their elation.

Elyria was but two paces ahead of him, seemingly frozen in place by the exaltation bearing down on them. He turned to see Kit, Thraigg, Nox, and Zephyr step through behind him, a similar kind of shock halting their movement.

He would have thought it out of place, the sheer amount of celebration happening in the remains of the Lost City . . . were that what they had returned to. But Cedric hardly recognized Castle Lumin. Gone were the dust-soaked carpets, the crumbling frescoes, the chipped stone. Billowing banners hung along the walls—the emblems of Havensreach and Nyrundelle embroidered in silver thread on each alternating flag.

Lit sconces made of crystal and glass cast shimmering light across a polished marble floor.

This wasn't the same rotted place Cedric had left behind when the Arbiter bound him to the Sanctum. It was made anew, as if conquering the Crucible had reawakened Luminaria's former glory. As if, in coming back through the Gate, he had stepped backward in time.

Cedric looked around the room, at the faces of the spectators—humans and Arcanians both, intermixed—welcoming them home. Most faces were beaming—bright, shining with happy tears. But some were . . . distressed. Chins quivered, eyes were frantic as they strained to see past the six of them, looking for *their* champion. And that's when Cedric noticed the layer of sad sound weaving in between the happy chatter in the room. His stomach clenched at the sight of a fae woman with short-cropped cobalt hair quietly sobbing off to one side.

Light swelled at Cedric's back, the Gate pulsing with shades of silver and pink and purple and green. A white-robed figure stepped through, and the light vanished. The Gate closed. Her hood was drawn low, her celestial features hidden beneath swaths of thick white fabric as Aurelia's voice—the Arbiter's voice, to everyone else present—rang out, an infinite chorus. "Your champions return!"

There was another surge of cheers from the gathered crowd before they fell into reverent silence, their collective breath held in awe. Cedric stumbled forward another couple of steps until he was at Elyria's side. He shot her a nervous glance, but she wasn't looking at him. Her focus was wholly on Aurelia as the celestial continued, her many voices carrying across the hall like the toll of a bell.

"Behold your victors, people of Arcanis. Forged by the trials of the Arcane Crucible. They have fought. Have suffered. Have sacrificed. And have emerged victorious. Elyria Lightbreaker and Cedric Thorne have conquered the Crucible."

A whoop pierced the quiet. Heart thudding, Cedric's eyes shot to a trio of men standing together at the far end of the hall. Hargrave leaned against a pillar, a grin on his gruff face, dark hair pulled back. Next to him, Thibault shifted uncomfortably as he eyed the Arcanians surrounding him, but when his gaze caught Cedric's, he lit up with admiration.

It was the third man, though, that had Cedric's full attention. Not the cool, judgmental visage of Lord Leviathan Church like he'd expected, but a far friendlier face. One Cedric hadn't realized how much he missed until this very moment.

Tristan's smile stretched across his face, the scar under his left eye curving up toward twinkling blue eyes. Pride burst from him, palpable even from where Cedric stood, and the back of Cedric's throat felt suddenly tight.

He came.

Even knowing how slim the chance was that Cedric would return, he still came.

Any disappointment at not seeing Lord Church among those waiting for him vanished. And if he was being honest with himself, Cedric wasn't sure he *was* disappointed. Something far more akin to relief spread through him, mixing with that ever-present simmer in the center of his chest. He did not begrudge the extra time to prepare, to sort through his thoughts and untangle his feelings before he would have to report to his benefactor on all that had occurred within the Sanctum. Cedric wasn't sure how much he wanted to tell him—how much he *would* tell him. There was, after all, still so much Cedric didn't understand about himself.

He gave Tristan a slow, grateful nod, then turned his attention back to Aurelia before that prickling tightness in his throat gave way to something more embarrassing. He was still very much on display, after all.

"See those who have conquered the Arcane Crucible, those who walk the path of unity rather than division," Aurelia said. "Those who have proven themselves worthy of a crown."

"But whose crown is it?" came a voice from the crowd. Cedric couldn't tell who it belonged to, but the question was only the first in a tidal wave of queries and calls suddenly barraging them.

"Which of them won?"

"Surely it cannot be both!"

"Does Havensreach or does Nyrundelle claim its power?"

Their fervor finally stirred Elyria from her frozen state. An odd expression on her face, she stared at the crown in her hand, tightening her hold around it. Cedric felt the presence of the other champions drawing closer behind the two of them, as if preparing for the crowd to rush them, for a mob to form.

They needn't have worried. Aurelia raised both hands, and a pulse of power spread over the crowd. They quieted again, compelled to listen. "The crown belongs to no one."

Some of the spectators exchanged sidelong glances, Hargrave and Thibault included, but their fervor did not climb out of control again.

"Not yet," Aurelia continued. "The Crucible has been conquered, but the power of the Crown of Concord has not yet been claimed. And it shall remain as such, until—"

Several things happened at once.

A blur of forest green darted into Cedric's field of vision.

A collective gasp echoed through the hall.

Elyria let out a sharp cry as she staggered back, colliding with Nox. She clutched one hand in the other, red blood dripping down the side of her palm.

Her empty palm.

And Zephyr now stood several feet in front of Cedric, the dagger she'd once used to save his life clutched in one hand, the crown in the other.

Anguish was stamped on every plane of her delicate face as she looked at Cedric with pleading green eyes. "I'm sorry," she said, her voice shaking. "I'm so sorry."

She took a step back. Cedric took a step forward. "Why?" His voice cracked on the word.

"The crown does belong to someone," she said. "And I have no choice but to bring it to him. He didn't give me a choice."

Cedric reached for her, but she was fast—so, so fast. Not weak, not frail, not spent, like he'd thought. No, that ashen quality, the nerves, the jumpiness he'd picked up on in the Sanctum wasn't due to her waning magic. It was because of her *guilt*.

"No!" shouted Aurelia, her layered voice sharp with ancient power. Her hand shot from beneath her robes, a galaxy of color swirling over her skin, an orb of magic forming in her hand. A godly strike meant to stop the sylvan from absconding with their hard-fought prize.

But Zephyr still was faster. With a flash of green light, her body was suddenly shimmering, shifting, shrinking—changing. Wings burst from her back. Sage-green skin gave way to viridian feathers. And suddenly it was not a sylvan standing before Cedric, but an eagle flying away from him, half of the Crown of Concord clutched in her talons.

Shapeshifter.

Changeling.

Aurelia's blast missed Zephyr by inches, ricocheting off the far wall and dispersing over the spectators with such force that most were knocked to the ground.

Cedric's head spun as Zephyr soared over the stunned crowd, a shriek tearing from her avian throat as she soared through the castle doors and out of sight.

"He didn't give me a choice."

Who was *he*? Varyth Malchior? Pieces of Cedric and Zephyr's time in the Sanctum knit together in his reeling mind, a quilt woven from each moment that informed her betrayal. He was suddenly examining every interaction they'd had since the moment he saved her from the gnarlings.

His thoughts stuttered. Had even that been manufactured? Her screams of terror, the gushing wound on her leg? Cedric stared at the spot where the eagle had disappeared, an image clawing at him. The green-tinged hide of the beast that had clawed Dissidua Pyr to death. He'd thought it a trick of the light, the reflection of the aurora overhead. He recalled the howl of pain as his sword sliced into the creature. Into its *leg*.

It was her.

She'd been playing Cedric from the *instant* he entered the Crucible, watching him, waiting for him. She killed Dissidua. Used the very injury Cedric had unknowingly given her to play on his sympathies. And he fell for her entire act. He had taken every shy smile he coaxed from her at face value. The *hurt* she'd exuded after his attempt to ally with the other human champions. Every anxious look, all that nervous wringing of her hands. He'd thought them indications that she actually cared about his well-being. Cared for *him*. That they were allies.

Worse, that they were friends.

Through sacrifice, darkness, and friendship betrayed.

Not once had he thought she was using him as a means to an end, pushing him to conquer the Crucible so that there would be a crown for her to steal. Had she known what the price of gaining said crown was when she propelled him toward it? Known that either he or Elyria would have to die in order to claim the final prize?

"It has to be you two . . . Take this to the end. For all of us."

Of course she knew. Surely, if she was working under Varyth's command, she knew *exactly* what to expect all along. He thought of her shock at seeing the pair of them reemerge after the final trial. Her utter disbelief.

She hadn't failed to fully heal Kit, Thraigg, and Nox after the battle with Evander because her magic was spent. She'd done it to keep them weak. To prevent them from being able to overpower her when the moment inevitably came for her to strike. For her to play her final hand.

Cedric turned, heat building in every stomp of his boots as he returned to the other champions by the Gate. Thraigg was still supporting a flagging Kit, both wearing identical expressions of appalled astonishment. Even Nox's typically unflappable face was scrunched with contemplation, as if they didn't understand what just happened.

Elyria clutched her injured hand tightly in the other, pressing the hem of her blouse upon it to stem the bleeding. Rage flared in Cedric's chest at the sight, though the wound Zephyr had slashed into her skin in order to pry the crown loose didn't look deep.

One look at Elyria's stony expression might have convinced others she was fine. A flesh wound. Just a scratch. But the pain in her eyes belied her stoicism. It mirrored the betrayal Cedric was sure shone in his own.

"We have to go after her," Elyria shouted. Shouted, because the stunned silence that had befallen the crowd was quickly fading, another wave of uncertainty taking over.

"What is this?"

"Arcanian traitors! They've stolen the crown!"

"You saw the way she exchanged words with the human victor. She's working for them!"

Another pulse of celestial power from Aurelia had their cries trapped in their throats, though the most vocal among them looked decidedly displeased about it. Cedric could see the restlessness in the eyes of those still present, the doubt creeping into their expressions as they exchanged wary glances. The celebration was over. Many spectators turned on their heels and stormed out of the hall, the start of an exodus that Cedric hoped wasn't a mistake. Who knew what tales and rumors would be spun from what they witnessed here.

"She is long gone already, I fear," said Aurelia, a simmering rage in her many voices that made the hair on the back of Cedric's neck stand on end. He understood her fury. Without their half of the crown, they had no way to find the other piece. And very soon, Varyth Malchior would.

A knot formed in Cedric's throat. "What do we do now?"

"We can't just let her get away," Kit said, voice weak. Cedric's blood burned at the sight of her, still feeble, still hurting. The knowledge that Zephyr had purposefully let her suffer like this stoked the furnace inside him.

"She's a fucking bird," Thraigg said with a grunt, shifting his weight so that he could support Kit more fully. "And alas, we aren't the ones who can fly, lass."

"I doubt you are in much of a state to do that either," Nox added.

Kit's answering nod was resigned. "Go, Ellie," she said. "Find her. Get it back. Without it, we can't—"

Elyria shook her head. "You need a healer. I stay with you."

"But—"

"I stay. With you." Her voice was resolute, her jaw tight, her muscles tense. Cedric knew there would be no changing her mind. He understood what she must have been thinking, that she had already left too much of Kit's health and recovery up to others. Relied on others, *trusted* others. Trusted Zephyr. She would not leave her again.

"Is there nothing you can do?" Elyria's head snapped to Aurelia, still standing a few paces away from the champions. "Can you trace the crown? Use your power to track her?"

Beneath her thick white robes, the celestial's shoulders sagged. "My domain is the Sanctum, not the world beyond," she said, her multitonal voice distant, detached. Like her focus—her very presence—was fading now that the Crucible was complete. "I cannot pursue her."

"Then tell us what to do." Cedric couldn't keep the panic from his voice. He jerked his eyes around the now mostly empty hall. Only Tristan, Hargrave, and Thibault, along with a handful of other observers, still loitered by the doors. The trio caught Cedric's eye, perhaps seeing the desperation in his gaze, and started moving toward him. "We don't know where she would be headed, where Varyth Malchior is. You must know *something*—"

Kit groaned, what little color remained leaching from her face. She needed that healer *now*.

Cedric turned to Elyria. "Go," he told her. "I will return to Havensreach. I'll need to explain everything that happened here to Lord Church, to . . . to the king. Perhaps they will know something of Varyth Malchior's movements, will have some information we can use to track them down." His voice was as solemn as he could make it when he added, "I will not let either of them get away with this."

A promise.

A vow.

Elyria's throat bobbed, reluctance written into every silver fleck in her eyes, but she nodded. "Try not to get yourself killed while I'm not around to save your ass, will you?"

Cedric huffed a laugh. "Wouldn't dream of it."

For a moment, they stood there, a silent understanding—a silent *farewell*—passing between them. Cedric wanted to reach for her, wanted to feel the grounding touch of her one final time. There was so much they'd never had the chance to talk about. So much they never would. Because the next thing he knew, Elyria was slinging Kit's other arm over her shoulder, and with one final meeting of emerald green and golden brown, she walked away.

"Sounds like you have *a lot* to catch me up on, Ric." Tristan's buoyant words had perhaps a touch of caution laced between them as he pulled Cedric into a quick embrace, rapping his fist three times on his back.

Cedric was surprised to feel the inner corners of his eyes pricking when Tristan released him.

"Seems like an understatement," Hargrave said, clapping Cedric on the shoulder.

"Should make for an entertaining trip home," Thibault added from a few feet away. The distance he maintained made Cedric realize that both Nox and Aurelia still lingered nearby.

"What will you do?" Cedric asked the nocterrian, who was tracking Elyria, Kit, and Thraigg's exit from the hall. It wasn't until they passed through the doorway and disappeared from sight that the nocterrian answered. It wasn't much of an answer at that.

"I'm afraid it's back to the shadows for me," they said, and with a final look at the vanishing form of Aurelia and no further explanation, they stepped into a shadow and disappeared.

The celestial had nearly faded, her white robes translucent. Through them, Cedric could see the Gate, no longer glowing, no longer beckoning. Sealed. Locked. Forever, he supposed.

And thank the stars for that, he thought.

"It is not over," she said, and once more, Cedric found himself doubting the star god's claim that she was not, in fact, omniscient. Sorrow filled every layer of her voice. "I fear it has only just begun. There is still much darkness ahead if we are to usher in a new dawn."

Cedric inhaled deeply. "As dawn brings a new day," he replied, citing the prophecy. But Aurelia was already gone, faded into the ether, swept back into her prison.

Tristan, Thibault, and Hargrave surrounded Cedric in a protective halo as they made their way to the end of the hall, navigating through the few spectators that lingered. They surged forward with their questions, requests, demands. Cedric did his best to answer what he could, to provide reassurance where he was able. And it wasn't until he passed through the city gates at the entrance to the Lost City—no longer lost—that he dug down deep inside himself, searching for the light at the end of that tether, still tied somewhere behind his ribs.

The Arcanian and human traveler camps were still assembled to his left and right as he exited Luminaria. Cedric let his gaze travel across each in turn, before turning his eyes to the horizon, where an unspoken promise held fast, stretching across the distance like a golden thread.

CHAPTER 58
RESOLUTION

Elyria
Eight weeks later

Aerithia had always been a little too bright for Elyria's liking. She stood on the balcony of her room at the Ravenswing estate, a cool coastal breeze lifting the ends of her loose hair as she stared out at the city. Her eyes roamed over the white stone streets, arched bridges, and gold-domed roofs of Nyrundelle's capital, gleaming under dusk's lavender sky. It all seemed too cultivated, a little too pristine. Too unlike the rest of the realm.

During the years Elyria spent living here with Evander and Kit, she'd never felt wholly like she fit in. Even now, with an air of cautious optimism palpable in the streets, rumors regarding the tenuous truce struck between King Lachlandris and King Callum in the wake of the

Crucible's completion whispered at every corner, Elyria still felt that deeply rooted sense of *unbelonging*.

True to his word, Cedric appeared to have told his noble lord the truth of what happened in the Sanctum. Of what they'd learned. That the Crucible had awarded only one part of the Crown of Concord, and that Varyth Malchior had been exerting his dark influence for too long. That Princess Selenae had not only escaped Malakar's wrath but might still be somewhere out there with the other half right now.

Lord Church told the human king, who, shockingly, believed the whole tale. Both kings did, in fact. Elyria learned from Kit's mother—the duchess—that Nyrundelle had been the first to extend the olive branch to the humans, willing to cede part of the Midlands for access to Havensreach's shores, that they might seek out Varyth and the Cult of Malakar.

Tensions were still heightened, the average citizens clearly waiting for the metaphorical boot to drop, but things were . . . changing. Reported skirmishes between Arcanians and humans in the Midlands were fewer and fewer, the last breath of a dying storm. The kingdoms had performed their first successful prisoner exchange since the Shattering. And though peace had descended upon Nyrundelle with all the pomp and circumstance of a sloppy coat of paint, it appeared that Aurelia's appeals to the value of unity had, in fact, had a foundation.

Ever the realist, Elyria suspected both sides had their own, very specific, very opposing, reasons for the agreement. Surely both kings had every intention of claiming both halves of the crown, and who knew how long this fragile peace would last once their location was discovered. All the more reason Elyria was determined to ensure she would be the one to discover it.

Her end goal had not changed. Celestial power did not belong in mortal hands. She would unite the crown and seal the Chasms, one way or another, and find a way to destroy it after. She would find Zephyr or find Varyth Malchior, possibly—hopefully—both.

And she would make them pay.

In the weeks that passed since returning from Luminaria with Kit, Elyria had plenty of time to pick apart her every interaction with Zephyr, her every defense of her. She recalled the reprimand she'd shoved down Cedric's throat after the first trial. Now, the thought of the sylvan Elyria had once protected, had *cared for*, working for the man who had ruined Evander and nearly taken Kit from this world left Elyria nauseated. She hadn't even been able to continue using the healing balm Zephyr had gifted Elyria for her scars, despite how well it worked.

The scars were somewhat faded now, an etched checkerboard of puckered pink skin that would always look slightly *off*, but not the grotesque tableau of pain they'd once been. It was enough. Elyria wore them like a badge of honor now—a testament to what she'd survived.

"Ellie?" One blue and one green eye peered out from a bronze face as Kit walked through the balcony doors, a breeze ruffling her shaggy moonlight hair. "Lost in thought again, are we?"

"Just wondering what a little bit of color might do to brighten up the stark streets of the city," Elyria said with a shrug. "Think your uncle would be open to it?"

Kit laughed. "I can have my mother float the idea to him, but I wouldn't hold my breath. The king likes what he likes."

"Don't we all." Elyria said it under her breath, though from the knowing look Kit was directing at her, she was certain she'd heard her.

An ever-present restlessness mixed with the nostalgia of being back in Kit's family home. Kit's recovery had been slower than Elyria would've liked, whether the result of whatever darkness had seeped into her through the injury made by Evander's darksteel blade, or . . . deeper wounds.

Sometimes, Elyria caught Kit staring at nothing, the light in her beautiful, mismatched eyes dimming, her hand going to her chest as if remembering the feel of that blade cutting through her. As if reliving the sting of that betrayal.

It was a feeling Elyria knew well, and it was clear the Crucible had left them all with scars that would never fade.

"Perhaps I'll attempt it anyway," Elyria said, eager to distance her thoughts from the dark feelings that arose whenever she thought about just how close Kit had come to death. She drew her hand to her chin and feigned contemplation. "Better to beg forgiveness than ask for permission, and I'm feeling . . . artistic." She grinned at Kit. "What do you say?

You whip up a few water orbs, I mix in a little paint, and we go to town. What's the king going to do about it?"

Kit shook her head, her expression settling somewhere between exasperated and entertained. "You may have the freedom to exercise your boredom in the form of vigilante art installations, but not all of us have that luxury. While the king might hesitate to throw the *Victor of Nyrundelle*"—Elyria shuddered at the reminder of her newest moniker, as if she didn't have enough of them already—"in prison, those same reservations hardly extend to me."

"You're his niece," Elyria deadpanned. "Somehow, I doubt that."

Kit skipped over to the balcony and placed a hand on the bone-white railing. The ease of her movement helped loosen some of the unrest in Elyria's soul—she was so, so much improved.

"Family's complicated," Kit said. "You know that better than most. Besides, don't tell me you've already forgotten what the wrath of Duchess Laeliana Ravenswing feels like. My mother's gratitude for you rescuing me has a limit *somewhere*, and in her overprotective current state, I doubt she would take too kindly to you riling up the king."

"Spoilsport." Elyria smothered the instinct to stick out her tongue. "Was there a particular reason you came here, aside from dashing my hopes for an entertaining evening?"

"You received another letter," Kit said, handing over a roll of parchment.

Elyria offered a wan smile as she pocketed the missive. "Artie again?" She'd long since given up on the stupid hope that she'd be receiving messages from anyone in Havensreach. She hated that she'd ever hoped at all.

Communication between kingdoms was reserved for the kings and their council. That was it. And even if Cedric had been able to figure out a way to communicate, why would he? They'd said their goodbyes before they left the Celestial Sanctum. This was what Elyria had prepared for before she even took that first step back through the Gate. She had taken her feelings about everything that happened between the two of them during the Trial of Concord—throughout the entire Crucible, if she was being honest—and had placed it in a neat little box, which she buried in the deepest part of herself. Deeper even than the knot of shadows curled in her chest.

A knot that had not loosened since she left the Lost City.

Kit nodded. "Sounds like your escapades in the Sanctum have made Tartanis's desire to speak with you swell to new heights. His men have been back to the Sweltering Pig several times over the past few weeks. Evidently, they haven't caused any trouble, but Artie recommends you continue keeping your distance from Coralith for now." She grinned. "He also offers his apologies that you will have to continue drinking, how did he put it, 'capital swill,' and says he'll endeavor to send a barrel of cider just for you at his earliest convenience."

Elyria's jaw went slack, her lips rounded in a perfect, shocked "oh." "What the fuck, Katerina? You read my letter?"

"Don't blame me; it fell open. Tell the dwarf to get better sealing wax. It's just as well, anyway. *Someone* had to start reading your messages." Kit cast a pointed look over her shoulder at the small pile of unopened letters sitting on a table just inside the room. Then, with a shrug and a final look that seemed to say more than Elyria was ready to hear, she waltzed off.

Elyria wandered the city streets with no particular destination in mind, as she did most nights. Now that Kit had recovered, Elyria wanted nothing more than to act with *purpose* again. She was antsy, aimless. Even the magic thrumming in her veins, knotted in her chest, felt foreign. Her shadows tugged at her, restless, as if drawn toward something always just out of sight and beyond her reach.

She wanted to fly straight across both Chasms and search every dark corner of every dingy tavern in Havensreach until she got a lead on Varyth Malchior's whereabouts. She wanted to hunt down members of the Cult of Malakar and put her woefully underutilized interrogation skills to use. She wanted to storm into Verdentia and demand that the sylvans help her figure out where Zephyr had gone.

But she couldn't do any of that. Not yet. Not without earning the true ire of the king and risking derailing his diplomatic efforts. She'd made her desires clear enough when she gave her report to King Lachlandris on what happened during the Arcane Crucible. She'd offered her platitudes and promises that she would find the crown for him, would win it back for Nyrundelle, so long as he allowed her to be among those seeking it.

In short, she lied.

It worked. He agreed. And then came the hardest part, the part she was the worst at—waiting.

Elyria had never been a patient woman. Had never dealt with boredom well. Unfortunately, the tried-and-true ways she used to kill time before she'd entered the Sanctum no longer held any appeal. She didn't want to spend her nights drinking and performing and fucking. She didn't particularly want to analyze *why* those things were of such little interest to her now, either.

And so, she walked.

Up and down the white stone streets.

Back and forth and back again, she walked.

She always waited until the quietest hours of the night, when fewer folks would be out, when she was less likely to be recognized. Alas, even with her wings under the constant cloak of her magic and a hood drawn tight over her periwinkle hair, inevitably, someone usually noticed her.

She still didn't like the attention, the stares that didn't bother to be subtle, the conversations that stalled the second she turned the corner. Admittedly, it felt different now. Not quite the same fear-filled apprehension she'd encountered as the Revenant. Rather, the Victor of Nyrundelle commanded adoration. Veneration.

She hated it just as much.

It made her feel just as alone.

Elyria turned her gaze inward, and though she told herself she shouldn't, though she knew better, she searched for that golden thread.

She didn't find it.

When Cedric died, the thread snapped. She felt it go limp, fade within her in the same moment he fell away. And whatever vestige of light had remained in him, that final flickering ember that she'd used to *tug* him back to life, she didn't think it was tied to her anymore.

Was it ever? she wondered.

She didn't know where it came from. Didn't know why from the instant she and Cedric set foot in the Sanctum they'd been drawn toward each other. Didn't know what it meant that she felt emptier now than ever before.

Or maybe she did know, but she wouldn't allow herself to dwell on it.

The palest rays of light were just starting to peek through the darkened sky as she returned to the estate. She was so lost in thought, so busy searching through the many shadowed layers of herself, that she didn't even notice the two figures lurking on the doorstep of the main house until she was almost upon them.

One was impossibly tall, a placid expression stretched over indigo skin, dawn's gray light highlighting the curved horns wrapping around either side of their head. The other was broad, squat, and only reached Elyria's chest, a massive hammer leaning against the wall at his side.

"Wh-what are you two doing here?" Genuine shock rang through Elyria's voice.

"Not a bad place ye've got here, Rev," Thraigg said, his gravelly voice familiar and warm.

"A bit ostentatious for my taste, but to each their own," added Nox.

Elyria arched a brow. "Uh, thanks?"

Nox grinned, flashing a hint of fang.

"Not that I'm not, um"—Elyria thought for a moment about what word to use—"pleased to see you, but again, what are you doing here?" She didn't know why she was whispering.

Thraigg slung his hammer up behind his head, bracing the handle behind his neck. "Figured ye might be wanting to do something about that crown. And about . . ." Elyria didn't have to be a mindwielder to know he was struggling with saying Zephyr's name. They'd all had a hard time dealing with the truth of what she'd done, all been hurt by her actions, but in the days after the Crucible ended, it became clear that Thraigg was taking it even more personally than the rest.

Nox nodded. "Kit sent for us."

Elyria's second brow joined the other at the top of her forehead, both of them now lifted in surprise. "What? Why?"

"Word came from the king earlier today. You didn't seem to be in the right mood to receive it." Kit's voice was smug as she flitted through the open window over the house's entrance and landed deftly between Thraigg and Nox.

Surprise stole Elyria's initial response. Then she said, "Liar. I was in a perfectly receptive mood."

Kit's blue eye twinkled as she folded her gold-and-silver wings against her back. "Fine, maybe I just wanted to be able to enjoy the drama of this little reunion. It's been rather boring around here lately, not sure if you've noticed."

Elyria nearly choked on the derisive laugh that formed in her gut. She stared at the three ex-champions for a long moment. Finally, she turned back to the nocterrian and the dwarf. "Why would you come help? Why do you care?"

"For fuck's sake, lass." Thraigg shook his head, the ornaments in his woven beard jingling. "I'm starting to doubt yer being 'pleased' to see us after all. Do we not have unfinished business here, same as ye?"

The nocterrian shrugged, a bafflingly casual gesture that seemed out of place in their body. "We cannot let Malchior get his hands on celestial power. And we all know you're the only one who can get it back."

Elyria did not, in fact, know she was the *only one* who could do this, but she sure as all four hells was going to be the one who tried.

Renewed purpose wove through her, the knot in her chest starting to unfurl.

Nox grinned again, as if they could sense the wave of resolution cresting inside Elyria. "So," they said, feline grin widening, "where to, Revenant?"

Elyria smiled, her inner shadow stirring. "Let's go hunting."

EPILOGUE

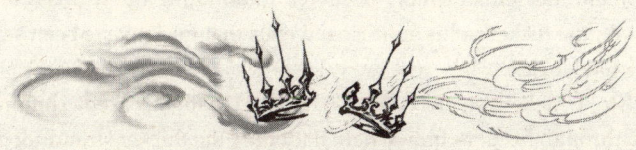

Leviathan Church

Firelight danced over the dark wood floor of Leviathan Church's office, casting long shadows across the overflowing bookshelves lining the walls, the piles of missives and tomes.

The lord sat behind his heavy oak desk, elbows perched on the edge, hands clasped under his chin. Boots echoed in the hallway outside, muffled through the heavy door, and his lip curled into a small, satisfied smile when a knock sounded.

He arranged his features into a neutral expression before opening his mouth and letting the gravitas of his voice flow through the room. "Enter."

With a creak, Sir Cedric Thorne stepped inside, the flickering fire casting the sharp angles of his face in shadow. The knight was dressed casually, his suit of armor forgone in lieu of a dark tunic and breeches beneath a stitched doublet. His chestnut hair had grown in the months since he returned from Luminaria, curling at the tips of his ears and around his face. A face that was just as carefully schooled as the lord's—stoic, respectful. No sign of irritation, of being inconvenienced by the last-minute nature of his summons.

Leviathan knew better than to trust it. Cedric was hiding something from him, had been since the day he emerged from the Celestial Sanctum. The knight had told the lord much of what happened, to be sure. A less-seasoned man might have thought he told him everything.

Leviathan was absolutely positive he had not.

"Sir Thorne," he intoned, his voice smooth and deep. "Thank you for coming on such short notice."

"Of course, my lord."

Leviathan gestured to a wide-backed chair in front of the desk. "Take a seat, my son."

Cedric's eyes widened at the uncharacteristic term of endearment, but he obeyed, dropping into the chair without hesitation. For a moment, Leviathan simply observed him, noting the stiffness of his posture, the flicker in his gold-ringed eyes that might have been something like unease.

"Do I make you nervous, Cedric?" Leviathan asked, running a hand through his dark brown hair, flattening the thicker strands of gray streaked within.

Cedric shook his head. "Of course not, my lord." Then he seemed to contemplate his words. "Not usually. This is just all a bit unexpected. The messenger made your summons sound rather urgent."

"Stole you away from your adoring fans, did I? I am sure many are clamoring for the Victor of Havensreach's attention these nights." Leviathan let a hint of amusement dance between his words, all too aware of how much Cedric disliked the designation.

The knight huffed something that sounded almost like a laugh. "Hardly, my lord."

A moment passed, then another. Leviathan allowed the silence to hang between them, to turn into tension, daring Cedric to cut through it. To see if he would let his knightly visage slip, let some of whatever truth he was hiding come to the surface. For a fleeting instant, Leviathan thought he saw Cedric's hand twitch, as if ready to reach for the dully glowing token hanging from his neck.

True to his role as the honor-bound knight, however, Cedric said nothing. Leviathan was almost disappointed.

"I've received word from King Callum. The accord has been finalized, the agreement sealed with blood." Displeasure curled his lip. "Havensreach will allow Nyrundelle to send some of their people into our lands as part of their search for Varyth Malchior. To hunt the Cult of Malakar." He drummed his fingers on the desk. "Arcanians have been officially sanctioned entrance into the realm of Havensreach. I never thought I'd see the day."

Some emotion flashed across Cedric's face, too quick for Leviathan to catch. It was a reaction, though. A strong one.

Cedric noticed the lord noticing. "This is a good thing, is it not, my lord? In exchange, they have given up part of the Midlands."

"Yes," Leviathan said. "A rather poor deal for them, is it not? Swaths of mana-rich land in exchange for passage for a few errant Arcanians. Does that seem like a trade their fairy king should be inclined to make?"

Cedric frowned. "I . . . I suppose not at first glance. But you are aware of the danger that Varyth Malchior poses. And I've explained the lengths to which he has already gone. You know what will happen should he get his hands on the other half of the Crown of Concord. Perhaps their king takes the threat just as seriously."

"Or, perhaps they know something they *think* we don't know about the power Malchior has stolen. Perhaps they race to get access to both pieces of the crown at once, to unite its power before we can."

"Perhaps," Cedric agreed, then somewhat hesitantly added, "Is that not what we are doing as well?"

Leviathan didn't answer. Instead, he leaned forward in his seat, eyes narrowing slightly at Cedric. "And you?"

"Me, my lord?"

Leviathan let the unspoken accusation hang in the air. Cedric's jaw flexed, his posture going rigid. "Are you not intrigued by this development? By this looming *peace*?" The very word curdled on Leviathan's tongue.

"Should I not be, my lord?"

"Perhaps I am simply curious as to the true reason for your interest.

The Arcanians will be sending a delegation to Kingshelm. Are you not the slightest bit curious who they will send?"

Cedric's shoulders sagged. "Of course I am curious, my lord, but no more so than the average citizen."

One side of Leviathan's mouth tipped up. "I'm sure."

Another few heartbeats of tense silence settled into the space between them.

Finally, the lord said, "And your own progress? Have there been any developments in your search for the other half of the crown? Any new information?"

"Nothing of substance, I'm afraid, my lord. I continue following what leads I can, but I will need time. Sir Hale suggests we consult the magisters in Paideus. I was going to ask your permission to travel there with him next week."

Leviathan allowed a small frown to crease his brow, a performance of contemplation. "Very well," he conceded. "Continue your efforts. Learn what you can. But remember, time is a luxury few can afford. And with Varyth Malchior and his stars-damned cultists doing Aurelia-knows-what in the meantime, we must be strategic and steadfast. Who knows how long this treaty"—he suppressed a shudder—"will truly last."

"Yes, my lord." Cedric inclined his head. "I understand what is at stake."

With that, Leviathan dismissed him, watching as the knight rose and left the room—shoulders square, movements sharp. He had changed in the Sanctum; there was no doubt about it. Truth be told, Leviathan hadn't expected to see Cedric come back at all. It was a pleasant surprise to be able to welcome him back with open arms. Or, to welcome whoever Cedric had become. It was clear he was not the same compliant student and obedient knight the lord had shaped.

He was something else entirely.

When the door clicked shut and Leviathan Church found himself alone once more, he stood, crossing the office with languid steps. He stopped in front of an ornate gilded mirror, its shining edges tarnished by time. One hand on the token dangling from his neck, he flicked his wrist. A darksteel dagger appeared in his free hand, and he wasted no time slicing it across the back of his arm.

Blood trailed down his wrist, dark and rich, and Leviathan smeared it onto the surface of the mirror. Crimson symbols appeared overtop his reflection, and the mirror slid aside with the whispered rumble of stone on stone, revealing a recessed compartment.

Leviathan's eyes roamed over the contents spilling over the shelves within—leather pouches full of gold coins, tokens pulsing with mana, gilded jewelry and shining gemstones, an array of small darksteel weapons.

And right in the center, nestled on a bed of black velvet between a ring of darkest onyx and a heavy gold locket, there it was.

Sharp golden spires, set with sparkling jewels. The jagged edges on either side where Daephinia's cursed arrow had shattered it.

The Crown of Concord.

Or one half of it, at least.

Leviathan's lips curled into a slow, satisfied smile as he let his fingers trace the delicate edges of the stolen crown. It was quiet. Still. He couldn't feel its power, but he knew it was there. Knew it wouldn't stay dormant for long. He just needed to stay vigilant, to stay the course a little longer.

He was close.

After all this time, after all he'd worked for, all he'd sacrificed, he was so, so close.

Wiping the blood from his arm with a handkerchief, Leviathan swapped out the token around his neck with a freshly charged one. With the wave of his hand, the mirror slid back in place, the compartment sealed, nary a drop of blood to be seen on its shining surface.

Soon, he thought. Soon all Arcanis would know, would remember, would fall before him. And the thought filled him with such dark joy that for just a moment, he allowed the serene mask he always wore to slip. He let the ruthless ambition that constantly burned beneath it bubble to the surface.

"Soon," he repeated into the empty room. And this time, it wasn't Leviathan Church that spoke.

It was Varyth Malchior.

GLOSSARY

TERMINOLOGY

ARCANIAN—collective term for the magical, non-human races of Arcanis

DWARVES—a race of master craftsmen and warriors characterized by their stout and muscular builds, standing between four and five feet tall.

FAE—a winged race born with elemental magic; the ruling race of Nyrundelle

NOCTERRIANS—a horned race that hails from Nocterrum with a nebulous reputation and an affinity for shadow magic; nocterrian society is genderless.

SYLVANS—a green-skinned, druidic race; masters of herbalism, known for their healing and nature-based magic.

Magic Wielders: Arcanian

FLAMECALLER—controls fire
NIGHTWIELDER—manipulates shadows
ORACLE—diviner of prophecy
STORMBENDER—controls wind and air
SUNBRINGER—controls light; extremely rare
TIDEWEAVER—controls water/ice
WILDSHAPER—controls nature/the earth

Magic Wielders: Human

SAGE—mindwielder/telepath
SAINT—possesses an affinity for healing
SANGUINAGI—blood mage
SEER—recipient of prophetic visions
SORCERER—wielder of powerful magic
SPELLWEAVER—wielder of small magics

PLACES

The Arcanian Realm of Nyrundelle (NEER-uhn-dell)

AERITHIA *(Air-ih-THEE-uh)*—the capital city of Nyrundelle
CORALITH *(KORE-uh-lith)*—a bustling seaside city

The Human Realm of Havensreach (HAY-vens-reach)

KINGSHELM *(KINGS-helm)*—the capital city of Havensreach
PAIDEUS *(Pie-DAY-us)*—a preeminent magical academy

The Midlands

FOREST OF VALANDOR *(Val-an-DOOR)*—a dense forest that cuts across the Midlands
LUMINARIA *(Loo-min-AH-ree-uh)*—the ancient capital of Arcanis, where Queen Daephinia and King Juno ruled the realm entire before the War of Two Realms; also referred to as the Lost City

Other

IRONPEAK MOUNTAINS—the mountain range that stretches across the northernmost part of Arcanis, home to the dwarven cities
NOCTERRUM *(Nock-TERR-uhm)*—the mysterious land from which all Nocterrians hail, also known as the Shadowlands, about which not much is known
VERDENTIA *(Ver-DEN-shuh)*—a sylvan settlement located at the southern tip of the continent

CHARACTERS

Arcanians

ARTEMICION "ARTIE" BONEJAW *(Art-ih-MEESH-un)*—the crotchety dwarven owner of the Sweltering Pig in Coralith

CYREN TENRIDER *(SAI-ren)*—a fae champion; stormbender

DISSIDUA PYR *(Diss-IH-dew-ah Peer)*—a nocterrian champion

ELYRIA LIGHTBREAKER *(Ell-EE-ree-uh)*—a famous fae warrior with a secret dark power and wounds from the past; wildshaper (and more)

EVANDER RAVENSWING *(Eh-VAN-der)*—a famed former fae champion, lost to the last Crucible attempt twenty-five years prior. Kit's brother and Elyria's former love.

GAEL WINTERS *(Gayle)*—a fae champion; flamecaller

KATERINA "KIT" RAVENSWING—fae champion; tideweaver. Evander's younger sister and Elyria's close friend (estranged at the beginning of the book).

KING LACHLANDRIS *(Lock-LAN-driss)*—the current ruler of Nyrundelle; fae

LAELIANA RAVENSWING *(Lay-lee-AH-nah)*—the duchess of Aerithia, Kit and Evander's mother; fae; stormbender

LORD CORLYN *(KORE-lin)*—the ruling noble of Coralith

MASTER TARTANIS *(Tar-TAN-iss)*—the leader of a Coralithian crime syndicate

OLYNDOR "OLLIE" OLEANDER *(OH-lin-dor Oh-lee-ANN-der)*—a fae member of the Coralithian city guard posted at the prison; Elyria's friend

PAELIN SALTWILLOW *(PAY-lin)*—a fae champion; wildshaper

PRINCESS SELENAE *(Sell-in-NAY)*—the mixedborn daughter of Queen Daephinia and King Juno, assassinated as a child at the same time as her father

QUEEN DAEPHINIA NERO *(Day-FIN-ee-uh)*—the fae queen, King Juno's wife, who ruled over a united Arcanis for many years until the Shattering; sunbringer

RAEFE *(Rayph)*—a member of Master Tartanis's criminal network; flamecaller

TARYN *(TAIR-inn)*—a fae member of the Coralithian city guard with a grudge against Elyria

TENEBRIS NOX *(TEN-ih-bris Nocks)*—a nocterrian champion, mysteriously fascinated with Elyria; nightwielder

THRAIGG IRONFIST *(Thrayg)*—a dwarven champion

ZARIC *(ZAIR-ick)*—the fae captain of the Coralithian city guard

ZEPHYR *(ZEFF-ur)*—a sylvan champion

Humans

ALDEN ASHFORD—a human champion; saint
ALOUETTE *(A-loo-ETT)*—Cedric's housemaid/nanny when he was a child
BELIEN LARKIN *(BELL-ee-en)*—a human champion; sorcerer and Belis's twin brother
BELIS LARKIN *(BAY-liss)*—a human champion; spellweaver and Belien's twin sister
BRANDON CORMAC—a human champion; sage
HARGRAVE—a guard/mercenary in Lord Church's employ
KING CALLUM—the current ruler of Havensreach
KING JUNO NERO—Queen Daephinia's husband, assassinated by Malakar
LEONA BLACKWOOD—a human champion; sorcerer
LORD LEVIATHAN CHURCH *(Lev-EYE-uh-thin)*—Cedric's benefactor and the lord he serves; took Cedric in as a ward after his family was murdered
MALAKAR *(MAL-uh-kar)*—the dark sorcerer whose assassination plot against King Juno led to the Shattering and the War of Two Realms
SIR CEDRIC THORNE *(SED rick Thorn)*—a human knight, orphaned at age six, destined to enter the Arcane Crucible at the behest of his benefactor and lord, Leviathan Church
SIR TRISTAN HALE—Cedric's close friend; a fellow knight in Lord Church's employ
THIBAULT *(TEE-bo)*—a guard/mercenary in Lord Church's employ
VARYTH MALCHIOR *(VAIR-ith MAL-kee-or)*—the *sanguinagi* leader of the Cult of Malakar, rumored to be a descendant of the dark sorcerer himself

Celestials

AURELIA *(Oh-RELL-ee-uh)*—the banished star god; Guardian of Balance
GAIA *(GUY-uh)*—Earth Mother
LUNARA *(Loo-NAH-ruh)*—Keeper of Time
NOCTIS *(NOCK-teese)*—Warden of Shadows
SOLARIS *(So-LAH-riss)*—Goddess of Light
THE ARBITER—presides over the Arcane Crucible on behalf of the celestials

ACKNOWLEDGMENTS

When I wrote my first set of acknowledgments for this book, I never could have imagined *Smoke and Scar* would have soared to the heights that it has. I had hopes, of course. Had dreams that it would find its readers—the people with whom Elyria's and Cedric's parallel journeys resonated. The ones who would help champion it. The reality of life since publishing *Smoke and Scar*, however, has been so far beyond what I ever could have predicted.

If you were one of the early readers of *Smoke and Scar*, thank you a million times over. You have single-handedly helped my dreams come true, and for that I will be forever grateful.

More of that gratitude needs to be aimed at my wonderful, patient, supportive family. Thank you to my husband, for bearing with all the late nights and continually replenishing my Sour Patch Kid stash (brain food, y'know?). Thank you to my beautiful kiddos for being the eternal lights in my life, and for constantly reminding me of the why beneath all of this.

Thank you to my parents—my father, the ultimate fantasy aficionado, and my mom, my number one fan. To both my awesome older siblings: my sister—my eternal first reader, and my best friend on this planet—and my brother, whose pride I aim to earn every day—thank you for your constant support. I have the raddest family ever, simple as that.

There are *so* many people I want to thank for being in my corner from the very beginning of my journey with this book, and anxiety has me fretting about how I'm sure to forget so very many. This feels like an apt point to remind anyone reading these that my brain is simply a colander filled with ADHD noodles, so make of that what you will.

Emily, thank you for being such a supportive, wonderful friend first, and the best PA second. You've helped keep me sane and are my best defense against the imposter syndrome constantly trying to creep into my periphery. Madi, thank you for being, well, the best. I cannot fathom what this past year would have looked like without you in my corner. Alex, thank you for being such a light in my life. Sheila, Jenessa, and Whit—thank you for being my lifelines and my rocks, as well as for the endless supply of meme perfection. Don't know what I'd do without you.

A huge thank-you goes to my inspiring and eternally helpful alpha and beta readers—KJ, Ai Rei, Ashley, Hope, Anne. Thank you for being such early champions of this book and for helping me cross the finish line!

To all the incredible authors I've connected with: thank you, thank you, thank you. Whether doling out advice or trading horror stories, I'm so grateful for this community and am truly inspired by you every single day.

And speaking of folks who spark inspiration, thank you to all the stunningly talented creators—content, artistic, and otherwise!—who have helped this book reach new eyes and ears. Extra special thanks to @amandathebookworm, @ashlynreadss, @bookmarked.byv, @bookish.girls.club, @caseygetsbooked, @shaesicles_bookwyrm, @gennareading, @jpreads7, @kirsten_isreading @thelostbooksofjess, @smut.slut.sisters, @thebookishanimator_, @swords.and.shapes, @theaviciouscosplay, @darkladycosplay, @celestarly, @indigowildcard, @dudakka_, @artofetherealm, @sunkissedillustration, and the myriad of other artists I've had the true honor of working with.

To my fabulous street and ARC teams: a very teary thank-you. Your excitement and support have been my staff and shield throughout this entire process, and I remain absolutely bewildered at how I convinced you all to take a chance on me (but I'm not giving you back!). The biggest ghost hugs for Adri, Allison, Amber, Ashley, Bea, Cam, Charlotte, Chloe, Christian, Dori, Emma, Jessica, Jessie, Joani, Justine, Katie, Kay, Lacey, Lexi, Linda, Liz, Melissa, Meredith, Michele, Michelle, Sara, Sarah, Shaley, Shayna, Sophie, Stephanie, Tori, Rachael, Ren, Vana, and oh my gosh, *so* many more, but I fear these acknowledgments will be ten pages long if I keep going, so I have to cut myself off. I hope you all know how important you are to me!

And then, finally, the biggest, most heartfelt thank-you to my agent, Katie, and my editor, Feather, as well as my entire team at Scarlett Press, for not only guiding me through this transition from indie to traditional publishing, but for just generally being the most delightful, wonderful people to work with. I feel so fortunate to have you on my team and can't wait to see where we go next together!

Smoke and Scar

by Gretchen Powell Fox

This reading group guide for Smoke and Scar *includes an introduction, discussion questions, ideas for enhancing your book club, and a Q&A with author Gretchen Powell Fox. The suggested questions are intended to help your reading group find new and interesting angles and topics for your discussion. We hope that these ideas will enrich your conversation and increase your enjoyment of the book.*

INTRODUCTION

For centuries, humans and the magical races of Arcanis have been bitter enemies. Their only hope for lasting peace lies in the Arcane Crucible, a brutal series of trials that demands sacrifice every twenty-five years.

Elyria Lightbreaker, once a celebrated fae war hero, is a shadow of her former self. When the man she loved was lost to the last Crucible, Elyria lost herself, too—but now that his sister has stepped forward as a contender, Elyria must rise to protect another person she loves from meeting the same fate. Which means entering the very nightmare she abhors and fighting like hell to get them both out alive.

Cedric Thorne, humankind's would-be champion, has lived only for vengeance. To him, Elyria is the enemy who stole everything: his family; his peace; his past, present, and future. But the Crucible doesn't care about grudges. To survive, Cedric and Elyria must fight side by side, even as their determination to win burns hotter than the desire they can't deny.

Dark magic. Betrayal. A slow-burn love that could ignite the world. In the Arcane Crucible, enemies could become lovers . . . or destroy each other before the trials are through.

Topics & Questions for Discussion

1. The world of Arcanis features a wide range of magical abilities: fire, shadows, storms, and more. Which would you say is the most powerful? Which would you choose to wield if you could?

2. At the start of the novel, Elyria is determined not to go anywhere near the Arcane Crucible, not even to save Kit. What convinces her to change her mind?

3. How would you describe Elyria and Kit's relationship? Do you have any similar relationships in your own life?

4. Arcanians and humans often have conflicting accounts of events, from their views of the goddess Aurelia to the prophecy. Why do you think their perspectives differ? Does anyone benefit from this dissonance?

5. Elyria saves Cedric multiple times, even though she doesn't like him. How does their dynamic compare to traditional gender roles and expectations? Did anything about it surprise you?

6. In the Trial of Spirit, Elyria relives the day she was reborn as the Revenant. Why do you think the darkness chose her? How did she make the choice to define *them*, rather than the other way around? Have you ever had to face a part of you that you were afraid of?

7. Discuss Elyria's and Cedric's changing feelings for each other. When and how do they each begin to feel a shift?

8. Elyria describes trust as "a blade sharpened on both sides. It can cut, yes. But it also protects." Does this match your understanding of trust? Why might Elyria and Cedric think of trust this way?

9. Which do you think is more torturous for Kit and Elyria: believing Evander died in the Crucible or facing the truth?

10. What was your reaction to Elyria's and Cedric's decisions in the Trial of Concord? Would you have done the same in their place?

11. Sylvans are described as a peaceful race prone to healing, not violence, which makes Zephyr's actions that much more shocking. How do you think she could have justified this decision? What effect did her actions have on your understanding of her character—and of her friendship with Cedric?

12. Compare Cedric's relationship with Lord Church before and after the Crucible. Have their feelings about each other changed during their time apart?

13. The Arbiter emphasizes the importance of working together and forging bonds in order to survive the Arcane Crucible. Knowing how the trials end, why do you think this is? If the champions had also known, do you think they would have done anything differently?

14. The trials are full of twists and revelations. Which did you find most surprising? Did you see any of them coming?

15. Elyria and Cedric are joined by a large ensemble cast. Who was your favorite supporting character? If you had to brave the Arcane Crucible, who would you most want by your side?

Enhance Your Book Club

1. *Smoke and Scar* is told through both Elyria's and Cedric's perspectives. How did this dual POV affect the story? Choose a side character (e.g., Thraigg, Zephyr, Kit) and discuss or rewrite a chapter of your choosing from their point of view.

2. Arcanian magic takes many forms, from tideweaving to flamecalling and beyond. What other kinds of elemental magic can you imagine? Give them names and describe them.

3. The Arcane Crucible was designed as a solution to a world of flaws and inequalities. Is it an effective solution? As a group, brainstorm alternatives to the deadly Crucible that could repair the disparities in Arcanis another way.

4. Elyria has an affinity for music and singing. Imagine a soundtrack playing throughout the Crucible. Which songs would best capture the essence of each trial: Strength, Spirit, Magic, and Concord?

A Conversation with Gretchen Powell Fox

Gretchen! You're one of the first authors to publish with Simon & Schuster's new Scarlett Press imprint. What's it like being part of that debut? How are you feeling?

It's been outrageously exciting! Amazing! Wild! Sometimes it still doesn't seem entirely real? Honestly, as a writer it's a bit hard to admit this, but I often feel at a loss for words when I think about it. It's been a whirlwind experience—and the most simultaneously exciting and stressful time of my life—but I couldn't be more grateful for the opportunity. I'm still a bit in disbelief that *my* book is among so many other incredible titles and authors as part of the inaugural lineup!

How does it feel to make the leap from indie to traditional publishing? Has the process been different from what you expected?

I think many formerly indie authors would probably tell you that there are growing pains that come with the transition. I mean, we're going from being in charge of *literally everything* to really working with a team and suddenly having external deadlines and input to navigate, y'know? But my editor and team at Simon & Schuster have been amazing, and I'm so grateful for all the doors that have opened for me (doors that are still locked up tight for even the most successful indie authors!). I can honestly say that things have moved both much faster and more smoothly than I expected, and it's beyond exciting that my stories and characters are getting in the hands of so many more readers, and I am just so thankful for the opportunity to forge this new path forward!

We can't wait for even more readers to fall in love with Cedric and Elyria and co.! Speaking of which: So many romantasy readers love enemies-to-lovers and a good slow burn. What drew you to these tropes for Cedric and Elyria?

I believe it was while watching the 1996 classic film *Harriet the Spy* that

I first heard the phrase "Write what you know." And while I can't say that I've personally experienced an enemies-to-lovers romance (my relationship with my husband is more of an "opposites attract" situation), what I *do* know is how much I love *reading* about two enemies slowly falling in love—against their better judgment, against expectations, against the odds. I wanted to write a relationship that would be full of yearning and pining and mental self-flagellation because I adore kicking my own feet and swooning right alongside every moment of it—and truly, Elyria and Cedric made it easy. There was never any other option for these two beautiful, stubborn idiots.

What other tropes do you love writing?
I'm a sucker for deadly trials, a found family you really want to root for, and the *delicious* tension that comes from forced-proximity situations. And yes, you do indeed find all those things in this book! Basically, if I love the trope, I probably found a way to squeeze it somewhere into the series, haha.

You chose to tell this story from both Elyria's and Cedric's perspectives. What made that dual POV essential, and did you find writing one character's voice more natural than the other?
Getting to write from both of their perspectives was so essential because I truly see this series as belonging to *them*, not just one or the other. Elyria and Cedric are opposites in many ways. They balance each other out, and I knew that in order to properly show that, they'd each need an equal stake in how the story is told. Thankfully, because they're so different, I found it pretty easy to write each of them and keep their voices distinct.

Elyria is bold and confident while Cedric is broody and steadfast. Do you see yourself in either of them?
I always say that I aspire to be like Elyria, but I personally relate more to Cedric, my overthinking king. I don't consider myself a particularly broody person, but I *am* introspective. And while I wish I could say I have even a modicum of Elyria's confident badassery, it's always good to have someone to look up to.

Elyria would probably want to know: How do you feel about bacon?
Y'know, I just said I don't relate to Elyria as much, but between the purple hair and our mutual love of bacon, maybe I am more like her than I thought!

Ha, we are *all* glad that bacon exists in Arcanis. This is an intricate world with its own history and magical laws. What's the hardest part about building a fantasy world from the ground up?
Historically, one of the hardest things for me has been establishing limits and maintaining consistency. When it comes to magic, the sky's the limit in terms of what you can create! But without rules and limitations, that creation can become boring. When magic can provide instant solutions, where is the tension? The conflict? So early on in my world-building process, I made sure to come up with limits surrounding the way magic works in this world. Yes, great power is attainable, but it always comes at some sort of cost—whether that's burning out from using too much magic, sacrificing some of your soul by becoming a blood mage, or draining mana from the world itself in order to access it. Once those rules were established, the most important thing to me was being consistent about them. It's not fun or interesting to readers if you're constantly retconning or making exceptions to the rules you've created. This is why I was very adamant about doing the vast, *vast* majority of my world-building before I even started drafting this story.

Every author has their own process. Are you a detailed outliner, or do you prefer to discover the story as you go?
I am a huuuuuuge believer in outlining and knowing all the major story beats ahead of time. I mean, it's natural that some things will change as you go along, of course. There is a lot of truth to the whole "my characters made me do it!" saying. But I need to have a pretty decent picture of how things are going to go in order to ensure the story is constantly moving forward and that what I want to happen, well, *happens* (eventually, at any rate). You always want to leave yourself a little bit of wiggle room, because some of the most earnest moments and best bits of dialogue came from "going rogue," as it were, but overall, I really tried to

be very intentional with both my world-building and my plotting when it came to writing this book.

Some scenes in *Smoke and Scar* are especially emotionally intense. Which was the hardest for you to write?

There are probably some obvious answers here. As a mom myself, Cedric reliving his parents' deaths was hard. Evander's betrayal, and the outcome of the battle that followed, was very emotional for me. And don't even get me started on how pretty much everything from chapters 51–54 was written through a veil of tears. But I have to say that it was the moments of reflection Elyria and Cedric have together before Evander's return, when he's tending to her burn wound and she's comforting him after his meltdown, that I found most emotionally challenging. At this point, we're catching both of them in moments of significant vulnerability—he's wrestling with his self-worth and identity, while she's still processing the burden of her grief and the actions she unwillingly took as the Revenant. It was very heavy to try to sift through their feelings simultaneously, with both of them knowing that they sit at a crossroads in their relationship and absorbing the implications of what that might mean. Of course, then they're conveniently interrupted by Evander, and we all get a momentary reprieve. Very momentary, heh.

Are you as much of a reader as you are a writer? If so, which genres or authors have inspired you the most?

Oh, goodness, yes. I'm a *voracious* reader. The year before I was inspired to write *Smoke and Scar*, I think I plowed through something like 160 books? I read across a range of genres, with a pretty significant skew toward romantasy, epic fantasy, and contemporary romance. I mean, write what you wanna read, you know?

Absolutely. You've spoken openly about managing ADHD while also juggling motherhood and a full-time job. How do you find the time and focus to write on top of all that?

Heh, I wouldn't really consider how I approach any of those three things as particularly "focused" if I'm being honest, but over the years

I've certainly learned a lot about myself and how I work best. For me, that means leaning into the things I'm super passionate about, because the satisfaction I draw from that seeps into the other areas of my life and makes everything better. My passion for writing and storytelling is at an all-time high right now, and it's easy to carve out time for the things I care about most (even if, okay, fine, it's sometimes at the cost of my sleep and/or sanity. Do as I say, not as I do, kids!).

Last question: What do you hope readers take away from this book?
One of the most important themes of this book, to me, is the idea that you are not your past. Elyria is haunted by all the things that she did as the Revenant. Cedric grew up with a very narrow worldview that rapidly changes when he meets the other champions (and Elyria, of course). They go on journeys of self-acceptance, in her case, and self-discovery, in his, and if a reader can relate to either of their struggles—to Elyria accepting even the darkest parts of herself or Cedric recognizing that there isn't just one right answer in life—and find hope in their stories, then I feel as though I did my job well.

(The following chapter takes place during the events of Smoke and Scar, *as the champions undertake the Arcane Crucible's second trial.)*

SMOKE AND SCAR BONUS CHAPTER

THE TRIAL OF SPIRIT

Kit

The door bounced twice before sealing shut with a rude sort of finality. Kit flinched, wings half flared, cursing when she looked to her back, then to either side, and realized Elyria hadn't followed her. She cursed again—far louder—when, with a zing of bright magic, the door disappeared entirely, leaving nothing but a solid wall of smooth stone in its place.

"Quite the mindtwist, isn't it?" drawled Tenebris Nox, their words sailing lazily across the small, windowless chamber.

"What are *you* doing here?" Kit spun to find the nocterrian already leaning against the far wall, their horned head tilted, red-black eyes assessing her with their typical look of simultaneous boredom and interest.

"Expecting someone else?"

"You could say that," she muttered. She could've *sworn* Elyria was right behind her. A pang of something that felt oddly like guilt swirled in her stomach. She still hadn't entirely forgiven Elyria for icing her out these past twenty-five years, but that periwinkle-haired pain in the ass *had* entered the stars-damned Crucible because of Kit. Elyria was here for her, and even if they hadn't wholly worked through their issues yet, it didn't feel right that they'd already been separated. What if this new trial proved just as deadly as the last?

Kit swallowed, avoiding Nox's assessing gaze. Boxed in as they were, there was no point in going farther down that path. If one thing in this cursed world was certain, it was that Elyria was the strongest person Kit knew—in all senses of the word. She would survive whatever came next.

And so Kit needed to survive it, too, if for no other reason than to get the closure, and apology, she rightly deserved.

"So, the Trial of Spirit," she said, blowing an errant lock of silver-white hair from her eyes. "What exactly are we supposed to be doing here, do you think?"

With a hum, Nox strode across the room to where golden swoops and swirls were painted on the opposite wall, creating a perfectly centered frame. Their expression gave nothing away as they lifted an arm to one of their horns, then tapped a blue finger against the pointed tip—the same way a person might tap their chin when lost in thought. "Things only get more and more fascinating, do they not?"

Kit blew out a breath as she stepped up beside the nocterrian. "Fascinating's one word for it. Is this supposed to be our way . . . what, in? Out?" She pressed her palms against the wall within the empty frame, beating her fists against it once, twice, as though sheer force might unlock it, might tell them what in all four hells they were supposed to be doing next.

There was a moment of silence, wherein Kit felt rather stupid. Then she startled backward as the painted border rippled, shimmering lines of gold moving and bleeding into one another, running across the empty space in the center until the entire frame was filled in with a pool of liquid gold.

Kit cursed again, the words falling out of her mouth on an awestruck breath.

"Mmm, so you've said," Nox murmured, taking a silent step forward.

Kit's wings twitched at the nocterrian's remark, though any irritation she might have felt was quickly overtaken by surprise as the golden liquid settled with a final ripple, revealing a smooth, mirrored surface.

She arched a silver brow at her gilded reflection, Nox looming more than a foot overhead as they swooped into place beside her.

"Excellent. A magic mirror," she griped. "What exactly are we supposed to do with this?"

"Enjoy the view, perhaps," Nox said with a dry huff of amusement.

Kit shot them a look, wholly unclear as to the purpose behind the nocterrian's . . . joke? Compliment?

What were they playing at? She still didn't like the close eye Nox had clearly been keeping on Elyria since before they'd even stepped through the Gate. Learning that the two of them had run into each other in that Coralithian jail—she certainly wanted to hear more about *that*—raised her suspicions even further.

Still, like it or not, it would appear that the two of them were stuck with each other for the duration of this trial, at least. No time like the present to get their side of the story.

"What's the deal with you and Ellie?" she blurted out.

Nox blinked slowly as they turned their head and pierced her with that crimson gaze. "What do you mean?"

"You're constantly looking at her. Watching her. Don't think I haven't noticed. And she told me that this isn't the first time the two of you have, er, run into each other. So what's the deal? Why *exactly* are you so interested?"

She swallowed as soon as the last words left her lips, unsure where that final bit had come from. She hadn't meant to sound quite so petulant.

If Nox even noticed the tone behind the words, however, they didn't let on. They seemed entirely unperturbed, in fact, as they interlaced their fingers in front of their chest and said evenly, "I find her fascinating too."

Kit waited for more.

More did not come.

"That's it?" she asked, fully recognizing that this wasn't doing much to counter her desire *not* to sound petulant. "That's all I get?"

Nox tilted their head. "Is there something else I am expected to give?"

With a roll of her mismatched eyes, Kit crossed her arms over her chest. "I don't have time for your cryptic nocterrian nonsense."

"Do you not? It feels as though time is the one thing we have no shortage of right now." Their tone and expression remained neutral, but Kit could've sworn she saw a quirk of the nocterrian's mouth, the barest flash of a sharp white fang behind indigo lips. "After all, we have received no further instructions."

"Yes, well, perhaps the goal of this trial is for us to have a spirited conversation in front of the mirror."

Another flash of fang. "Trial of Spirit indeed."

Kit blinked. Cleared her throat. "If that's the case, why not start by telling me how, precisely, a nocterrian ends up in a Coralithian jail with the Revenant?"

Nox pursed their lips as though considering how best to respond, and for one fleeting, hopeful moment, Kit really did think she would get an actual answer.

But then they spoke.

"How does anybody end up anywhere, really?"

And Kit flung her hands into the air with a frustrated sigh, only for one of them to accidentally collide with Nox's sturdy arm as they lifted it once more to their horn. The touch was so unexpected, so surprising, that Kit found herself leaping aside reflexively, her other hand grazing the gilded surface of the mirror.

A surface that was not, in fact, solid and smooth at all.

It was *liquid*. And it was wrapping itself around her hand, crawling up her arm, pulling her inward.

"Careful," Nox warned, but it was already too late.

Gold surged, a vise around Kit's wrist, yanking her forward. Her wings flared as her boots left the floor, a word strangled in her throat as she cried out a single "Nox!"

The nocterrian swore, a word in an unfamiliar tongue tripping from their mouth, and then the same arm that had been the startling impetus for this entire mess was wrapped around Kit's waist.

Kit felt herself being hauled backward, the rope in a game of tug-of-war between the mirror at her front and the bewildering nocterrian at her back.

The leash around her wrist loosened, just a fraction, and for a second, Kit thought Nox was winning.

But then, with a burst of golden light, the mirror claimed them both.

Kit stumbled, her wings flaring again for balance as her boots crunched on gravel. The weight of recognition was heavy on her shoulders as her eyes adjusted and she took in her surroundings.

She knew this place.

The Ravenswing estate was imposing under the veil of night, its white stone walls stark against the midnight sky. Though, admittedly, the streaks of color raining down from the aurora overhead was a new touch.

Kit's stomach knotted.

It had been, well, *a while* since she'd been home. And even knowing that this couldn't possibly be the actual place, that this was some sort of trickery or illusion, and that she was almost certainly still within the Celestial Sanctum, it felt so stars-damned real.

It even smelled like home.

Smelled like *him*.

Sea salt and sunbaked earth and the subtlest undercurrent of cherry almond. Because, of course, where there was him, there was her.

At least, that's how it used to be. Before.

Before Evander sacrificed everything to enter the Crucible.

Before he threw away his entire life in the name of glory and honor for Arcanis.

Would he still have gone, Kit wondered, if he'd known that doing so meant Elyria throwing *her* life away too? If he'd known that his great love would spend a quarter century running away from everything, and every*one*, that reminded her of him?

The air shimmered, the world around Kit shifting. The backdrop of the estate blended with the night sky in a kaleidoscopic swirl of color, but before she had a chance to even try to discern what was happening, the scene cleared.

It had changed.

And Kit was no longer standing outside her family home.

She was inside it, in a warmly lit, tapestry-lined office, staring at a desk covered with letters.

Her desk.

Her *returned* letters.

She stepped forward, plucking one of the many unopened missives from the piles on the desk, her mismatched eyes tracing her own handwriting on the front.

She didn't have to open them to remember what they said.

Didn't need to see the pathetic words she'd scrawled out time and time again.

But alas, the Trial of Spirit was not satisfied, it seemed, by the mere *memory* of the fruitless letters Kit had written to her friend—to her sister. No, despite her lips remaining tightly sealed together, Kit's own voice carried through the room, a recital of her humiliation.

"Please, Ellie. Please. Talk to me. I miss him. I miss you. You have to come home. Mother won't talk about it."

Blessed silence returned, and Kit exhaled.

Her relief was premature.

"Nothing's the same," said the voice brokenly, *"and you left me. You weren't both supposed to leave me. I can't do this anymore, not without you. I can't . . . do this anymore."*

A tear slipped free from Kit's eye, trailing a fat track down her cheek before she wiped it away with the back of her hand.

The scene changed again, her surroundings swirling together once more, the letter in her hand dissolving into mist. And suddenly she was no longer standing in a firelit office but rather at the edge of a sharp, crumbling cliff.

With clenched fists, Kit watched the waves break roughly against the rocks far below.

"You still think about it, don't you?" The words curled into Kit's

ears—a voice that was still her own, but with something *else* there, too. A low undercurrent, an insidious echo. *"You stood here, just like this. You looked down at the crashing waves and wondered if your mother would even notice if you were to vanish into them."*

"That was—" There was a tremble in her real voice as Kit spoke aloud. "That was a long time ago."

"It wasn't as though you had anyone else waiting for you. Nobody else to miss you. And that was the worst part, wasn't it? It hurt so much, being that alone.

"You didn't want to hurt anymore." A beat of silence. *"You don't have to."*

The bitter wind ripped through her hair, ocean spray kissing her cheeks. Each crash of water against rock was like a beckoning call in her ears, summoning her gaze. She couldn't look away. She didn't know if she wanted to.

"You could still do it, you know. It would be such sweet relief. No more pain. No more loneliness. All you'd have to do is keep those wings down, keep your magic at bay, and let the water pull you down, down, d—"

"Shut up." The words were weak, nearly swallowed by the hissing wind.

"You weren't enough," murmured the voice, gentle at first—a comfort. Then louder, firmer, it continued. *"You weren't worth staying for then. What makes you think you are now?"*

She hated the idea that she was even listening to this phantom voice, that she was letting her own darkness get under her skin. But Kit couldn't deny the very real sting of the words, the way they picked at scabs that had only *just* begun to heal. And the path ahead, one where she and Elyria might have a chance of sealing the rift between them . . . it just seemed like it would be so *hard*.

And Kit was already so, so tired.

Her boot shifted a fraction toward the edge of the cliff.

And then something colder than the salt-laced air brushed her back, ran across her wings.

Kit stiffened. Slowly, she turned her head.

There was nothing.

Wasn't there?

She squinted at the empty cliffside beside her, where the light of the aurora was bending, refracting in midair. And the barest shimmer of a figure, kneeling in the dark, materialized before her.

This most definitely was not part of her memory.

It was like trying to see through a veil. Shadows twisted in the air, obscuring her vision, but Kit could make out the horns curving from the figure's head. She could see the black chains coiled around their wrists and throat. She could sense the defeat in the shadowy mist leaking from them.

That villainous perversion of her own voice cut through the air again. *"No one is waiting for you."* It was a tidal roar pushing against Kit's will, not noticing or not caring about the other champion, who was still barely visible next to her, clearly fighting through a memory of their own.

The intention of the voice was clear enough. Had it been able to, Kit thought it might have physically pushed her toward the cliff's edge. But the jagged cut of the words was softened by her concern for the bound nocterrian, and suddenly, she found herself confused as to why she had ever even contemplated jumping.

She rolled her shoulders back, tilted her chin. "I don't think that's true."

And with a sharp inhale, she stepped back from the cliff.

Kit was in the chamber once more, the golden mirror at her back. She didn't know exactly when she'd stepped through or exactly how her twisted memory had come to an end. She just knew that the stone under her feet and the torchlight flickering off the walls were real—as was the nocterrian staring at her with raised brows.

Kit stared back, her head tilted to one side.

"Are you well?" Nox finally asked.

She tried very hard not to notice the way they rubbed at their wrists before crossing their arms over their broad chest. Nodding, she replied, "And you?"

Nox hesitated for a beat, then inclined their head in return.

The air in the chamber felt suddenly thick—heavy with the words that neither of them seemed willing to speak. Had Nox seen her on that cliffside? Kit wondered. Did they know how close she'd come to jumping?

Did they know she'd seen them, too?

Kit's gaze lingered on them a heartbeat longer than she'd intended, the vague image of the nocterrian in those dark shackles sending a chill through her. She cleared her throat, as if doing so might banish the thought from her mind. She certainly couldn't ask about it. So instead she narrowed her eyes and said, "Don't get any ideas. This doesn't mean we're friends."

There was a flicker of fang as Nox's mouth curved, their shoulders dropping. "Perish the thought."

And before Kit could come up with a snappy retort, they gestured to the far wall . . . and the open door that had magically rematerialized there.

"Shall we rejoin the others?" Nox asked, and something that felt dangerously like hope sparked in Kit's chest. There were others. There was more than loneliness in her life now. There was one specific person who could be waiting for her at this very moment. Who had indeed thought her worth staying for—worth risking everything for.

And even if Elyria hadn't come back through yet, even if she wasn't quite done with whatever the Trial of Spirit had thrown at her, that was all right too.

Kit would wait.

(The following chapter takes place after the events of Smoke and Scar *and before the beginning of* Splintered Kingdom.*)*

SMOKE AND SCAR BONUS CHAPTER

BARDS & BALDRICS

Elyria

"Well, it's no sweltering pig, but I guess it'll do." Elyria grimaced as a squelching sound emitted from where her boot met something suspicious on the ground.

Kit was already three steps ahead, skipping through the open tavern doorway. "You're the one who wanted to avoid your adoring fans, Lady Victor," she said, tossing a grin back over her shoulder. "It doesn't get much farther off the beaten path than the Rook & Ruse."

"We wanted off the beaten path, not outside of common sense." Tenebris Nox brushed past Elyria, sniffing the air. "This place looks more likely to gift us some new disease than a relaxing evening."

"Who said we were in the market for a relaxin' evening?" said Thraigg with a laugh. The dwarf bounced on his heels beside the nocterrian, surveying the squalid tavern with appreciation. "Have heart there, Noxie. Ye can tell this is the kind of place that has *character*."

"Ah, so *that's* what that smell is."

Elyria's lips curved into a lopsided smile as she caught up with Kit. "All right, all right. Far be it from me to presume I know better than you when it comes to the fine establishments of this city, Kitty Kat. I'm just happy to be out doing literally *anything* other than waiting for your uncle to finally make a stars-damned decision about going after the crown."

Kit blew out a breath as she ushered the group farther into the tavern. Elyria's shoulders relaxed as soon as the door swung shut behind them. With peeling wooden walls and a floor that seemed entirely too wet for how early it was in the evening, the Rook & Ruse was hardly the height of luxury, and it had the patronage to show it. Aside from a sour-faced fae seated in a booth and a pair of dwarven traders perched by the bar, the place was entirely empty.

Just how Elyria liked it.

No nobles. No council members. No whispers about the Revenant or the Victor of Nyrundelle or what happened in the Sanctum.

"You can say that again," said Kit with a snort, taking a seat at a round table in the center of the tavern. "Noctis take me if I have to sit through one more council meeting without any progress."

"There's a saying that feels pertinent to our current situation. Something about the inherent virtue in having patience?" Nox slid into a seat beside Kit.

Elyria held her breath as the rickety chair creaked under the nocterrian's weight. When it failed to immediately collapse into a splintered pile of soon-to-be-firewood, she took a seat at Kit's other side and said, "Not once in my life have I ever claimed to be virtuous."

Thraigg's raucous laugh drew the eyes of the other patrons, along with the tavern master, who ambled over with a tray full of mugs. He set them down with a grunt, spilling ale across the tabletop, before ambling right off again.

"Alas, I suppose I cannot blame you for your patience wearing thin," said Nox, picking at the sleeve of their coat. "Even I must admit that all this waiting around has not been particularly fun."

"Luckily for all of ye, fun happens to be a specialty of mine," said Thraigg with a chortle, his gaze moving to a spot behind Elyria's head. "Seems like we made it here just in time for it to really begin."

Elyria raised a brow, twisting to follow the dwarf's line of sight. "What are you—" She took in the elevated wooden stage butting up against the far side of the tavern . . . and the curvaceous fae woman settling into a chair beside it, lute in hand. "Oh. Oh, no. Katerina Ravenswing, what is this?"

Kit beamed. "Thought you might appreciate the opportunity to dust off your vocal cords, Ellie. It's been a while since you graced our ears, after all."

Thraigg huffed in agreement. "Aye. And some of us have never had the pleasure at all."

"This is not exactly what I had in mind when I agreed to come here tonight," Elyria said with a groan. "But . . . I suppose that since it's only us and a handful of stragglers, I could—"

As if on cue, the tavern doors swung open and a long line of new patrons filed into the room, chattering excitedly among themselves. They plunked down into booths and chairs, rapidly filling the empty space.

With the flick of his wrist, the tavern master sent a flicker of fire to light the torches that lined both sides of the stage. "Good people of Aerithia!" he boomed, stepping onto the platform. "Welcome to Minstrel Night!"

There was a smattering of applause, a few rowdy cheers.

"It is an extra special evening for the Rook & Ruse, as tonight we are graced with the presence of none other than the Lady Lightbreaker, Victor of Nyrundelle, herself!"

The cheers grew louder, and Elyria buried her face in her hands. "Stars a-fucking-bove." She lifted her head just enough to glare at Kit. "You planned this."

Thraigg's shoulders shook with laughter as he lifted a mug from the table and took a long swill. Kit's grin could not possibly have been wider. Even Tenebris Nox looked faintly amused, one dark brow arching more sharply than a crescent moon.

"Who, me?" Kit blinked her mismatched eyes innocently. "Who would have the *time*? He must have recognized you."

"Mm. Must have," Elyria said drily.

The tavern master was still talking, regaling the now-bustling tavern with tales of Elyria's bardic prowess and her long history at the Sweltering Pig. Admittedly, hearing Artie's name among the heraldry had her ears perking up—as did the fact that the speech ended with an invitation for Elyria to take the stage.

"For fuck's sake," she grumbled.

"Time to make a decision, Revenant," said Nox, flashing a hint of fang, "or the crowd's going to get rowdy."

"Ah, let the *Lady Victor* finish her drink first," Thraigg said with a wink. He threw back the final drops of ale in his mug with a flourish before adding, "I'll warm 'em up for ye, lass."

Before Elyria could protest, the dwarf was already lumbering toward the stage, wiping at his beard with the back of his hand. "Don't suppose ye know 'The Hymn of Stonehold,' do ye?" he asked the musician. She shook her head. "Bah, never ye mind. I hardly need accompaniment."

And then he launched right into a solemn work chant, his surprisingly smooth baritone stretching over the room.

Well, it was *mostly* solemn. Dwarven songs were generally a mix of somber reflection and coarse humor. And though Elyria was unfamiliar with this particular tune, it was quickly evident this one would live up to expectations.

> *By stone, by flame, by callused hand,*
> *We carve our fate through bedrock's stand.*
> *Through scar and blood and ache and soot,*
> *And still we march with steadfast foot.*
>
> *Lift the pick, raise the hammer,*
> *Raise your mug—don't mind me grammar.*
> *Don't dig too deep nor drink too fast,*
> *And kiss yer wife 'fore the caves collapse.*

By the time Thraigg had launched into the fifth verse, with no end to the song in sight, folks were starting to shift in their seats.

"This is warming up the crowd?" Elyria whispered, her eyes

roaming over the patrons, who seemed to be growing more antsy with every passing word. Many of their gazes, heavy with expectation, were trained solely on Elyria.

Kit's grin had faltered into a sort of half grimace. "You can't say he didn't have good intentions. But we all know who the people are really here for."

"And if I said I *really* don't want to do this?"

"Ellie . . ." Kit's voice bordered on pleading, and a kernel of guilt sparked in Elyria, rattling the box of emotions she kept buried under the knot of shadows in her chest.

"Need me to go next?" offered Nox.

Elyria sighed. "Entertaining though I would find that, it's fine. Might as well get this over with. Since *someone*"—Kit flinched—"has apparently made promises that *I'm* on the hook to fulfill."

Flexing her fingers at her sides, Elyria rose slowly. The energy in the room immediately lifted, excited whispers and claps sounding from the crowd, cutting into the final notes of Thraigg's refrain.

He didn't seem to mind—the opposite, in fact. Thraigg was smiling broadly at Elyria as he stepped down from the stage, reaching up to clap her on the shoulder before sauntering back to their table and helping himself to the still-full mug of ale she'd left behind.

"'The Ashen Promise'? Can you play that one?" Elyria asked the musician, who gave a short nod in reply. For a moment, she thought maybe she should pick something a little more upbeat after Thraigg's confusingly somber song. Thought she should give the crowd a jaunty drinking song or bawdy sailor's tune.

But something about this one—an old-fashioned ballad from the days before the War of Two Realms, before the Shattering, before *all* of it—felt right to Elyria. It was a feeling that settled further into her bones as she took her final step onto the stage.

The crowd hushed.

The musician plucked the strings of her lute.

And Elyria began to sing.

> *When fire fell from celestial breath,*
> *And ash replaced the bloom,*

> *I swore beneath the cindering sky*
> *I'd find you through the gloom.*
>
> *The stars above forgot to shine,*
> *The sun forgot to rise —*
> *Yet still I knew the shape of you*
> *By soul, if not by sight.*

Her voice wrapped around the room like silken smoke—low and lilting. The ballad spun through the air, weaving through the captivated crowd, and though Elyria tried not to look too closely, she didn't miss the reverent looks on their faces nor the way it seemed like their collective breath was caught in their throats.

Kit sat frozen in her seat, as though she didn't dare move.

Nox nodded their head softly in rhythm with the words.

And Thraigg was once again pawing at his face, though instead of wiping ale from his beard, he seemed to be rubbing at his eyes.

Elyria noticed this all dimly, but it fell away just as quickly.

Because as she sang—the words soft, the melody aching—her gaze kept dragging to a spot at the back of the room. To a table tucked far into the corner.

An empty table.

There was no one there. Nothing but flickering shadows cast by the torches. She knew this.

And yet.

For one impossible moment, Elyria thought—

But no, that was impossible.

> *So if the wind should bear my name*
> *On some far eastern shore,*
> *Know I was yours, in ash and flame —*
> *And will be yours once more."*

She finished the song with a trembling flourish, the lyrics cracking open the lid of that rattling box inside her, some unnamed emotion flooding her veins.

The room was utterly silent.

For a single suspended heartbeat, it was as if time itself held its breath.

And then—

It took Elyria a moment to catch up to the crescendo of clapping and cheering that exploded through the room. Took a moment to absorb the fact that every single person in the Rook & Ruse was on their feet.

With an awkward bow, Elyria descended the stage, bypassing Kit and Thraigg sitting slack-jawed at their table, next to a somewhat stunned-looking Tenebris Nox. The feeling stirring in her chest was too big, too real, pulling and pushing at the knot of shadows there.

She just needed some fresh air. A moment to breathe. It had simply been a while since she'd performed a song like that. Since she'd performed at all.

That must be it, she thought as she pushed open the tavern door, letting the cool night air hit her skin.

It had nothing to do with the way her eyes had slid once more to that darkened corner of the room as she walked past. Had nothing to do with the way the shadows there had flickered strangely once again.

And it most definitely had *nothing* to do with the way that, just for a heartbeat or two, they'd seemed to form a familiar silhouette.